Praise for Earl Murray

"Murray is a gripping storyteller who knows the land and the people he writes about."
—Elmer Kelton, multiple Golden Spur Award winner and author of *The Pumpkin Rollers*

"Today there are possibly a scant dozen writers of the Native American experience who really understand and feel its spirit. One who must be included on that short list is Earl Murray."
—Don Coldsmith, author of *The Spanish Bit*

"There is nothing less than exquisite beauty in the power Murray wields to enfold the reader in the simple, yet explosive world of his very real characters."
—Terry C. Johnston, award-winning author of *The Plainsmen*

"Murray is a master at capturing the historical moment . . . Readers will be swept upward into a flaming sky, borne on a wind that cries out like a thousand eagles . . . and they will see, as never before, the last grand, desperate moments of Sioux culture."
—W. Michael Gear and Kathleen O'Neal Gear, authors of *People of the Lakes*

FLAMING SKY

A NOVEL OF THE LITTLE BIGHORN

Earl Murray

A TOM DOHERTY ASSOCIATES BOOK
NEW YORK

This is a work of fiction. All the characters and events portrayed in this book are either products of the author's imagination or are used fictiously.

FLAMING SKY: A NOVEL OF THE LITTLE BIGHORN

Copyright © 1995 by Earl Murray

Cover art by Brad Schmehl
Maps by Victoria Murray

A Forge Book
Published by Tom Doherty Associates, Inc.
175 Fifth Avenue
New York, NY 10010

Forge® is a registered trademark of Tom Doherty Associates, Inc.

ISBN: 0-812-51320-7
Library of Congress Card Catalog Number: 95-2065

First edition: August 1995
First mass market edition: July 1996

Printed in the United States of America

0 9 8 7 6 5 4 3 2 1

To the memory of Butch, my childhood friend, who showed me the pathway.
I'll remember you always, my brother.

ACKNOWLEDGMENTS

Grateful acknowledgment is extended to Kitty Deer Nose and John Doerner of the Little Bighorn National Monument, who provided maps, books, and periodicals from the archives as well as their own expertise, as did Tim Bernardis and Carson Walks-Over-Ice of the Little Bighorn College Library.

Thanks to Chip and Sandy Watts and their family, who extended gracious hospitality at their ranch near the Little Bighorn River during my surveys of the battlefield, and to Hank and Kennard Real Bird for their oral history contributions.

A deep appreciation goes to my good friends Ben Cloud, Larson Medicine Horse, and the Henry Rides Horse family for oral interpretations of the battle and for including me in the spiritual ceremonies and traditions of their families, enabling me to better understand Plains Indian culture.

A special thanks also to Dan Old Elk and his family, and Dexter Falls Down and his family, who also provided oral histories and included me in the sacred ceremonies that bring strength to their lives.

Many thanks go to Jack and Carol Bailey for their help with Northern Cheyenne traditions and culture.

Also, my thanks and appreciation to Bill Tall Bull, who has shared Northern Cheyenne history and traditions with me over the years.

And thanks also to Howard Teten, FBI Behavioral Sciences, retired, for his expertise in helping me with the psychological motivations of George Armstrong Custer during that fateful day in June of 1876.

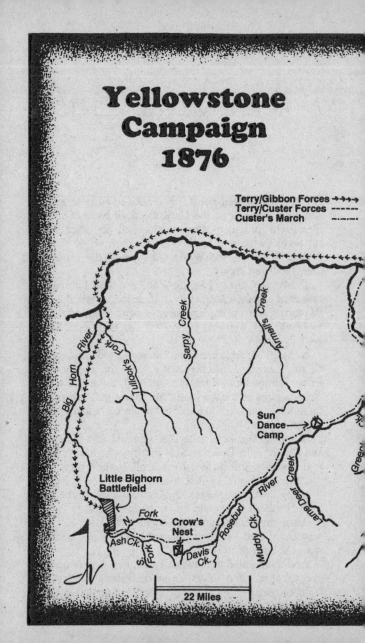

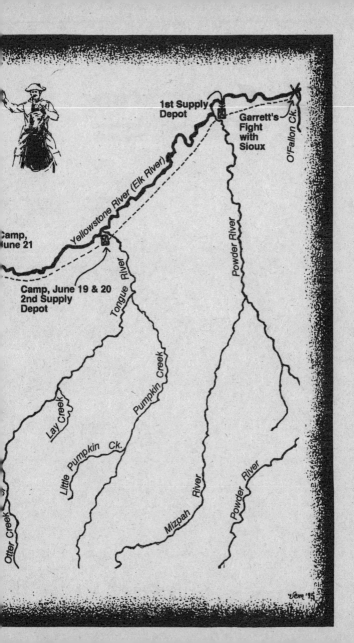

Little Bighorn Battlefield

1876

Troop Movement ————
Indian Movement ╌╌╌►

Deep Ravine

Gall

Crazy Horse

Two Moon

Lame White Man

Medicine Tail Coulee

Little Bighorn

Indian Village

River

Custer's Advance

Skirmish Line

Reno's Retreat

Reno's Advance

Ash Creek

1 Mile

ONE

The night sky was swirling. Huge tongues of red rose into the darkness like inverted tornadoes. The plains were ablaze in every direction, farther than the eye could see.

He stood in smoldering ashes, his bare feet black with soot. Surprisingly, his toes were not hot, but pleasantly warm, which puzzled him. His body felt awkward, unable to move. Could he have walked anywhere, he wouldn't have known where to go, anyway. So he remained still, watching the firestorm.

He had thought that he was alone, but turned to see a huge animal standing before him, staring into his eyes. At first he was gripped by fear. He wanted to turn and run, but couldn't move. Finally, the fear left when he realized that the animal meant him no harm.

The animal was massive, far bigger than anything he had ever seen. Confused, he stared as the beast turned sideways to him, the large hump in its back silhouetted against the crimson night, its thick horns curving upward, the tips polished and gleaming.

A bull buffalo! he told himself. *But why? What's happening to me?*

The fire, raging in all directions, had encircled them both, but now remained at a distance and would come no closer. Where he and the buffalo stood had already burned, the last haven of safety in a world of smoke and flame.

He continued to wonder. *What are you doing here? What do you want?*

He got no answer. From above came a trailing snake

of fire that singed the back of the huge animal, igniting it.

His eyes widened in horror. The buffalo stood passively as the hair along its hips and back burned with a crackling sound. He tried to step back but couldn't. Rooted to the ground, he could only stare.

The fire continued to engulf the animal, burning forward along its massive back and shoulders, consuming its sides and legs, finally stopping short at the neck.

As the flames receded, the buffalo remained upright, tears streaming from its large brown eyes. He reached out to touch it. The buffalo stood motionless as he sank his fingers into the thick black hair on its neck. He suddenly felt a tremendous surge of power rush through him. He felt united with the huge animal, as if he had become one with it, and it with him.

Startled, he pulled his hand back. Then, as his mouth fell open, the singed hair turned a stunning white— shining, filling the night with a strong glow.

He stared and wondered again, *What's happening? Why am I here like this? Why has a buffalo come to me?*

The buffalo lunged away from him, its coat now a stunning white. It ran toward the ring of fire, and at the edge of the flames, turned to look at him. He stared as the flames parted.

The buffalo watched him a while longer, then turned and lumbered through the break in the fire line, pulling the flames with it until all was totally black.

Adam Garrett awakened in the darkness, drenched with sweat. He sat up quickly, struggling to catch his breath. Overhead, stars filled a vast ocean of sky. In the distance a wolf howled, answered by another, their calls echoing across open plains.

Nearby, the Yellowstone River surged through the valley bottom, powered by late spring snowmelt. There were no more wolf calls. The river was all he could hear.

Garrett fought panic. He was alone. He couldn't call out for anyone; he had been told by his scouts not to make unnecessary noise. The last thing he wanted was for the Sioux to hear him. They could be anywhere out here, and if they found him, it would be the end.

There was a small fire burning in camp. It had to be late, Garrett knew, maybe even close to dawn. He climbed from his bedroll and searched the eastern horizon, where the black was turning to light gray.

But where were the scouts? They had to be somewhere near.

Garrett took his rifle and saddlebags and settled near the fire. He took a deep breath and tried to shake the feeling of the dream. But it wouldn't leave. It stayed with him—the leaping flames, the huge buffalo burning into white.

He took paper and pencil from his saddlebag and made an entry in his diary:

Dawn, 18 June 1876
Yellowstone River, near mouth of O'Fallon Creek

Another day and, finally, without rain. Awakened to the strangest dream of my life. I stood in a ring of fire with a huge bull buffalo that burned up and turned white. He ran from the circle. I think he wanted me to follow. Strange. Reaches clear into my gut.

Am uncertain of everything at this juncture. Am tired and my bones ache. Have yet to catch up with the Terry–Custer forces. Scouts have found sign that the entire battalion was once camped near here, within a week's time. Hope to find them by afternoon at mouth of Powder River.

Out of food. Scouts want to hunt, but have no time. Still no signs of hostiles, which I'm glad for. The three of us would be hard-pressed to survive.

Little Crane still trying to make me an Indian. Says I need to learn a lot if I'm to survive. Am doing well with their sign language, however. Will keep working and soon will be able to understand more.

All in all, though, I feel lost without the ability

to converse in the way I'm accustomed. Little Crane and Red Moon go for hours without talking. They say little but seem to understand one another perfectly. A great mystery to me.

Will focus my attention on reaching Custer. Nothing more important than that. Must find him soon, otherwise it may be too late to join him and my mission will be ruined.

Garrett set his notebook down and stared into the fire. A lone figure emerged from the darkness. Garrett jumped.

Little Crane, one of two Arikara scouts Garrett had hired to accompany him out from Fort Abraham Lincoln, sat down beside him. Little Crane, who spoke good English, had laughed at him the entire trip.

"You jump like a grasshopper. Are you a grasshopper?"

"Where were you?" Garrett asked. "Where's Red Moon?"

"He's watering the horses. Will be here soon."

Garrett stuffed his paper and pencil back into his saddlebag.

Little Crane pointed. "You make the paper talk again. Always making the paper talk. Will that get us to the soldiers faster?"

"I'm just keeping track of what's happening," Garrett explained. "That's all."

"You don't come to the fort when everyone else is ready. Everyone leaves and you are slow. We should have left with the soldiers, a long time back. Now we get killed trying to catch up. Are you ready? The Sioux are coming."

Little Crane had said it over and over during the trip, shaking his small frame as he laughed. His face was round, with a deep knife scar across his chin that stretched when he smiled. His long hair, parted along the left side and braided into two plaits, held three eagle feathers and the dried body of a large mouse. He wore nothing but a blue breechcloth and moccasins.

The other scout, also Arikara, would be in camp momentarily. He wanted no mention of himself in Garrett's notes, and he had sworn never to have his picture taken. It was Red Moon's personal feeling; he didn't care what other Indians did.

Tall and slim, his face long and sad-looking, Red Moon spent most of his time gazing into the distance. He wore a tattered buckskin shirt and a black breechcloth. His hair was cut short and was unkempt, as if he cared little about life.

It was usually Red Moon, however, who noticed things, and Little Crane who would talk endlessly about it later. The two took turns with chores and watching the horses, but Little Crane always spent more time in camp. Garrett couldn't decide if Little Crane hated being by himself, or just preferred to be around so he could be a pest.

"You didn't tell me if you're ready for Sioux," Little Crane continued. "You should thank me for getting you a fast pony. Maybe we outrun Sioux. Maybe not."

Garrett stared into the fire, trying to ignore him.

Little Crane ran his finger in a circle around his neck. "The Sioux, some of them, take heads off. If you weren't slow, we wouldn't worry about our heads."

"Why do you keep talking about the Sioux that way?" Garrett asked. "It's as if you want them to find us."

"I like to see your face when I talk about them." He smiled. A wolf howled, again on a nearby hill. "Don't worry. Sioux not around here. They gather together in big village. They won't be here."

"I don't believe you any more," Garrett said. "I thought you told me we would catch up with the soldiers yesterday. That didn't happen. And you told me the same thing the day before." Garrett threw his hands up. "I might as well just spit into the wind."

Little Crane shrugged and reached into a skin bag. He grabbed a handful of pemmican and tossed the bag to Garrett.

"Eat. You need strength. You won't let us hunt."

Garrett ate from the bag. "When we find Custer, then you can hunt."

Little Crane swallowed and laughed. "Six Fingers shouldn't worry. Today. We'll catch Bluecoats today. Then for sure. Or maybe one more day. No longer. For sure. Don't worry. Anyway, if we don't, Six Fingers will have more time to make the paper talk."

Little Crane had named Garrett Six Fingers because of Garrett's pen. Little Crane would laugh while Garrett wrote, putting a stick between his own fingers in imitation.

Though he didn't show it, Red Moon was as curious about the talking paper as Little Crane. Both men knew that words had a powerful medicine, something that would allow people with this medicine to see the signs on the paper and know things.

But it was Little Crane who was becoming obsessed. He'd wake Garrett from sleep, giving him ideas, insisting that he put something down, even when nothing of interest had happened.

Both scouts were familiar with hide paintings that depicted great battles or hunts, but they couldn't imagine how Garrett's tiny markings, on small pieces of paper, could tell someone about an entire moon of travel.

Though Little Crane had an on-again, off-again dislike for whites, he had apparently decided that Garrett wasn't a bad sort and had begun to train him in the ways of the frontier. Garrett had shown him the marks that meant Little Crane, and he knew when Garrett was making the paper talk about him.

Garrett hoped to find the Terry–Custer forces and to do a lot of writing in the coming weeks. His mission, for which he was being paid very well, was to find George Armstrong Custer and document as much as he could about the "Boy General" during the campaign against the Sioux. The information gathered was intended not to flatter Custer, but to prove to the American people that the man could never lead a nation.

Garrett's employer was Orvil Grant, brother to Ulysses

S. Grant, the president. There was bad blood between Custer and the Grants; a lot of it. Custer had recently taken the Democratic side in some touchy political issues. It was Garrett's job to slay Custer in the field of public opinion, to lay his bones out to bleach in Republican newspapers across the land.

Garrett, a veteran journalist, had been a war correspondent throughout the Southern Rebellion, sending copy to the St. Louis *Democrat*. His nights had often been spent riding from the battlefield to the nearest rail or telegraph head, where he would send his story, then turn and ride back to the front, getting precious little sleep before joining the Union forces preparing again for battle.

Garrett had learned to use firearms well. He had killed soldiers from both sides to stay alive, some who had mistaken him for the enemy, others who didn't want certain news stories getting into print. Now he carried a Henry repeating rifle and a newly made Colt .45 revolver. He had learned, and learned well, the value of adequate defense.

Garrett had mixed feelings about his mission. He had accepted the Grants' offer to spy on Custer both for the money and for the potential of additional opportunities. Should he do a good job, he would be given other assignments that could further his career considerably.

He was certain, though, that his mission would endanger his life and leave him with a deeply bitter taste in his mouth. Viewing the field after the Battle of Gettysburg, he wrote in his journal: "I believe the nation will never recover from what has happened here, and throughout this conflict. Brothers lie near brothers, dead or dying, many in pieces. Those still alive have hollow eyes and hollower stomachs. They have aged a thousand years. I fear they will carry their grudges forever."

Garrett had been just nineteen at the time. Raised in an affluent St. Louis family, he had enjoyed the comforts of the city. But the Rebellion had taken him into the woods and hills, where he now wanted to stay.

He had never been West, and he had never met any

of the Plains Indians, before hiring Little Crane and Red Moon. They were taking him across a land open and vast beyond his comprehension. It was a land of beauty and majesty, breathtaking in every detail. And all Little Crane could do was talk about death.

Little Crane reached over and touched Garrett's hand. "Sioux will not take your head. They also make necklaces from fingers. Your fingers have medicine. They would probably still move, trying to make the paper talk." He laughed. "A good necklace. The Sioux will be looking for you."

Garrett hadn't taken much time in picking his scouts, and he lamented that fact often. Little Crane tested his limits. The two Arikara, called Rees by the soldiers and frontiersmen, had been the only scouts available when he had arrived at Fort Lincoln. The others had left with the Terry–Custer forces or had gone back to the Fort Berthold Indian Agency.

Garrett had offered Little Crane and Red Moon twice what the army would have paid them. He had been given a large budget and had been told to spend it wisely. The two Rees had accepted Garrett's offer unconditionally.

"I'm tired of hearing this," Garrett said. "The Sioux aren't going to take my fingers."

Little Crane motioned to the west. "Another Six Fingers, a man-who-makes-the-paper-talk, went with the Bluecoats. Maybe Sioux already got his fingers. Maybe they don't want yours anymore. Which fingers are better?"

Garrett was aware that a journalist named Mark Kellogg had gone with Custer. He knew how Kellogg fit into Custer's plans for a glorious campaign and an equally glorious write-up in the New York *Herald*.

"I will tell the *truth* about Custer," Garrett told Little Crane. "Fingers or no fingers, I'm out here to tell the truth."

Little Crane made two fists and slid them under his armpits, making his arms stick out like wings. "You hide fingers. Sioux won't want you." He laughed.

Little Crane knew that the man-who-makes-the-paper-talk, the Six Fingers, had to listen to what Little Crane said. No matter how strong in body or mind, Little Crane knew, the Six Fingers couldn't do without his two scouts. Not if he wanted to find the Bluecoat soldiers.

Little Crane again offered pemmican to Garrett. "Eat. Can't ride if you're hungry."

Garrett accepted a handful of pemmican. "I need to find the Bluecoat soldiers as soon as possible. That's why I hired you. I didn't hire you to eat and talk, but to find the Bluecoats."

Of above average height and well muscled, Garrett was not easily intimidated by anyone, and not shy about asserting himself. He seldom asked for trouble and prided himself on his good nature. But this trip had brought new meaning to the word patience.

Except for his notepads, which he kept at hand, Garrett would never be mistaken for a journalist. He wore boots and light cotton trousers, and a broad-brimmed hat that he had purchased in a sutler's store at Fort Lincoln.

He had discarded the cotton shirts he had brought from Missouri for a thin buckskin pullover that Little Crane had given him as a present. The beading and designs on the shirt were made just for him, according to Little Crane, even though Little Crane admitted that the shirt had been worn by his grandfather.

"You wear it like it was always yours," Little Crane had said. "When your hair is long, like mine, you'll be Indian. Maybe."

The gray light in the east had begun to turn light blue. Under the trees, however, the shadows remained thick.

"Where's Red Moon?" Garrett asked. "I thought he was bringing the horses."

A howl rose from a hill just outside of camp. The wolves had come nearer. Little Crane swallowed more pemmican and listened. It was hard to hear over the rush of the Yellowstone.

From the trees came the sound of a night bird. Little Crane hurriedly doused the fire with dirt and a cloud of smoke enveloped the camp.

Garrett coughed. "What are you doing?"

"Sioux!" Little Crane hissed. "Get up! We go!"

Garrett scrambled to his feet. Red Moon, holding the horses, materialized out of nowhere, speaking to Little Crane in Ree.

"He says we'll have to fight," Little Crane translated. He jumped on his pony. "Use your little gun! Come on!"

Garrett jumped on his horse and pulled out his Colt, knocking his notebook from his waistband. He cursed and jumped down to get it.

As he grabbed it, a shadow appeared to his left from behind a tree, drawing a bow. Garrett turned and fired. The shadow doubled over at the middle.

As Garrett jumped back on his pony, the trees came alive with screaming shadows. The two Rees were gone. Garrett could hear their ponies just ahead, crashing through the brush along the river. He started after them, running down a warrior who tried to block his way.

Another seized his pony's bridle, swinging a war club at the same time. Garrett took a glancing blow against his upper left arm. He fired his Colt into the Indian's face and kicked his pony's ribs.

Garrett raced through the trees, holding the pony to the trail along the river. *Got to stay in cover!* he reminded himself. Little Crane had told him that over and over. In the open he wouldn't stand a chance; the Sioux would run him down.

Garrett stayed low, allowing his pony free rein, trying to catch up to the Ree scouts. He saw them just ahead as shafts of morning light reached through the trees. He would catch them. He had a good runner, as good as the Ree horses. They had chosen one for him from their herds, telling him that the country they were going into was rough and only stout horses were good.

His shoulder aching, Garrett struggled to hold on. The pony ran full speed, dodging brush and jumping fallen logs. Tree limbs whipped and snapped, and the thorns of rose and gooseberry grabbed at his pantlegs.

Just behind, Garrett heard another pony running, gaining steadily, a screaming warrior on its back. Ahead, the trees broke into an open bank, where O'Fallon Creek joined the Yellowstone. Filled with runoff, the creek was nearly fifty yards wide and rushing with power.

The Rees were just crossing, splashing in the half-light. Garrett's pony stopped at the bank, then jumped in. Garrett fell sideways and off the pony, the current momentarily sweeping him under.

The Sioux warrior was into the stream, turning his pony toward Garrett. Leaning over, the warrior swung the war club. Garrett reached up and grabbed the warrior's wrist, twisting. The club fell into the current.

Desperate to stay above water, Garrett grabbed the pony's mane with one hand and clutched the warrior's hair with the other. The warrior slid thrashing into the water.

They fought, the two slamming one another unmercifully with their fists. Garrett landed a hard blow to the warrior's nose, knocking it sideways against his face. He then clamped both hands around the warrior's throat. The two spun through the frothy water, kicking and gouging, until Garrett got the warrior's back firmly against a fallen tree.

Pinning the warrior against the tree with his knees, Garrett renewed his choke grip. The warrior coughed heavily, water gurgling in his lungs. Little Crane and Red Moon had dismounted on the bank and were shooting their rifles, driving the remaining Sioux back.

Garrett felt the warrior die. He stood in the current, shaking, the warrior's lifeless body limp, lodged against the trunk. Little Crane and Red Moon rode up to him, shouting triumphantly. In the east, the light had grown into a pink-scarlet streak across the heavens.

Red Moon jumped from his pony and pulled the Sioux warrior's body from the water and onto the bank. Garrett came out and sank to his knees, breathing heavily. Little Crane jumped down and handed him a knife, pointing to the Sioux warrior.

"The scalp is yours."

"No, I don't want it."

"Take it!" Little Crane said. "Keep it with you. You will gain much favor."

Red Moon turned the Sioux over onto his stomach and stood back. Little Crane knelt and repeated, "Take it!" running his finger along the warrior's head where the knife should cut.

Garrett thought about the pain in his left arm and the deep bruise that was already beginning to swell. He thought about the warrior's face, the desperate rage, the intent to kill.

Little Crane looked into his face. "Good! It is good!" he yelled. "You will do it!"

Garrett grabbed a forelock of hair and, holding the head up, ran the knife in a semicircle around the warrior's hairline. He pulled back forcefully and the scalp lifted with a sucking sound. He tore backward, pulling the scalp free near the nape of the neck, and held it up, staring at it.

Both Rees were singing a war song, shouting and whooping. Garrett dropped the scalp and vomited.

"Six Fingers is a warrior now," Little Crane said. "Show the scalp and all Sioux enemies will be your friend."

Garrett retrieved the scalp and climbed on his pony. He hugged the horse tightly, grateful for its speed and endurance during the chase, thankful that it had saved him. He stared into the rising sun while the Rees circled him on their ponies, singing songs of praise.

Garrett touched his belt. His pistol was gone, as was his notebook. Little Crane yelled at him, holding up a handful of paper that he had taken from his own saddle-bag.

"Six Fingers not worry. Have more of the paper. Lots more. You can make it talk. You have great medicine. Make the paper talk about what you have done this day! Tell everyone what you have done!"

TWO

Garrett rode stiffly, his injured arm in a sling that Little Crane had made for him. Each jolt in the saddle was a rush of agony. Little Crane stayed back with him while Red Moon rode ahead a short distance, going from hill to hill, looking over the country around them.

To Garrett, the incident at O'Fallon Creek was hazy. He could recall bits and pieces, but not everything. He had never been so frightened, not in four years of covering the Rebellion. He had seen soldiers fight each other—white soldiers—but none of them had shown the intensity displayed by the Sioux warrior he had drowned in the muddy water.

"They were Sioux?" Garrett asked Little Crane. "How did you know they were coming?"

"Didn't know they were coming," Little Crane said. He shrugged. "But they came, a small band of scouts, likely moving ahead of a village. Santee. Part of the Sioux nation." He pointed north, then made a circular sweep with his hand. "Coming from up there. Coming from all over to join Sitting Bull. Big village to the south. Very big. Many Sioux and Cheyenne down there. Too many."

"There are a lot of soldiers out here now," Garrett said. "If they all come together, it will be a huge force."

Besides the Terry–Custer forces, a regiment from the west, led by Colonel John Gibbon, was already in the field, as was another large force to the south, under the command of Brigadier General George Crook. The hunted Indian nations, trapped between the three commands, would be forced to return to their reservations, or be crushed to extinction by the fighting power of the soldiers. That was the plan.

Garrett had been informed of the plans before coming out, and had learned the officers' biographies and their particular tendencies. He was to be able to analyze for himself how the campaign was going so that he could pick everything apart in print.

Arrangements had been made by Orvil Grant to have Garrett's correspondence published in the Democratic press under the nom de plume A. J. Becker. Garrett would dispatch his findings in letter form to his fiancée's address in St. Louis, where a Grant associate would retrieve them and make the necessary forwardings to get the information to the Grants. They would then see to it that the appropriate newspapers published the columns for the American people to see.

The plan seemed simple enough, except for the fact that General Terry had specific orders that no journalists accompany the campaign. Garrett had already notified the Grants that Custer had taken Mark Kellogg of the New York *Herald* along, against Terry's better judgment. Should anyone ask Garrett whom he was representing, he would report the St. Louis *Democrat.* And should he be asked to remain behind, he would counter with the example of Kellogg. If Kellogg was to go, he would go as well, or there would be a political stir about playing journalistic favorites. One had to be fair about things, especially during such an important campaign as this.

"There's going to be a big fight," Little Crane remarked, "a bad one. That's good with us, the Arikara people, because Sioux and Cheyenne have killed many of us off. But I don't think there are enough Bluecoats to stop them."

"The army believes they can outfight the Sioux with one man to every ten warriors."

Little Crane laughed. "Bluecoats are stupid to think that. They fall off their horses. How can they fight when they fall off their horses?"

Garrett remembered how hard it had been for the new

recruits during the Rebellion. Many country boys could ride well, but many could not. Still, the men should be seasoned by now—those who were still in service.

"I've been told that a lot of the soldiers on this campaign have had Indian fighting experience," Garrett said. "Some have been in the army over ten years. They should be able to ride well by now."

"What you call 'ride well' is nothing compared to a warrior," Little Crane said. "Warriors live on their horses. Bluecoats fall off."

Garrett thought about his own pony and how well it had performed in the chase with the Sioux scout. He wondered if he would have another event like that to look forward to in the future.

"Besides," Little Crane continued, "the Bluecoat horses never keep their strength up. They might be bigger and maybe faster, but Bluecoat horses need extra feed and need grain. Warrior ponies live only on grass and do very well. You'll see. Bluecoat horses tire very quickly."

Garrett tested his arm, which was aflame to the touch. He wondered how he could stay on a horse or report the upcoming events in this condition. With his injury, he was forced to ride much slower than he would have liked. But he had no choice.

At midmorning, Garrett grew dizzy.

Little Crane rode over. "Pain in your arm too much?"

Garrett didn't answer. He reeled in the saddle. Little Crane reached over and caught him.

"Time to get down. Rest." Little Crane took them into the trees.

"We've got to find the soldiers," Garrett protested.

Little Crane pointed upriver. "Just a short distance. We'll reach them easily. I'll make drink for you to ease the pain."

Garrett dismounted and settled with his back against a tree. Merely moving his arm filled him with misery and it was good to sit quietly.

Red Moon remained mounted, saying nothing. He stared behind them and a little to the south, looking long and hard. He pointed and said something to Little Crane.

After looking, Little Crane shrugged. "Some dust, way out," he told Garrett. "Shouldn't worry."

Garrett tried to see what had alarmed Red Moon. He stood up, but Little Crane sat him back down.

"What's out there?" Garrett asked.

"Shouldn't worry." Little Crane took a forked stick and a small pot from his saddlebag. "I'll dig plants. Be back soon." He motioned for Red Moon to dismount and tend to Garrett.

Red Moon, as usual, remained silent and pensive. He seemed saddened by life in general and unable to change it for himself. He brought a bladder of water and set it next to Garrett, then began gathering twigs and sticks. Soon, a small fire crackled.

"Why the fire?" Garrett asked, pointing. "I'm not cold."

Red Moon cupped his left hand and stirred a stick in his palm with his right hand, then set his palm over the fire.

"Cook?" Garrett said. "We can't stop to eat!"

Red Moon shrugged. He stood and looked into the distance, his eyes holding on the dust toward the south. Garrett watched him, wishing Little Crane would return so he could learn what was really going on.

Little Crane hurried back from the river. The pot was filled with roots he had dug and washed at the river. In his other hand he carried two flat stones. He took a bladder of water from his pony and sat down next to the fire.

"Don't take time to cook, for God's sake!" Garrett bellowed. "Custer will be gone!"

"Long Hair's not far," Little Crane insisted. He pointed upriver. "Over there." He began crushing the roots between the two flat stones.

"I said I don't want you to cook!" Garrett repeated. "I'm paying you, and I want you to listen!"

"You should listen!" Little Crane held up a mashed root, his eyes narrowed. "This will help you. Listen!"

"What is it?"

Little Crane took a portion of the crushed roots and

mixed them in the pot with water. He set the pot next to the fire. The remainder he mixed in his hands with water and two other roots he had crushed. He held his hand out to Garrett. "Eat!"

"I don't want it!"

"Eat! Or you can't ride well. You'll never find Long Hair!"

Garrett extended his hand and Little Crane dumped the mixture into his palm.

"How will this help?" Garrett asked.

"Eat!"

Garrett downed the mixture, choking. He nearly vomited. Little Crane held the bladder of water up. Garrett drank deeply. "What is it?"

"Roots. They'll calm you inside." He rubbed his stomach, then pointed to Garrett's arm. "They'll help with pain. Take off your shirt."

Little Crane took the pot from the fire and tested its contents with his fingers. Satisfied, he smeared the concoction on Garrett's bruised arm and held it there by tying a cloth in place.

"Wait for a time," he said. "Don't touch."

"How long?" Garrett asked.

"A while. Maybe all of today. Don't touch. I'll tell you."

Garrett drank more water and settled back against the tree. The day was open and very warm. Birds filled the trees along the river. In a patch of buffalo berry, two mourning doves cooed softly. Nearby, a woodpecker drummed against a hollow trunk.

Little Crane went into a nearby bog. He returned with a small willow, cut it, and bent it into a hoop, fastening the ends tightly with sinew. He smiled and retrieved the scalp from Garrett's saddlebag.

"I will dry it for you."

Garrett didn't reply. He watched while Little Crane methodically spread the scalp across the hoop and sewed sinew through the edges with a porcupine quill. Carefully, he stretched the scalp, attaching it to the hoop with the sinew.

"Leave it on your saddle," he said. "When it's ready, you can tie it on your rifle."

"Why don't you just keep it?" Garrett suggested.

"You won that scalp," Little Crane said. "It's not mine. You have great honor. Why don't you want honor?"

Garrett moved his left shoulder. The pain had dulled. "Honor's good." He hoped that Little Crane would then drop the subject. "Honor is very good. When the scalp is ready, I'll tie it to my rifle. Satisfied?"

Little Crane grunted. "I now have a warrior for a boss. That suits me fine."

Red Moon hurried over to Little Crane and spoke in Ree. He was pointing to the south. The cloud of dust was bigger.

"What's the matter?" Garrett asked.

"Could be buffalo," Little Crane said. "Maybe not. No matter what, we'll go and hide, and watch to see what comes."

The two Rees mounted. Little Crane held Garrett's pony while Garrett eased himself on. Red Moon had already kicked his horse into a gallop.

"Are there more Sioux coming?" Garrett asked. "Is that what the dust cloud was all about? I thought you said they'd left. You don't know anything, do you?"

Red Moon had ridden upriver into a thick patch of trees and brush. Little Crane pointed. "We go there and watch. No one will see us."

"Answer me," Garrett insisted. "You really don't know anything, do you?"

Little Crane was gone, kicking his horse into a gallop. Garrett followed him into the trees, grimacing with pain. As Garrett dismounted, Little Crane put his index finger to his lips. "No talk."

Little Crane muzzled his and Garrett's ponies with strips of rawhide. Red Moon had already muzzled his horse and was crouched in a thicket of wild plum, studying the approaching dust cloud.

Garrett watched while the dust grew closer. Suddenly, a small herd of buffalo surged over the hill and into the valley bottom, running directly for the river. They stopped in the shallows, breathing heavily, their tails held out behind them.

Garrett stared. The dream came back to him in full force. But no flames appeared. Instead, the buffalo stood knee-deep in the water, catching their breath.

Red Moon and Little Crane were speaking in Ree. Little Crane was laughing, scratching his feet and rubbing between his toes. He turned and noticed Garrett's puzzled face.

"Heel flies," he said. "The buffalo have heel flies. They run to the water for help."

"Hell flies?" Garrett said.

Little Crane laughed. "Heel flies, not hell flies. Foot flies. Flies bite up into the heel and cause pain." He turned to Red Moon and told him what Garrett had said. Red Moon rolled on the ground with laughter.

Garrett began to laugh, realizing his mistake. Maybe he had been quite accurate, though, at that.

"Maybe the buffalo call them hell flies," he told Little Crane.

Little Crane laughed harder. "Maybe the Black Robes talked to the buffalo, and told the buffalo about little devils sticking them in the feet with little forks. Yes!" He howled.

Little Crane and Red Moon laughed uncontrollably, rolling, pounding the ground. When they finally tired, both rose to their feet, teary-eyed. Red Moon walked over by himself and sat down on a log. He lowered his face into his hands and began to sob.

"What's the matter with him?" Garrett asked.

"This is the second thing of honor you've done today," Little Crane told Garrett. "First, you gained a war honor by killing the Sioux, you counted coup. Now you help Red Moon with his grief."

"I don't understand," Garrett said.

Little Crane pointed to Red Moon. "He's not laughed like that for nearly four moons, when his wife and two children died of sickness. The laughter broke through to his grief. You broke it out of him. He'll be good now. He'll talk more; laugh more. Your honor.''

Garrett looked perplexed. Little Crane took the muzzles off the ponies. Red Moon came over and mounted, taking a deep breath. Little Crane helped Garrett up and then slid onto his pony's back.

''Good day already,'' he said. ''The best day we've had. We'll go now and find Bluecoats.''

In late afternoon, the Powder River appeared. At its mouth was a large contingent of soldiers bivouacked under the cottonwoods. Despite his throbbing arm, Garrett shouted for joy. But his pleasure was short-lived. They had merely found the wagon train and the infantry, left behind to guard what had become the campaign supply base. Terry and Custer had left two days earlier with the cavalry, en route to the mouth of Tongue River.

The commanding officer, Major Orlando Moore, tried to console Garrett. ''Sorry you missed him. They were in a rush to catch the Sioux. The word is they're headed for the mountains to the south, the Big Horns.''

Moore thought that Garrett and the two Rees were additional scouts. Garrett didn't tell him otherwise. Little Crane got everyone's attention by displaying the scalp and pointing to Garrett, indicating that he had killed a Sioux warrior that morning in battle, hand-to-hand. Garrett explained to Moore that the warrior had been part of a small scouting party and that there was no use in pursuing them.

Before long, Garrett was helped onto a cottonwood stump and asked to relate his story to everyone. The soldiers gathered, whooping and yelling. They asked questions endlessly, until nearly sundown, and wanted to see the scalp. Many of them displayed their own grisly items taken over the years, including bullet and tobacco pouches made from human skin.

After a meal of bacon, beans, and hardtack, Little Crane and Red Moon curled up in their blankets and fell sound asleep. Garrett began work on a new diary, using paper given him by Little Crane. He felt confident that he could reconstruct the events of the past four days without losing details. Luckily, he had started a new notebook not long before the attack had come. Prior to reaching the Yellowstone, he had filled three volumes, which lay bound securely within his saddlebags.

A skiff was scheduled to leave the following morning, carrying mail to a steamboat docked below Fort Lincoln, and from there to points east. Garrett prepared a letter for Orvil Grant:

Supply Depot at mouth of Powder River
Montana Territory
Midafternoon, 18 June 1876

Dear Orvil,
   This finds me well, but shaken. I had an encounter with a Sioux warrior early this morning and am hoping it was the first and last of its kind. I was forced to kill the man and, at the insistence of my Ree scouts, now have his scalp. Before falling, the warrior gave me a knot on my arm from his war club. All in all, I am not hurt. Yet this is not what I expected.
   Regarding my mission, I am told that I will find Custer in another day at most, likely in the vicinity of Tongue River. General Terry is bivouacked there while Custer and Major Marcus Reno are scouting the country. Have been inquiring here about Custer and find mixed feelings. There is no shortage of stories about him, many in his disfavor. I do not want to divulge who I am, however, and the commanding officer considers me a scout.
   I am told that the steamboat *Far West* is shuttling men and equipment up and down the river. Would find it easier to board and travel in that manner, but my scouts are afraid of the boat. I will honor their request to remain on horseback. They have certainly been of good service to me.

Will remain here until dawn, at which time we will commence upriver to join the Terry–Custer forces. Have been treated very well by the major and will receive what I need in the way of arms and ammunition, as well as provisions for two days.

Cannot say when my next dispatch will be, but likely from Tongue River. I am told the mail goes out regularly on river by skiff, or on land by courier. Many ways to keep in contact, which I shall, as I have promised.

I remain, your obedient servant,
Adam Garrett

Relieved that Custer was less than a day's ride away, Garrett relaxed for the first time since leaving Fort Lincoln. The poultice on his arm had begun to reduce the swelling and he knew his sleep would be sound. But there was one matter that needed attending to first, the matter of a promise he must keep. He took paper and an envelope and walked off by himself to the edge of the river, where the falling sun had cast a vermilion sheen over the water.

Ann Malone, his fiancée in St. Louis, was on his mind. He could feel her hair, red and light, soft as the breeze that whispered through the trees, soft as her tender lips. He wondered if her eyes were now closed in sleep, or large and brown, filled with tears at his leaving.

It had been hard to leave her, especially since she had tried desperately to dissuade him from going. He had told her that should his mission be a success, their future was assured. He would be of rank in the next presidential administration.

What more could a journalist ask? What more could he want for a new wife and a family-to-be? The mission would be a success. He would see to it.

With the light fading, he sat on a cottonwood log to compose his words.

Supply depot at mouth of Powder River,
Montana Territory
Evening, 18 June 1876

Dearest Ann,

Hope you received my last letter of 13th June. I
miss you so much and long for your touch. If only
you were here to see this sunset with me! If it were
that I could have you here, I would bring you post-
haste.

I am joyous this night, as I have finally reached
the soldiers. It's not Custer, not yet, but I'm told my
scouts and I will reach him by the morrow noon. I
am so interested in meeting him face to face and
learning of his temperament.

It is good that we have reached the soldiers, for
this morning I was forced to fight for my life against
a Sioux Indian. They came at us in our dawn camp.
My left arm sustained a deep bruise. Nothing worse
than that. I was forced to kill the man. Will detail
the experience when we next meet, but suffice it to
say that I gained a coup and am honored in the eyes
of my scouts and the soldiers.

This comes after having had the strangest dream.
It was of a huge buffalo standing in front of me.
We were encircled by fire. The buffalo caught fire
and burned, turning white. It then ran and the flames
opened up, much as the waters of the Red Sea parted
before Moses, I suppose. I couldn't understand it
and my scouts told me to think about it, that they
would find someone I could talk to when we reach
Custer and the other scouts.

This late morning brought buffalo to the river,
very close to us, shaggy beasts that they are. As you
can imagine, the dream returned to me. I don't know
what it's all about.

I feel that the fight with the Sioux warrior will
help me with my cause. I will now be able to talk
with the scouts about the campaign. Meeting Custer
will be the biggest coup. I am beginning to think,

though, that nearly as important as my mission against Custer is my fascination with this great land. I must tell you that it is a marvel! You can see forever out here, forever and beyond!

My Ree scouts understand this land so well. They call it their mother, with a reverence as strong as if they were speaking of flesh itself. I can understand their point. Each day and each night brings me closer to her bosom. I am in awe of her grandeur. Especially the waters. In all the world there cannot be anything so powerful as these waters out here in this vast land. They rise and fall and rush with the force of legions. If the Sioux are only half as formidable, Custer shall have his hands full.

It is a different world out here and, when the land is more settled and we are married, I think it would be grand to pay a visit. I have no doubt that you will feel as I do, touched in your very soul. You need to see it with me. You need to see it before it changes. There is something here that is vanishing, sadly. A way of life going into the past. I see it in my scouts' eyes. They don't speak of such things, but I know they feel this way. I want you to partake of it, before it's gone.

I don't want you to think I've forgotten about your cousin. I haven't. As soon as I reach the soldiers, I will inquire about him.

I think of you always and see your beautiful face in the sky above me each morning. I see you in a bridal gown, coming down the aisle to meet me. Soon, my dear. Very soon.

Until my next letter, then,
My love always,
Adam

THREE

The darkness was dense, blacker than any night she had ever known. She felt so heavy that she could barely move. Her paralysis, she knew, was fear.

This was the third straight night of her ordeal. She wondered if it would ever end, making her fear that she was dying. She struggled against it, but the fear grew stronger, pushing against her so hard as to make it difficult to breathe.

As it had the previous two nights, her fear suddenly grew to panic. Once again huge flames of red appeared in the distance, a long line of crimson racing toward her. As before, she lifted her feet to run, straining against some force that made her entire body as heavy as stone.

But tonight was to be different. Just ahead of the flames ran a huge animal, humpbacked, with large horns that curved upward. More astounding, it was pure white.

The animal came ever closer, the flames right behind. She tried to run, but could barely walk. As the animal drew nearer, she could see someone riding on its back. A man, who called to her, waved frantically.

She stared, unbelieving, as the animal approached. The man waving to her was Adam! It was her fiancé, Adam Garrett!

Adam? What are you doing? Where are we? The huge animal came alongside her. Adam reached down to pull her up with him. She held out her hand a fraction of a second too late, clutching only the hair of the white beast. Adam's fingers, inches from her own, clutched only air.

Adam! Adam, wait! Please!

The white beast carried him beyond her, he looking

back, until the darkness swallowed them. Tears streamed from her eyes. *Adam! Come back! Please come back!*

In her left hand she held a clump of the white hair. It felt alive to the touch.

She heard a roaring behind her and turned. The flames were there, nearly upon her, coming faster, ever faster. She began to run. Her feet were heavy. The flames drew closer, huge and jagged, roaring through the blackness. Closer, ever closer.

Ann Malone sat up in bed and gasped. She looked around her, unsure of where she was. Her cheeks and brow ran with perspiration, mingled with tears that streamed from her eyes.

The house was still, the darkness complete but for a hint of moonlight shining through her window. She rubbed her moist cheeks and took a deep breath. She was in St. Louis, safe in her home. There was no huge white animal. No Adam Garrett. No flames. The sheets were smooth, the headboard solid. But the dream had been so real!

She had been on a vast plain alive with fire, trapped and alone, screaming after Adam as he rode away on a white beast, lost forever in the darkness beyond her. It was the third night she had dreamt this way, but the first night she had seen Adam. For the past two days she had contemplated going to find him, to talk him out of his assignment and bring him back to St. Louis. Now, after this dream, she was determined to go. As soon as possible.

Fully awake, Ann swung her feet to the floor. The letter lay on the nightstand, as it had since arriving three days before, when her dreams had started. Reaching inside, she felt the clump of thick, black hair that Adam had enclosed with his letter.

The hair felt the same as that of the white animal in her dream.

Adam had talked about hoping soon to see a buffalo. So why had she been dreaming of fire, and now of a white buffalo? And why had Adam swept past her on the buffalo's back? Was he going someplace without her?

She couldn't bear to consider the possibilities. Death was foremost in her mind. Was Adam going to die? Was her own death soon to come? She fought against the thoughts now racing through her mind.

Ann lit a lamp. She took Adam's letter from the envelope. Her fingers trembling, she read:

Ft. Abraham Lincoln,
Dakota Territory
13 June 1876

Dearest Ann,

I hope this finds you well. I have barely begun my journey and already miss you so. I look at your picture constantly and wish that you were by my side.

Soon, when my mission is finished, we will be together once more, never again to part. The fruits of my labor will enable us to secure a very good life within the Grant administration. At that time our lives will be splendid. You will see.

It is a cool morning here. A thunderstorm passed through at dawn and the grass now sparkles in the sunlight. The train arrived yesterday at noon, without incident. In fact, the trip was rather boring, with the exception of a stop for water somewhere on these vast and open plains.

That is where I collected the wool enclosed in the letter. It seems that a herd of buffalo had passed through, and in rubbing against the supports for the water tower, had brought it crashing to the ground. Needless to say, we were detained for some time until repairs to the tower were made and water could be taken on. I was disappointed in not seeing one or more of the beasts, but thought I would collect a memento of their visit, and share some of it with you.

Other than that one episode, there was little to view or remember. This is an open, treeless land.

The air here is drier than you can imagine. I am told that the mountains to the west take all the rain and leave little for the open plains. Nevertheless, it is a fascinating area, and I will be calling it home for a while.

I will be leaving the fort as soon as possible. As I had suspected, the Terry–Custer forces have already departed—a full three weeks ago! I am not concerned though, as large forces of men travel very slowly. I can catch up in a matter of days, not weeks. I will need to secure scouts, however, as soon as possible.

Having been all around the post and having talked with many of its inhabitants, I am confident that I can help the Grants. My wages may not be all that hard to earn. I don't even have to mention that I want unfavorable news about the "Boy General." Such news is offered to me openly. The mere mention of his name causes severe frowning among all but the most devoted Custer followers.

Among those who admire him, I would consider his wife, Libbie, foremost. I met her by chance late yesterday afternoon—she had heard that I am a journalist and that I will be securing scouts to catch up with the troops. I believe she had intended to ask me to take her along, but reconsidered, thinking it imprudent.

I found Mrs. Custer an agreeable person, but discovered that she can talk about little else than her husband. She calls him Autie and stated any number of times that I would have no trouble finding him, for he would be the handsomest man on the Plains.

Though pleasant, Mrs. Custer does not impress me as a woman who cares to see the truth. She goes into a trance when she talks about her rogue, a kind of dreamy swoon that takes her far away, to wherever he might be. I believe she has a good and devoted heart. But there's no room for anyone else but her hero.

I am sure she thinks that my desire is to embellish

her husband's campaign, as Mark Kellogg is surely doing, and I will not lead her to believe otherwise. I hate to think how she will feel, though, when she learns that I have undermined him. She will surely learn that even before the campaign is finished.

I have inquired here about your cousin, Mason Hall, but have met with no success in learning anything about him. The post has no record of who is serving under General George Crook on the campaign out of Fort Fetterman. Will keep trying and hope I can learn something of him while with Custer's forces.

The courier is calling for mail, so I will close. I hope you think of me often. I will write you again as soon as I can.

My love always,
Adam

Clutching the letter, Ann rose and peered from the window. Light was breaking over the city. Below, a gardener was already at work, trimming the lawn's edge near the entrance to the estate, while birds flitted among the bushes, singing their hearts out. She wished she was watching the dawn from a guest room at Fort Abraham Lincoln, preparing to leave for Yellowstone country.

Ann had long ago become used to life in St. Louis, but had also had a taste of the frontier. A small taste, but enough to teach her about life outside the city.

Having lost her mother to illness at the age of five, she had grown up under the guidance of her father, a loving man but one unaccustomed to the tutelage of little girls. He was in the fur trade and often made forays into the mountains.

Ever eager to please Ann, he taught her to ride horses and even took her on an occasional trip to a nearby fur post, where she saw Indians who had once been wild. Nothing close to St. Louis was wild anymore.

Though Ann had asked to go often, her father never

consented to take her very far from the city. Any number of things could happen, he had always insisted. And something had happened to him during Ann's sixteenth year.

Word had come, just before Christmas, that Ann's father had drowned when his canoe capsized in the Missouri River. His fortune had gone to Ann in trust, to be disbursed when she was twenty-one.

During his frequent absences, Ann had lived with Cora Malone, her spinster aunt, on the large estate, also born of money from the Rocky Mountain fur trade, where she now made her home. It had been during a trip to the St. Louis *Democrat,* owned in part by her aunt, that she had met Adam Garrett. At the time he had just begun to write dispatches on the escalating Indian wars in the west.

Ann had been too young at the time even to consider a relationship, but had never forgotten him. Nor had he forgotten her, for he had begun to write to her last year. When he returned they began to see one another frequently, despite her aunt's insistence that Ann find someone more gentlemanly.

Ann knew that Adam was the only man she would ever want. When with him, her very being burst with happiness. And now he had secured this career-making position working for the Grants and had promised to marry her after completing his time with Custer's Yellowstone campaign.

But that depended on his safe return, and there were too many variables to suit Ann. This latest dream had convinced her that something terrible was going to happen. She didn't want Adam in the middle of something where he might surely die.

Besides the Indians, there would certainly be some soldiers who thought the world of Custer and his mission. What if one or more of those men discovered that Adam intended to tear the campaign apart in the press? What if Custer himself discovered this?

Ann couldn't bear the thought of what might happen. She had asked Adam to reconsider his mission many times. They could do well enough if he just took a normal job with the *Democrat*. Such a job had been offered.

But Adam had a silly notion that he could help the country by working with the Grants. He was certain that while among Custer's forces he could log the truth about the controversial commander and steer the country in a better direction by stopping Custer from gaining the Democratic nomination for president.

Ann shook with frustration. How could Adam be so vain? How could he think that even if he did succeed in his campaign to ruin Custer in the press, the Grants would necessarily come through on their end?

Adam had justified his dangerous mission by telling Ann any number of times that working for the Grants would establish them far better and far faster than anything else he could possibly do. The campaign against the Sioux and Cheyenne was the most politically charged issue since the close of the Rebellion.

Ann thought Adam naive. The Grants were politicians, too. What would make them so loyal to Adam?

Ann returned to the bed and sat down heavily. She slipped the letter back into the envelope and laid it down on the nightstand. She realized that she needed help in getting to the frontier. She would never be able to find Adam on her own.

There was a man, though, whom she could turn to. Tyrone Banks, who had worked for her father, had comforted her during the funeral as best he could. He had been separated from his own mother and father at the age of six, when they were sold during a slave auction, and knew the pain of separation well. "I know you don't feel it's fair, Miss Ann, losing your mother and now your father," he had told her, "but these things happen. Just remember that the Good Lord is taking care of you. It won't seem that way to you for a while. But it's the truth."

Tyrone had always been a paid employee of Ann's father, finally the second in command in her father's company at a time when it was not polically prudent to allow blacks equal social status. He had accompanied her father on numerous journeys into the mountains.

Of all those who had known her father, the only one to console her had been Tyrone. "Always remember that you're a strong one," Tyrone had said. "Otherwise the Good Lord wouldn't be putting this burden on you now. And remember that I won't be saying goodbye—just so long for a little while. I'll be looking in on you from time to time. When the time's right, we'll see one another a great deal more."

Ann had thought of him many times over the years. As promised, he had looked in on her from time to time. The visits had been short, during Aunt Cora's infrequent trips away from the mansion.

It had been just three days before, when she had gotten Adam's letter, that she chanced to meet him at the train station.

"You looking to go over them tracks somewhere, Miss Ann?" he had asked, a broad smile covering his face.

After hugging him, she had told him about Adam and how she was seriously thinking about joining him in the west. Tyrone, now frowning, told her that the west was a dangerous place to go.

"They say those Indians don't want to see no more people go out that way. It's different than the old days. A lot different. They kill folks. Man, woman or child, they'll kill you."

"I've got no choice," Ann told him. "The man who means the whole world to me is out there. I need to be with him."

"Don't he plan to come back?"

"Not without my help. I know that sounds crazy, but it's true."

Tyrone, shaking his head in his usual manner, said, "You've not changed a bit, Miss Ann. When you're bound to do something, you'll do it. But you won't be going out there alone. You hear? I know trains and I been out there a time or two. Promise me you'll let me travel with you. Promise me!"

Ann spent the next three days packing. By midmorning of the third day, she was ready. Tyrone had made traveling arrangements that same day he had talked with her.

Somehow he had known that she would be leaving very soon.

Ann would be meeting him at the train station. Rail travel was much faster and far more dependable than travel by water.

Ann again stood at her window. Dakota Territory was like another world, distant and dangerous. Possibly not as dangerous as her Aunt Cora would have her believe, but certainly uncivilized.

Aunt Cora had objected strenuously to Ann's decision to leave, especially after hearing that Ann's traveling companion would be a colored man twice her age. Ann would hear nothing of "scandalous" or "outlandish." She had made up her mind to leave; nothing would change that.

A carriage rolled along the cobblestone street, its driver turning the horses onto the roadway that led to the Malone mansion. Ann took a deep breath and turned from the window. She tucked Adam's letter into her purse and closed the door to the room behind her. Her bags already waited near the front door.

The servants watched curiously as she descended the stairs. They had been ordered by Aunt Cora not to help her with her things. This order had brought on mixed emotions; but for the sake of their positions, they had obeyed. Miss Malone was leaving, after all. There was no sense in risking their own departure as well.

Ann stopped at the foot of the stairs. Outside, the carriage waited. In front of the door stood a stooped, gray-haired woman, a cane in one hand and a glass of bourbon in the other.

"Aunt Cora, must we make a scene of this?" Ann asked.

Aunt Cora's eyes flashed. "You really are going, aren't you?"

"Of course I am. Can we say a friendly goodbye, or must it be ugly?"

"You've made the choice, Ann."

"Yes, and I'm certainly old enough to do so. Now, I must ask you to move, please."

"Your father wouldn't approve, Ann."

"My father's not here, Aunt Cora. And I'm a grown woman. Must we go over this again?"

Aunt Cora slurped from her glass. Her eyes were red and swollen. Ann had rarely seen her cry.

Ann stepped forward. "We've talked about this, Aunt Cora. I feel I must go. Otherwise I would stay and wait for him. I've explained that. I'll be back before you know it."

Aunt Cora moved away from the door, jabbing her cane into the hardwood floor as she walked. "Don't tell me that, Ann. I refuse to hear it. A lady doesn't travel into the frontier—a wilderness filled with Indians, at that—and live to tell about it. It's ludicrous! Sheer nonsense!"

Ann came closer to her aunt. "Do you remember the story you told me when I was a little girl, the story of how you rode the horse through the wilderness to find Uncle Bill?"

"That was different! That was a necessity. I didn't have a choice." She raised her handkerchief and blew her nose loudly.

"I'm sure someone else could have gone. One of the townsmen, perhaps. I'm sure they didn't want a lady out in that kind of country. That's what you said when telling the story. Do you remember?"

"Oh, fiddlesticks!" Aunt Cora jabbed her cane into the floor. "Nothing I can say is going to stop you. I can see that. Let me give you a hug goodbye."

Ann held Aunt Cora closely, as closely as she could ever remember. She hadn't known her aunt could possess such affection.

"You be careful, young lady," Aunt Cora said. "And you write to me. You hear?"

"I shall," Ann promised.

Aunt Cora turned to the servants, directing them with her cane. "Well, what are you all waiting for? The young lady needs help with her bags. She's a long way to go. A very long way."

FOUR

The next day Little Crane and Red Moon led Garrett to the top of a knoll and pointed downriver. A large steamboat lay moored along the riverbank. Spirals of campfire smoke drifted into the late morning sun.

Garrett wanted to shout for joy. Little Crane spoke in Ree to Red Moon, who pursed his lips and made a loud, birdlike call.

"Our Ree brothers will hear that," Little Crane told Garrett. "They will certainly be out from the camp, watching for signs of the enemy. They will come to greet us."

Little Crane had no more than spoken the words when a similar call came from among the hills to the south. Soon a party of eight Ree Indians appeared, waving their arms in salute.

Garrett rode forward with Little Crane and Red Moon. The Ree scouts from the Tongue River military camp laughed and shouted in greeting. With them was a white man who introduced himself as Fred Gerard, hired to interpret for General Custer.

Gerard, wiry and dark complected, appeared uneasy.

"I have the responsibility of telling the General what the Ree scouts have found," Gerard told Garrett. "Who are you and what are you doing here?"

Before Garrett could answer, Little Crane spoke in Ree to Gerard, holding up his fingers, making sign into the palm of his hand that Garrett was a writer.

"You rode all the way out here to write about the campaign?" Gerard asked.

"Yes," Garrett said. "I got a late start. I'm lucky to have made it here."

"I don't have the authority to let you stay," Gerard said. "You'll have to go through the ranks, starting with Lieutenant Varnum, chief of scouts. He'll tell you who you'll have to talk to for permission."

"General Custer would be the one to give that, wouldn't he?" Garrett asked.

"It's not that simple," Gerard said. "I don't know how much you know about the army, but nothing's simple. You have to see someone, then wait and see the next person."

"He shouldn't have to wait," Little Crane said. "He has medicine fingers. Long Hair should be proud to have him."

Gerard studied Little Crane. "You speak English very well. How come you weren't hired back at Fort Berthold?"

"I was sleeping and forgot to get up." Little Crane laughed. He said it again in Ree and the scouts howled. He pointed to the hoop hanging from Garrett's saddle and talked about the fight at Glendive Creek. The scouts nodded and yelled war cries.

"Show them," Little Crane said to Garrett. "Hold up the scalp and show them. Tell them what you've done."

Garrett lifted the hoop from his saddle horn, the long, black hair hanging loosely. Little Crane took the hoop and held it up for the scouts to see. They all nodded their approval and pointed at Garrett, raising their index and middle fingers together, indicating that they wished to be friends with Garrett.

Little Crane indicated by sign that he had grown up with most of the scouts present. "We learned the ways of warriors together," he said. "We are all brothers."

Little Crane took the hoop back from the scouts and cut the scalp loose. He worked it with his hands, nodding in approval. It was ready. He rode up and tied the scalp to the trigger guard on Garrett's rifle with a piece of sinew, while the scouts cheered.

"Show your medicine to Long Hair Custer," Little

Crane said. "Tell him you've come to make the paper talk and that he'd better do something brave, because you already have."

The Ree scouts laughed and shouted, turning their ponies toward the river. Garrett rode with them at full speed, while they bunched around him in a circle, shouting and yelling, pointing to him. Gerard rode alongside him.

Garrett and the scouts caused considerable commotion when they rode into camp. The entire contingent of Ree scouts, forty-one in number, were gathered, shouting their approval of Garrett. Garrett dismissed Little Crane and Red Moon to take care of the horses and spend what time they wished with their friends.

Garrett found Lieutenant Charles Varnum, a medium-sized, slim-faced officer with stern features. Varnum had been expecting him.

"You've caused a considerable stir here, Mr. Garrett," he said, eyeing the scalp. "What's the meaning of all this?"

"I would say that your scouts have been celebrating my recent killing of a Sioux warrior, downriver at the mouth of Glendive Creek."

"You fought Sioux down there?"

"Just a handful. They came into our camp at dawn."

"I guess I don't understand all this." Varnum was studying Garrett. "When did you meet the Sioux? How did you and the two Rees come to be separated from us? In fact, I don't even remember ever signing you or the other two on."

"I'm not a scout," Garrett told him. "I hired the two Rees on my own. I'm an independent correspondent."

Varnum was still puzzled and a little put out. "A correspondent? Out here on your own? I can't give you authorization to travel with my scouts. You'll have to go to General Terry."

"That is my intention," Garrett said. "Where can I find him?"

"You'll find him aboard the steamboat. But I should warn you, he's not in the best humor. We're waiting for another officer on scouting assignment to arrive with his troops. The officer is late and the general has little patience with that sort of thing.''

''Thank you for your help,'' Garrett told Varnum. ''And thank you for the warning. I trust I'll be talking to you again soon.''

Garrett made his way toward the steamboat. The camp was alive with activity. Soldiers were scattered over the river bottom, mending tack or working their horses, while others lounged, playing cards or telling stories. At one edge of camp a number of men were butchering cows from a herd that had come with the column, and a number of antelope that had been shot on a hunt earlier in the day.

In the middle of camp was a sutler's tent where soldiers were purchasing food, straw hats, and whiskey. Off to the side, a party had gathered to compare Indian weapons and dress items. Garrett recognized them as members of Custer's family.

Custer's brothers Tom and Boston, his nephew Armstrong ''Autie'' Reed, and his brother-in-law, Lieutenant James Calhoun, were passing around a bow and arrows, and a set of finely beaded moccasins, the bottoms of which had also been beaded.

Garrett recognized the men from the pictures he had studied prior to coming out. He thought about approaching them, then considered that his first business was with General Terry.

Approaching the river, Garrett began to rehearse in his mind his audience with Terry. He would just knock on the commander's cabin door and hope for the best.

The *Far West* was nearly two hundred feet long and close to thirty-five feet at the beam. She had been built for speed and strength, and had two steam capstans, one on either side of the bow. She was the first boat of her kind. Garrett had learned from the Grants that the government was paying $360 per day for her use.

Her captain, Grant Marsh, had thirty years of experience boating the major rivers of the midwest, including a tour of duty on the *A. B. Chambers No. 2,* together with a young man of that time named Sam Clemens.

Garrett stood on shore, watching men stack armloads of cottonwood on the deck, wondering how he would find the general's cabin, when an officer suddenly erupted from a tent near him.

The officer's stripes showed him to be a lieutenant. He was moderately tall, slender in build, with short strawberry blonde hair and quick, piercing blue eyes. As he approached Garrett, two large staghounds got up from lying in the sun and followed him. He pointed and the dogs retreated to the tent.

Garrett recognized the man immediately. "General Custer, I believe," he said, using Custer's brevet rank to address him. "What a fortunate pleasure! So nice to meet you, sir."

Custer wore a wide-collared campaign shirt and a bright red cravat, knotted neatly in front, that flowed halfway down his chest. He did not extend his hand but stared inquisitively from under his broad-brimmed felt hat.

"Are you the 'white warrior' the scouts are all yelling about?" he asked. "Were you and the two Rees who came in with you recently hired as scouts?"

"I'm no scout, General. The Rees work for me."

Custer's eyebrows raised. "Really? May I inquire into your business here?"

"Certainly, General." Garrett straightened himself. "I'm a correspondent on assignment to cover your campaign." Garrett was careful to use the word *your.* "I'm sorry I got such a late start, but I'm glad I finally found you. You see, General, there are countless readers who want to know about every moment of your coming victory."

Emerging from the tent and taking his place beside Custer was a large, calm, dark-haired officer with long, sweeping sideburns, Dundreary whiskers, as they were called. He studied Garrett with curiosity.

"General, I believe that it's critical to America's history that this campaign be fully covered," Garrett continued. "I feel extremely proud that the *Democrat* chose me to accompany you."

"The *Democrat*?"

"Yes, General, the St. Louis *Democrat*. An excellent paper devoted to the new, emerging leaders of our country. I'm sure you concur."

Custer eyed Garrett up and down. "I see. You understand, though, don't you, that General Terry is not prone to correspondents. He may wish to leave you aboard the *Far West* when we begin our travel south."

"General," Garrett said, "I've read your great book, *My Life on the Plains*, backwards and forwards. In addition to reporting, I want to learn from you. I want to see what you see and be able to capture it on paper, as you have, sir."

Custer nodded. "I see. What previous experience have you had?"

"I worked correspondence during the Rebellion, sir, reporting for the *Democrat*."

The officer with the Dundreary sideburns smiled. "Yes, that's right, General. I remember his dispatches."

"I believe I do as well," Custer commented.

"You see, General," Garrett continued, "I've never been west or covered an Indian campaign. That's why this mission is so important to me. I want to learn from the best Indian fighter our country has ever seen."

The sideburned officer extended his hand to Garrett. "My name is Lieutenant William Cooke, adjutant to the General. You took your life in your hands coming out here. And I have heard the stories circulating of your encounter with a Sioux warrior. You have quite a reputation, Mr. Garrett."

"I was lucky," Garrett said. "I now feel quite safe, thank you."

"Indeed." Cooke turned to Custer. "He seems like a proper man to me, General. He could be of good service, I would think."

"It would seem so," Custer agreed. He turned to Garrett. "Are you aware of the other correspondent, Mr. Mark Kellogg?"

"I heard mention of him back at Fort Lincoln," Garrett said. "I have never met him, though."

"Well, why don't we kill two birds at once, then," Custer suggested. "I'll take you aboard the boat and we'll talk to General Terry. Mr. Kellogg should be in his cabin. He likes to rest this time of day."

Custer dismissed Cooke and led the way aboard the *Far West*. Garrett felt he now had more than half the battle won. With Custer on his side, plus Kellogg already going along, he didn't see how Terry could hold him back.

Yet he knew Terry would be difficult. Though not the soldier Custer was, he was a deep thinker. Before serving for the Union in the Rebellion, he had been a practicing attorney in Connecticut. He had gathered many accolades as a commander in the Rebellion, but had no experience against Indians.

Garrett knew that Terry had been instrumental in getting Custer to command the Seventh Cavalry under him. Terry had to know how difficult it would be to keep Custer in check, but Custer's knowledge of Indian warfare was all Terry could count on to make the campaign a success.

On the boat, Custer rapped on Terry's cabin door. A junior officer answered and announced Custer's arrival. Terry looked up from his desk and waved them in.

Garrett stared. General Alfred Terry was an imposing presence, his dark eyes flashing from under heavy brows, one hand working his beard. His desk was awash with maps and paper of all sizes and shapes, from letters and memorandums to small snitzles bearing hurriedly scribbled notes. With his free hand, he tapped a pencil impatiently against his desk.

Custer saluted. "General Terry, this is . . . is—" He turned to Garrett.

"Adam Garrett, General Terry, sir, correspondent for the St. Louis *Democrat*."

"Yes," Custer said. "He and Mr. Kellogg could work together quite well, I believe."

Terry remained seated, eyeing Garrett, tapping his pencil. "A journalist, you say?"

"Yes, sir. I'm hoping to—"

"Mr. Garrett, I don't want to appear rude, but this is not a trip for journalists. I've made that regulation. This is a dangerous mission." He stared at Custer. "I would have hoped you could have made this clear to him, Lieutenant, *before* bringing him in here to interrupt me."

Custer frowned. "Maybe you should hear him out."

Terry tapped his pencil harder. "I haven't time for this, Lieutenant."

"Excuse me, General," Garrett said. "Did you say that you're not allowing any of the press along?"

Terry stopped tapping and stroked his beard harder. "I'm sorry if you've been inconvenienced, Mr. Garrett, but you'll have to remain behind with the boat."

"That is disappointing, General," Garrett said. "I'm certain Mr. Kellogg will be equally unhappy, especially since he made the long trip from Bismarck. He is a correspondent, isn't he?"

Terry cleared his throat. "He was not authorized to come along."

"But his intentions are to accompany the campaign when it turns south," Garrett said. "Am I correct?"

After thinking a moment, Terry said, "I haven't decided yet."

"Let me put it this way, General," Garrett said. "If I stay with the boat, so does Mr. Kellogg. If he goes along, I go along as well. Can you understand my position?"

Terry stood up. "Mr. Garrett, you will not dictate terms to me!"

Garrett stood firm. "I'm only asking you to be fair, sir. After all, why should one paper be allowed coverage of the events at the exclusion of all the others?"

Terry grunted, his face red.

"How would it look if I reported to my editor that the U.S. Army had granted the New York *Herald* exclusive rights to report this campaign?'' Garrett asked. ''Not good politics, General.''

Terry sat back down, picked up his pencil, and resumed his impatient tapping. ''Mr. Garrett, I'm not as concerned with politics as I am with doing my duty. And that is to subjugate the Sioux and Cheyenne and force them onto their reservations, once and for all. That comes first, before anything else.''

''I understand that, General,'' Garrett said. ''By the same merit, I feel it is my duty to chronicle each and every event during the course of operations. This is the most important campaign in the history of the Indian wars. There should be more of us along, don't you agree?''

''I'll not lie to you,'' Terry said. ''I'm not partial to journalists. Neither are my commanding officers. We've had some unpleasantries with your kind.''

''Unpleasantries?''

''Mr. Garrett, the majority of your colleagues tend to be fatalistic and to exaggerate the facts to suit their own point of view. That makes it hard for a commander to perform his duty as he sees fit. It's uncomfortable having someone with a notepad watching your every move, eager to tear you apart in the newspapers.''

Garrett noted that Custer was listening intently to every word. He frowned often, as if concerned that Terry might change his mind about Kellogg and leave him aboard the *Far West* also. Custer was intent on having Kellogg along and wanted nothing to spoil his chances of being written up in national newspapers immediately after the encounter with the hostiles.

''I don't agree, General,'' Garrett said. ''Not all journalists are so eager to criticize. I believe that Mr. Kellogg and I both understand the situation out here. This is a country waiting to be settled. That cannot happen as long as there are Indians stopping the movement.''

Custer smiled. ''Mr. Garrett does know the circumstances, General. I believe that he will be of help to us, just as Mr. Kellogg will be. Don't you agree?''

Terry studied Garrett. "Did I understand you to say, Mr. Garrett, that you believe this land is destined to receive civilization, destined for farming and for development of the natural resources, its minerals, timber, and other wealth?"

"Certainly, General," Garrett said. "What good is this land out here if it isn't used properly?"

Terry thought a moment. "That being the case, Mr. Garrett, how would you go about performing my duties? How would you go about returning the savages to their reservations?"

"I would likely do the same as you, General," Garrett said. "I would see to it that they got my message, loud and clear. I would send my best commander to carry that message to them, a man such as General Custer here. I would allow him all discretion to carry out the duty of doing what's best for this great country of ours."

"There's been a lot of bloodshed, Mr. Garrett," Terry said. "The hostiles have caused untold grief among the settled population out here. There is little we can do but fight the way they do, to show them that we cannot and will not tolerate their behavior."

"Whatever it takes to get that message across, sir," Garrett said. "Whatever it takes."

There was a knock at the door. Terry's adjutant answered and took an envelope from a courier, who stepped inside and stood calmly, awaiting further instructions.

The adjutant addressed him as Mr. Boyer. He was dressed like the other scouts, a mixed-blood of above average height and strong appearance, his dark eyes filled with confidence.

"From Major Reno," the scout told Terry. "Important."

Frowning, Terry leaned across his desk, his hand extended. The adjutant handed him the envelope. Terry ripped it open and read, frowning. He slammed the paper down. "Damn him, anyway!"

"Has he ruined our plan?" Custer asked. "I knew you shouldn't have sent him out. Never, never."

"That's enough, Lieutenant," Terry said. He sat down.

"It appears that we'll have to draw up new plans."

"Where is Reno now?" Custer asked.

Ignoring Custer, Terry addressed Garrett. "You can go, Mr. Garrett, with this understanding. You will not be listed as a member of this campaign, on any rolls, U.S. Army or otherwise. And, as such, you shall not draw rations. You are on your own completely, Mr. Garrett. Is that understood?"

"Understood, General," Garrett said. "You won't even know I'm along."

"I should hope not." Terry took a deep breath and picked up the letter. He spoke into his beard. "That's all I need from you, Mr. Garrett. Just stay out of the way. Lieutenant Custer, I'll ask you to remain behind." He looked up at the scout. "Mr. Boyer, you can go as well. I'll call for you when I need you."

Garrett left, the scout behind him. On the deck, Garrett took a deep breath and stared into the current, a boiling and splashing brown soup laden with branches and brush.

The scout stood alongside Garrett, smiling. "I'm Mitch Boyer." He extended his hand. "You must have come for an important purpose. Not many men can have Custer and Terry talk to them in the same room."

Garrett shook Boyer's hand. "What do you mean?"

"The two white chiefs have power and don't see their lesser men very much. They tell them what to do by sending their lesser chiefs to talk for them."

"You seem to know how the army works."

"I've scouted for many Bluecoat leaders. I came from up the river, where I live among the Crow people. I came after the snows left to scout for One-Who-Limps, the one called Gibbon. The main chief, Terry, called for me to join him. Why are you so special that you can have both Terry and Custer talk to you at the same time?"

"Well, I want to write about this campaign," Garrett replied. "I want to make the paper talk about what happens." Garrett took a notebook from his pocket. "Do you know what I mean?"

Boyer smiled. "You're a writer. There's another one here, Mr. Kellogg."

"Did you attend school or something?" Garrett asked.

"I can't read or write," Boyer said. "I've been around trading posts and have scouted for whites a long time. I've seen writers come into the mountains before. I know about writing."

"Yes, I'd say that you do," Garrett agreed.

The door to Terry's cabin opened and his adjutant came out. "Mr. Boyer, the General will see you."

Boyer shook Garrett's hand again. "Come to me when you have time and I'll tell you some things."

Garrett watched Boyer disappear into Terry's cabin, thinking that this man might have valuable information about the campaign and its conduct. He would definitely take Boyer up on his offer.

On shore, a group of soldiers had organized a foot race. Eight men had taken their place at the starting line, preparing for a dash of some eighty yards along the river bottom. Lieutenant Cooke, Custer's adjutant, was among the sprinters.

As he descended to the main deck, Garrett watched them. He was eager to begin a letter to Orvil Grant. Upon leaving the boat, he was approached by a slim, youthful-looking man with short, graying hair, wearing spectacles and dark cotton clothes. He extended his hand to Garrett.

"Mark Kellogg is my name. I represent the Bismarck *Tribune* and the New York *Herald*." He looked out at the race, which was just getting underway. "Lieutenant Cooke is very fast afoot. He'll be hard to beat, I'd wager."

Garrett shook Kellogg's hand. "Adam Garrett. Yes, I can see by the way the race is going that the Lieutenant has already won."

Soldiers cheered and yelled as Cooke crossed the finish line well ahead of the others. Bets were paid and others made as another race was organized.

Kellogg stood back from Garrett, looking up at him. "I hear you're a journalist, like myself, and one who has counted coup at that."

Garrett noted a wry smile. Kellogg was trying his best to present a calm front, but his irritation showed through.

"There is room for both of us, Mr. Kellogg," Garrett said. "There'll be more news than we can both cover, I can assure you."

"It appears to me, Mr. Garrett, that you possibly want to create the news. I see that your buckskin shirt is beaded and all. You're trying to upstage General Custer, are you?"

"I'd hate to see you worried so," Garrett said. "Rest assured I'll leave the Indian fighting to Custer. And I hope that you can keep up with both of us."

Kellogg cleared his throat. "Listen, Mr. Garrett, I'm not worried about you. I'm handling General Custer personally."

"What do you mean you're 'handling him?' " Garrett asked. "You make it sound like you've got him trained."

"I don't appreciate your caustic airs, Mr. Garrett," Kellogg snapped. "My job is to follow General Custer into battle. I'll see what he does and record what he says. I'd be happy to share my notes with you."

"I can take my own notes, Mr. Kellogg. Thank you just the same."

Kellogg shifted his feet and adjusted his spectacles. "We can't be making a press conference out of this, you know. General Custer invited Clement Lounsberry, my publisher at the Bismarck *Tribune,* to accompany him on this trip. As things turned out, Mr. Lounsberry's dear wife took ill and he sent me in his stead. Am I to understand that General Custer invited you personally as well?"

"You don't have to understand any of it, Mr. Kellogg," Garrett said. "Now, if you'll excuse me, I have business to attend to."

Kellogg adjusted his spectacles again and cleared his throat. "One thing before you go, Mr. Garrett, and I hope you'll hear me plainly. General Custer is a fine man and the best leader the U.S. Army has. There is only one like him and that's the reason General Terry insisted he be along. No one fights Indians better than George Armstrong Custer. This campaign would be lunacy without him. You couldn't possibly believe otherwise."

"I've already told you, Mr. Kellogg, my business with the General is my own. I had hoped we could be friends, but that doesn't appear possible. Rest assured, I won't lose any sleep over it."

From the boat came a horn blast. Custer was on the upper deck, turning in a circle, waving his hat in the air. He was yelling something, but the horn drowned him out. He started down off the boat, accompanied by Mitch Boyer.

Custer's staghounds, excited by their master's return, dashed past Garrett and Kellogg. On shore, Custer greeted the dogs, scratching their ears and calling both by name, Bleuch and Tuck. When he reached Garrett and Kellogg, he was beaming.

"Gentlemen! Good news! Come along with me. This expedition is about to get underway again."

"We're marching, are we, General?" Kellogg asked excitedly.

"On the morrow we leave to join Major Reno down-river," Custer said. "I want everyone ready early. I mean business. We're finally getting someplace on this campaign. We'll not let the hostiles elude us. We'll catch them and, by God, they'll surrender or wish they had never met the Seventh Cavalry."

FIVE

Garrett began filling pages with notes as Custer spoke. The message delivered by Mitch Boyer had been from Major Marcus Reno, a commander sent on reconnaissance with six companies of cavalry. The note from Reno stated that he had scouted as far as the Rosebud and then down to its mouth. His intentions had been to rejoin the main battalion on Tongue River, but he had camped eight miles out because of rough terrain.

"The fool!" Custer commented. "He flagrantly disobeyed orders by going over to the Rosebud. A worthless man and even less of a commander. I hope he hasn't alerted the hostiles. If he's caused them to run away I'll flog him myself!"

Mitch Boyer had already left with an order from Terry to Reno, telling him to stay where he was, that Custer would lead the command out from Tongue River the following morning to join him. They would all march to the mouth of Rosebud Creek, the new command base.

Garrett continued to take notes while Custer marched through camp, inspiring the troops for the renewal of the campaign. "We'll give them their due, boys!" he yelled, waving to all. "Our mark in history is about to be made!"

While Custer stopped to make a speech, Garrett moved to where Little Crane and Red Moon stood with some of the Ree scouts. Their faces were somber.

"What's bothering you?" Garrett asked Little Crane. "I thought you were ready to go after your enemies."

Little Crane pointed to Custer. "Long Hair is crazy. I hear that he's doing bad things around here."

"He's just trying to get the soldiers ready to march," Garrett explained. "He's trying to ready them for battle."

"Maybe he should stay away from the river," Little Crane said. He pointed. "See where he's leading the soldiers? This was a winter camp and there were burials made back in the trees. He's going to a sacred place and he should stay out of there."

Garrett watched as Custer led a large group of soldiers into a grove of trees filled with platforms.

"That is how the dead are sent to the Other Side Camp," Little Crane explained to Garrett. "They are laid to rest in their finest clothes, wrapped in robes and blankets. Their weapons are laid with them, and other possessions that they want to take with them. Long Hair shouldn't be going there. I've heard that some of the Bluecoats have already violated the dead."

Garrett remembered having seen some of the soldiers, two of them Custer's relatives, comparing moccasins and clothing. He had thought little of it at the time.

Custer was shouting, leading a group of frenzied soldiers through the trees like a mob fixed on a hanging. Along the way, the soldiers attacked the burial scaffolds, disrobing the bodies and kicking the remains to pieces.

Mark Kellogg stood back and watched, impassive.

A number of soldiers, looking for more burials to violate, gathered around a large scaffold painted red and black, set in a small clearing. "That was a strong warrior," Little Crane said. "The colors mean he was brave and died a proud death."

Custer made a flippant motion with his hand and the soldiers began kicking at the support poles. The scaffold toppled and the body was quickly stripped and thrown into the river. The soldiers began fighting over the warrior's clothes, bows and arrows, and other belongings.

Elsewhere, more soldiers climbed into the trees or knocked the platforms down with poles made from cottonwood limbs, tearing through the belongings, each struggling to claim the best prize for himself.

Tom Custer was a rampaging wild man, smashing corpses with his pistol butt as if striking a living enemy, subduing them with a rage that Garrett thought almost inhuman.

Little Crane and Red Moon turned and walked away. Garrett stared at Custer, who seemed to be surveying a battlefield, drunk with the glory of his conquering soldiers. He was reveling in the atmosphere, smirking at the fevered men, as if watching dogs tearing at rabbits.

Many soldiers stayed back, shaking their heads, talking among themselves. Garrett chose from among them a commander with thick white hair, grown long and combed back, whose light blue eyes were filled with deep contempt. Despite the pure white hair, Benteen was just over forty years of age, and was nearly as large as Garrett. His features suggested the face of an early adolescent.

Captain Fredrick W. Benteen. Garrett had read about Benteen in the material supplied to him by the Grants. He had surmised that this man, of all those on the campaign, probably held the greatest dislike for Custer.

Garrett introduced himself. Benteen stared at him. "Another one of Custer's diary keepers? How are you going to write this up? Custer's over there fighting *dead* Indians, for God's sake! That's the best he can do!"

"I have no intention of glorifying this," Garrett said. "I just wanted to know if you'd be willing to grant me an interview."

"An interview? What for?"

"I'm interested in an unbiased view on General Custer and this campaign. Could you help me?"

Benteen laughed. "An *unbiased* view of Custer? There is no such thing. Men either follow him without question, like his pack of hounds, or they hate his every living breath. Need I tell you whom to count me among?"

"I think I've got the picture, Captain Benteen. Therefore, you would be a very good interview, I believe."

"Who did you say you were writing this for?" Benteen asked.

"I'm a correspondent for the St. Louis *Democrat*," Garrett replied. "I need all sides of this campaign, not just the glory. Do you understand what I mean?''

"I believe I do,'' Benteen said. "I've written a few things myself about Custer that ended up in the *Democrat*. Do you know much about Custer?''

"I've tried to learn as much as possible." Garrett had no intention of discussing his motives openly. No matter how much contempt Benteen showed for Custer, it would not do to confide in him. "I've read the General's book, *My Life on the Plains*, but that only represents his side of things.''

"That's an understatement,'' Benteen said. "The book would be more properly titled *My Lie on the Plains*.''

"Is there a chance I might get some comments from you, off the record, of course?'' Garrett asked. "My reports to the *Democrat* need not mention sources.''

Benteen smiled. "Why don't we take a walk toward the blacksmith quarters across camp? I need to check on my horse.''

During the walk, Benteen talked about his association with Custer, notably the winter campaign on the Washita, where Custer had led his troops against a Cheyenne village, killing a number of women and children.

"To think of that day still makes me sick to my stomach,'' Benteen said. "In fact, a letter I wrote to a friend of mine on the matter ended up in the *Democrat*. A commander named Elliott was killed, along with his soldiers, while Custer showed off in the village by shooting captured horses in front of the women and children. He ordered them all shot, hundreds of them, and killed them at close range. Those women and children were screaming and crying. Custer even shot their dogs.''

"For what purpose?'' Garrett asked.

"Oh, it's standard practice to destroy the enemy's food and lodging during a winter campaign,'' Benteen replied. "But Custer goes too far. He wants them to see how hard he can make things on them if they don't obey him. You don't slaughter dogs and ponies in front of your captives and laugh at them for screaming.''

"What about Elliott, the commander?'' Garrett asked.

"You said he was killed while Custer was entertaining himself."

"Yes, the Cheyenne surrounded him and his command. They were butchered, cut into pieces, and their remains thrown around in the snow. I don't know if Custer ever felt to blame or not. It doesn't matter now. He wants to make this campaign his stairway to the White House. Everyone knows that."

Garrett and Benteen reached the blacksmith quarters, where five men worked feverishly to shoe lame cavalry mounts. Benteen picked out one of the blacksmiths, ordering him to stop his work.

"Where's my sorrel?" Benteen asked. "I thought he'd be done by now."

"He's next up, Captain," the blacksmith said.

"No, he's up now!" Benteen snapped. "You put that horse aside and get mine done. I want him done right away."

The blacksmith frowned. He led the horse he had been working on out to the picket and returned with Benteen's sorrel. Benteen was glaring at him.

"It won't be long, Captain," the blacksmith said, readying the horse for shoeing.

"I told you earlier to start on him," Benteen said. "Why did you disobey my explicit order?"

"You didn't give me an explicit order," the blacksmith argued. "Besides, there are other horses in much worse condition." He bent over and lifted a front foot.

"Well, I'm now giving you an explicit order," Benteen said, grinding his teeth. "I want my sorrel done right now. Is that understood? And you'd better hurry up about it."

The blacksmith straightened up. "Listen, do you want me to get to it, or do you want this hammer so you can do it yourself?"

"Draw your pay and get out of here!" Benteen ordered.

The blacksmith held his hammer tightly, the muscles in his arms bulging. Benteen's hand went to his Colt.

"You'd better do as you're ordered," Benteen said.

"I'll see you another day, sir," the blacksmith said coldly. He threw the hammer at Benteen's feet and stomped off.

The other blacksmiths were all staring. Benteen picked the next closest one and led his sorrel over. "Unless you want to lose your job as well, you'll work on this horse. Now!"

The blacksmith took Benteen's sorrel and without a word, tied it to a tree and began checking each hoof. Benteen turned to Garrett.

"I believe I'll stay and see to it that he finishes."

"Very well, Captain Benteen," Garrett said. "I'll look you up another time."

Garrett left. Benteen had been a waste of time. The man hadn't said anything about Custer that wasn't already public knowledge. In fact, most of the public agreed with killing Indians, by any means possible.

Should Benteen have control of the Seventh Cavalry, Garrett thought, he would likely be no different from Custer. He had fought in the Rebellion just as hard as Custer, and had gathered even more honors. Yet his application for promotion to brevet Brigadier General had been denied. Perhaps that was the reason for Benteen's bitterness: Though five years his junior, Custer was his commanding officer.

Garrett stopped at the sutler's tent to purchase a dozen eggs, a delicacy he hadn't enjoyed since Fort Lincoln, and was approached by Lieutenant Cooke, Custer's adjutant. Garrett congratulated him on winning the footrace earlier in the day.

"Do you have a moment, Mr. Garrett?" Cooke asked. He showed none of the casual air he had worn at their first meeting.

"Certainly," Garrett said. "Is there something wrong?"

"The General would like to speak to you right away," Cooke said, "if that wouldn't inconvenience you."

"Not at all," Garrett said, dismissing the idea of buying the eggs.

Cooke led Garrett to Custer's tent, where the General was outside playing with his staghounds. He was on the ground with them, laughing and pulling their ears, while they growled and bit him playfully.

"Mr. Garrett has arrived," Cooke announced.

Custer either didn't hear the message or ignored it. Garrett couldn't determine which. Finally, Custer came to his feet, brushing grass and dirt from his hair and clothes.

Custer took his hat from Cooke and said, "Mr. Garrett, would you like to take a walk?"

"Certainly," Garrett replied.

Custer led the way, upriver through the trees. Garrett and Cooke followed. At the edge of camp, Custer stopped and threw a stone into the river.

"Are you taking a lot of notes, Mr. Garrett?" he asked.

"Quite a few," Garrett said. "Why?"

Custer turned to Garrett, his eyes ablaze. "I understood you to say that you wanted to write about *me*, Mr. Garrett, not Captain Benteen."

"My intentions are to write about you, General," Garrett said. "I merely thought that I would—"

"You can't be writing about *me* if you're talking with Benteen," Custer interrupted. "What could you possibly learn about me from Benteen?"

"I was just asking the captain about the campaign in general," Garrett said. "I just wanted to know which regiments he commands and what he does. I can see no harm in that."

"I can tell you what every officer on this campaign does and doesn't do, Mr. Garrett," Custer said. "You don't need references from anyone else. If you want my cooperation in this matter, you'll adhere to that. Is that clear?"

"I don't understand, General. I—"

"Let me make it perfectly clear, Mr. Garrett. I don't care whether General Terry gave you authorization to go along or not. *I'm* the commander of the cavalry and it will be the cavalry that does the fighting. So, if I don't want you with the cavalry, you'll remain behind. Do you understand me?"

"Yes, General, I do."

"Now that we understand one another, I'm certain that we can work together just fine."

"Yes, I believe we can, General."

Custer lifted his chin and again challenged Garrett with his eyes. "There is one other, very important consideration, Mr. Garrett, that we haven't yet discussed. And that is your ability with firearms. That's very important, you know. Can't be going along if you can't handle yourself properly with a firearm."

"I told you, General," Garrett said, "I was a correspondent for the North throughout the war. I had to defend myself many times. I'm more than adequate with both a pistol and a rifle, sir. I can hold my own against most."

"Perhaps," Custer said. He pointed to Cooke. "The Lieutenant here is a marksman of great quality, as am I. There are few, if any, who can top the Lieutenant, though. I come as close as anyone."

"I'm feeling safer all the time," Garrett said.

"Yes," Custer said. "We'll need steady hands during this campaign. I'm certain you can wield a pen—and you shall learn more from me—but I wanted to be sure you could use a weapon as well. Very, very important."

"Rest assured," Garrett said. "I can take care of myself in that department."

"Maybe we'll have the opportunity to do some shooting along the way," Cooke suggested. "Grouse are a good test of marksmanship."

While Cooke was talking, Garrett thought of Ann's cousin, whom he had been intending to ask about. The discussion of marksmanship had brought him to mind.

"Speaking of good shots," Garrett said, "I've been interested in locating a soldier with General George Crook's regiment. His name is Mason Hall. He's my fiancée's cousin and I promised her that I'd look into his welfare. You know how that sort of thing goes."

Custer smiled. "Yes, it's nice to be accommodating of

the womenfolk, isn't it? You say he's with Crook's forces?''

"Yes," Garrett said. "I understand they're south of us.''

"Is he an officer?" Custer asked.

"I don't believe so, General. An enlisted man, as far as I know.''

Custer immediately lost interest. "Well, I doubt if I can be of help. You see, we have a list of the officers, but to try and find an enlisted man among all the names would be very difficult.''

"I brought him up because he's an excellent shot," Garrett said. "Maybe he's risen in rank by now.''

"I suppose that possibility exists," Custer said. "What is his standing in life? You know, his upbringing?''

"His father, I understand, was a fur trader. I believe his mother died when he was still fairly young.''

"So he grew up a ruffian I would assume," Custer surmised. "Not officer material. You'll have to do your investigating if we meet up with Crook, which I doubt we'll ever do.''

"Why wouldn't we?" Garrett asked. "Crook's supposed to be coming up to meet you, isn't he?''

"It will all be over by the time he finds us," Custer said. "We'll be traveling fast. It's either that or lose the hostiles. They'll be on the run. Thanks to Reno, we've lost precious time already. I just hope he hasn't alerted them. We can't be waiting around any longer.''

Custer turned and started back to camp. Cooke followed. Garrett watched them a moment.

From a distance, Custer turned. "Are you coming?" Custer yelled.

Garrett looked up. "In a minute, General.''

"Remember," Custer said, "I'm your source of information on this campaign. Stay close to me and keep your weapons loaded. We'll do well together." He waved and disappeared into the trees.

Garrett took a deep breath and pulled his notebook from the waistband of his pants. He started to write, then set the pad and pencil down on the log. He entwined his fingers and twisted them, working to stop his shaking. He didn't want to write while his hands were trembling.

A sudden gust of wind burst through the trees. To the west, a thunderstorm had developed and was moving through the valley.

Overhead, four large crows appeared, gliding into the cottonwoods. They perched in the top branches, cawing loudly, their black wings spread halfway as they struggled for balance against the gusty wind.

Garrett stared up at them; they turned their heads toward him and continued their racket. Unnerved, Garrett lifted his hand and shouted, "Go on, you black devils! Get away from here!"

The crows lifted off together, catching an updraft that swept them skyward toward the south.

Opening his notebook, Garrett wrote:

Evening, 19 June 1876.
Yellowstone River,
Camp at mouth of Tongue River.

Have met Custer. Volumes will not describe him. If I'm to remain in his confidence, I must be very careful. The same with Benteen. I will stay away from him, though. Would do so even if I hadn't been warned by Custer.

Am very troubled at this moment. The sky is darkening. Four crows came into the trees above me and flew south, I'm certain toward the eventual battlefield. Can remember them so well from the Rebellion. There were times when they would be waiting at the field before the armies even showed up. Indeed, before the armies even *knew* they would meet one another. Those birds of hell bother me considerably.

Will have to tell Ann in my next letter that it will be difficult to find her cousin. Nothing has changed from the Rebellion: Officers and enlisted men do not mix.

The rain is starting to come in big drops. I dislike

the mud intensely, but will likely have no choice.
Will look forward to the dawn, when the march begins. Where the march will end, though, I cannot
say. I wish I hadn't seen the crows.

SIX

The evening was cool, brought on by a thunderstorm that had just passed, leaving the air fresh. A breeze carried a lone crow into the branches of a cottonwood beside the Missouri River. Ann followed its flight from the back of a small chestnut mare named Jill, marveling at the open sky.

Tyrone rode next to her. "Don't worry yourself, Miss Ann," he said. "We're going to find him. You can bank on that."

Fort Abraham Lincoln rested on a flat plain adjacent to the river, at the base of a gently sloping hill. Rows of white buildings—barracks, Officer's Row, storage and utility areas—surrounded a large parade ground. Here and there stood young cottonwoods, planted in hopes of future shade on an otherwise treeless expanse of prairie grass.

As they approached the fort, they were met by two men in uniform, who listened to Tyrone's explanation for their visit, and led them into the grounds. One of them pointed to the sutler's store, the informal center for information on what was happening on the frontier to the west.

Tyrone, who had been talking nervously ever since disembarking from the rickety ferry that had taken them across the Missouri, hoped to find his contact as soon as possible.

"I know he'll be here," he kept saying. "There's no other place he can be, is there? Where else would he be?"

Tyrone was talking about an Arikara named Water,

said to be the younger brother of a scout who had been hired by a man-who-makes-the-paper-talk, a man named Adam Garrett. Tyrone had learned that Garrett had hired Water's brother, Little Crane, and another Ree named Red Moon, to help him catch up with Long Hair Custer and the Bluecoat soldiers.

Tyrone had gotten his information from an old fur trade comrade who now worked nearby at the Fort Berthold Agency. Tyrone had wired the man from St. Louis. The friend, a Métis trader named Julian Landreaux, had agreed to meet them at the Bismarck train depot.

"Water told me that he and some others would take you and the lady out," Landreaux had said at the station. "But he's not at the agency now. It is said that he went to Fort Lincoln to work as a hunter."

"Maybe you can come with us," Tyrone had suggested to Landreaux. "We can see some of the country we used to trap."

"No, I'm too old for that," Landreaux had said. "Besides, it's all different. I don't want to lose my hair to the Sioux. I have a woman and two children who depend on me. I can't go, no matter how well you pay."

Tyrone had been disappointed, but had insisted to Ann that he would find someone to take them.

"I'm going, even if it means just the two of us," Ann had told Tyrone numerous times. Each time she said it, Tyrone grew more nervous.

"Let's not get hasty," Tyrone would say. "It'll all work out. The Good Lord'll see to it. He will, I know He will."

Ann looked up. The crow had flown from the distant cottonwood and was sailing straight overhead. Ann craned her neck to watch the bird, large and coal black, flap into the distance.

Tyrone had already dismounted and was talking to the sutler, who had come to the doorway. Inside the store, a woman turned to watch.

"I think Water left yesterday," the sutler was saying, "headed back up to Fort Berthold. He didn't think you were coming." The sutler pointed to some Indians gathered near the enlisted men's barracks. "Ask them. They might know more."

Ann climbed down from her horse. "What do you suggest we do, Tyrone?"

"I'll find this Water as soon as I can, Miss Ann," he said. "Maybe you'd care to look around, if you're not too tired."

"I can't afford to be tired," Ann said, "either now or later. We have too far to go for that."

"Ah, well, Miss Ann, you've got the spirit in you. I'll say that." He threw up his hands. "Sorry things aren't running so smooth yet."

"Don't apologize, Tyrone. You're doing the best you know how. No one can fault you for that."

"I'll be back soon," Tyrone promised. "I'll have scouts and horses enough to do us well."

Ann watched him leave, half-trotting across the parade ground toward the men the sutler had pointed out. Some were soldiers and others Indians. Soon he was among them, talking and pointing west.

Ann turned her gaze to the west, wondering at this land she had come into. It looked every bit as formidable as Adam had said. She wondered what lay ahead; and despite her weariness from the train rides, she was anxious to get going, to find Adam and take him into her arms and hold him for a long time. If she could do that just once more, she promised herself, she would never let him go and never again consent to anything as foolish as what he was now doing.

The woman from inside the store came out. She was dressed in a blue cotton dress and a sunbonnet. Her soft voice interrupted Ann's thoughts.

"Good afternoon. I'm Elizabeth Custer. I'd like to welcome you to Fort Lincoln, if I might."

Ann turned. Before her was a slim, dark-haired woman with a girlish face and a warm smile. Her brown eyes, though searching, were friendly and filled with expression.

"You have heard of my husband, haven't you? General George Armstrong Custer?"

"Yes, I've heard of him," Ann said. "Forgive me. I was just deep in thought, I guess."

"Well, we've all been there. Think nothing of it. You can call me Libbie if you'd like."

Ann introduced herself and motioned across the parade ground toward Tyrone. "Mr. Banks is assisting me in my mission to secure scouts and travel into the Yellowstone country. He was a dear friend of my late father, and equally as dear to me. With his help, I intend to reach your husband's command before the end of the month."

Libbie's eyes widened. "You intend to travel into the Yellowstone country, did you say? To find my husband's command?"

"That is my intention, yes. I intend to find my fiancé and bring him back with me before it's too late." She realized she had blurted the words.

"Too late?" Libbie asked.

"His name is Adam Garrett and he's a journalist," Ann explained. "He's gone in search of your husband, for the sake of chronicling the battles with the hostile Indians. I want to reach him before he goes into battle beside your husband."

"I was just heading back to my quarters," Libbie said. "Would you care to join me for tea?"

"I'd love to," Ann said. "Thank you very much."

"Think nothing of it. It's not often that we have visitors." She noted Ann's split riding skirt and loose cotton blouse, as well as her broad-brimmed hat. "I see you're a lady after my own heart, one who's not afraid to ride the range, as they say."

"My father was a fur trader," Ann said. "He taught me the outdoors, not the ways of polite society. However, I'm comfortable in both situations."

"Well, you certainly are a lady of my own heart. How nice to meet you."

Ann felt self-conscious befriending Libbie Custer. After all, Adam's sole mission was to discredit her husband. As they walked, she wondered if the General was as at ease with strangers as was his wife.

"You said you intend to travel into the Yellowstone

country to find your fiancé?" Libbie asked. "Do you know the dangers there?"

"I'm well aware of the dangers. Too aware," Ann replied. The fire-and-buffalo dream passed before her eyes. "But Adam doesn't think about danger. He tends to take chances when trying for the great story. You know how that is."

"Certainly, I do," Libbie said, smiling. "You know, I believe I've met him. Wasn't he here in early June? A rather strong-looking man who hired two Ree scouts?"

"Yes, that's him. He had wanted to arrive earlier, but couldn't make the connections. He must be very close to catching up with your husband by now."

"I suspect he has caught up," Libbie said. "And quite possibly they've met the Sioux by now."

Ann's stomach dropped. "Oh, not really. Not so soon."

"Autie said that they wouldn't linger, but would go as quickly as possible. Autie fears that the hostiles will scatter if they know he's coming after them. He mustn't let them get away."

As they crossed the west end of the parade grounds, Ann heard the sounds of a guitar and women singing "Nearer My God to Thee." "That's pretty," she told Libbie. "A good way to pass the time."

"Yes, but it's gotten to be too regular for me," Libbie said. "We all gather and sing hymns on the sabbath; but now, since the men's departure, they want to sing more and more. It wears me down, the continual sad lyrics. Everyone seems to be wanting God more and more."

They reached a white two-story house, trimmed in blue, with an abundance of flowers along the front porch. In the back was a large fenced garden, where a caretaker was pulling weeds. Three large staghounds came racing from behind the house, their tales wagging. Elizabeth ordered them back to their kennel.

"They're not bothering me," Ann said, petting them in turn. "Are they yours?"

"No, they belong to Autie. He's had up to forty at a

time. I've taken the liberty of giving some of them away, but there are still over a dozen left.''

Another staghound trotted from behind the house. She stopped at Libbie's feet and leaned forward to have her ears scratched.

"This is Lulu," Libbie said. "She'll be having a litter in the next couple of months."

"One would not have to go far at this post to look for a dog," Ann said.

Libbie laughed. "Autie loves them all and usually takes them with him. But not this time. Two of them ran after him upon his leaving, and he kept them. But the others are here, waiting. They seem so quiet and subdued. I often hear them whining in the night. They miss him as much as I do. Well, let's go inside and have some tea."

Ann followed Libbie onto the porch. A small table and chairs sat near the door. Resting on the front railing, not far from the door, was a large white pelican.

"I suppose she's waiting for Autie as well," Libbie commented with a laugh. "So many ladies in waiting. So many." She pointed to the pelican. "That's Lily. One of the housekeepers found her in the garden with a hurt leg. The dogs were barking at her trying to get through the fence. Autie helped nurse her back. He won't think of taking her back to the river, though I think that would be best. She has such a difficult time getting around. I think that even if she hadn't had her misfortune, she wouldn't do well on land. Too much bill in front and not enough tail feathers in back."

The pelican sat contentedly, unmindful that she was being discussed derisively.

"The housekeepers feed her mashed potatoes," Libbie added. "She seems to prefer them to fish. Or maybe she's just gotten spoiled."

"She seems perfectly content to me," Ann observed.

"Autie would make a zoo of this entire post if he could," Libbie continued. "He even kept a porcupine for a time."

"A porcupine?"

"Oh, yes. Sally. She slept at the foot of the bed off and on. The dogs remained on the floor whenever Sally decided to spend the night. Otherwise, the dogs all came onto the bed and sprawled out everywhere. Did you ever try to sleep with a pack of hounds on your bed?" She laughed. "I'm still trying to catch up on my sleep."

Libbie opened the door to the house. Ann stepped into a living room over thirty feet long, complete with a bay window that overlooked the parade ground. The room was furnished with hardwood chairs and endtables, each polished to a glorious sheen. On two of the walls hung the mounted heads of a deer and an antelope. The floor was partially covered by a black bear rug, complete with head mount.

"Autie is quite a sportsman," Libbie bragged. "You mentioned that your fiancé is a writer? Autie has published extensively. He does hunting stories for some of the eastern magazines."

The walls without mounted heads were adorned with pictures of Custer in buckskins kneeling over a fallen bear; Custer in buckskins kneeling over a fallen elk; Custer in uniform; Custer and Libbie together, and Custer and Libbie with Custer's brothers and friends.

Ann stared. She had never seen so many photographs of one individual in a single room in all her life.

"He is striking, isn't he?" Libbie said. "We were meant to be together, he and I. He has a truly marvelous history. Everything, for us, fits together, you see. It always has. Our lives are meshed like a great, wonderful puzzle. I am awed by it all."

A maid entered the room. "I see you've returned, Miss Libbie. You've decided not to join the ladies for songs?"

"Not today, Maria."

"Are you ready for tea, then, Miss Libbie?"

"Yes, thank you, Maria," Libbie said. "This is my new friend, Ann Malone. She will be staying with us tonight."

"Oh, that's not necessary," Ann said. "I appreciate the offer, but I couldn't impose."

"Nonsense!" Libbie said. "I love to make new friends. Besides, you'll find this house quite comfortable. The visitors' quarters are frightfully dusty."

Libbie instructed Maria to serve tea on the porch. Ann followed Libbie back out and watched her gently lift the pelican and deposit the large, awkward bird farther down the porch railing.

"I don't mind her, but she spoils the view at times," Libbie said. She offered Ann a chair and sat down. "I much prefer the outdoors this time of year, don't you?"

"Yes, I do," Ann said, looking out across the parade ground. Tyrone was nowhere in sight.

"If you're looking for your servant, you needn't worry about him," Libbie said. "Before I talked with you, I told the sutler to inform him of where you would be. He'll be here soon enough. You must trust him deeply to have him accompany you alone. Did you travel far?"

"From St. Louis," Ann replied. "And, yes, I trust him implicitly. I don't consider him a servant. As I said, he's a dear friend."

"Oh, certainly. They make wonderful companions. Maria is a darling, as is Mary, her sister, who's with Autie on the campaign. You could never find two ladies more loyal."

Ann sipped her tea. Overhead, a thin sheet of clouds was absorbing light from the falling sun. They looked red and lavender in places.

"The sky out here is something, isn't it?" Libbie commented. "You see some unusual things in the clouds."

Libbie went on to talk about the morning that Custer and the other officers had led the Seventh Cavalry out from the fort, toward the Yellowstone.

"It was a very odd morning," Libbie said. "Fog was lifting from the ground, and there was a radiance that reflected Autie and his soldiers into the sky. I actually saw them riding in the clouds."

"Riding in the clouds?"

"Yes, their images were imprinted on the clouds. Just for a short time. I can't tell you how it made me feel inside."

Ann recalled her dream in full, seeing the white buffalo coming toward her, and Adam's hand extended toward her. She wanted to tell Libbie about it, but reconsidered. Instead, she closed her eyes and took a deep breath.

"Is anything the matter, Ann?" Libbie asked.

"No, I'm just anxious to find Adam, is all. Thank you for asking."

Maria came out and refilled their teacups. Libbie started again with the conversation, her face sad and reflective.

"Yes, I've been told by even those in the highest offices that my days with Autie will be numbered."

"What do you mean?" Ann asked.

"It was a very strange thing," Libbie replied. "Autie and I had the most wonderful time just after our marriage. It was toward the close of the Rebellion. We attended balls and dinners in New York and Washington, more than I can count. Everyone was wonderful, all wishing us the best. Then, while we were in Washington at the theater, I had a chance to meet President Lincoln."

Ann listened with fascination. "You met Abraham Lincoln?"

"He was every bit as stately as his reputation, but oh, such a careworn face! At our introduction, he shook my hand and asked if I wasn't married to the man who charged into battle with a whoop and a shout. I told him that I was. 'Well, I'm told he won't do so anymore,' he said to me. I told him that I hoped that he would. He then said to me, and I thought he was joking, 'Then you wish to become a widow.' I laughed, but I must admit it unnerved me at the time."

Ann's stomach was churning. She could barely hold her teacup steady. Across the parade ground, Tyrone was approaching with two men.

"See, there's your friend," Libbie said. "Perhaps he has done well and you're now outfitted to go. You can get a good night's sleep and begin early tomorrow."

Tyrone removed his hat and approached the porch. The other two remained a short distance back. One was Indian, a short man with a round, lively face, wearing a red breechclout and moccasins. He had long hair braided in two strands with an eagle feather attached in the back.

The other man was dressed in worn buckskins. His long graying hair fell from under a red scarf tied in a kind of cap over his head. His features were rugged, but his smile was friendly.

Tyrone was beaming. "Miss Ann, I believe we're in business. I found Water and my old friend Lareaux has decided to go with us."

"That's great news," Ann said. She introduced him to Libbie and waited for her to invite him to tea, which didn't happen.

"Ann tells me that you're most loyal," Libbie said to Tyrone. "I find that most agreeable."

Tyrone smiled. "Thank you."

Ann rose from her chair. "I believe it's time to get on the trail," she said. "Thank you for your hospitality, Libbie. It was good to meet you and talk with you."

Libbie rose. "Oh, surely you don't want to leave until morning."

"I wouldn't be able to sleep anyway. I think it's best if we begin our journey this evening and get some rest later on."

"I would love to have you stay. I find you to be much like myself."

"Under different circumstances, I would accept," Ann said. "I certainly appreciate it. But knowing we're so similar in nature, do you think you could restrain yourself if you were me?"

"No, I think not," Libbie said. "I had seriously thought of asking to go with you. Earlier, I had wanted to go with Captain Marsh on the steamboat, but he said it wouldn't be wise. Perhaps not. So I shall remain here until Autie's return." She leaned forward and hugged Ann. "Be careful on your journey, and when you see him, give Autie my love."

"I shall," Ann said. She stepped down off the porch. "Is there any other message that you wish me to take him?"

Libbie looked into the sky and back to Ann. "Tell him to think of me and how much I love him. Tell him that I think of him always and will always continue to do so. And . . . tell him never to forget that our Heavenly Father watches over him. Always."

SEVEN

A hee-ia! Eee-ia! Hoi-ia!
  Driven by the pounding drums, their near-naked bodies smeared with red and black, the dancers circled the flames, screaming war songs and waving coup sticks and lances lined with enemy scalps. They gleamed in the firelight, their knees rising alternately, up and down, up and down, their moccasined feet pounding the loose soil around the campfire.

  Eee-ia! Hoi-ia! Hoi-ee!
  Leaning forward, now leaning back, they screamed to the Powers below and the Powers above. They tossed their heads, adorned with feathers, in wild abandon, their arms thrashing the air as if churning desperately for life through the dark depths of an endless sea.

  The celebration was underway in all the camps. A massive village of Northern Cheyenne and Lakota Sioux filled the valley of the Greasy Grass, just above the Little Bighorn. The dancing had begun early in the evening, after the lodges had been erected, and had not stopped even during the thunderstorm that had passed through just before sundown. The celebration would continue throughout the night.

  Mason Hall, his body dripping sweat, left the circle of dancers and sat down, breathing heavily.

  In his mind he relived the Battle of the Rosebud. He saw himself leaning over the side of his buckskin, racing headlong, together with a blur of painted warriors, toward a line of U.S. soldiers. The smoke of army Springfields puffed from the blue line. Bullets whizzed past him. Warriors loosed arrows and shot repeating rifles. The blue line faltered, then broke.

The warriors passed through and circled for the kill. A line of Crow and Shoshone warriors suddenly formed in front of the Bluecoats. The two lines came together, the Cheyenne and Lakota, the Crow and Shoshone. The Bluecoats fell back, taking new position on a different hill, while the Indian forces raced their ponies across each other's lines, battling to count coup.

The Cheyenne and Lakota would have ended it all for the Bluecoats two days ago, had it not been for the Crow and Shoshone warriors who had fought savagely in their defense. They would have killed General George Crook and his soldiers to the last man. Still, it had been a victory, and they celebrated this night.

Mason Hall, his breath returning, stared through the dancers at the fire. Hall had known George Crook. He now lived among the Cheyenne, his given name Nighthawk, a Bluecoat soldier who had deserted to the Indians.

Four months earlier Hall had been a private in Crook's command, riding through snow and subzero cold to fight the Sioux. On a frigid St. Patrick's Day, he had found himself deserted in a Cheyenne village along the Powder River. He would have died at their hands had he not saved the life of the Cheyenne woman named Ghostwind who was now his wife.

Since then, his life had changed so dramatically that his days as a U.S. cavalry soldier seemed a lifetime past. Though he still could not explain it, his new world among the Cheyenne felt more like home than his prior existence among his own people, a people he now wished would never enter these lands.

Nighthawk's part in the fight had earned him high ranking as a warrior. For a man so new to the ways of the Plains Indians, it was a great honor. A man of white skin, he had won the admiration and respect of many in a world where the white race was hated. There were many who disliked and distrusted him, but there were none who did not respect him.

A warrior approached and sat down beside Nighthawk.

"The look on your face makes me think you're lost," he said. He spoke in Cheyenne, mixed with sign language.

Nighthawk turned. His close friend and war brother, Eagle Wing, seemed concerned about him.

"You are far away, my friend, not here," Eagle Wing added. "Has the dancing affected you badly?"

"I was thinking about the battle," Nighthawk said. "I was wondering if there will soon be another like it. Or maybe one worse."

"We've sent them on the run," Eagle Wing said. "They won't be back. They'd be foolish."

"They could join up with others and return," Nighthawk suggested. "That's what the plan is, for them all to join together and attack us."

"You would know the Bluecoat plans, it's true," Eagle Wing agreed. "But when have the Bluecoats ever kept to a plan? Their leaders all fight among themselves. Each wants all the glory for the victory. They are all hard on their men. They push them like slaves. After that fight on the Rosebud, those soldiers will no longer want to fight. They'll leave and we won't see them again. Trust me on that."

Nighthawk stared into the fire. "I hope you're right. But I don't think so."

"Why should you be worried?" Eagle Wing asked. "You fight as bravely as any of us. And you shoot like no other can. You should hope for another battle. There are many more honors to win."

"You know, the more we fight them the harder it will be for us," Nighthawk said. "You say they'll decide to leave, but I know better. The army I fought with will never quit. They *have* to win."

"I know you've told me that before," Eagle Wing said. "I don't understand your people. I'll never understand them."

"Why do you call them *my* people?" Nighthawk asked. "I'll never live among them again."

"Maybe your heart has become Cheyenne," Eagle Wing said, "but your skin is still white. You can't change that."

Eagle Wing got up and joined a number of warriors feasting nearby. Nighthawk looked into the fire, his mind returning to the Rosebud, seeing the air filled with dust and gunsmoke, hearing the shrill cries of warriors on horseback.

That day had been a turning point for him. He had shown himself a true member of his adopted people. With no friends among the soldiers, he had fought as strongly as any of the warriors. He had worried only about a mule packer named Kincaid, who had cared for him as if he were his only son. He would always wonder what had happened to Kincaid.

But that was in the past. The real concern now was in the immediate future. Despite what Eagle Wing believed, Nighthawk was sure there would be more Bluecoat soldiers. Even if Crook didn't return for another fight, another command would surely come along.

But no one seemed concerned about this. No one seemed to think a Bluecoat force would ever come that would be large enough to attack a village this size, with so many warriors who had fought so many times before. The Bluecoat leaders, who had often shown poor judgment, could never be *that* foolish.

Nighthawk knew better. There was no doubt in his mind that the U.S. Army intended to drive all the Lakota Sioux and Cheyenne back on their reservations or, better yet, kill them.

While with Crook, Nighthawk had learned of the forces led by Terry and Custer, who were advancing from Fort Abraham Lincoln, moving along the Yellowstone. And he knew of the column led by Colonel John Gibbon, whom the Indians called One-Who-Limps, resting by the Yellowstone, awaiting Terry and Custer's arrival. Nighthawk had in fact been part of a horse raid against Gibbon's camp at Fort Peace, the night he had been given his warrior name.

"You've come a long way in a short time," Eagle Wing had told him that night. "There are few men, even among my people, who are as determined as you to learn new ways. This is good. You'll be strong, and we will always ride together in battle."

Nighthawk realized that if the three forces joined there would be a terrible battle, one that could destroy the future of the Cheyenne and Lakota people.

Nighthawk's wife, Ghostwind, approached, carrying a bowl filled with stewed meat. With her was her three-year-old daughter, Talking Grass, holding two pieces of fry-bread, which she held out for Nighthawk.

Nighthawk thanked her and took the bread. He set her in his lap and handed her back one of the pieces. She giggled and took a large bite.

He always noticed Talking Grass's left hand. The last two fingers were missing. She had lost them to frostbite the day Nighthawk had come to the Cheyenne.

He couldn't forget that day. His cavalry uniform stiff with frost, he had charged with the other soldiers through the snow on a white horse, the temperature at minus forty degrees Fahrenheit. They had attacked the village at daybreak, driving the Indian people into the hills above the lodges. The soldiers had been yelling, "Get Crazy Horse! Get Crazy Horse!" But it hadn't been Crazy Horse's village. Instead, they were attacking a peaceful camp of Cheyenne, mixed with a few Lakota Sioux. Crazy Horse had been camped downriver.

Ghostwind set the stew down in front of him and took a seat. "Why aren't you dancing?"

"I'm resting. Where did you get the fry bread?"

"More Cheyennes came into camp from the agency," she replied. "They came with some Santee from the north. They brought flour and shared. I just cooked it for you."

Nighthawk swallowed a mouthful of bread and stew. "They're still coming from the agencies?" he asked. "Why don't they stay back there? It's dangerous out here now."

"The Santees lost a warrior to a white man, up on the Yellowstone," Ghostwind said. "They know it's dangerous, but they can't stay on the reservation. There's no food. The rations are very low. They say someone is stealing them before they get to the agencies.''

"Probably the agents themselves," Nighthawk said. He let Talking Grass go to her mother, where she lay down and fell asleep immediately. "Where's Young Horse?"

"He and Tall Deer are watching the dancing," Ghostwind replied. "They've never seen so many dancers in one place. They likely will never see it again."

"It would be good if they didn't," Nighthawk said. Ghostwind's son was only eight. *Would* it be the biggest group of warriors he saw in his entire life? "When people come together like this, it's for safety. They're afraid something's going to happen." He studied Ghostwind. "Are you still having your visions?"

"You know that I am." Her voice had an edge to it. "Do you think they're going to stop?"

"I didn't mean to upset you. I just hoped maybe they had stopped."

"No. They won't stop until something terrible happens. I've told you that. The visions will be with me until the terrible battle comes."

Nighthawk had listened to Ghostwind tell of her visions ever since first knowing her. He had known early on that his wife would someday become a greatly respected prophet.

She had told him of her coming to the Cheyenne during a winter storm. "As I walked through a terrible blizzard," Ghostwind had told him, "I heard the spirits talking to me. I couldn't see anything, so terrible was the storm. I thought I would surely die, but the voices kept saying, 'Turn this way. Now go this way.' I might have fallen over cliffs, or fallen through river ice, were it not for the voices.

"Then I found Old Bear's village. I saw that the voices that had led me there belonged to owls. There were four of them. Large and white, they sat in the trees around the village. Many of the people thought I was a spirit, bringing them harm. Many ran. But it was Mountain Water, my adopted mother, who touched me and told the others that I was only lost, and not a spirit.''

"I felt Ghostwind had come to me, to be my child and to teach me things," Mountain Water had told Nighthawk. "Then we all heard her say that we should not join Black Kettle's band on the Washita. When the council decided not to move, I knew that Maheo, the Creator, had sent her to us.''

The reverence shown in the word Maheo had made a lasting impression on Nighthawk. He realized that no people could ever show more respect for their Creator.

A woman named Day Lily, Ghostwind's closest friend, had also spoken to Nighthawk of that day with a look of wonderment in her eyes. "Ghostwind told us not to join with Black Kettle on the Washita. She said we must stay put, that the Washita was not a safe place. She saved our lives from Long Hair Custer and his Bluecoat soldiers. They killed Black Kettle and his people, slaughtering them in the snow. We could have been with them.''

Nighthawk watched his wife as she smoothed Talking Grass's hair. The child slept peacefully while all around the singing and dancing continued.

Ghostwind turned to him. "You've had your own vision, my husband. Why do you deny it?''

Nighthawk finished the last bite of stew. "I just don't want it to be real, I guess.''

"It's all too real. Learn to accept that." She rose and took Talking Grass in her arms. "I'll be in the lodge. I'm through celebrating.''

Nighthawk stared into the empty bowl. As much as he would like to forget, the vision had been very powerful, and had left him shaken. As many times as he had reviewed it, he couldn't shake the foreboding it brought.

The vision had come while he had been a soldier in Crook's army. They had found an old Sioux campsight and the skeletal remains of a butchered warrior. "Likely Crow," his friend Kincaid had told him. "Warring Indians don't like to have their enemies come back to haunt them, so they chop them up. You see, they believe that everything they have in this world goes across with them. If his weapons are taken or destroyed, then he can't use them in the next life. If his body's mutilated, he won't be able to live properly. They want to make sure of that.''

It had been the first time Mason Hall, the soldier, had seen anything like it. It had reached deep into him, touching his own mortality. Now that he was no longer a soldier, it affected him even more.

Nighthawk looked deep into the bowl, the vision returning. Still a soldier, he stood on a wide plain below the mountains, surrounded by warriors on horseback, their war paint gleaming, their feathers dancing in the breeze. Behind them, a sunset flamed over the peaks, the light swimming in long streaks, like huge snakes in a darkening sea.

They rode toward him single file, chanting. The dust from their ponies' hooves formed whirlwinds in the sky, streaming upward, mixing with the strange crimson light.

Hall wanted to turn and run, but found he couldn't move. His arms hung dead and his feet felt rooted solidly. Only his head could move, turning to and fro, watching the oncoming warriors riding their horses toward him in a zigzag line.

The warriors closed in, circling him, each waving a weapon in one hand and a body part in the other. Arms and legs, and rings of fingerbones, hung out from their ponies. From the circle of warriors came one, painted in red and black, riding a blue stallion. The warrior thrust a severed head into his face, the dark hair tangled and matted with blood, the mouth gaping, the eyes rolled back in their sockets.

"Pray to your God for him," the warrior commanded, and rode away.

A second warrior, painted blue and white, rode forward, holding another head. Hall could not turn away, nor close his eyes. The warrior thrust the head into his face, the man's hair red this time. The warrior spoke the same words as the first had: "Pray to your God for him."

A third warrior, painted entirely in dark yellow, his mouth and eyes ringed with black, rode forward with a third head. This head was much larger and covered with yellow hair. The sockets held large, grayish blue eyes filled with horror. The warriors behind him chanted loudly.

As the warrior approached, the chanting increased. The warrior held the head up and it began to spin in a circle. Hall yelled, "Stop!" but the sound only echoed dully in his head. The head seemed to explode before him, the yellow hair and skin flying off, the skull exposed, the huge, grayish blue eyes turning into burning coals.

Nighthawk jerked back from the bowl and threw it aside. Some of the people sitting nearby stared. Nighthawk rose and paced for a time. He went to a small skin bag he had left in a blanket back from the fire. He sat down again, and with trembling fingers, opened the bag.

After taking out a mirror, Nighthawk began to paint his face, covering the old paint that had been sweated off. He took a deep breath and steadied his hand. He applied three bars of bright yellow paint crossways along each cheek, from the nose back to the jawline. He crossed his forehead with three bars of red, then with a single, thicker streak of red running down from his lower lip, over his chin, ending at the base of his throat.

The face he now saw in the mirror was wild and un-tamed—unconquerable. It was his medicine, his coat of protection during battle. He made certain that the dried nighthawk, which he had tied into his hair, was firmly secured, and rose to rejoin the dancing.

Nighthawk entered the twisting and turning circle of dancers, writhing with them, struggling to push the vision from his mind. But the heads stared at him, and all he could do was scream into the night sky.

EIGHT

Ghostwind awakened early. Talking Grass was curled up next to Nighthawk. Both were fast asleep. Nighthawk had danced through the night, as had many of the warriors. None of them would likely rise soon.

Ghostwind took four water bags from beside the door. Though small and trim, she could carry nearly her own weight in water or wood. She stepped outside, where the sun was barely topping the horizon, an arc of bright gold rising into a deep, cloudless blue. Smoke curled upward from campfires that ran along the bottom farther than the eye could see.

The Big Village, as the people called it, was the largest camp of its kind that any of the tribes could remember. Lodges filled the valley, which was nearly a mile wide and over two miles long. The Cheyenne were camped the farthest north, with the Unkpapa Sioux, Sitting Bull's people, at the southern end.

In between were the rest of the Lakota Sioux—the Oglala, the Sans Arcs, the Minneconjou, and the Blackfeet. Along the west edge of the six major camp circles were smaller numbers of two Lakota divisions—the Brulé and the Two Kettle. Small numbers of Assiniboine were also mixed in, as well as a few Santee Sioux who had just joined the village.

Along the west edge of camp flowed the Little Bighorn River, called the Little Horn by the Indian People, swollen and swift. The bottom was boggy in places, allowing for bathing and for easy access to water, but the main channel was treacherous, churning with high water. Winter had held tight in the mountains and snowmelt had only just begun.

Outside her lodge, Ghostwind set the water bags down and breathed deeply of the morning air, which still held a hint of coolness. Though summer had come and the days were very warm, the darkness still held a chill from the snowfaced slopes of the White Rain, or Big Horn Mountains to the south and the Pryor Mountains to the northwest. The nearby Wolf Mountains held little patches of snow at the very highest points, very unusual for this time of year. Normally, the nights were much warmer, but as yet winter wouldn't leave the high country.

The village elders said that the spirits were unsettled, that the nights and the days hadn't formed normal patterns this year. That meant prayer ceremonies should take place more often. The old people all were restless.

Ghostwind leveled her blue eyes on the horizon, raising her arms toward the sun to say a morning prayer in thanks to the Creator for another day of life. Her light hair hung nearly to her waist.

Though dark-skinned, Ghostwind carried both white and Cheyenne blood. The *Wiheo,* the whites, were not liked among the Cheyenne, and in the eyes of some, she was still an outcast.

But her adopted mother, Mountain Water, and her own warning not to join Black Kettle and his people on the Washita, had made it possible for her to stay. She had saved Old Bear's people from Long Hair Custer and his murdering Bluecoats.

As a woman, Ghostwind had been given as wife to a warrior named Kicks-the-Fox, to whom she bore two children. Kicks-the-Fox had been killed during a horse raid on a Bluecoat camp the previous winter, Nighthawk's camp; it had been Nighthawk who had killed him.

Yet Nighthawk had filled a yearning deep within Ghostwind. He had come into her life and had become a part of her. She could no more understand it now than the day she had first met him. She just knew it to be true.

The sun had risen fully and Ghostwind had just finished her prayers when her son, Young Horse, and his friend, Tall Deer, rode in on their ponies. Young Horse had an enthusiastic flair for adventure. At eight, he could already outrun and outwrestle many of the older boys and could also ride better than most of them.

His best friend, Tall Deer, was without question the best rider for his age in the entire Big Village. Just twelve, Tall Deer was as tall as many of the warriors and could trick ride better than all but a few. His goal was to be the best ever among all the Cheyenne people.

Tall Deer's mother, Pine Woman, was a Minneconjou of the Lakota nation. She had married Nighthawk's father, Shot-in-the-Throat, many years before, when Shot-in-the-Throat had come out to trade for furs. Tall Deer had been born of their union.

It had been very hard for Nighthawk to meet his father, the man who had left him to begin a new life of his own, but Ghostwind had helped him as much as she could. Tall Deer was Nighthawk's half brother by blood, a full brother in the Indian way. Nighthawk still wasn't used to the situation.

Young Horse and Tall Deer rode their ponies to a stop in front of Ghostwind. Both were smiling broadly.

"Good morning, Mother," Young Horse said. "It's a very fine day."

"Have you had any sleep yet?" Ghostwind asked. "Or did you and Tall Deer watch the dancing all night?"

"We got some sleep," Young Horse said. "But we don't need much." He jumped down from his pony, entered the lodge, and began to rouse Nighthawk from sleep.

Ghostwind darted inside and jerked Young Horse's arm. "Come out and let your father sleep. And you're going to wake Talking Grass. Do you want to take care of her for the entire day?" She pushed him through the doorflap. "What do you want with your father, anyway?"

Young Horse pointed to Tall Deer, who was smiling broadly. "Ask him."

"I'm not trying to cause trouble," Tall Deer said. "I was hoping that Nighthawk would go out on the flats with us and work on his riding. I want to teach him some things."

"He's too tired for that right now," Ghostwind said. "Besides, his leg hurts from all the dancing. You can teach him later."

Tall Deer smiled. "He should work on his riding before long. The men are going to hunt buffalo. There's a big herd to the west."

"I'll tell him when he awakens," Ghostwind said.

Tall Deer had been trying to talk Nighthawk into learning trick riding in exchange for lessons in rifle shooting. Nighthawk had been hesitant. He wasn't interested in trick riding, and he didn't want to give Tall Deer a reason to be shooting all the time. A rifle was dangerous, especially when you weren't used to it. And Tall Deer was one who wanted to learn things too quickly.

Tall Deer wouldn't be deterred, though, and pressed as often as possible. Some day he was going to have to learn how to take no for an answer.

"I'll give you something to eat," Ghostwind said. "Then you can go back out until Nighthawk awakens. He'll come to see you then."

The boys waited while Ghostwind filled bowls with stew, then sat down and ate in silence. Ghostwind watched them, noting how nervous they were.

"Why are you fidgeting?" Ghostwind asked Young Horse. "Are you worried about something?"

"I'm not fidgeting," Young Horse said. "I'm just anxious to have Father come ride with us."

"Why is it so important right now?" Ghostwind asked. "You two usually have more fun by yourselves. Why do you want your father with you so badly?"

Young Horse set his bowl down and jumped to his feet. "We'll wait for him over toward the hills." Tall Deer set his bowl down quickly also. Both jumped on their ponies.

"Don't go far," Ghostwind said. "You know the limits. Not beyond the edge of the valley over there." She watched them mount. "You hear, Young Horse?"

"Yes, Mother. Don't worry. There are camp police out there. They'll send us back and never let us go again. We don't want that. We know how far we can go."

Ghostwind watched them leave. Along the distant east rim of the valley, horses grazed in vast numbers, a mottled sea of movement. Horse tenders watched the perimeters, each keeping the horses from his own village separate from the others as much as possible. At any time warriors could come out and ask for their horses. It was easier if they weren't all mixed together.

Ghostwind looked to the edge of the village. The police, members of the Fox warrior society, rode in small groups of three or four, watching the camps and the country above the valley. It was their duty to enforce the rules and watch for scouts who had ridden out to look for game and possible danger.

Ghostwind turned to the north. Something in the clouds caught her eye. Suddenly, she saw the sky redden deeply. It began to churn and boil, and numbers of men dressed in blue began to fall toward the earth, kicking and screaming.

Ghostwind gasped. She covered her eyes. When she looked toward the sky again, it was a peaceful, deep blue, with scattered, puffy clouds.

Young Horse and Tall Deer were near the edge of the village. "Young Horse!" Ghostwind called. She saw him stop and turn. She wanted to call them back and make them stay near the lodge. But that was silly.

"What is it, Mother?" Young Horse shouted.

"Remember, don't go too far!"

Young Horse nodded and rode off with Tall Deer. Talking Grass came out of the lodge, rubbing her eyes. "Why are you yelling?"

"Young Horse and Tall Deer have gone riding," Ghostwind said. "I just told them to stay close."

Talking Grass squinted into the distance. "Young Horse wants to learn to ride like Tall Deer. I don't think he should try. It's dangerous."

Ghostwind scooped Talking Grass into her arms and

picked up the water bags. "I see you're worried about your brother. Well, he'll be just fine. Let's go to the river and bathe. How does that sound?"

"What about Father?"

"Let him sleep," Ghostwind said. "He's just an old bear when he's tired, you know."

Talking Grass giggled. "Just an old bear. He even growls like one."

"We don't want a bear growling at us, now do we?"

"No," Talking Grass said. "Sometimes bears aren't any fun."

Near the river, Ghostwind was joined by her mother, Mountain Water, who had been bathing some of her other grandchildren.

"There's a shallow pool over there," she told Talking Grass, pointing. "The water's warm. I'll bet you'd like to play in it with the other children."

"Do you want to go over there?" Ghostwind asked Talking Grass.

Talking Grass smiled and jumped in the air. She hurried over to the pool, where a lot of children were playing and older women were watching over them.

Mountain Water was a large woman in middle age, with braids that hung down to her waist. Her eyes were quick and her hair was as dark as a young woman's. She understood Ghostwind well and always knew when something was troubling her.

"I've been watching you," she told Ghostwind. "Are you having your visions again?"

"Every night, and sometimes during the day."

"You look as if you just saw something."

"I did," Ghostwind said. "Something happened in the sky."

"Do you want to tell me what you saw?"

"No. It's better to just forget it."

"Now that you're with child," Mountain Water said, "you shouldn't worry so much about everything."

Ghostwind had conceived two months previously. Now she wondered how she could possibly bear a child and face the coming problems at the same time. "There's much to worry about,'' Ghostwind said. She stepped into the shallows and lowered the skin bag into the current. "I can't help it. Bad things are coming."

"But what can *you* do to change those things?"

"I don't know."

"Does it do any good to worry unless you have a plan to change things?"

Ghostwind turned, water dripping from the bag. "Plan? How can I *plan* against something like this?"

"That's my point. What's coming will come, no matter how much you worry. This makes your children worry about you, then. It's good to watch over them and guard them closely, but you cannot stop what the Creator is bringing."

"But why am I seeing it?"

"That's between you and the Creator. Pray. Find out if you can. I'll see if I can't organize a sweat ceremony for you. Maybe you can learn something."

"I don't think a sweat will get rid of my visions."

"I didn't say it would. You need to ask the Powers for help. Do you understand?"

Ghostwind came to shore and traded her full bag for an empty one. "I saw the vision to the north. Maybe I can go someplace where they'll leave me alone."

"And where would that be?"

"I don't know." Ghostwind stood staring into the water. "I have been thinking. Something will come to me." She lowered herself to fill the second bag and put a hand over her eyes to hide the tears.

"Come out of there and sit down," Mountain Water said.

Ghostwind joined her mother on shore, and the two sat with their backs against a fallen log. Overhead, a great blue heron swept over the treetops and landed upstream, where a number of large stick nests rested in the forks of the cottonwoods.

"The visions must be terrible," Mountain Water said. "I haven't seen you this disturbed since you entered the village as a child."

"This world is going to blow up into fire," Ghostwind said. "I know that will happen."

"Is that what you've seen?" Mountain Water asked.

"Yes. Fire and death. That's what I've been seeing. It won't go away."

"Take a deep breath," Mountain Water said. "And another."

"Being calm won't change things," Ghostwind said.

"Maybe it will help you understand, though. If things are rushing through your head, you can't be open to learn."

"I prefer things rushing through my head. Then maybe I won't keep seeing the things that I do."

"You just told me that nothing can stop what you're seeing. So look at it and learn."

"But it's too horrible."

"Stay with it anyway," Mountain Water insisted. "Let the visions come. Don't fight them. See what they tell you. Maybe you can save our people again."

Ghostwind's best friend Day Lily arrived, holding two water bags. Ghostwind and Mountain Water rose to their feet.

"I'll go and watch Talking Grass and the other children," Mountain Water said. "I'll see you back in camp."

"I didn't see you at the dancing last night," Ghostwind said.

Day Lily filled one of her bags. "Red Bear didn't want to watch, so we stayed in the lodge."

"So Red Bear's having a hard time," Ghostwind said. "Is that why you're so late in coming for water?"

"You know how it is with a badly injured husband," Day Lily said. "Life can be very hard."

Ghostwind did know what it was like. A month before he was killed on the Bluecoat raid, Kicks-the-Fox had fallen with his horse. He had sustained a serious groin injury that had kept him bedridden for nearly a week. For many more days he couldn't ride. During that time, he had been very hard to live with.

"If a man cannot live as a warrior, or a medicine man, or whatever he has chosen to do, he doesn't feel like living any longer," Day Lily added. "Red Bear is getting worse instead of better."

"Give him time to heal," Ghostwind said.

"He will never be the same," Day Lily said. "His upper lip was shot away at the battle and some of the front teeth have come loose. He can hardly talk. There is no way to repair that. And his knee that was torn will likely always be bad. It's swollen and hard like a large rock, a large blue rock."

Ghostwind filled another bag. "Has he talked to Horned Bull or the other medicine men?"

"He's been chewing roots that Horned Bull gave him, but they don't seem to take away the pain."

"Maybe Horned Bull can hold a ceremony and help heal him," Ghostwind suggested.

"Maybe. But that must be later," Day Lily said. "We have nothing to give him. We lost everything when the Bluecoats came into the winter village. And we haven't had time to gather more."

"I'll give you some things that you can use as presents," Ghostwind offered. "And I'm sure Nighthawk will give a pony or two. We'd be glad to."

"I thank you," Day Lily said, fighting tears, "but you're no richer than I am right now. And after losing Kicks-the-Fox, you lost even more than me. Besides, the presents must come from us."

"We'll give you the presents now," Ghostwind suggested again, "and you can pay us back when you want to."

"No. I don't want to do it that way." Day Lily rubbed tears from her eyes. "We want to give Horned Bull good things that we've made ourselves. Red Bear wants to give him a buffalo robe. There has to be a hunt first. It will take a while to get things together, but we will—if peace ever comes again to our people."

"Times have been very hard this year, it's true," Ghostwind said. "I wonder if things can get better, if they ever will."

"I heard you talking to your mother," Day Lily said. "I know, too, that you've been acting strangely. And I know how you are when you're having visions. That's not good for any of us."

"I don't like having the visions," Ghostwind said. "But I can't help it."

Day Lily closed the ties to her water bags. "How long will it be like this? How long do we have to fear the Bluecoats?"

Ghostwind picked up her own bags. "I'm afraid we're always going to have to fear them. They don't want us to live on our lands any longer. They want to herd us onto the reservations and make us stay there. As long as we want to be free, we'll have to fear them."

"And if we give in to them?" Day Lily asked. "Are you saying we won't have to worry any longer?"

"I don't like sounding this way," Ghostwind said, "but I believe we'll have to fear them no matter what. I don't think it matters either way. So we might as well try and stay free. I don't believe there's anything else."

NINE

The sun was well into the sky, and the village was alive with activity. Nighthawk walked toward the horse herd, having awakened and eaten his fill of stew. Ghostwind had told him that Young Horse and Tall Deer wanted him to go riding with them.

Nighthawk wanted no part of horseback riding just now. He was lucky to be able to walk. His right leg, heavily scarred from a prison knife fight, was stiff from dancing. It was slow to loosen up, even in the warm summer air. The injury had taken place six months earlier, but it had been very serious and was still in the healing process.

In addition, Nighthawk was still fighting the fear within him. The vision of the warriors and the severed heads was lurking in the back of his mind, waiting for the right moment to reappear. That could be any time, and he didn't want to look foolish in front of anyone.

Still, it would be good to watch Tall Deer perform his riding tricks. That was a treat anytime, and usually drew a number of spectators.

Nighthawk reached the edge of the village. A light wind blew through his hair, now grown much longer than in his army days and showing streaks of blonde from the hot sun. His trim body was naked but for a breechcloth and moccasins, and his clear blue eyes offset a face deeply tanned.

Young Horse and Tall Deer were riding their ponies along a terrace below the hills. Young Horse was standing on the back of his pony, while Tall Deer circled them on his red pony. A short distance away a number of women and children watched.

Tall Deer, his pony running at full speed, slid under the belly and up the opposite side, then stood on the pony's back. He did a handstand, then flipped back to his feet; the pony ran full speed the entire time.

Seeing Nighthawk, Tall Deer turned his pony by applying pressure to its left shoulder. He rode headlong toward Nighthawk, veering only at the last second. Upon passing, he flipped backward into a full somersault, landing a few feet from Nighthawk, smiling broadly.

"It's a good day for riding."

"I see that it is," Nighthawk said. "That was impressive, but what are you going to do about your pony? He's running away."

The horse was headed toward the herd at a gallop, its tail held high. Tall Deer whistled. The pony immediately turned and galloped back, stopping at Tall Deer's side. The women and children cheered and began to disperse.

Young Horse arrived, riding Big Spot and leading Nighthawk's buckskin. "It's hard to stand on top of a pony, much less jump around on it," he said. "I've got a long way to go."

"Take your time," Nighthawk said. "Your mother worries about you. Don't go too fast. You don't want to break an arm or leg."

Leading his pony, Tall Deer walked over to a nearby tree and picked up three long sticks painted red and black.

Nighthawk knew they were coup sticks that the young warriors used in training. Tall Deer had a game in mind.

"Father, do you know what he wants?" Young Horse asked.

"Yes," Nighthawk replied. "I knew some day he would want to test me."

"Maybe it shouldn't be today," Young Horse said.

"You're right," Nighthawk said, "he could have picked a better day. We'll see."

Tall Deer rode back and tossed one of the coup sticks

to Nighthawk, smiling. "You've learned a lot about riding as a warrior, but you need to learn a lot more."

"I'm not interested in riding today," Nighthawk said. "I came out to watch you two."

"Watching is no fun," Tall Deer said. "It's *doing* the riding that's fun."

"Maybe another day," Nighthawk said.

"Maybe tomorrow," Young Horse said to Tall Deer. "You can see that his leg is hurting him."

Tall Deer was rubbing his pony's neck. His persistence was showing. "Just what if you *had* to ride today?" he asked Nighthawk. "What if you had no choice?"

"Why wouldn't I have a choice?" Nighthawk asked.

"Bluecoats," Tall Deer said. "What if Bluecoats came? You'd have to ride, no matter how your leg felt. Maybe you should get on your pony and loosen up."

"Are you expecting more Bluecoats?" Nighthawk asked.

"You can never tell," Tall Deer replied. "You know what the old people are saying: Anything could happen this year. The spirits are restless."

Nighthawk jumped on his buckskin, grimacing, knowing that he must meet the challenge. "You know," he told Tall Deer, "you sound like a commander I had, a guy named Buckner, who loved to push me, especially when my leg hurt the worst. He liked to see men in pain. You're not that way, are you?"

"I don't see you bleeding anywhere," Tall Deer remarked. "You can't be too bad off."

Tall Deer kicked his pony into a gallop and rode out a distance. "Are you ready?" he called to Nighthawk.

"I'm ready."

Nighthawk had seen this game played often by older horse tenders and young warriors, a match between horses and riders that showed the riders' skill and the ponies' abilities to turn at full speed. The game was used to train buffalo ponies for the hunt and for warfare.

Tall Deer, by making the challenge, had declared himself the aggressor. He would try and count coup on

Nighthawk. If he succeeded, Nighthawk would, in turn, have to give chase. The older warriors played the game as well; but they played it with an enemy, often for their very lives.

Tall Deer kicked his pony into a full run, bearing down on Nighthawk, yelling as a warrior would when rushing to count coup. Young Horse had moved his pony out of the way and sat watching. "Come on, Father!" he yelled. "You can win!"

Nighthawk felt the tension mounting. He had a good pony in Dancer, every bit as good as Tall Deer's red stallion. Guiding the pony and staying on, though, was going to be a test of endurance.

Tall Deer was nearly upon him, reaching out with the coup stick. Nighthawk waited until the right moment and leaned over his pony, kicking the buckskin's flanks. The pony lurched into a dead run, and Tall Deer's coup stick narrowly missed Nighthawk's shoulder.

Nighthawk, his mind on the game, stayed low over the buckskin's back. Tall Deer had turned his pony in a tight circle and was giving chase. Nighthawk felt the blood rushing in his veins, obscuring the pain in his leg. He knew he would have to teach Tall Deer something one day, and it would have to be today.

Nighthawk touched his knee to Dancer's left shoulder and the pony turned a quick, sharp right. Tall Deer's red stallion made the turn equally as quickly, with Tall Deer leaning way out over the pony's back, trying to touch Nighthawk.

The two riders turned their ponies in sharp zigzags all across the flat before Tall Deer finally touched Nighthawk's shoulder with the coup stick. Then, in the blink of an eye, the ponies changed directions and Nighthawk was the one giving chase.

Tall Deer laughed aloud as he rode, taunting Nighthawk, turning his pony this way and that. He rode magnificently, darting from one side to the other, contorting himself so that Nighthawk couldn't touch him.

But Nighthawk persisted. Tall Deer had ridden his

pony all morning. Very soon, he knew the red stallion would tire.

Nighthawk was right. Tall Deer's pony, winded, began to slow. Its turns became less sharp. Nighthawk took advantage and drove the coup stick into Tall Deer's ribs.

Angered, Tall Deer gave chase. Nighthawk rode his pony through a small coulee and up the other side, turning back through the coulee as Tall Deer circled. Nighthawk, far out in front, slowed his buckskin. Tall Deer had given up, knowing he couldn't push his pony any harder.

Nighthawk rode up to Tall Deer. "Don't challenge a man like that unless you have a fresh pony."

Young Horse came galloping over. "You did very well, Father! Very well!"

"If my pony hadn't tired, I would have won," Tall Deer said.

"You should have thought about that," Nighthawk said. "Tomorrow would have been better."

Tall Deer began to smile. "And you're very good, especially for one with a bad leg. Maybe I won't try you when it's healed." He leaned over his pony and extended his hand to Nighthawk. "I should have expected as much from my brother."

They dismounted and led their ponies to a spring at the base of a hill. When the animals had watered, Nighthawk and Tall Deer began to rub them down with dried grass. Young Horse helped Nighthawk, smiling broadly.

"If you have a good pony, most often you can survive," he told Nighthawk. "But you have good medicine *and* a good pony. That's why many call you a warrior already. I'm proud that you came to be my father."

"Thank you, Young Horse," Nighthawk said. "You're a fine son. I know I can never repay you for taking your real father from you."

"Mother says that you punish yourself too much for that," Young Horse said. "I believe she's right. My father was an unhappy man. I could see that. The Creator took him to the Spirit World. If it hadn't been you who had shot him, it would have been another. That's the way it is. So don't worry any longer."

"I'll do everything I can to protect you and your mother," Nighthawk said. The three sat down on the slope, letting the horses graze.

"I know you will protect us," Young Horse said. "You'll do a very good job."

"Yes," Tall Deer agreed. "He's right. You have very strong medicine. I've heard the warriors talk about you. Death has come to take you more than once, and you've turned it away."

"I've just been lucky, is all."

"What your people call luck we call good medicine," Tall Deer said. "Just look at how things are for you. You've learned much about horses and riding since I first helped you. A lot. And it hasn't been that long. Some day you'll be as good as me, maybe."

"I doubt that," Nighthawk said. "You'll get better and better. I'm happy with the way things are now."

Young Horse asked, "Don't you want to be a trick rider? You already are a trick shooter."

"Shooting is enough for me. I can't do it all."

"Think of it, though," Tall Deer put in, "riding on the side of your pony, then sliding under the belly and shooting from the other side. Maybe you could shoot a bird from the sky that way. Everyone would stare at you all day long, like they did when you shot the turkey feathers from behind your back. That was something!"

Nighthawk laughed. "You'd make a good circus promoter, Tall Deer."

"Tell us about your circus days," Young Horse begged. "Tell us how you learned to shoot so well."

"That wasn't fun," Nighthawk said. "No matter what you might think, things were hard for me. I learned to shoot very well, it's true. Trick shooting became the most important part of my life. Nothing else mattered. I had to shoot better than everybody else so that nobody could come along and steal my job away."

"Mother says you had to kill the circus owner," Young Horse said. "Is that why you went to prison?"

"He had taken a brand new rifle that I had won in a shooting contest," Nighthawk explained. "I asked to have it back and he tried to hit me over the head with it. He went crazy. It was him or me."

Tall Deer noticed Nighthawk rubbing his sore leg. "How did the fight in the prison happen?"

"It's a long story. Maybe I'll tell you about it another time."

"It seems that you don't like to fight, even your enemies," Tall Deer observed. "Among my people, there is much glory in defeating an enemy, especially if you touch one while he's alive and you get away to tell about it. That's the highest honor."

"I suppose," Nighthawk said. "But I've tired of trying to save myself. And I feel it's only just begun."

"Do you know there'll be more battles with the Bluecoats?" Tall Deer asked, his eyes wide.

"The Bluecoats who came to fight us will be back," Nighthawk said. "I know those people. I know they won't quit. They'll push the Cheyenne and the Lakota until there are either no people left, or the survivors are back on the reservations."

"They can't stop all of us together," Tall Deer argued. "There are too many of us."

"A village this size can't stay together long," Nighthawk said. "This many people eat a tremendous amount of food. The horses need a lot of grass. The village will have to split soon. The Bluecoats will be after us again."

"I think you're wrong, Father," Young Horse said. "I hear everyone saying the soldiers were afraid of our warriors, and they would have all died on the Rosebud if the Crow and Shoshone hadn't been with them. They won't come back. Everyone says that."

"I wish that were true," Nighthawk said. "I'm not saying it to scare you. It's a fact. There are more Bluecoats than just those we fought on the Rosebud. They have orders not to fail. They cannot fail."

"How did it feel to be out there?" Tall Horse asked, thinking of the Rosebud fight. "What was it like to be fighting the same people you camped with?''

"I didn't have many friends among them," Nighthawk replied. "The only one I truly cared about was a mule packer. His name was Kincaid. He was like a father to me."

"Did he adopt you?" Young Horse asked.

"No. He just treated me like I was his son."

"He should have adopted you," Young Horse said. "If he treated you that way, he should have given you presents and called you his son."

"It's not that easy among the white people," Nighthawk explained. "People don't accept one another very easily. Some do, but most don't."

"Kin . . . caid?" Tall Deer struggled with the English. "What does Kincaid mean?"

"It's just a word," Nighthawk replied. "Jordan Kincaid. Just two words that say who he was."

Tall Deer laughed. "The *Wasichu* name themselves with empty words. I don't understand."

"Maybe in times past, in the language of his ancestors, it had a meaning. But now it's just a word. My name used to be Mason Hall. I'm sure it had a meaning long ago. But it's just a name now."

"Did he die?" Young Horse asked. "Did Kincaid die?"

"I don't know," Nighthawk said.

Another rider appeared on the hill. Eagle Wing waved and rode down at a gallop.

"Do you need to raise so much dust?" Nighthawk asked as Eagle Wing reached them. Eagle Wing pointed up the hill. "You two boys ride back to camp. Go now!"

The two hurried to mount their ponies. They knew not to ask questions. When one of the camp police gave an order, it was carried out immediately. There was always good reason for it.

Eagle Wing watched the boys ride away. "Why did you bring those two out here, past the boundary lines?"

"I didn't know," Nighthawk said. "I didn't think we were in any danger."

"Do you see any camp police out here?"

"No. But they're not that far away. The village is just over the hill."

Eagle Wing said, "I should punish you for this, you know that. You put the boys at risk. Yes, the village isn't far, but if Bluecoats somehow got a jump on you, it would be very bad."

"I didn't mean to break the rules," Nighthawk said. "I was riding with the two boys and we just went too far. I'll be more careful next time."

"There may not be a next time," Eagle Wing said. "Other camp police saw you out here as well. When the council meets again this afternoon, many will want you to leave the village. Leave or be killed."

"I didn't know there were so many against me."

"More than either you or I thought. There is much bitterness against the white man; and regardless of how you fought at the Rosebud, there are many who feel uncomfortable with you here."

"But I'm married to Ghostwind. Doesn't that mean anything?"

"You know that there are many who fear her. She has owl medicine. And she is a mixed blood. Many want her to leave, also. They want you both gone."

"How do you feel?" Nighthawk asked.

"You know how I feel," Eagle Wing said. "We have become brothers. I can speak for you at the council and tell them that we need you on the upcoming hunt, to shoot many buffalo. We can only hope they agree with me."

"What hunt?" Nighthawk asked.

"Scouts have seen many buffalo moving toward Rotten Grass Creek. It will be a couple of days before they're close enough to hunt. Each of the villages will send hunters, their best. I'll ask the council to hold on their decision so that you can help us. It's important that we succeed. We need the meat badly. If you shoot a lot of buffalo, it will make the people happy. It's your only chance."

TEN

The sun was falling behind a dark wall of clouds that rolled down from the uplands into the valley. Distant thunder and jagged flashes of light pushed ever closer to camp.

Moored two miles downstream from the mouth of the Rosebud, the *Far West* rocked gently with the current of the Yellowstone beneath her. Men worked feverishly to unload and inventory the last of the supplies. White tents and blue uniforms covered the river bottom.

Adam Garrett sat on a cottonwood log near the water's edge, notepaper in hand, watching the approaching storm. The lightning to the west was dazzling—jagged streaks of white that burst from the clouds to the valley floor. The huge, heart-shaped leaves of the cottonwoods began to dance with the breeze, their rustling growing ever heavier.

A short distance away, four crows flew with the wind, sailing over camp. Garrett quickly grabbed his rifle; if the crows landed, in the trees or on the ground, he intended to open fire on them. Oh, how they made him churn inside!

But they flew past, cawing, as if laughing at him, the wind sweeping them into the distance. Garrett set his rifle down, the trophy scalp dangling from the trigger guard. He ran his fingers through the long, tangled hair. It felt alive to his touch. He let go quickly, rubbing his hand against his pants leg, trying to get rid of the feeling.

He considered cutting the scalp loose and throwing it away. But he realized how much the trophy meant to Little Crane and Red Moon. They and the other scouts considered him a warrior now, worthy of honor and a place of distinction. To continue receiving their help and information, he had to keep the scalp.

Garrett picked up his pencil and took to writing once more. Since arriving near the mouth of the Rosebud and making camp at noon, the rest of the day's events had been the most important to date. Garrett knew that this might be his last letter to the Grants for some days to come.

Garrett resumed the letter he had begun to Orvil Grant.

Yellowstone River, near mouth of Rosebud Creek
MT Territory
Evening, 21 June 1876

Dear Orvil,
    Custer, Terry, and other commanders held a major conference aboard the steamboat early this afternoon. I would love to have heard what was said but couldn't find a way to be invited. Kellogg was not allowed, either, so I have surmised that Terry is frustrated with the way the campaign is going and called the meeting to upbraid his officers, especially Major Reno, who disobeyed orders by scouting past the Powder River to the Rosebud.
    I find it odd that Terry and the other commanders should be so at odds with Reno. After all, it was his reconnaissance that told them the Sioux and Cheyenne are not on the Powder River.
    Terry will now have to revise his plans for approaching the hostile village, which is certain to be somewhere along the upper Rosebud, or over in the Little Bighorn River country. It's my guess that Custer will be the one to lead the next detachment out.
    This seems to be certain, as some of Gibbon's forces have joined us, including a hunter and scout named George Herendeen, along with the top six Crow Indian scouts. They know the country better

than the Rees and scouted the area earlier while with Gibbon.

Mitch Boyer, the half-Sioux scout, has told me that he helped select the six Crow scouts. I had a chance to talk with Boyer briefly and he tells me that, while with Gibbon, the Crows crossed the trail of a very large village, with more lodges than they have ever seen together. They feel that it will take a lot of men to fight, and since they have heard good things about Long Hair Custer, they hope that he will be the leader.

The Indians all want Custer, and none of the other commanders have one ounce of faith in him. It is a curious situation. Terry is having a hard time, and I don't envy him his position.

Despite Custer's rank, I cannot imagine that Terry believes this man to be able to command an operation of such importance as this. I don't know Terry's political persuasions, but I am wondering if Terry doesn't think he can help Custer regain his status. The word among the men is that the Seventh Cavalry has been promised the first shot at the hostiles. It seems that Terry may be offering Custer the opportunity to make himself a hero by allowing him the discretion to chase the Sioux at his own whim. Custer has somehow mastered the art of pleasing Terry. Maybe Custer has learned how to please all of his commanders, at least those he believes matter to him.

Perhaps Terry is relying mostly on Custer because of his faith in Major Reno. Custer's distaste for Reno is quite evident, as is all the other officers' dislike for Custer. I can't, however, get any of them to discuss Custer, other than the obvious. That he is hard on the men is no secret to anyone. Perhaps no one will talk for fear of reprisal by Custer, should he hear of them plotting against him.

There is little doubt that Custer sees this campaign as the most important of his life. He's preparing himself, he says, by "praying in his own way." He told me that he prays within his heart and puts his trust in the Almighty to "guide me through each battle that I face. This makes me calm and gives me the courage that I have."

Those were his very words to me while we stopped to water the horses early this morning. He pointed to the sun and said, "The Indians think that the Creator put the secrets of life into that round ball of light. Well, I admire them for that. They say their prayers morning and night, which is more than I can say for the great majority of my soldiers. Praying is a good thing. I do a lot of it myself."

When I asked him if his prayers were always answered, he told me, "So far I've been saying them correctly, I believe. Wouldn't you agree? I can't foresee any changes."

I don't know what to make of him. It is interesting to note also that Custer will not drink liquor and makes it doubly hard on those who do. The last night at Tongue River, I watched him take sport with a drunken infantryman passed out on the ground. Custer ordered him packed into an empty supply barrel and had the barrel turned upright and pinned to the ground, trapping the soldier inside. Custer laughed until it hurt while the soldier screamed from inside the barrel.

Later, I asked Custer what he thought of drink. He said, "Alderney, Mr. Garrett. Yes, Alderney is my preference. Don't you understand?" He laughed and curled his lip and informed me that Alderney is a breed of cattle. "Yes, Mr. Garrett, I prefer milk!" He then scowled at me and told me not to mention it again.

It surprises me so that the Indians consider him such a great leader. Maybe it's his accomplishments. He certainly has been hard on them in the past, especially the Cheyenne.

But this is going to be a lot different. And I believe he knows it. As of yet, what mistakes he will make that will be of help to you I cannot say. He portrays himself as unstoppable. If there are as many Sioux waiting as the scout Mitch Boyer says, he will have to prove his mettle indeed.

Garrett signed the letter and placed it in an envelope. He rose to his feet as Little Crane and Red Moon approached, accompanied by four of the six Crow scouts who had been assigned to Terry's forces. They were lithe and strong, their hair well groomed, cut short in front and combed straight back. They wore skins and beaded moccasins, and feathers in their long, braided hair. Each one wore a small medicine pouch that hung low on his neck.

The four studied Garrett, smiling. Little Crane was also smiling, pointing to the folder under Garrett's arm.

"Ah, Six Fingers. You're making the paper talk."

"Yes, I've been at work." Garrett wondered if Little Crane wasn't putting on a show for the benefit of the Crow scouts. After all, anyone who knew a man-who-makes-the-paper-talk must have some special medicine of his own.

Little Crane pointed to the sky. "Maybe you're good at it, yes. But can you make the paper talk when the storm strikes?"

"No," Garrett replied. "Not unless I'm inside somewhere."

"These Crow men have some shelter," Little Crane said. "Red Moon and I are going there with them. They have asked me to invite you. Will you go with us?"

"I should continue my work."

Little Crane pointed to the storm. "You stay out here and the thunder spirits will send down lightning to sting your fingers." He laughed.

Red Moon had been standing impassively. Now he stepped forward and put an arm around Garrett. He gestured in a circle, including all of them. "Come," he said. "Good. All us. Come. Together."

Garrett was amazed. When had Red Moon learned any English?

"He has asked me to teach him the white man

tongue," Little Crane explained. "He wants you to be his brother. You did a good deed for him when you made him laugh the other day. He will always remember how you broke his heartache and made him feel better. He wants to be able to talk in your language. He's working very hard at learning."

Garrett felt both honored and embarrassed. He thought back on the scene at the river on the way out, when the buffalo had come running in from the hills. He hadn't done anything but misunderstand what Little Crane had said about the herd running into the water to escape heel flies. "Hell flies" is what he had said. That's all. He hadn't heard them right. An honest mistake. It had been funny to them. But funny enough to make Red Moon want to become his relative?

"You must understand," Little Crane continued. "Red Moon feels like a new man now. He can open up again. His sadness is still there, but he can live once again without disliking life around him. Do you understand?"

"I guess so, yes," Garrett said. "I'm glad I helped him, though I can't see how." Red Moon was still holding Garrett's shoulder, smiling broadly.

"So, will you join us then?" Little Crane asked.

"Sure," Garrett said, picking up his rifle. "Why not."

The Crows nodded in approval. They all walked a short way downstream to a large platform shelter under the trees. It was constructed of small cottonwood saplings placed in two rows so that branches of willow and cottonwood could be tied crossways to form a roof. The cross members on top were then layered heavily with willow and cottonwood limbs, to provide shelter from the sun and rain.

They seated themselves, cross-legged, in a circle. Thunder boomed overhead and streaks of hail began pounding the camp, little balls of ice the size of fingernails that bounced off the ground, soon falling so heavily as to become layered.

Little Crane smiled, pointing outside the shelter and then at Garrett. "We saved you, Six Fingers. If we hadn't gotten you inside here so quick, your talking paper would have turned to mush.'' He made sign to the others and they all laughed.

Garrett chuckled. He made sign to the Crows that Little Crane was very careful to take care of him, that he even cleaned his fingernails for him, so that the paper would talk good.

When the Crows had stopped laughing, Little Crane nodded and said, ''You can talk with the sign better than I thought. You're learning.'' Little Crane turned to the Crows and made sign. The Crows nodded and smiled. ''I told them that you like them and wish to be friends. It's good. They wish to be friends and believe that you have great medicine.''

''That's good,'' Garrett said. ''I'd like to be friends with them also.''

One of the Crows, large and strong, opened a bag of pemmican and passed it around. Garrett took a handful and thanked him in sign.

''His name is White-Man-Runs-Him,'' Little Crane told Garrett. ''He wants to end the fighting with the Lakota people forever.''

Another of the scouts, smaller and younger, reached forward and touched the scalp hanging from Garrett's rifle.

''I've told them about your honor,'' Little Crane said. ''They would like to see the scalp.''

Garrett untied the scalp from his rifle barrel and handed it to the young scout.

''His name is Curley,'' Little Crane said. He made gestures with his fingers. ''Curley is but sixteen winters old.''

Curley was of medium height, slim and strong, and quick to notice things. He smiled broadly as he examined the scalp, talking to the others in Crow.

Garrett was amazed, but not surprised, that a scout so young would be on such a dangerous mission. It did not surprise him, as he had seen boys of twelve and fourteen fighting for the Confederacy during the last six months of the Rebellion. Boys became men when it came time to fight. There was no adolescence in the world of war.

Curley handed the scalp to White-Man-Runs-Him, who passed it on to Hairy Moccasin and Goes Ahead. As they examined the scalp, the remaining two Crow scouts arrived and entered the shelter. They sat down, crowding in next to Garrett, eager to see the scalp.

"You are famous!" Little Crane told Garrett. "Hold up your hand and put the talking stick between your thumb and first finger, like you do when you make the paper talk. I want them to see why you're called Six Fingers."

Garrett looked at the Crows. They were watching intently. "They don't care about that," he said.

"Yes, they do," Little Crane insisted. "Show them how you do it. You'll be friends then, and they will tell you a lot that you can put on the paper."

Garrett nodded. While the Crows shuffled closer, he took a piece of paper from his folder and pointed to one of the two scouts who had just entered.

"What's his name?" he asked Little Crane.

"White Swan," Little Crane replied. "He's the leader of the Crow scouts, Curley's older brother."

Garrett wrote White Swan's name on the paper, followed by the word *Leader*. Beneath it he drew six stick men on stick horses, all in a row. He then made sign to White Swan, telling him that he had written out his name and his position among the Crow scouts, in the white man's tongue.

White Swan looked at the paper. He took the paper from Garrett and held it up for the others to see, putting his finger on the words and then on the stick figures, talking in Crow.

The other scout who had just arrived with White Swan made sign that he wanted his name drawn as well.

"Write Half Yellow Face," Little Crane told Garrett. "Then you can write all the others down. Show them all their names drawn in the white man's tongue. If you do it for one, you must do it for all of them."

When Garrett had finished writing each scout's name, Little Crane made sign to the Crows that Six Fingers made the paper talk about Long Hair, whom they called Son-of-the-Morning-Star.

"They talked with Long Hair just a short while ago," Little Crane told Garrett. "Mitch Boyer took them to Custer's tent, the one with the big flag on top."

Everyone knew Custer's tent. You could see the flag from anywhere in camp. Since the officers' meeting, it had become a haven of activity.

The young scout, Curley, leaned forward and made sign to Garrett. Little Crane helped him interpret.

"Curley says that he talked with Long Hair Custer, the Son-of-the-Morning-Star, and heard Long Hair's words about tracking the Sioux, that he will never give up, even when food is gone. Curley told Long Hair that he and his Crow brothers like that kind of leader and will stay with him. They will eat mule like he does, if they have to."

"Ask Curley if he believes Long Hair can beat the Sioux."

Little Crane studied Garrett. "He just said he would follow Long Hair for as long as it takes."

"I know that," Garrett said. "I want to know how many Sioux and Cheyenne there are. Really. I believe they know. And I'm wondering if they think this army can fight them and win."

Little Crane made sign and translated Curley's reply. "There are many Sioux, and it will be a big fight. The biggest. If Long Hair can meet with the other Bluecoats who went to the Big Horn River, if they can come together at the village, the Sioux will be finished. This is what they hope will happen."

Garrett studied the Crows. He believed they had too much faith in Custer. Far too much. He said as much to Little Crane.

"Do they even know about Custer?" Garrett asked. "How can they believe in him so totally?"

"Don't misunderstand," Little Crane said. "It's not that they think that highly of him. They know that he kills without honor, that he will shoot women and children and count them as slain warriors. In fact, the Crow elders were not in favor of sending scouts with the Blue-coats. They knew that Son-of-the-Morning-Star would be a target.''

"Then what did Curley mean by saying he liked a man who would march to his enemy, even if he had to eat mule?''

"Curley was building Long Hair up, hoping to make Long Hair feel he could win no matter what.''

"I don't think Custer needed any help from them,'' Garrett said. "He believes the Seventh Cavalry can whip any number of warriors, anywhere.''

"I believe the Crow scouts are hoping that if they make Long Hair hurry, they will meet up with Three Stars Crook, the Bluecoat chief who is coming up from the south.''

Garrett knew about Crook and wondered why Custer had never mentioned him. Not once had Custer stated that he hoped Crook and his forces would be waiting for them, so they could attack the village with the combined forces. If Crook, Custer, and Terry arrived at the same time, and surrounded the village, as Terry hoped, there would be no battle, but certain surrender.

On the other hand, if the village was as large as the scouts believed, Custer would have to wait for the other commands.

"What if the three separate divisions don't come to-gether?'' Garrett asked. "What if one division or the other meets the Sioux, without the help of the others?''

"Why bother to ask that?'' Little Crane said. "The Crow scouts will do whatever is asked of them.''

"They would ride into certain death?''

"They gave their word to Long Hair. By saying that they would follow him, even if they became hungry, they gave their word to complete their duty. It is the same with the Arikara.''

"How do you feel about that, Little Crane?''

"I came with you, and I gave my word to you. If you wish to ride into the battle, I will go as well. So will Red Moon.''

"I wouldn't ask you to do that," Garrett said.

Little Crane shrugged. "But maybe I would want to. It might be the last time I have a chance to die with honor, on the field of battle against my enemies." He waved his arm in a large circle. "All this land is changed. The Crow have fought the Sioux and Cheyenne a long time. The Sioux and Cheyenne are pressing across here, farther into Crow homelands." He pointed toward the west. "And the trouble is not just here. Everyone is fighting everyone else for hunting grounds. There has been a lot of hunting the buffalo for hides, and the whites moving around out here in their wagons, using up the grass with their animals, have caused trouble.

"It used to be that there were enough buffalo for all the tribes. Fighting was mostly for honor. Stealing horses was the greatest honor. But now it's a matter of survival. The Crows feel that if they don't fight with the whites, they'll be killed off. It is also that way with the Arikara, even though there are reservations. Many Sioux and Cheyenne will not live on a reservation. They want to roam free. But they will still attack an enemy, an Arikara or a Crow. So we must fight until it is over, one way or the other."

"Making the paper talk about this will not be easy," Garrett said. "There is a lot to understand."

"It would be good if we could all live as brothers," Little Crane said. "Maybe some day that will happen." He pointed into the west, where the sun had fallen. "We Indian people will always pray, whenever the sun comes and when it leaves, that life will be good for everybody. But that will take a long time. That's what the old people say."

The Crows were assembling to climb a nearby hill and sing their evening songs. Little Crane and Red Moon would soon go to find their Ree friends and do the same.

Garrett thanked the Crows for inviting him, and said good night to Little Crane and Red Moon. He needed some time to himself, some time to prepare before the morning came. He had more to think about than he wanted.

With the sun gone, the sky had turned a deep red, a trail of crimson along the skyline, bathing the underbellies of scattered clouds. The hail had melted into puddles, with scattered drops of rain still pattering the tents and the ground. Everywhere campfires burned and soldiers gathered for discussions and card games. But there was not the laughing and joking that was the usual fare.

Perhaps everyone was too tired, Garrett thought as he arranged his bedroll. He had found a spot under a thicket of small cottonwoods, crowded densely together, that would keep him dry and away from the wind. He had thought of starting a letter to Ann and maybe catching up on his diary, but building a fire would take too long and he wasn't up to it.

Outside camp, coyotes howled into the darkness. Garrett settled into his bedroll, wondering at the coming events. A few days would tell the tale. There was going to be a lot of blood, no question. Who would shed the most remained to be seen.

The Crows, so sure of themselves and so sure they could make Custer a real warrior, alarmed him. They were a straight and true people, amazing to watch and learn from, and he believed the Sioux and Cheyenne were likely just as proud and as interesting. People of the same race so bitter, ready to kill each other to the last man. It reminded him of the Rebellion—so many had been so ready to fall for the survival of a cause.

Garrett wondered if his notes and letters would actually mean anything in the end. He had entered a struggle that was going to be tremendous in scope. It seemed already written, with an ending that would do no one any good.

Perhaps Ann had been right. Perhaps he should have listened to her and just stayed in St. Louis, content to gather stories of everyday life for the *Democrat*. Certainly, then there would have been no sense of impending doom.

Garrett struggled to fall asleep. The buffalo dream crept into his mind. He erased it. It came back.

Finally, he concentrated on the sounds around him,

blocking his mind from other things. He could hear horses snorting at the edge of camp, chomping oats, and the low murmur of the Yellowstone behind him. Not far away, a steady beat of Indian drums began, small, hand-held drums that Garrett knew were accompanying the evening songs, the Arikara and Crow scouts praying to the Creator. Their singing rose and fell, rose and fell, as the intonation of the songs changed. It was soothing; and though the buffalo came back into Garrett's mind, it didn't alarm him.

And somewhere in the middle of it all, just as Garrett was falling asleep, there came the high, mournful howling of Custer's hounds, long and forlorn, echoing out into the darkness.

ELEVEN

The sun was a ball of orange yellow on the eastern horizon. The trees and brush along the river were alive with birdsong. But Ann was much too tired to enjoy it.

She slid from her horse and settled back against a cottonwood. With just five hours of sleep in sixty hours of hard riding, she realized she would need to get some rest before going any farther.

Barely able to keep her eyes open, she listened to Tyrone as he settled down beside her.

"Can you hear me, Miss Ann? Water and Lareaux tell me that this was a soldier camp, a very big one, but that it's old. They wonder if we shouldn't leave the river and cut cross country. Can you hear me, Miss Ann? They said we can find one of the travois trails we've seen and follow it. It will be dangerous, and very rough going, but maybe we'll catch up a lot sooner. Miss Ann? Miss Ann, can you hear me?"

"We'll do whatever you think is best, Tyrone," Ann said, yawning. "You know this country. I don't."

"I worry about getting you to Mr. Garrett," Tyrone said. "Anything can happen out here, Miss Ann. Anything."

From a short distance away came a high, piercing wail, long and drawn out. Despite her weariness, Ann rose to her feet, her eyes bulging.

"What in the world was that?" she asked. "It's not a wolf. We've heard them all the way out here. What in God's name is it?"

Tyrone listened. The wailing began again. "I'd say it's

an Indian woman crying over a death. Maybe her husband. Maybe her son, or father. That's what I'd say it was. Haven't heard it for a long time, Miss Ann. Wish I wasn't hearing it now."

Water and Lareaux came riding back. Water, ordinarily a fun-loving sort prone to teasing, was as serious as Ann had ever seen him. Lareaux, who had spent most of the trip from Fort Lincoln bantering with Tyrone, looked equally concerned.

Lareaux jumped down from his horse, while Water stared into the cottonwoods along the river, looking for signs of movement.

"Sioux. They've been here," Lareaux said. "Someone killed one of them. Soldiers maybe." He pointed. "A woman is up near the creek crossing, grieving."

Tyrone told Ann to stay put, that he would go with the other two and check it out.

"I'm coming with you," Ann insisted.

"It's not necessary, Miss Ann. Water will stay here with you. Why don't you try and get some rest?"

"Rest? When I don't know what's going on? I might be tired, but I'm not that tired."

Tyrone helped Ann onto her horse. She trembled from weakness, but maintained that she must go with them. They were four in number, only four, and needed to stay together.

They rode through the shadows of the trees, Tyrone and Lareaux in the lead. Water, who rode beside Ann, was carrying a medicine shield. He took the cover from it, exposing a buffalo painted on the front. He took an arrow from his quiver and fitted it to his bow, holding it across his saddle in front of him.

Tyrone checked his rifle, a forty-four caliber Henry repeater he had purchased at the sutler's store before leaving Fort Lincoln. He had bought four boxes of ammunition, prompting the sutler to ask Tyrone if he intended to take on the whole Sioux nation himself. "You just never know," Tyrone had told him. "You just never know."

Lareaux carried a hatchet in his belt and a large Green

River knife. His rifle was a Hawken, one of the early models measured in weight instead of caliber. He had carried it throughout the latter years of the fur trade and swore by it. "Lucy, she has never let me down," he would often say. "*Oui*, she is my best lover." He molded the balls himself, carrying them in a large skin pouch on his right hip.

"Why don't you get rid of that old gun?" Tyrone had asked Lareaux. "Get a repeater. You need something that you can shoot and reload in the same day."

"I'll do more with Lucy than you with your little pop-rifle," Lareaux had replied. "We shall see. *Oui*, when the time comes, we shall see."

Under her father's tutelage, Ann had learned about firearms, including rifles and pistols. Her father had insisted that if she were to go with him to the posts, she must know how to protect herself.

When Tyrone had purchased the Henry rifle, Ann had gotten herself a Colt Army thirty-two, small enough for her to handle yet large enough in caliber to stop an enemy at close range. She carried it in a holster across her left hip, in the same fashion as Adam wore his side arm. If it worked for him, she reasoned, it should work for her.

She touched the grip of the pistol as she rode, searching the trees ahead for a glimpse of the Indian woman, whose loud wailing continued to tear the morning stillness.

At the confluence of Glendive Creek and the Yellowstone, they found her. The lone Sioux woman sat cross-legged at the foot of a tree, rocking back and forth, her voice lifted to the sky in a wild, loud tremolo.

"She looks to have been here maybe three, maybe four days," Lareaux said. "She is worn out badly. *Oui*, very badly."

"Let's see what we can learn from her," Tyrone said, dismounting.

Lareaux got down from his horse and said something in Ree to Water, who was looking all around them.

"He thinks something is going to happen," Lareaux told Tyrone. "He doesn't feel good."

"I don't know why they would leave this woman by herself," Tyrone said. "Maybe he's right. Maybe they're coming for her."

"Then we'd better hurry," Lareaux said.

Ann dismounted with Tyrone and Lareaux twenty feet from where a burial platform rested in the lower branches of a cottonwood. The woman's hair was short and uneven, hacked off in her despair. Her buckskin dress was torn, and she was a mass of blood from head to foot, where she had sliced and gouged herself. A bloody knife lay in the grass beside her.

Lareaux eased around in front of her, speaking in Sioux. "We are sorry for your grief. Are you alone?"

The woman ignored him and continued to wail. She took a large rock resting next to her and placed it between her legs. She laid the little finger of her left hand on the rock and brought the knife down forcefully. The last joint of the finger rolled from the rock, leaving a bloody trail.

Ann stared in shock. Tyrone took her by the arm and led her away. "I told you not to come, Miss Ann. You just won't listen, you won't."

"The poor woman," Ann said. "The poor, poor woman."

Lareaux again asked the woman if she was alone. The woman turned hateful eyes to him and pointed to the south. She spoke with rage.

"She says her dead husband's brother will come to get her, that he will bring warriors with him. We will all be killed."

"So why are we here?" Tyrone asked. "We should go, I'd say."

"I will try to get some information from her," Lareaux said. "Maybe she knows where Long Hair Custer is."

"What makes you think she'd tell you?" Tyrone asked.

The woman suddenly rose to her feet, and began chasing Lareaux with the knife. Ann rushed out of the way. Water, watching from his horse, shouted in English, "Kill her! Kill her!" then said it again in Ree.

Lareaux turned on the woman. She thrust the knife at

him. He grabbed her wrist and twisted. The woman sank to her knees, the knife dropping into the grass.

"Kill her!" Water yelled again.

"What honor would there be in it?" Lareaux asked.

"There will be no more Sioux babies from her," Water shouted.

"Don't kill her!" Ann yelled. "Why should she die?"

Lareaux pointed toward the south. At the top of a rise five warriors sat their horses, looking down on the scene.

"Sioux!" Lareaux said. "They've come back, as she said they would."

The Sioux sat their horses, pointing, talking.

"They're talking about which one of us to challenge," Lareaux explained. "They want to kill the leader."

As Lareaux talked, the woman came to her knees. She grabbed the knife and lunged at Lareaux, plunging the blade into the back of his leg, just above the knee.

Lareaux yelled and pulled away, sagging to the ground. The woman was yelling loudly. Water rode over and loosed an arrow into the woman's neck. The shaft went straight down, clear to the fletching, and the woman fell onto her side, kicking and thrashing.

Ann stood speechless, unable to believe what the woman had done.

Tyrone rushed to Lareaux's side and pulled the knife from his leg. The blade had cut to the bone, but the blood flowed evenly, with no gushing, and Tyrone believed no major artery had been severed.

"Ah! It's but a scratch!" Lareaux said, rising to his feet. "We have Sioux to fight!"

One of the Sioux warriors had come forward, brandishing a war club. He rode back and forth in challenge.

"I will take him," Water said. "I need a Sioux scalp."

Lareaux pulled the hatchet from his belt and tossed it to Water. "Go get him, my friend." He turned to Ann. "You stay in cover."

Water rode to the flat, yelling, the hatchet raised. The Sioux warrior charged him, his pony running full speed. Water kicked his pony into a run and met the charge.

The two came together and exchanged blows. The

Sioux warrior's stone club bounced against Water's shield. Water struck with the hatchet, the blow glancing off the Sioux warrior's shield. The two maneuvered their ponies for position, striking again and again. Finally, Water got in a decisive blow.

The Sioux warrior raised his club high, lifting himself, exposing his upper chest over the shield. Water swung the hatchet, caving in the warrior's collarbone, slicing deep into a lung.

The warrior sagged on his pony. Water brought the hatchet down again, nearly severing the warrior's head. The warrior fell to the ground, his head at an awkward angle. Water jumped from his pony, grabbed the warrior's hair, and pulled his knife.

"Ah! He's done it!" Lareaux yelled.

"Yes, and here come the others," Tyrone said, handing Lareaux his Hawken. "Get ready."

Ann stepped from cover and cocked her pistol, ignoring Tyrone's yells for her to stay back.

The other four Sioux warriors were screaming war cries. One of them fit an arrow to his bow and charged down the hill at Water, who was holding up the scalp.

Lareaux, who had limped to a nearby tree, leveled his Hawken across a limb and fired. Water had his shield raised, hoping against hope to deflect the arrow that would soon be loosed by the warrior charging him.

As the warrior raised his bow, the ball from Lareaux's Hawken took him in the lower stomach, doubling him over. He fell from his pony at Water's feet. Water raised his knife, still gleaming red, and plunged it into the warrior's neck.

Tyrone had jumped on his pony and was riding full speed to Water's aid. Two warriors were charging down the hill toward Tyrone, who raised his rifle and fired.

The bullet tore through the first warrior's upper shoulder, spinning him around on his horse. He held on, screaming, and rode past Tyrone, firing his rifle. The bullet singed Tyrone's left arm, leaving a furrow just above his elbow.

Lareaux had reloaded and now fired at the second warrior coming at Tyrone. The ball slammed into his left thigh, shattering the bone, sending fragments into the pony's rib cage. The pony squealed and bucked, losing the warrior.

The warrior with the shoulder wound had turned his pony for another run at Tyrone. Water loosed an arrow at him, the shaft running clean through the warrior's lower abdomen. Tyrone fired his rifle at the same time, hitting the warrior in the forehead.

Lareaux, breathing heavily, was counting the fallen warriors. "I only see four," he said to himself. "Where's the last one?"

Ann stood with her pistol cocked, numbed with shock and fright. She saw Lareaux turn and point behind her, his mouth wide, yelling.

She turned in time to see the warrior running toward her, his war club raised. She raised her pistol and fired. The bullet plowed into the warrior's neck. He staggered, but did not fall, staring at her with blazing eyes, gagging, as if choking on a piece of meat. She fired again and again, into the warrior's chest. He fell and lay still.

Ann sank to her knees. Tyrone rode his pony over to her and dismounted.

"You all right, Miss Ann? Can you hear me?"

"I'm all right, Tyrone."

Lareaux hobbled over. "Ah! Such a brave woman. Maybe she should be leading the soldiers instead of Long Hair Custer." He laughed.

"We should look at that stab wound in your leg," Tyrone suggested.

"It's just a scratch, I told you," Lareaux said.

Out on the flat, Water was collecting scalps, holding them up, screaming at the top of his lungs. Ann sat down on a fallen log.

"Your arm is bleeding, Tyrone."

"I'll tend to it, Miss Ann. Where should we go from here?"

"I'm so tired," Ann said. "We'll talk about it later. I just need to sleep. I feel if I don't sleep, I'm going to die."

*   *   *

Bloody Knife was the best known of all the Ree scouts and considered Custer's favorite. His presence commanded respect. As the sun rose on the camp near the mouth of the Rosebud, he sought Garrett out to talk to him.

Little Crane, who was interpreter, told Garrett, "Don't get angry at some of the things he says. He doesn't care for whites, but would rather fight with them than let the Sioux live."

"What does he want with me?"

"He says that he's heard that you can make the paper talk and that he wants you to make the paper talk about him."

Garrett studied Bloody Knife, of medium height and strongly built, with fine features hardened by age and anger. He was dressed in buckskins and wore a clam shell–bear claw necklace and a black neckerchief covered with blue stars—a present, he had told Little Crane, from Long Hair Custer.

"What does he want me to say about him?" Garrett asked Little Crane.

"He wants you to know that the Sioux are a terrible people, and that he will guide Long Hair to them, to get rid of them once and for all. It will be he, Bloody Knife, who will take revenge for all the things that have happened before."

Garrett was jotting notes. "Why does he hate the Sioux so deeply?"

"His father was Sioux," Little Crane replied. "His mother was Ree. When he was young, he lived with his father's people and was beaten often because of his Ree blood. Corn Eater is what they called him. Lower than a dog. He has scars to show of those days." As Little Crane spoke, Bloody Knife pointed to various marks on his body. "He wants to give some scars back to them."

Bloody Knife said something else to Little Crane, raising his fist into the air, yelling a war cry.

"He says," Little Crane interpreted, "that he wants to kill all the Unkpapas, the one named Gall especially. He says that Gall killed two of his brothers and cut them up for the wolves. When he finds Gall, there will not be enough left for the wolves.''

Bloody Knife stepped close to Garrett and lifted his chin. His eyes were red and his breath smelled faintly of whiskey.

"He wants you to know that he is proud of who he is," Little Crane said. "There is no man prouder than he, and the Sioux will learn this."

"Where did he get the whiskey?"

"He doesn't want to say. He asks you to promise that you won't tell Long Hair."

"I don't care what he does," Garrett said. "But I'll bet Custer will be angry with him."

"He knows that," Little Crane said. "He wants to keep Long Hair from finding out."

"Ask him how he knows Long Hair Custer so well."

Little Crane talked with Bloody Knife and turned to Garrett. "He has scouted for Long Hair many times. Two summers past he led Long Hair and other Bluecoats through the Black Hills, to the east of here."

"Is that where they found gold?"

"The same place," Little Crane replied. "Many whites came into the land after that. A lot of bad feelings started. The Sioux began killing everyone."

"Ask him if he believes Custer to be a good leader."

Little Crane asked Bloody Knife the question. Bloody Knife got up and jumped on his horse. He motioned toward Custer's tent.

"He says he has to go, that he cannot answer that question. He has vowed to follow Long Hair and he wants to kill all the Sioux. That is what's important."

When Bloody Knife was gone, Garrett asked Little Crane, "Are you and Red Moon ready to go the rest of the way?"

"Are you saying you want to go back, that you no longer want to make the paper talk about Long Hair?"

"It seems to me that everyone is following him blindly. Everyone who's Indian on this campaign hates the Sioux. Everyone else is either a commander or a regular soldier who has to follow orders. I don't have to follow any orders.''

Little Crane studied Garrett. ''When you first talked to me about bringing you to Long Hair, you thought you knew how everything would be. You thought you could make the paper talk and see how Long Hair made mistakes. It is not so simple as that. Can you understand? There are many who help Long Hair, who cover for his mistakes. That makes him look good. It's not so easy to say that he makes mistakes when everything is good in the end.''

''Do you think Bloody Knife and the rest of the scouts can lead Long Hair to the best position against the Sioux? Can they take him to a position where he will win without question?''

''With Long Hair there is always question. He does what he wants, no matter what anyone says to him. He thinks he is always right. That's why all the scouts are worried. He wants them to take him to the enemy, but he doesn't want to believe what they say about how strong the enemy is. With Long Hair there is always question.''

Little Crane left to find Red Moon. The column would soon begin the march up the Rosebud, at a grueling pace, to locate the hostile village and attack it before the hostiles tried to run. But maybe the hostiles wouldn't run, as Little Crane had already suggested. Maybe they would want to fight, to get out all their bitterness.

Garrett began to assemble his things. He still needed a lot of information before he could be of help to the Grants, so there was no reason to think he was through with his assignment. He would go up the Rosebud with Custer and the Seventh Cavalry and face whatever might come.

As he sat down to write a letter to Ann, he wondered what he was going to say. She had warned him. She had told him that his bullheadedness would someday get him killed. Nothing, she had said, was more important than their love—not money, not position. Nothing. Yet he was going up the Rosebud to fulfill his promise to the Grants, knowing full well that meeting the Sioux and Cheyenne would be every bit as dangerous as any battle he had covered during the Rebellion.

But he would tell her none of that. Instead, he would write again about the beautiful country, about the clouds that rolled across this endless sky. He would tell her anything but what was going to happen. And he was so very glad that she was back in St. Louis, away from the blood and death that afflicted this land to its very core.

TWELVE

The air was filled with screaming and the waving of weapons and war trophies. The Ree scouts, high with the thrill of the hunt, sang their death songs and showed their desire to destroy the Sioux and Cheyenne.

Garrett sat his horse, holding his rifle high in the air, while a group of warriors led by Little Crane, Bloody Knife, and Red Moon rode circles around him, whooping and yelling, aiming their rifles and bows at the Sioux scalp that dangled from the trigger guard.

Garrett knew that none of them would shoot, yet it made him uneasy, knowing that the scalp he held above his head was the object of such strong reaction.

"We are on the trail of the Sioux," Little Crane had said earlier. "Now is the time for glory."

After the Rees had completed their show, the Seventh Cavalry lined up for review. They paraded before commanders Terry, Gibbon, and Custer, even more eager than the scouts to reach the Sioux and Cheyenne village.

As the Seventh concluded their review, Garrett was approached by Mark Kellogg. Two canvas bags straddled the back of Kellogg's mule, no doubt filled with coffee, bacon, and sugar enough for fifteen days, plus his pencils and paper. Kellogg had been watching the proceedings with General Terry, including the display by the Ree scouts. He held his mule with a stiff rein and stared contemptuously at Garrett.

"What can I do for you, Mr. Kellogg?" Garrett asked, arranging his provisions in his own saddlebags.

Kellogg cleared his throat. "I see, Mr. Garrett, that you continue to insist on making a show of yourself."

"A show of myself?"

"You know very well what I mean," Kellogg said. "Holding that rifle up, with that scalp on it. That was ridiculous."

"Why aren't you in the spirit, Kellogg?" Garrett asked. "Everyone else is."

"Do you really think you're going to get anywhere acting like one of the Indians?"

Garrett tied his saddlebags tightly. "I'm not trying to *act* like an Indian, Mr. Kellogg, or even like a soldier for that matter. We're all in this together. Everyone's whooping and yelling. Or haven't you noticed?"

"I don't feel obligated to take part in that manner, Mr. Garrett," Kellogg said. "I feel better taking note of the activities."

"Get yourself a scalp, Kellogg," Garrett said. "Maybe you'd like to do more than watch from the sidelines. Take a chance for once. Everyone else is taking a chance here, or don't you quite grasp that either?"

"I thought you were a journalist, not a savage!" Kellogg snapped.

"Are you saying that savages can't be journalists?" Garrett steadied his horse and checked the latigo strap on the saddle, making sure it was secure. "I'll bet any number of these scouts can draw a better description of what's happening on a rock than you can on paper." He wanted to tell Kellogg that he should do something for himself other than kneel at the feet of Custer, but he knew that would reach Custer and might not sit well.

Kellogg adjusted his spectacles. "I take serious offense to that remark, sir. And I will say further that what you're doing here, trying to impress the General by killing Indians and taking their scalps, makes you look like a clown. It does our profession no good."

"And just what good are you doing *our* profession?" Garrett asked, climbing into the saddle. "Do you intend to become famous by licking your pencil every time you jot down a note on Custer, bathing yourself in his sweet smile?"

"I beg your pardon!"

"Does he dictate every word to you, or are you capable of original thought on your own?"

Kellogg stared at Garrett. Garrett knew he had said too much. He had let Kellogg get the best of him.

"You say you know a lot about journalism," Garrett added, "but you can't know what you're writing about unless you can feel it. I'm trying to live it, as much as I know how. That way I'll be better able to translate the experience to others. Does that make sense to you?"

Kellogg wouldn't be deterred from Garrett's previous comments. "I want you to explain something to me, Mr. Garrett. Exactly what did you mean when you referred to the General's 'sweet smile'?"

"Let's put it this way," Garrett said. "I don't think any journalist should agree wholeheartedly with every word his subject speaks. I believe you've never questioned the General about anything. Have you?"

"It's just as I suspected," Kellogg said. "You don't care for the General, do you? You're out here to do him harm. I knew it!"

"Don't jump to conclusions, Kellogg."

"Oh, on the contrary, Mr. Garrett. I have always believed, and now see that it was rightfully so, that you are a scoundrel. You've come to do this mission harm. I believe you to be on the side of the Indians. I believe that you're against civilization entirely. Am I correct, Mr. Garrett? You, who dress like an Indian and carry a scalp on your rifle."

"Mr. Kellogg, you'd be amusing if you weren't so ridiculous."

"Nevertheless," Kellogg said, his jaws tight, "I shall report my findings to the General. You shall answer to him."

Kellogg turned his mule and kicked it hard. It broke into a slow trot. Garrett watched him bounce up and down on the mule's back like a large rubber ball. He wanted to call Kellogg back, to start the entire conversation over again.

But it was too late. He had said too much and he could only hope that Custer took Kellogg to be exaggerating.

Should the General take offense, it could mean that he would have to stay with the *Far West,* which would be the worst thing that could happen.

That would be more than disaster to Garrett. There would be no coverage of the events to come and no success to be measured by the Grants. In short, he would have the rest of his professional life to think about the few minutes he had spent with Mark Kellogg just before starting up Rosebud Creek, and to wish that he had never said a word to the man.

The march began at noon. Custer, dressed in buckskins and a broad felt hat, took the lead. Directly behind rode his two sergeants. One bore the regimental standard and the other Custer's personal campaign flag, a red-and-blue forked pennant with crossed sabers in white.

Directly behind rode Bloody Knife and Mitch Boyer, followed by the Crow scouts and Custer's orderly, John Burkman, who was in charge of the two staghounds. Garrett rode with Little Crane and Red Moon, together with the other Ree scouts, along the flanks of the troops.

With Custer using hand signals to direct, the columns, in order, rode southwesterly, covering the two miles to the Rosebud. Each troop rode mounts of the same color—bays and sorrels, mostly. Company E, the Gray Horse Troop, stood out from the others dramatically.

In early afternoon, the Seventh Cavalry splashed across the Rosebud and began the march southward along the western bank, toward the Little Bighorn. The valley was narrow, with patches of pine and juniper growing on rocky buttes and ridges along both sides. Thick grass rolled across the bottom in a carpet of heavy green, now beginning to burn at the tips in the continuing heat.

Garrett rode in silence, his mind blocking the sounds of the marching cavalry—the snorting horses and the constant creaking of saddle leather. He thought about the peaceful expanse of country around him, wondering how he could be here under the circumstances of death. He knew that, along with everyone else's, his life was on the line.

This would be different from the Rebellion, where everything was planned and armies took time for strategy. At the fore of Rebellion battles, both sides assembled themselves in some form of order. Little Crane had let Garrett know that Indians didn't fight that way. Surprise, and quick, deadly assault were their chief weapons.

And there would be no quarter given the press. Garrett knew that when it came time to meet the Sioux and Cheyenne, they wouldn't care if he wore a uniform or not. He was with the Bluecoat army and that made him one of them.

But maybe he wouldn't be going much farther. He thought about his indiscretion with Kellogg, wondering if he would have to pay for it soon. There was no saying how Custer might react. The farther they got from the Yellowstone, though, the less he would need to worry. Surely Custer would have said something to him right away had he no longer wanted him along.

As the afternoon passed, Garrett's thoughts turned to Ann Malone. Her beauty continued to fill the lonely moments before he fell asleep and after he awakened in the dawn. Seeing the land around him brought her to mind even more, knowing how she loved to walk in the springtime, touching the flowers and smelling their blossoms.

Had the circumstances been different, he would have loved to have Ann with him. The Rosebud was lined with wild roses, their pink-and-scarlet petals coating the green along open banks and under low-growing trees. The cottonwoods were sparse here, replaced by scattered colonies of box elders and green ash, mixed with an abundance of shrubs. Little Crane rode up to Garrett and offered him a handful of chokecherries that he had stripped from a bush while riding past.

"Take these and eat. They're still not fully ripe, but they'll be good for you."

Garrett studied the reddish berries. He found them very tart. "Don't bring me any more," he said, spitting out the seeds.

"I've told you that you'll need to be strong," Little Crane said. "You can't stay strong on Bluecoat food. I'll find some gooseberries for us. They'll be better.'' He handed Garrett more chokecherries. ''Eat the rest of these and don't spit them out. Six Fingers must have all fingers working well all the time.''

Garrett reluctantly finished the chokecherries. He trusted Little Crane's judgment and his abilities to find food and medicine plants. The bruise on his shoulder from the Sioux warrior's club had nearly healed. He had Little Crane to thank for that.

Red Moon rode nearby, listening intently. His sole purpose in life now seemed to be learning English, so that he could converse with Garrett. In time, when he felt he could speak well enough, Red Moon intended to make a formal offer to adopt Garrett as his brother.

Little Crane, having ridden off into the brush along the creek, returned with a handful of gooseberries, light green in color. They were plumper and much sweeter.

''This is more like it,'' Garrett said. ''I could eat more of these.''

A rider approached Garrett. It was John Burkman.

''Mr. Garrett, the General requests your presence at the head of the column. Immediately.''

This is it, Garrett told himself. He's heard Kellogg's dialogue and now he wants me to turn back.

Burkman turned his horse and returned to the head of the column. Garrett tried to rehearse things he would say. Little Crane laughed at him.

''Six Fingers should be able to make up words that please Long Hair. Don't work so hard. They'll come. Let Long Hair talk all the time. He likes to hear himself.

''Maybe you ought to go instead of me,'' Garrett suggested.

Little Crane laughed harder. ''Long Hair would surely become angry. I would tell him that you sent me because you can't be bothered with him. You have more important things to do than listen to his childish babbling.''

''I'd better go alone,'' Garrett said.

Custer was alone at the head of the column. His two hounds, Bleuch and Tuck, were roaming up the valley, sniffing excitedly, just behind Boyer and Bloody Knife, who were scouting the valley ahead.

Garrett rode alongside Custer, his Indian pony dwarfed by Custer's favorite horse, Vic, a blaze-faced sorrel with white stockings, of Kentucky Thoroughbred stock. The customary saber at his side was missing. He had ordered no sabers on the march, to keep the noise at a minimum.

"I was told you wished to speak with me," Garrett said.

Custer adjusted his red cravat. "Mr. Garrett, are you enjoying the day?"

"It's a good day for a march, General," Garrett answered.

Custer continued to toy with his cravat. "How do you like this?" he asked Garrett. "I think it complements my buckskin well, don't you?"

"It looks very nice, General. Very nice." Garrett tried to control his nervousness, wondering if Custer wasn't postponing the announcement just to watch him squirm.

"Did you ever consider wearing one?" Custer asked. "I think you would look nice. Very nice. I wouldn't want you wearing scarlet, though, you understand. That's my color. Perhaps yellow. Canary yellow. Or a very light blue. Yes, you would look very nice, Mr. Garrett."

"That's not my style, General," Garrett said.

"You're a striking-looking man, Mr. Garrett. You shouldn't be afraid to dress up a little."

Garrett frowned.

"Yes, Mr. Garrett," Custer repeated. "You're a fine-looking man. Accentuate yourself."

"I don't wear cravats, General. Certainly not red ones. Not even a yellow one."

"Would you do it for me?" Custer asked. "If I requested it? Maybe if I ordered it."

"I don't see the point, General."

"You don't see the point?"

"No."

Custer changed the subject. "Have you been taking some notes regarding this new leg of the campaign?"

"We've barely started, General. I intend to, though."

"Good. Tell me, Mr. Garrett, do you keep track of the negative statements made about me?"

"I don't hear many of those, General."

"Who are you trying to fool, Mr. Garrett? Most certainly you hear negative comments about me. Lots of them. I'm just wondering how much credence you put in them."

"A man can't please everyone, General. Especially a man in command, like yourself."

"I need to know the names of the men who've been conspiring against me," Custer said. "I need to know who they are. Especially the officers."

"These soldiers are careful what they say around me, General," Garrett said. "They know I've got a pencil and paper."

"Well, perhaps," Custer said. "But if you hear anything, you'll come to me with it, won't you?"

"I will, General. But I expect not to hear much. Everyone is too busy trying to keep from overheating in their woolens, or wiping the dust from their mouths."

"Ah!" Custer said. "Those men don't care if they sweat a little and their faces are dirty. Most of them grew up that way. They don't know any better." He pointed to his hounds. "Those two dogs, they don't have a care in the world. Everything's an adventure to them. It's too bad we don't share that real zest for life's adventures. We should all loosen up a bit. Instead, though, we mire ourselves down with what-ifs and what-do-we-do-nows. Don't you think, Mr. Garrett?"

"No question about it, General."

"It's the journey that counts, Mr. Garrett, not the destination. We need to live each moment as if it were our last."

"Isn't that a bit of a fatalistic outlook, General?"

"But how can we know, Mr. Garrett? What is there to tell us when the end is to come? Why not live as if the end were coming with the setting of the sun?"

Garrett wondered why Custer had called him to the front. It didn't seem that the General had any notion of dismissing him. Or, if he did, he certainly had lost his train of thought.

"I share your idea that life should be as pleasant as we can make it," Garrett said. "But I don't like to think of death as being on my doorstep."

Custer studied Garrett. "I know you've seen a lot of death. Your time recording the fall of the Rebel cause can attest to that."

"That's certainly true, General. But I don't dwell on it. I'd like to think of that as a forgotten chapter."

"There's nothing about that conflict that we shall ever forget, Mr. Garrett, you can count on that, sir." Custer took a more rigid stance in the saddle. "Those people that we subdued rose unjustly. It's much the same now, with the Indians out here. Wouldn't you agree?"

"Can you really say that fighting for one's land and way of life is an unjust cause, General?"

Custer was silent a moment. At length he said, "Mr. Kellogg is of the mind that you're out here to record the Indian's plight, and that you yourself are more savage than civilian."

Garrett held his response. Any demeaning remarks about Kellogg could well be his last remarks to Custer before being dismissed from the campaign.

"Mr. Kellogg shouldn't be concerned about me, General," Garrett said. "He really shouldn't. I live in St. Louis and I get into the country rarely. While I'm out here, I like to 'feel my oats,' as they say."

Custer smiled. "Well, I can certainly understand that, Mr. Garrett. Tell me, are you married?"

"Engaged, sir, to a wonderful woman. We'll be married after the campaign is finished."

"My congratulations, Mr. Garrett. As you're well aware, I'm sure, my Libbie is the light of my life. Have you heard me talk of her before?"

"No, General, I haven't."

Custer rode silently for a time. Garrett thought he had suddenly become saddened.

"I shan't bore you with a long dissertation about my Libbie," Custer said. "Needless to say, she's all I have at the moment. I've taken her on campaign with me often. This time I felt it better that she remain at the fort." He cleared his throat. "Now, getting back to Mr. Kellogg and his concerns about you, I would like to know how you place his writing in regard to your own."

"I can't say that I've ever read anything by him, General," Garrett lied. He had read one of Kellogg's diatribes against the Sioux and Cheyenne the previous year in the St. Paul *Daily Pioneer-Press,* under the pen name "Frontier," where Kellogg had stated that he would support measures to "turn the dogs of war loose, and drive them off the face of the earth."

"Maybe you should read some of Mr. Kellogg's work," Custer suggested. "It might be something you could aspire to."

Again Garrett had to hold his tongue. Custer was waiting for a response when the hounds began to bark. The column had just topped a ridge and there, on an open flat a few hundred yards distant, stood a large herd of antelope.

The antelope immediately became restless and began to mill in circles.

Custer laughed. "There you are, Bleuch! And you, Tuck! There's your dinner! Run for it!"

The hounds broke instantly, tearing through the grass, baying noisily. The antelope were now moving at a fast gallop, forming a long line that stretched through the bottom and across the creek to the opposite bank. At the sight of the pursuing hounds, they scattered in terrified confusion, running in all directions.

The hounds jumped this way and that, unable to decide which animals to attack. Custer laughed again.

"You'd better make up your minds!" he yelled out. "Don't let your dinner get away!"

The hounds finally settled on a young doe, dazed and crippled after being trampled by the confused herd. One grabbed a foreleg and the other a hind leg, tearing her to the ground.

Boyer and Bloody Knife watched from a nearby hill.

Fred Gerard, translator for the Rees, had joined them. Garrett could see Bloody Knife making hand gestures and pointing. He was obviously angry.

Custer continued to laugh at the dogs, who were now tearing the doe to pieces, eating noisily.

"It's about time!" he yelled. "I thought you would both go hungry." He turned to Garrett. "How are you going to write that up?"

Garrett momentarily forgot himself. In disgust he said, "Why should I write it up? There was nothing heroic about that."

Custer studied him. "Maybe I should decide for you what's heroic."

"I'm capable of that, General."

Custer frowned. "I don't know that you are, Mr. Garrett. In continuing our discussion, it has come to my attention that you believe Mr. Kellogg to be nothing more than my own personal diarist. What have you to say about that?"

"I don't think Mr. Kellogg is capable of being anybody's personal diarist, General. He hasn't had a fresh thought of his own during the entire campaign. How, may I ask, could he think fast enough to write down someone else's concepts?"

"I should advise you, Mr. Garrett, that Mr. Kellogg is a personal friend of mine. He was invited to join me on this campaign."

"It was my understanding that his boss, a Mr. Lounsberry, was to come along, but that his wife took ill. Kellogg came at the last minute, didn't he?"

"You seem to know a lot about it, Mr. Garrett. Did you get your information from Mr. Kellogg?" Custer didn't wait for a reply. "I think not, Mr. Garrett. I think you've done some thorough research on your own before embarking on your little trip to find me. Might I be right?"

"I wanted to know as much as I could, General. You can't fault me for that."

"And I suppose you thought you could join up and

immediately enjoy the status Mr. Kellogg holds?''

"I don't know, General. I don't think I thought about it.''

"Oh, I believe you did, Mr. Garrett. Tell me, are you jealous of Mr. Kellogg's position?''

Garrett took a deep breath. He saw a chance to keep himself on the campaign. He had to allow Custer to be right. Sure, he envied Kellogg, if that's what the General wanted. Garrett realized that no matter how disgusted he might become with his mission, he had to stick it through if he meant to gain any status with the Grants.

"Perhaps that's it, General,'' Garrett said. "I feel I could document the events of the campaign far better than he. But you're right. I shouldn't expect preferential treatment. Mr. Kellogg was here first.''

"I'll tell you what, Mr. Garrett,'' Custer proposed. "I'll allow you with me as much as Mr. Kellogg. You can take notes, as many as you please, along with him. I'll read yours and his, and tell you which I prefer. How does that sound?''

Garrett thought a moment. "I'm afraid it wouldn't work. Mr. Kellogg and I cannot get along, not for a moment.''

"You could tolerate one another, I'm sure.''

"Not a chance. I'm afraid I'd have to take his scalp and add it to the one on my rifle. I wouldn't be able to stop myself.''

Custer seemed amused. "Can't you behave better than that, Mr. Garrett?''

"I'm afraid not, General. You can keep him at hand and I'll do what I can to ask you questions at opportune times.''

"As you wish, Mr. Garrett,'' Custer said. "And from here forward, do your best not to disturb Mr. Kellogg.''

"Fine, General,'' Garrett said. "I'll do my part if he'll do his.''

Gerard rode down from the hill where he had been talking with Boyer and Bloody Knife. He rode to Custer's left side and said, "I figure we'll have some trouble with Bloody Knife.''

"What do you mean, Mr. Gerard?" Custer asked.

"Your hounds taking after the antelope, and all. That made him a little sore," Gerard said. "He thinks you don't care one whit about giving them Sioux and Cheyenne warning we're coming."

Custer slapped his leg. "What's the matter with him? We're a long way from any hostile camp. He told me that himself."

"Well, you know how things are with him," Gerard said. "He takes this fight serious. And he knows you think he's the best scout you've got. He wants things on an even keel is all."

"You tell him, Mr. Gerard, that things are on a very even keel." Custer's jaw was rigid. "You tell him that when he rides with me, leading the Seventh into battle, his wishes will all come true and his glory shall be great. He'll get his revenge against the Sioux, and then some. You tell him that, Mr. Gerard. You tell him exactly that."

THIRTEEN

Evening, 22 June 1876
Camp on Rosebud Creek

Strangest night of the campaign so far. Camp subdued. In fact, the complete opposite of this morning when we cheerfully started up the Rosebud. Card playing, but no laughter. Men singing, but no happy tunes. One soldier not far away singing *An Irish Lullaby*. Exceptional voice but oh, so mournful. Can remember the lyrics from school days.

Don't know what to make of it. Rumors around camp are that Custer called a meeting with his officers and, in effect, begged them to support him in the campaign. It seems that he's certain everyone is out to sabotage the campaign.

This afternoon, I have seen another side of Custer. Don't know what to make of him suggesting that I wear a cravat, a yellow one, and that I am a "very good-looking man and ought to accentuate it." Don't want to think of the implications.

Little Crane has grown silent. Very unsettling. Red Moon never was one for talk, but Little Crane hasn't said a word all evening. Can't even make him talk by holding up my fingers.

He goes back and forth from anger to looking afraid. Told me earlier today, after I talked with Custer, that the ghosts of those in the burial site on the Tongue River were following us. Told me Custer never should have disturbed their graves. The items Custer's brothers and cousins took and kept will cause death. He doesn't want to turn around, though. He says that if death is coming, he will meet it straight on, not running away.

Feel I may have gotten in over my head. Nothing right about this campaign.

Garrett stuffed his diary back into his saddlebag. He sat alone for a short time, growing ever more uneasy. Finally, he searched out Little Crane and Red Moon, who were talking with a large group of scouts, Arikara and Crow combined. All were in an animated exchange.

"What's all the excitement about?" Garrett asked Little Crane.

"Bloody Knife was here, and he was drunk," Little Crane said. "He's still angry with Long Hair about the hounds chasing the antelope. He said that he told Long Hair that this trip was just for a good time, that Long Hair never intended to find or fight the Sioux. Long Hair said that he was in command and could do what he pleased, and that he intended to fight the Sioux. But he isn't sorry that his hounds go off, chasing game in all directions, causing us scouts to worry about the Sioux knowing that we're coming."

Mitch Boyer had been listening. He added, "It doesn't seem that Long Hair cares about that. And he won't listen to us about how many there are to fight against. I don't think these Bluecoats can win this battle."

Garrett studied Boyer. "If you think that, then why stay with Long Hair?"

"I gave my word that I would scout for him. That's what I will do. That's what the others will do."

"But you could be killed."

"I knew that when I agreed to come along. Any warrior who goes to a battle believes that the Creator will decide whether or not he will die. Every warrior prays and makes his medicine, but it is still up to the Creator. I'm not afraid to die."

Boyer left, announcing that he was going to try to

sleep, that the march would begin early and go a very long time.

Little Crane told Garrett, "I said to you earlier that a warrior meets death head on. That's how it is."

Red Moon, who was standing next to Little Crane, asked, "Six Fingers afraid to die?"

"I don't think so." Garrett felt himself tightening inside.

"It's either yes or no," Little Crane said.

"Then it's yes," Garrett admitted. "I hadn't given it much thought, I guess. All I've had on my mind was writing about this campaign."

"Making the paper talk," Little Crane said. "Does it go with you when you cross over?"

"No, that stays behind," Garrett said. "The marks remain on the paper for many people to see, long after the writer dies."

"If it is truth," Little Crane said, "then it's good medicine. If the signs are lies, it's bad medicine."

Garrett stood in silence. "Yes, I suppose that's true. I guess I'll go to bed."

Red Moon put a hand on his shoulder. "Do not fear to die, good friend. Brother. Creator take care of you."

"I believe that, Red Moon," Garrett said. "Thank you."

Garrett lay in his bedroll. His entire world view had changed. Though he had thought about death before, now it seemed very real and very likely. And in a land he had never seen before, a long way from home. He was aware that he was trembling.

Overhead hung a nearly full moon, surrounded by stars that shone brightly in a vast expanse of endless space. One fell. Garrett immediately thought, *God, please don't let me die. What would Ann do?* Even more important, he realized, was his own deep fear of this unknown condition, where everything necessarily must change drastically. He didn't know any other way to think of it. He didn't want it. Not now. He didn't know when he would be ready.

Little Crane and Red Moon saw death in the right form as an honor, as did Boyer and the Crows and the rest of the scouts. This was astounding. Dying young on a battlefield was the best of all possible ends, facing it straight on with no fear. How could a person get to see things that way?

Still restless, Garrett left his bedroll and walked to the edge of camp. He sat down on the stream bank, his knees under his chin, as he had often sat in contemplation as a child. He stared into the stream, the water gurgling past him in the darkness, shimmering where shafts of moonlight bathed the surface.

All was silent; the camp and even the wilderness outside of camp were in a deep calm. Not a single coyote howled in the distance. It seemed the end of something.

He sat quietly, letting the bubbling stream relax him. The current seemed to be singing in a small, soothing voice, like time running past him on the breath of moving water. "Nothing stays the same," Little Crane had often told him. "Nothing lasts forever but the earth and sky."

Garrett heard footsteps and turned. A voice called out to him. "That you, Garrett?" Captain Benteen's voice. "Can I join you?"

"Be my guest," Garrett said. "This is a good spot to relax."

"I could stand to relax some," Benteen said, taking a seat beside Garrett, "but I don't think it's possible. We're headed into hell and there's nothing anybody can do about it."

"It seems everyone feels that way," Garrett said.

"Damned right, they do. And for good reason. You'd know why if you'd come around to interview me. Did the General forbid it? Has he got you running scared?"

"I might as well be honest," Garrett said. "Custer was downright ugly about my interviewing you. I was afraid he'd stop me from going along."

"He'll make a Kellogg out of you yet, he will," Benteen said. "Too bad. I thought you to be made of stronger stuff."

"Put yourself in my place, Captain," Garrett said. "If

you were teetering on the edge to begin with, would you take a lot of unnecessary chances?''

"*Unnecessary* chances? Talking to me is unnecessary? How else, in God's name, would you ever learn the truth?''

"There are a lot of ways to learn the truth, Captain Benteen," Garrett snapped. "And one of them is to steer clear of people filled with hate.''

Benteen sat in silence. Garrett thought he might get up and leave. Instead, he said, "You don't know the circumstances, Mr. Garrett, so how can you be both judge and jury?''

"Captain, I'm not judging you, and I don't care about the circumstances. My mission is to gather substantiated facts. I can't use anything else. And if you want to consider me a coward for avoiding you, that's your prerogative. But I intend to complete my task by any means possible.''

"You're an odd one, Garrett," Benteen said. "You dress and act like one of the scouts, but you talk like a qualified politician in the hunt for the governorship.''

"As a matter of fact," Garrett said, "you might consider me in such a position.''

"Really?" Benteen laughed. "If I consent to help you, might you give me one of your cabinet assignments?''

"Most certainly," Garrett said. "One good turn deserves another. I've been hearing rumors about the officers' meeting tonight. Why did Custer call it?''

"Custer thinks everyone is out to stab him in the back," Benteen said. "His paranoia is getting the best of him, even more so than usual on this campaign. I think he's scared, right down to the marrow of his bones.''

"He's afraid of the Indians?''

"Underneath it all, he's afraid of everything, if the truth were known. If he doesn't get the job done, he'll be dead politically and socially, not to mention his army career. There's reason to believe, also, that he might have to face a court martial after this is over. If we whip the hostiles, he'll get the credit and maybe erase all his problems, plus he'll likely get the Democratic nomination for president. I believe he figures it's all or nothing.''

"Are you saying that he's going to go against the hostiles for his own personal reasons, without regard for his officers and men?''

"That's precisely what I'm saying, Mr. Garrett. You can call me bitter if you so choose, but I know for a fact that George Custer has never had a bit of consideration for anyone but himself. Others might think he does; he might even think he does himself at times; but, really, all he thinks about is what's in it for him.''

"Do the other officers believe that?''

"Anyone who's fought with him or under his command thinks it. He knows his tactics, but he's too reckless. He won't listen to reason. He thinks he knows it all and can do it all. When we left the Rosebud, Gibbon told him not to be greedy, to leave some of the Sioux for them. Custer just laughed. Giving him this command was the craziest thing anyone could have ever done.''

"I was led to believe that Custer was quite subdued during the meeting,'' Garrett said. "I heard he wanted to make peace and gather everyone's support.''

"Oh, he was begging at the end, that's true. But he wasn't fooling anybody. We all know that when it's all over, he'll say he did everything.'' Benteen doubled one hand into a fist and rubbed it with the other. "You know,'' he continued, "I just about shot him during the meeting.''

Garrett turned. "You did? How did it come to that?''

"At the beginning, Custer ranted and raved about officers in his command trying to undermine his campaign. I saw him looking at me, like a challenge. So I unsnapped my holster and asked him who he might be talking about. He assured me and everyone present that I wasn't one of those he was concerned about. He backed down, he did. After that he got all friendly with everybody. The coward!'' Benteen rose to his feet and began pacing. "Nothing but a miserable, glory-hunting coward of a bastard!''

Garrett waited for Benteen to calm down. "Can you

give me information that will prove that Custer shouldn't be in command? I mean other than your own personal opinion.''

Benteen sat down again. "I told you that Custer wanted just the Seventh to march up the Rosebud. We could have been four companies stronger. We could be bringing hell to the hostiles. But, no, not with Custer in charge.''

"What do you mean?" Garrett asked.

"Major Brisbin offered to join us with his Sixth Cavalry, and the use of two Gatling guns," Benteen replied. "Brisbin's men would have been four more companies, more than enough to do the job. But, no, Custer declined. He told Brisbin that the Seventh could do the job, that the Seventh could handle anything we meet. The fool! The stupid bastard!''

"Custer declined additional manpower?" Garrett said. "Is there a legitimate reason why he did so?''

"No, of course not.''

Garrett wished he'd brought pencil and paper. "You say it was Major Brisbin who offered his services?''

Benteen was running his hands through his long white hair. "He's so crazy! So very, very crazy! I wish I knew how to get out of this and save face. Oh, I can see why he declined the Gatling guns. They're cumbersome and this is rough country. They'd hold us up. But four more companies of men? To decline that is totally insane! I told him as much. I did. I told him as much.''

"How many Sioux and Cheyenne are there?" Garrett asked.

"Custer believes between a thousand and fifteen hundred warriors. Those are the figures he got when he was in Washington. They're stuck in his head. He says the agents know how many Indians they've got around the agencies. But the scouts laugh at him. You know that. They can read sign and tell within two or three lodges. You know that. You've watched them work.''

"They're good," Garrett agreed. "I've never seen anything like it.''

Benteen shook his head. "The strangest part of this is,

I wonder if Custer doesn't realize there are a lot more warriors. Somehow, I think he knows, but he's bound and determined to stick to his own plan. Oh, he's so very crazy! The stupid bastard!''

"What about his notion that the Indians are bound to run?'' Garrett asked.

"And what if they don't?'' Benteen said quickly. "The smaller villages, sure. They ran like coyotes. What choice did they have? But if you're part of a fighting force of, say, two thousand to twenty-five hundred men, would you feel afraid? Hell, no! You'd feel like stomping somebody's ass into the ground!''

"You know, Captain,'' Garrett said, "I might think you fly off the handle rather easily, but I will tell you that you make a great deal of sense. Now, will you go on the record as stating that Custer refused to take additional men when the offer was made?''

"Ask the other officers. They'll tell you the same thing. Certainly Major Reno will. Get them all to sign your story. Send it in. If Brisbin were here, you could ask him yourself. I'll bet he'd sign it.''

"I'll write up a story, as long as you and the other officers sign it with me.''

"Fine by me,'' Benteen said. "Send it in as soon as you can. But there won't be any couriers leaving until after we meet the Sioux. By then history will have made its mark. We will have seen what we're up against and we will have gone into the battle, like men, like the soldiers we are.''

Ann lay in her bedroll in the midnight stillness near the Tongue River, looking up at the stars. Her whole world seemed to be spinning out of control. Nothing was as she had envisioned it.

Lareaux lay nearby, groaning in half-sleep from the pain in his leg. Tyrone had cauterized the wound by building a fire and heating the same knife the dead widow had used. He had then inserted the blade, white-hot, into the cut. Lareaux had passed out from the pain and Tyrone had wept.

Water, who now had five Sioux scalps to his name, had spent all his time on lookout. He seemed more tense and had begun to talk about his twin brother, Little Crane, saying, "He shouldn't have gone to find Long Hair. Never." Now, though, he was silent in the darkness, watching over the horses as they grazed nearby.

After the fight, Ann had rested for a time, awakening to the white buffalo dream, screaming for Adam. Tyrone had comforted her, assuring her they were safe and would remain safe. They would travel along the river and not cross country out in the open. With so many Sioux traveling to find the main village, they would take no chances. Staying to the river would take longer, but it would allow them cover should they encounter more hostiles.

After the rest, they had ridden until well after sundown, watching for more Sioux along the way. At Powder River, they had found signs of a massive military camp. Now, near the mouth of Tongue River, Ann wondered if Libbie Custer hadn't been right: The army had already met the Sioux and Cheyenne, and everyone was dead.

Bothering her the most was the fact that she had been forced to kill the Sioux warrior earlier that day. She had seen people die, but she had never before taken anyone's life. Despite the fact that it was self-defense, the event weighed heavy on her mind.

She climbed from her bedroll and wrapped herself in a blanket. Water and Lareaux had each given her one; they had plenty. Lareaux had said that a blanket was the most usable, versatile item on the frontier.

"Is everything all right, Miss Ann?" Tyrone was sitting up in his bedroll.

"I'm fine, Tyrone," she answered.

"If you've a mind to talk, I'd listen."

"I don't know what I'd talk about, Tyrone."

"Maybe about today, Miss Ann. Things got hard for us."

Ann covered her face with her hands and began to weep. The tension and the worry of the trip, and the added shock and horror of the afternoon all came pouring out. Tyrone came over and sat down beside her.

"It's good that you're crying, Miss Ann. Troubles can ball up inside you and make you real sick."

"I had no idea it would be this hard," she said. "No idea. We didn't even bury those people, Tyrone. I feel so awful."

"Don't worry much about the burial part," Tyrone said. "In their way of thinking, lying out in the open is a decent burial. That way they join with their brothers the wolves and the crows and the magpies and such. Everything is one in their eyes, and all come together in the end."

"Do you mean that wolves scattering their bones is what they want?"

"It's a good thing. The Grandfathers, those who've passed on, live in the rocks and the trees and the waters. That's not the way folks in the city see it. We put people in boxes, but sooner or later they mix with the earth. Among the Indians, it's just sooner."

"Today still bothers me," Ann said. "Maybe I should have listened to Aunt Cora and stayed in St. Louis. But I just couldn't. I had to come."

"What made you feel that you had to come, Miss Ann?"

Ann stared out into the night, across the vast open, lit by starlight from above. "I had a dream, Tyrone, the strangest dream of my life. Adam was in it, and it scared me."

"I don't know much about dreams, Miss Ann, except that you should pay close attention to them."

"Then I guess you understand. I had to come."

"Would you like to tell me about the dream?"

Ann related what she had seen: the surging flames curling into a vast darkness, and Adam bursting through on the back of a white buffalo.

"The Indians would say that you had a medicine dream," Tyrone said. "A powerful one at that."

"Do you know what it means?"

"I can't say that I do, Miss Ann. But I can see why you're afraid for Adam. There's a reason you saw him, though, and the Good Lord will tell you in time.''

"It's between now and then that's driving me crazy,'' Ann said. "I wish I knew what I was supposed to do. I believe that I must find him. But it seems so hopeless.''

"Nothing is hopeless, not if you want it bad enough. And I'll help you, any way I can. You know that, Miss Ann.''

Ann took Tyrone's hand and held it tightly. "You're a good friend to have, do you know that? The best friend anyone could ever have.''

"Well, I've told you before, Miss Ann, you're a special lady. You're father was so proud of you that he could bust. He would talk about you and he would just beam. And I can understand why. I feel privileged to know you, ma'am.''

"Do you think we'll get through this, Tyrone?''

"I can't say what will happen, Miss Ann. All I can say is that I don't forget my prayers, not out here.''

"I thought you were going to tell me not to worry a bit, that everything would be just fine.''

"Why would I tell you that, Miss Ann? You know what happened today wasn't just fine. It was awful. More awful things could happen, but I'd like to think everything will turn out for the best. I believe that.''

"That doesn't make me certain that Adam won't die. Or that all of us won't die.''

"Nothing's certain, Miss Ann. You know, the Indians say that only the earth and the heavens are immortal. Everything else passes. There's something to that; and if you believe it, you'll rest easy.''

"How can you believe in the Indian sayings and be a Christian, Tyrone?''

"I don't see that much difference in the teachings. If you think like the Good Lord, you'll treat everyone the same, you'll care for your brother. The Indian believes that he who takes care of others will come to power and glory. He will stand out among his fellow man. Seems like the same thing to me.''

"Doesn't feeling that way make it hard for you to kill an Indian?''

"It's hard to kill anything, Miss Ann, but there's times when there's no other choice. I don't ask for answers because I don't know the right questions to ask."

Ann was silent. Lareaux was resting easier, drifting into a deep sleep.

"Water mixed up some plants for him earlier," Tyrone said. "They'll put a man to sleep no matter how bad he's feeling. Maybe I'll go back over and try to get some rest myself."

"So you don't think this was a bad idea?" Ann asked. "You think it was right for me to insist on this trip to find Adam?"

Tyrone shrugged. "Like you said before, you had to come. Your dream told you something and you have to look for it. So it wasn't a bad idea. To some folks it might seem downright crazy, but that don't make it a bad idea."

"Well, that surely answers my question," Ann said. "You make me feel a whole lot better."

"Glad to be of help, Miss Ann. Glad to be of help."

Tyrone went back to his bedroll and Ann settled in again, hoping that sleep would come quickly. Nearby the river spoke, the tumbling water singing in the darkness. In the distance, wolves howled back and forth across the open, perhaps talking to one another about the fallen Sioux warriors and how they had joined with their Grandfathers to sleep the endless sleep.

FOURTEEN

The sun rose into a cloudless sky on the day of the hunt. Scouts had reported that two herds of nearly three hundred head each had moved onto the divide between Rotten Grass Creek and the Little Bighorn. The hunters would form a northern group and a southern one. They would swing apart and ride parallel on the outer flanks of the two herds.

All of the villages had sent their best hunters. Each village had chosen a leader, and all the hunters had chosen one from among them to be the main leader. Crazy Horse, the Oglala war chief, had accepted the hunters' request to carry the pipe.

Nighthawk saw this as a mixed blessing. Crazy Horse respected him and believed him to have great medicine, for he had said more than once that no other man he knew could shoot as well. But Crazy Horse had deep feelings for Ghostwind, which he had not hidden. Only when she had decided that Nighthawk would be her husband did he step back.

At the Battle of the Rosebud, Nighthawk had fought beside Crazy Horse. Since then he had seen little of this warrior who was so well known among all the camps, considered by many to be the finest and fiercest in all the Big Village.

Crazy Horse was not a large man, like Gall or Sitting Bull of the Unkpapa. He was of moderate height and build, with light skin and hair. He had a high, sharp nose and deeply inset eyes, dark and unsettling. He often wore an Iroquois shell necklace with his blue leggings and red blanket. For the hunt, he wore only a breechclout and moccasins, with a small medicine bundle around his neck.

There was always talk of warriors in the camps; and among those most talked about was Crazy Horse. He had gained a large number of war honors, due to his belief that *Wankantanka,* the Creator Spirit, had endowed him with special powers. Everyone believed him, for he had often ridden back and forth in front of Bluecoat rifles without being hit.

Crazy Horse believed he had been given the power to cross into the Spirit World, the Real World as he called it, whenever he wished, thus evading his enemies. He had spoken often of how his horse would dance in a strange way when he was in the Real World, and thus his name, Crazy Horse.

Anyone who wished for victory in battle followed Crazy Horse. The most recent battle on the Rosebud, the biggest with the Bluecoats to date, had proved his abilities to lead and protect his people.

But there was no room for battle talk today. No one thought of anything but getting to the buffalo and having a successful hunt. The plan was to drive the two herds onto one another, creating mass confusion. The hunters would then surround the combined herds and· make as many kills as possible.

The council had decided to let Nighthawk stay in camp at least until after the hunt, but not without intense debate. Eagle Wing had explained how valuable Nighthawk would be in bringing home badly needed meat, but many had argued that his disobedience would overshadow the value of his skill. His having taken two boys well beyond the village boundaries, especially in the face of grave danger, had proved this. If he took it upon himself to go to the hunt ahead of the others, he could chase the herd away. That would be disastrous.

Eagle Wing had replied that Nighthawk had proven himself at the Rosebud battle. "You know how bravely he fought·against the Bluecoats," he had pointed out.

"He counted coup and saved Red Bear from death. With the two boys, his judgment may have been poor, but he's not our enemy."

As they traveled to the hunt, Nighthawk rode alone, at the very back of the line. He had been placed under strict supervision. Everyone realized that he was a good hunter; but they would give him no chance to spoil the hunt by trying to prove himself too soon.

Nighthawk realized he couldn't be angry with Tall Deer, for he had made his own choice in playing the tag game with him. It would be important to show his abilities with a rifle once again.

"You'd better do very well on this hunt," Eagle Wing told Nighthawk as they joined the northern group. "If you don't, there will be nothing more I can do for you. You and Ghostwind will be sent away. I don't want to lose you as a war brother."

"You won't," Nighthawk said confidently.

At midmorning, the hunters stopped to prepare for the hunt. Scouts who had ridden ahead of the main body reported that the two separate herds were grazing peacefully along the high ridge above Rotten Grass Creek. Crazy Horse stood on the back of his pinto to address the hunters.

"When the hunt is to begin," he said in Lakota and sign language, "we will divide into two groups. The Oglalas and the Cheyenne will go to the north, and the other camps to the south. I will ride to the top of a hill, where all can see me. When we are ready to push the two herds together, I will signal with my red blanket.

"At that time, the northern group will push their herd southward and the southern group will push their herd north. The two herds will run together, giving us a good chance to surround them. We will have a good hunt."

Ordinarily, the hunters would have cheered. Today it was important to keep quiet. The buffalo were too close.

Crazy Horse lit the pipe and offered it to the earth and sky, and the four directions. He prayed for a successful hunt and for the safety of the hunters. He asked that the

Buffalo Spirit be kind to them and provide them with nourishment.

When the ceremony was finished, the hunters divided. As they neared the northern herd, Nighthawk made sure that the rope tied around his pony was tight and that the smaller rope around his middle was securely bound to the larger one. He didn't want to be leaning over his pony's side and have the knots slip.

Crazy Horse led the northern hunters into position. They lined up, facing south. The herd grazed peacefully less than a mile away.

As he took his place in line, Nighthawk checked his rifle, a Henry repeater that held seven shots. He had more bullets in a leather pouch at his side. He was allowed the ammunition only because he had proven his shooting ability. There was precious little to waste.

One other hunter had a Henry rifle, and another had brought a long-barreled Springfield, called a Long Tom, that he had taken from the Rosebud battlefield. Most of the hunters, including Eagle Wing, used a bow and arrows. A few carried lances. Everyone sat their horses, eagerly awaiting the signal to go.

Crazy Horse rode up to Nighthawk. He spoke in Lakota and in sign. "You got yourself into trouble, I hear."

"Bad judgment. I'll be more careful next time."

Crazy Horse pointed behind his left ear, and then to Nighthawk's ear. "Do you still have the medicine stone that I gave you?"

Nighthawk lifted the hair just above his ear, revealing a rawhide string that kept the stone in place. "I will always have it. No matter what. But today will be a good day."

"You don't seem to be worried," Crazy Horse said. "Do you think the Cheyenne will keep you?"

"I know they will."

Crazy Horse smiled. "Yes, I believe you're right. If I could shoot like you, I would go on foot and save my pony."

Crazy Horse rode to the top of a hill. He waited a short

time, his face raised to the heavens, his lips moving. Then he waved his blanket wildly, yelling.

Nighthawk kicked his pony into a run. The column of hunters surged toward the northern herd, screaming loudly. The buffalo, startled by the yelling, began a wild scramble southward, grunting loudly, churning the earth with a heavy drumming tread that sounded like thunder.

The column raced behind the surging buffalo. To the south, the second herd appeared, driven by the southern hunters. The two herds rushed headlong together, creating instant confusion, and the hunters closed in, forming a circle.

Yelling hunters rode alongside, sending arrows and lances into the hearts of the buffalo. The buffalo bawled wildly, their mouths open, tongues hanging out, eyes wide and rolling.

Leaning over his pony, Nighthawk quickly dropped three yearling cows, shooting them directly behind the ear. He killed two more, his pony dodging in and out of the herd. The churning and trampling buffalo tore the grass to shreds and soon the area lay under a thick fog of dust.

Fallen buffalo lay everywhere, tripping those trying to escape, creating immense pileups. Those badly wounded that had not fallen began turning on the hunters, charging in crazed fury.

Nighthawk pulled back to reload. Ready again, he turned his buckskin just as a huge bull with an arrow in its shoulder emerged from the haze. Nighthawk's pony turned about face and dodged the bull's furious lunge. A nearby hunter, though, didn't see the bull in time.

Nighthawk yelled. At full speed, its huge head lowered, the bull rammed the hunter's pony. The pony, disemboweled, squealed and fell. The hunter, trapped, was lifted on the bull's horns and tossed several feet away into the horde of milling buffalo.

Nighthawk turned his pony again as the bull swung around, ripping the air with a massive horn. He fired into a glaring red eye and the bull thudded to the ground.

Turning his buckskin into the herd, Nighthawk rode up alongside the fallen hunter. The hunter grabbed Nighthawk's arm and swung up behind, holding tight as Nighthawk maneuvered his pony out of the milling buffalo.

At a signal from Crazy Horse, the hunters retreated from the herd, allowing the buffalo to scramble down into Rotten Grass Creek to safety. The dust began to clear. With a loud series of cries and yells, hunters rode among the fallen, marking their kills by recognizing their arrows. Nighthawk had the most kills, with twelve.

The hunter who had been tossed from his pony, a young Oglala named High Road, had somehow managed to escape injury. He was downcast nonetheless, as he hadn't killed a single buffalo, and had lost his rifle.

Nighthawk saw the rifle, the long-barreled Springfield, lying in the grass a short distance away. He jumped from his pony and examined it. It was still intact.

High Road was glad that Nighthawk had found his rifle, but he said he still felt discouraged. He was the only hunter who hadn't downed at least one buffalo.

"Do you have any bullets left for this rifle?" Nighthawk asked High Road.

High Road took off his cartridge pouch. "A lot. Why?"

"I propose to make you a trade," Nighthawk said. "Three buffalo for the rifle and all the ammunition."

High Road answered immediately. "It's a good trade. I can't shoot very well. The rifle and bullets are yours."

"Pick any three of my fallen buffalo that you'd like," Nighthawk said.

High Road hurried out among the fallen buffalo and located those he wished to claim. Eagle Wing watched and rode up to Nighthawk.

"Why did you make that trade?"

"I'll show you," Nighthawk said.

Crazy Horse, who had been sitting his pony a short distance away, said, "Are we going to see some more trick shooting?"

"Not trick shooting," Nighthawk replied. "Long-distance shooting. This rifle wasn't made to chase buffalo with. It's too awkward to carry."

Nighthawk rode to the top of a nearby hill. Eagle Wing and Crazy Horse rode behind. Some of the other hunters followed to watch.

The herd had run nearly two miles away before slowing down. A number of injured straggled behind, limping badly or lying on the ground, waiting for the wolves.

Nighthawk picked a yearling bull that had stopped about a mile distant. Balancing his elbow on his knee, Nighthawk aimed carefully and fired. The rifle spit powder and the bullet whizzed out over the open plain, slamming into the bull just behind the foreleg.

The bull jumped and leaped forward a few steps, wobbled, and fell onto its side. Eagle Wing and the other hunters cheered. Nighthawk took aim at a dry cow standing not far from the fallen bull. Again the rifle boomed and the buffalo lurched with the impact of the heavy slug, slumped to its knees, and over onto its side.

"I'll drop one more. Then I'll be back to even," Nighthawk said.

Another shot and another buffalo fell. Many of the hunters held their hands over their mouths, shaking their heads in amazement.

"If you learn to cross into the Spirit World when you want," Crazy Horse said, "you will be unstoppable."

Eagle Wing, declaring his own glory in having been right about Nighthawk, made up a song:

> *Ah-heee!* His medicine is strong!
> They fall before him, the buffalo.
> They fall before him, his enemies.
> Behold him, he is my war brother!
> Behold him, he is my war brother!

Crazy Horse lit the pipe, giving thanks to the Creator for a successful hunt.

The women began arriving, leading packhorses. Ghost-wind hugged Nighthawk tightly. "I couldn't bear to think of losing you," she said. "But I knew that you would show everyone your power. Tonight I will say to everyone that I have a husband who is both hunter and warrior. The best hunter and warrior!"

With nightfall, the dancing and feasting began. There was plenty of buffalo for everyone. To show their gratitude, the Cheyenne gave a lot of meat to their Oglala friends, who had so graciously taken them in after the battle on Powder River the previous March.

In addition to scalp dances, each hunter told of his part in the day's success. Nighthawk's story was saved until last.

Nighthawk told his story in sign and what little Cheyenne he could comfortably use. The people listened intently, their hands over their mouths, some yelling at the end. Even those who had doubted him now gave him homage.

Ghostwind, though, was absent. It bothered Nighthawk and he asked Day Lily, who pointed into the hills above the village.

"She told me earlier that she had to go out and pray. Something was happening inside her, she said. She hasn't come back. She wouldn't have missed this if something important hadn't happened."

As Nighthawk walked through the village, he was greeted with honor. One warrior shouted, "Nighthawk, when are you going to teach me to shoot like you?" Another one called, "I'll trade you for that big, long-shooting rifle of yours. Five good horses! Seven? No more than that!"

Eagle Wing stopped Nighthawk, insisting that he come and feast with him.

"I'm going into the hills to find Ghostwind," Nighthawk said. "I'll join you after I've found her."

Eagle Wing looked concerned. "She's up there so late? And when there's feasting and dancing for all? Something must be wrong."

Nighthawk made his way out from camp, village firelight flickering through the shadows. The singing and dancing and the pounding of the drums followed him, a throbbing rhythm that echoed through the darkness.

He started up the main trail he had taken with Young Horse and Tall Deer earlier in the day. He stayed in the hills, where he knew Ghostwind would be. Not far away, he saw the light of a small fire, its smoke rising from the edge of a bluff, its flame outlining Ghostwind as she sat praying.

He walked a way farther and sat down. Careful not to interrupt Ghostwind's ceremony, he waited until she called down to him.

Ascending to her, Nighthawk found her standing before the fire, wiping her eyes.

"What are the tears for?" he asked.

Ghostwind took a deep breath. "A great battle is coming. Very soon."

"Have you learned what your visions mean?"

"Not yet," she replied. "This is different. This is something else."

Nighthawk came close and held her. "What have you seen?"

Ghostwind pointed into the darkness. "Do you see them, the Little People, sitting on the rocks?"

"The Little People?"

"They come when major change is happening, often when there will be death."

"You mean little beings. Manlike."

"Yes. Very small. They look a great deal like humans, but much smaller and in different proportion. Do you see them? They're moving around. I think they're leaving."

Nighthawk stared into the darkness, afraid of what he might see. But he saw nothing.

"I don't understand," he said. "I don't see any little people. I don't see anything but shadows."

"They live in the shadows," Ghostwind said. "It's good that you cannot see them. You would likely become very frightened."

"I'm frightened as it is," Nighthawk admitted. "Why haven't you told me about them?"

"You wouldn't have understood. They came just before the Rosebud battle. Now they're back.''

Nighthawk felt his spine tingle. He thought he saw movement in the rocks, but he could have been imagining it.

"You can't see what you don't believe in," Ghostwind said. "I've seen them helping spirits across to the Other Side."

"Does this mean we're going to die?" Nighthawk asked. "You and I?"

"I can't say. I don't feel death coming for me. I still feel it coming for others, as I've been feeling for a long time. I don't know about you. But not for me."

"Have you seen the owls?"

"Not tonight," Ghostwind replied. "They haven't come yet. But they will."

"Maybe you should come back down to camp and rest," Nighthawk suggested. "You're very tired."

"I need to know what's going to happen," Ghostwind said. "I have to know what's coming for our people. It's important."

"Maybe you're not supposed to see what's coming," Nighthawk said.

"But I've already *seen* it," Ghostwind argued. "I just need to interpret exactly what it means. Maybe the Little People came to help me."

"Take some tobacco and some presents to Horned Bull," Nighthawk suggested. "Tell him what you've seen. His medicine is strong. He can help."

"Horned Bull helped me greatly that first day, when I came to the village as a child," Ghostwind said. "He brought my mind back to this world and made it stay here. Before that winter, I had wandered a very long time, going back and forth from this world to the Spirit World. I don't know how I survived. I believe the Little People helped me. I saw them often. Then I hadn't seen them until just before the Rosebud fight."

"Why don't you want to ask Horned Bull about this?" Nighthawk asked.

"After I came back that day, Horned Bull told me that it would be the last time he could help me. He said that he had helped me as much as he could. He said that any answers I needed would have to come through my own spirit helpers.''

"Then no one else can interfere?" Nighthawk asked. "No one else has the medicine to help you see the things to come?"

"No one. I'm alone with this. Maybe after the bad event has passed I can learn things from others, but not until then.''

"What about Sitting Bull?" Nighthawk said. "Maybe his vision of the soldiers falling into camp means the same as yours."

"Maybe," Ghostwind replied. "They say that he believes a big battle with the Bluecoats is coming. But he hasn't told anyone when it's to come."

Nighthawk watched smoke curl from the fire into the night sky. "Maybe you should ask to speak with him."

"I can't do that," Ghostwind said. "I know he respects me, but I'm not going to his lodge. Maybe you could. You've done great things, especially today. Maybe you could learn some things from him."

"Maybe so. But I'm not certain. There are rumors that he's clearing his village of anyone who isn't a full blood.''

"Do you know that for certain?" Ghostwind asked.

"That's what I've heard. They say that Sitting Bull is having a bad time because of his vision. He's very worried for his people. He believes that white blood nearby will spoil his medicine."

"Then don't go to see him," Ghostwind said. "He might have you killed."

"I don't know him to be that kind of man," Nighthawk said. "He's always been very fair to me. Maybe I should go anyway. Maybe he will talk to me away from the village, so I'm not close to his medicine bundle. I'll tell him it's to help you, that it's for my family. He'll understand that."

"Don't go if you don't want to," Ghostwind said. "I shouldn't have suggested it."

"I don't feel bad about it," Nighthawk said. "If he doesn't want to see me, he won't. That's all. He won't have me killed, though. You don't have to worry about that."

Ghostwind thought a moment. "If you feel right about it, then go and talk to him. It's important for me to learn what I've been seeing and what it means. I'm having trouble singing the right songs to our coming child. When I wait for a song to come, all I see are the terrible sights and sounds of war. I don't want our child hearing and seeing those things."

"How can that happen when the child isn't yet two months in the womb?" Nighthawk asked.

"If the child is to live, then she is already learning things, through me," Ghostwind said. "That's what we believe."

"She?"

"Don't you wish for a daughter, to carry on the people?"

"Oh, I don't care if it's a son or daughter," Nighthawk said. "I don't see how you can know."

"Mountain Water told me," Ghostwind said. "I've told you, older women know a lot of things."

"I believe you," Nighthawk said. "Maybe you should come down with me now."

"It's not time yet for me to leave here." Ghostwind looked into the fire. "If you want to stay up here with me, you must sit quietly. Otherwise, you can go back down. I'll come when I'm finished."

"What should I tell Young Horse and Talking Grass?"

"You don't have to tell them anything. They're staying with Mountain Water tonight. They know where I am and that I'm safe."

Nighthawk knew, of course, that the children were accustomed to their mother's unusual ways. There was no use worrying.

Nighthawk started back down to the village, the drumming and singing growing louder and louder. It had been hard enough to adjust from his white upbringing to the

Cheyenne and Lakota ways. Now he was among them, and they were struggling for their very existence. It was going to be the strongest test he had ever had to face, and he wasn't sure he was ready for it.

FIFTEEN

Nighthawk paced in front of his lodge. It was nearly midmorning and still no word had come from Sitting Bull. It appeared as though the great leader wouldn't see him.

Ghostwind sat near the entrance, beading a vest to be used in dancing. Talking Grass, who was nearby playing with friends, would soon begin to learn fancy dances.

"You shouldn't worry so much," Ghostwind told Nighthawk. "You know that he'll see you. Just be patient."

"How can you be so calm?" Nighthawk asked. "This concerns you more than it does me."

"I'm always calm when I'm beading," Ghostwind said. "Just as long as I'm beading."

Young Horse stood nearby, listening. He had been grooming his pony and another that Nighthawk would load with presents for Sitting Bull. Next to the pony lay a Hudson's Bay blanket, a fringed saddle blanket, a buckskin halter, and a pouch filled with twist tobacco.

Young Horse looked up from his grooming and pointed to a rider who had entered the Cheyenne village and was approaching the lodge. "I'll bet he comes from the Unkpapa camp. He's coming to talk to you, Father."

Indeed, the rider halted near Nighthawk and pointed toward the river, at the southwest edge of the Big Village.

"Sitting Bull has sent me to tell you that he will meet you there," the Unkpapa said. "Go when the sun is straight overhead."

The messenger left and Young Horse jumped up and down. "I haven't been grooming this pony for nothing," he said. "You can load the presents now, Father. I'm going to get the chance to see Sitting Bull!"

"Calm yourself," Ghostwind told him. "He won't want to meet a boy who acts like a grasshopper."

Young Horse smiled. "Not every grasshopper gets to meet Sitting Bull."

Nighthawk packed the presents onto the second pony with trembling hands. Ghostwind watched and said, "Come, both of you. Have something to eat. Then you can go to Sitting Bull."

Inside the lodge, Nighthawk sat but couldn't eat. He shifted nervously.

"You seem more anxious about learning my visions than I am," Ghostwind said. "Or maybe it's your own visions that are troubling you."

"It's both," Nighthawk said. "I don't know what I'll say to Sitting Bull."

"Maybe he'll talk mostly," Ghostwind said. "You can listen, and learn much."

"I'm afraid of what he might tell me. I've had visions before, but nothing this vivid and horrible." He got up and left the lodge.

Ghostwind and Young Horse came out. Nighthawk was already on his pony. Young Horse mounted his and took the halter rope to the pony laden with gifts.

"As my mother told me," Ghostwind said, "there is nothing we can do about what's coming. Maybe we can learn, though, what to do when it happens."

"Maybe," Nighthawk said, turning his pony. "Let's hope so."

Nighthawk sat his pony at the west edge of the Unkpapa camp, waiting patiently, watching the approach of two figures on horseback. The sun was directly overhead, burning the air throughout the valley.

Young Horse sat his black and white pinto, holding the halter rope of the other pony. He watched the riders approaching with anticipation.

As the two riders drew nearer, Young Horse grew excited. "It's him! It's Sitting Bull!"

"Stay calm," Nighthawk said. "When I've greeted them and Sitting Bull has accepted the presents, go back and tell your mother."

Nighthawk and Young Horse sat their ponies silently while Sitting Bull and the other rider, a lean warrior near Sitting Bull's age, drew nearer. Sitting Bull wore a breechclout and leggings, and heavily beaded moccasins. He wore nothing from the waist up but a medicine pouch that hung around his neck.

His hair was braided in two long strands, wrapped in otter fur, that trailed past his waist. At the back of his large head was a single eagle feather tipped with horsehair, tilted to one side.

Sitting Bull stopped his pony, a strong gray stallion with sweetgrass braided into its mane and tail, and made a gesture of greeting to Nighthawk. He said in Cheyenne, "It's a very fine day, isn't it?"

"Yes, it is," Nighthawk said. "Thank you for coming." He noticed that Sitting Bull's arms were both lined with bloody scabs from shoulder to wrist. He had given flesh offerings during the recent Sun Dance along Rosebud Creek, where his vision of soldiers falling into camp had come to him.

"Who's the fine boy with you?" Sitting Bull asked.

"My son, Young Horse," Nighthawk replied. "He is firstborn to Ghostwind. He shares my honor in greeting you."

Sitting Bull smiled. "Some day he will make the Cheyenne people proud."

Young Horse sat straight on his pony, smiling broadly.

Sitting Bull introduced his companion. The man was his brother-in-law, Black Bull, who had helped him during the Sun Dance ceremony. He smiled also.

Sitting Bull then said, "I've learned that you would like to speak with me about sacred matters."

"I would be honored if we could talk," Nighthawk replied. "It's important to my wife, Ghostwind, for she's worried about all the people. Her own visions are coming often and she cannot understand them."

Sitting Bull nodded. "I will listen and help, if I can."

Young Horse led the pony up and Nighthawk took the presents. He handed them to Sitting Bull, who took them and shook Nighthawk's hand. He handed them to Black Bull, who loaded them on his pony and turned back toward the village.

Young Horse then turned his pinto and galloped across the open flat toward the Cheyenne camp.

"I've come to talk with you because you have an honest heart," Sitting Bull said. "And I've heard about your honors, both as a hunter and a warrior."

"I was afraid you wouldn't see me," Nighthawk said.

"I know you've heard that I want no white blood near my medicine articles, and you respect that," Sitting Bull said. "You're willing to speak with me away from my lodge. Normally, that would be an insult to a guest. But I can't help the way things are now. Do you understand?"

"I understand," Nighthawk said. "I'm not insulted. Besides, it is calmer out here. Don't you think?"

Sitting Bull smiled. "Much calmer. Why don't we go to the river? It's cooler under the trees."

At the river, Nighthawk dismounted. Sitting Bull slid from his horse and looked to the village, where women worked and children ran and played.

"I can see why your wife is troubled," Sitting Bull said. "I worry for my people, also. Look at them, just living, not bothering anybody. What have they done that the Bluecoats should want to kill them all?"

"The Bluecoats want the land for white people to settle on," Nighthawk said. "There are a lot of people to the east who want to move out here. Maybe they feel they can live better if the Indian people are confined to one place on a reservation."

Sitting Bull frowned. "No, it's more than that. They don't want us anywhere around. They want us to go away, to die, so that it will be easy for them. They don't want any of us left to bother what they do. They want to ruin the land and they don't want us to stop them. They are coming to kill us, all of us, if they can. Why do they think that way?"

"I can't answer that," Nighthawk replied.

"You don't know? You were once a Bluecoat."

"You know that I was *forced* to become a Bluecoat," Nighthawk said. "I never believed as they do." Nighthawk tried to keep from showing his nervousness, but he realized that it was useless. Sitting Bull missed nothing.

"When you put the colors on, you became one of them," Sitting Bull insisted. "You must have learned the thinking."

"I have white skin and I once wore a Bluecoat uniform," Nighthawk argued, "but I've never approved of fighting for no good reason. A lot of those men don't know anything else. They've been in the army all their adult lives. They were in the war when the North fought the South. Their lives have been lived as soldiers, nothing else."

"Our men live as warriors all their lives," Sitting Bull pointed out. "Yet they don't lose their minds. Don't these men have families?"

"Many came back to find their families had been killed while they were gone fighting," Nighthawk replied. "I believe a lot of the younger ones had nothing better to do than join this army."

"So now they all want to kill us," Sitting Bull said. "But that will not happen. The Creator will not allow it."

Nighthawk took a deep breath. "I hope not."

"You don't have to worry," Sitting Bull said. "It won't happen. Bad things are coming, but my people will survive." He picked up a stick and walked to a thatch of thick grass just back from the river. He ran the stick over the grass. "See how the grass springs back after being pushed down? Your people will push us hard, but we'll never break. We'll bend back. That's what will happen."

"So you don't believe the soldiers will win?"

"I don't know any more than what I've seen myself." Sitting Bull was walking toward a cottonwood, where a large woodpecker was feeding its unseen young through a hole in the trunk. "I know that life moves in a circle. Everything always moves back to the same place. Always. Some of it is good, some is bad. I cannot stop it. No one can stop it. I only know that my people will suffer terribly, but that we will not perish.''

Nighthawk watched the woodpecker, wondering how the process of life worked. The mystery was too tremendous to contemplate, yet in the eyes of the woodpecker, so very simple. There was nothing more important than gathering food for its young.

"You see how that bird is," Sitting Bull continued. "That bird is sacred, as are all living things. But the birds can fly through the air and feel the Creator holding them up. You and I can't do that. The Creator loves those birds or he wouldn't be so kind to them. I've asked them this, and they've told me. They will tell you secrets, too, if you believe they can.''

"Secrets?'' Nighthawk asked.

"Yes. They can tell you secrets that will help you. It's from the birds that I learned that my people will never perish completely. They say that we will survive because we have been given sacred ways of life and sacred ways of talking with the Creator.''

Nighthawk watched while Sitting Bull made a low, purring sound in his throat. The woodpecker stopped its feeding and looked down, then flew to a stump near Sitting Bull and stared at him. Sitting Bull made another sound and the bird flew back up to its nest.

"My people know the sacred ways,'' Sitting Bull continued. "A bird like that once saved my life. I was sleeping under a tree like that one where the nest is, along a river trail, when a large white-tipped bear came by. I awakened when the bear started pulling berries from a bush right beside me. That bear was huge. The woodpecker told me to lie still and everything would be good. The woodpecker flew at the bear and the bear left. I owe my life to the birds.'' He looked hard at Nighthawk. "Do you have a story like that?''

"Yes, but it was the Cheyenne and Lakota people who saved me from the bear,'' Nighthawk replied. "I was told to join the army or be hanged. I chose the army, not knowing that I was choosing a life that would eventually lead to good. I was delivered from the army that brought me out here. Now I'm glad that I chose that army, because I've learned what a good life is really like. You have to see the worst before you can understand the best. I didn't have anything good in my life until I came out here.''

Sitting Bull smiled. ''You're trying hard, I'll give you that. But your skin is still white. And your father, Shot-in-the-Throat, loves this land, also. But he, too, is white, and many of my people are very uneasy about your people now. He is thinking about moving away from the village. Have you talked to him about this?''

''I've seen him once, right after the battle up on the Rosebud. He was glad that I wasn't injured. Then he went back to his wife. I didn't know he was thinking about leaving.''

Nighthawk's father had gone west to become a fur trader, leaving his son at home with a sick mother. Nighthawk had carried a lot of contempt for his father throughout his life and wanted to get over it.

''Maybe you understand that your father carries guilt for having left you behind,'' Sitting Bull said. ''I think you know that. I think you know it's hard for him to see you, because he knows how badly he hurt you.''

''He could have brought me out here with him,'' Nighthawk said. ''I would have been fine.''

''You can't live someone else's life,'' Sitting Bull said. ''It often hurts you badly when they do things you don't understand. You can't hold anger toward them for that.''

''All I understand is that he should have brought me with him,'' Nighthawk said.

Sitting Bull shook his head. ''That's what you always tell yourself. But how do you know anything for certain? You don't. Maybe you'd have been killed out here. Did you ever think that the spirits that guide your father might have told him to leave you at home, that you would some day come out on your own? And maybe those same spirits are telling him to leave the village now.''

''He's never said anything like that to me.''

''You don't understand. The spirits speak to your inner

mind. You can't hear them. They tell you things that help you through life. You have to do things that make you learn. The Creator wants you to learn. I've never understood why your people don't want to learn. In fact, they make it very hard for people who do want to learn. So don't blame your father so much. He has much to learn, and so do you."

Nighthawk watched the woodpecker fly away. He had come to talk with Sitting Bull about Ghostwind's visions and had instead learned more about himself.

Now Sitting Bull seemed to be reading his mind. "As for your wife, she will need to pray a great deal. And she shouldn't stop, even if she doesn't get answers. The Creator doesn't have to tell us everything. We should be glad for the life we've lived and not think we're owed any more than we've been given."

"She worries about our unborn child," Nighthawk said. "And she worries about the future of Young Horse and Talking Grass."

Sitting Bull pointed into the village, alive with midday activities. "She isn't alone, would you say? That's why everyone is coming to this village. They're calling it Sitting Bull's village. The Big Village! Sitting Bull's village!"

Nighthawk sensed that Sitting Bull was both proud and deeply troubled by the honor. Things were going to happen that he had no control over, yet thousands of people depended on him to make their decisions for them.

"I feel as though there are stones around my neck," Sitting Bull continued. "Large stones that are weighing me down to the ground. I want to take them off, but I can't move my arms. I have to carry them, and I don't know for how long."

"There are others who help you share responsibility for your people," Nighthawk said. "It's not up to you to carry it all."

"It is mostly up to me," Sitting Bull said. "The people look up to me. They ask me things. They want me to give them wisdom. Yet, lately, when I speak to them no one listens."

Nighthawk knew that Sitting Bull was referring to the young warriors who had taken guns and ammunition from the Rosebud battlefield, even after being ordered not to. Many were dancing nightly with their new weapons.

Sitting Bull's face clouded. "*Wankantanka* told me that there should be no robbing of the dead. 'The Bluecoat soldiers are yours,' he told me, 'for they have no ears for listening. But do not take their spoils.' " Sitting Bull bowed his head. "I cannot stop what might happen now."

"But you don't believe that Three Stars was part of your vision, do you?" Nighthawk asked. "He didn't fall into the village. We fought on a battlefield away from the camp."

"You're right, there is another battle coming," Sitting Bull said. "I cannot tell when it will be, but the soldiers will have to come into the village."

"I can't imagine any force large enough to attack the village," Nighthawk commented. "No commander in his right mind would challenge so many warriors."

Sitting Bull stared hard at Nighthawk. "Wasn't it you who said that many of the Bluecoats are crazy, especially the leaders?"

"Yes, I did say that," Nighthawk replied. "There were many crazy ones, at least among the soldiers I marched with. I can't say anything about other commands."

"Why would they be any different? When a mind is so driven as to cause total ruin, there is no thinking straight. There is only the desire to kill. Nothing else."

"You speak as if you know that mentality."

"I have been ashamed of myself many times," Sitting Bull admitted. "I know it's not good to wish the total destruction of other human beings. It's not good to destroy *anything*. That makes the mind sick. I'll admit that I've wished for death on our enemies, the Crow and the Shoshone to the west, and the Pawnee to the east. I've wished this often, for I've lost war brothers, many of them. But it's not good to hate. This is something a young man doesn't know."

To the north and west, a thunderstorm was moving down the Yellowstone valley. A wind gusted through the trees along the river. Nighthawk watched four crows sail into the branches, cawing loudly. Sitting Bull stared at them.

"Are they talking to you?" Nighthawk asked.

"Yes," Sitting Bull said. "They came down here from the north, three days ago. They've been talking to me about my vision. They've visited the Other Side Camp and say that there are relatives coming soon to take some of my people across." He took a deep breath. "They keep saying that."

Nighthawk got a sick feeling in his stomach. "Ghostwind says she saw the Little People last night. Does that mean she'll die?"

Sitting Bull continued to watch the crows. "I cannot say."

"She says the Little People help deceased souls across to the other side. I hope they aren't coming for her."

"Did you speak with them?" Sitting Bull asked.

"I don't know. She didn't tell me."

"Maybe she won't see them again," Sitting Bull suggested.

"What if she does?" Nighthawk asked. "Should she try and talk to them?"

"She should do what her heart directs her to do," Sitting Bull said. "I can't tell her. And I can't tell you about your own visions, the ones that trouble you now."

"Why did you agree to see me if you can't help me?" Nighthawk asked.

"I am helping you," Sitting Bull said. "You're not listening."

"What should I be hearing?" Nighthawk asked.

"Listen to the inside of yourself," Sitting Bull instructed. "I'm trying to tell you that no man can see clearly into you. Only *you* can do that, with *Wankantanka*'s help." He pointed to a small, dome-shaped lodge covered with buffalo hide a short distance away. "This

evening I will take you into a sweat ceremony. There
will be some other warriors. We will all go in and pray.
Give yourself to *Wankantanka*. Ask Him to help you. He
will hear you, if you're sincere. You'll learn some things,
I can promise you. That's how I can help you.''

Overhead, the crows continued to caw in the trees,
while the wind grew stronger. The tops of the cottonwoods swayed and thunder boomed through dark clouds
that covered the sun. Big drops of rain began to fall.

Sitting Bull pointed at the crows as they took flight.
''There will be more of them coming,'' he said. ''They
won't tell me the exact day when my vision is to become
real, for they cannot do that. But they have told me that
it will be very soon. Someone is coming to find us, one
who hunts Indian people. And when that man finds us,
there will be a very big fight. The biggest our people
have ever seen.''

''Have the crows told you what will come of this battle?'' Nighthawk asked.

Sitting Bull was staring into the sky, watching the roiling clouds. ''It is a battle that is both an end and a beginning,'' he replied. ''It's the end of something that has
been for a long, long time. Something else will take its
place. This will not be good for my people. We will all
suffer greatly. But in time the circle will turn again and
the old ways will come back. I don't know how long it
will be, but this will happen. That's what the crows have
told me.'' He took a deep breath. ''That's what they
say.''

SIXTEEN

Nighthawk lay on his back, looking into the sky, his body a steaming cloud of vapor. His heart pounded in his chest, a heavy thumping that echoed in his ears.

The second round of Sitting Bull's sweat lodge ceremony had just concluded, and the twelve participants had crawled outside to cool off. Among them were the warriors Crow King, Hump, and Pizi, the one named Gall.

Nighthawk was enjoying sensations that he had never felt before. His body had opened up to allow the world around him to come in. The sweetness of the air filled his nostrils and lungs. The sounds of birds in the trees overhead, the silky rush of the Little Bighorn, were clearer and sharper than he had ever known before.

Inside the sweat lodge, though, he had faced the deepest fear he had ever known.

The fear had come at the beginning, even before the start of the first round. Everyone had entered the lodge, naked, and had taken their places, sitting around a pit in the center of the lodge. Nighthawk had sat quietly while a warrior used a forked branch to fill the pit with white-hot rocks.

Sitting Bull had spread cedar on the rocks, praying to *Wankantanka* for blessings and a good sweat for all the participants. He had then dipped each man's switch into a large kettle of water placed near the edge of the pit, and shaken it over the rocks. The rocks had sizzled, while Nighthawk had trembled. Remnants of ash from the fire that had heated the rocks were washed away, leaving the stones clean for the ceremony.

Sitting Bull had then handed each participant his switch, a collection of eight to ten chokecherry branches, each about eighteen inches long, covered with leaves, and bound together with buckskin on one end. Sitting Bull's attendant, the doorkeeper, had then lowered the flap, creating total darkness within. The stones were pulsing red-hot in the pit.

Sitting Bull had poured water onto the rocks from a buffalo horn, and it had hissed into clouds of suffocating steam. Nighthawk had folded forward, experiencing the most intense heat of his life. If he had to describe it to someone, it would be impossible. There had been a moment when he had believed that he might be scalded alive.

No matter how Nighthawk had prepared himself for it, there was no describing how the heat had searched out his deepest fears.

"It will test your faith," Sitting Bull had warned him. "You must give yourself to the Creator, *Wankantanka,* and say prayers honestly for good intentions. Use the switch that I made for you and slap your back and your sides, and all over yourself, so that the heat can enter and the spirits nurture you."

Nighthawk had used the switch, slapping himself on the back and sides, along with the others, feeling the sting, opening his body to the intense heat.

"Keep your head lowered," Sitting Bull had told him. "The steam will make it hard for you to breathe."

Sitting Bull had poured more water, and still more, the rocks popping and hissing. Nighthawk had thought that he wouldn't be able to endure it any longer. A warrior beside Sitting Bull was asked to pray. The prayer seemed never to end, the heat burning like fire itself. Under his breath, Nighthawk prayed for mercy from the Creator, asking God to understand and grant him relief.

Relief had come when the doorkeeper lifted the flap, allowing the steam to rush out. Everyone had lain down flat, reviving, praying.

What kind of a church is this? Nighthawk had asked

himself. *You don't come in here unless you're ready to learn the real meaning of prayer. And prayers under these conditions must certainly be heard.*

The second round had been even hotter. Nighthawk realized that the participants were praying that their people might be spared from death from the Bluecoats, that their lives might return to normal, that they might be allowed to roam free as their grandfathers before them. They had been praying for good fortune for all.

"I don't want you to think that we pray for death to our enemies in a sweat lodge," Sitting Bull had said earlier. "We never do that. The sweat lodge is a sacred place. We do not ask for bad things to happen. We only ask for protection. We ask for good things—health and happiness for our people."

In the middle of the second round, Nighthawk had resigned himself to the pain. Nothing would make the heat scorch him any less than complete resignation to it. If it killed him, so be it. He was dying anyway. The sooner the better.

It had worked. Relaxing, opening up. Giving in to the heat, accepting the pain, rising above the physical, had granted him a new world and a new way of seeing. Eagle Wing, his war brother, and Sitting Bull had both said that the Creator demanded a lot from an individual. If you gave yourself totally to the Creator, you got back a great deal in return.

Now, while resting for the third round, dripping sweat and enjoying the wonder of life with open senses, Nighthawk watched the clouds moving overhead, sifting past like loose, floating cotton. As the clouds moved, the sun shone through ever different gaps and holes, forming shadows that came and went, melting away into nothing.

Suddenly nighthawks appeared, soaring and swooping about, singing their quick, raspy songs. Their small bodies on long, thin wings, with white feathered bars underneath, darted with the wind, dancing their summer dance.

Nighthawk sat up and noticed a warrior sitting next to him, wiping sweat from his brow. It was Gall.

Nighthawk made sign, exclaiming how beautiful the evening was. Gall nodded and spoke in Cheyenne.

"So you like the sweat, eh?"

"I do like it," Nighthawk said. "How do you know the Cheyenne tongue?"

"We camp with them a lot," Gall replied. "We sit in council with their leaders. We know each other's language."

Nighthawk said, "You're Gall, aren't you?"

"Yes, and you're the one with rifle medicine. You can take the heat, too. I thought you might run out the first round. It's a good thing you didn't. I don't like someone spoiling my sweat."

Gall was well over two hundred pounds, tall and heavily muscled. From his boyhood days he had acquired a reputation as a fierce competitor in war and endurance games. His wrestling prowess was known throughout the Sioux tribes, few being able to stay on their feet against him for more than a few seconds, much less defeat him.

His eyes were every bit as intense and disturbing as those of Sitting Bull. Sitting Bull had, in fact, adopted Gall as a brother, placing him in a high position among the Unkpapa war leaders.

But Gall was also a devoted father and family man, preferring time in his lodge to extended conversation within war societies. Even though he made his own decisions about when to fight or go on raids, he still held a high office among the Strong Hearts, an Unkpapa war society. Anyone who disagreed with him was subject to his wrath, or worse yet, his indifference, the biggest insult of all. His gruff ways had made him as many enemies as friends among his people.

Nighthawk's previous interaction with Gall had been limited to a single meeting, during one of the victory dances after the Rosebud battle. Gall hadn't spoken to him. Nighthawk hadn't expected him to. Most of the Lakota and Cheyenne avoided Nighthawk either out of mistrust or feelings of superiority. How could this white man adopted by the Cheyenne simply for a few brave deeds be equal to them? How could he so easily give up his white ways? No, he was white, and that's how he would remain.

Nighthawk had certainly felt out of place. It had been a good lesson, he had told himself, a way of learning how it must feel for Indians in the white culture.

Gall studied him. "Do you want to become an Indian?"

"I'm living with the Cheyenne," Nighthawk replied. "I married a Cheyenne woman. I should learn the ways, don't you think?"

"You don't have to. If you do, it still won't make you Indian."

"Well, I don't fit in the culture I came from," Nighthawk said. "Maybe I don't fit in anywhere. But I won't worry about it."

"You are different from any of us," Gall said. "I've heard that you can shoot the rifle better than anyone else probably ever could, and that when you wish it, there's nothing that you cannot bring down, at any distance. Is this so?"

"I can shoot well, but not perfectly. I don't believe that's possible."

"Have you ever tried to shoot a warrior who has the medicine with him, who cannot be hit by bullets?"

"I've never shot at a warrior before."

Gall looked puzzled. "But you were once a Bluecoat."

"I was forced to become a Bluecoat," Nighthawk explained. "I was among the Bluecoats that attacked the Cheyenne village on Powder River, back when the snow and cold was on the land. But I fell from my horse and hit my head. When I awakened, I shot only Bluecoats."

This intrigued Gall. "You shot your own people?"

"I shot a Bluecoat leader who would have shot me," Nighthawk explained. "I can never go back among the Bluecoats, and I would never want to."

"You fell from your horse and hurt your head?"

Nighthawk pointed to the scar on his leg. "I had a bad knife wound at the time. I had very little strength. Riding for many days took the last of my strength from me. The charge into the village in the cold was too much. I couldn't stay on my horse.''

"When you fell," Gall said, "did you go away and come back again to be someone else?"

Nighthawk didn't know how to answer. He had never thought of it that way. "Perhaps," he replied, "but I don't feel like a different person. Yet since that day everything has changed for me.''

"Yes, and now you're trapped with a people you don't understand. Our ways are far different from the ways of the white man, the *wasichu*.''

"Your ways are more open. I like life as a warrior better than life as a Bluecoat.''

"If more Bluecoats come, you would shoot them?''

"Just as fast as I could.''

Gall asked again, "Have you ever thought of trying to shoot a warrior with the medicine-that-keeps-bullets-away?"

"No," Nighthawk said quickly. "I have no desire to shoot a warrior.''

"I didn't say to shoot a warrior. I said to shoot *at* a warrior. What makes you think you could hit one with medicine?''

Nighthawk had heard Eagle Wing speak of warriors who, just prior to battle, invoked the help of their medicine powers to avert injury or death. There were warriors who challenged their enemies by riding back and forth in front of their rifles, drawing fire to show that they couldn't be hit, bringing confidence to the rest of the warriors.

Nighthawk had seen Crazy Horse do this at the Battle of the Rosebud. A few other Sioux and Cheyenne warriors had done it, also. While with Crook's forces, he had heard his mule packer friend, Kincaid, tell of this.

"I don't know if I could hit a warrior with great medicine or not," Nighthawk told Gall. "I'm saying that I don't even care to try.''

"Wouldn't you like to know if your medicine was strong enough to do that?''

"No.''

"What kind of warrior are you?"

"What kind of honor would I gain if I shot a warrior who had the medicine?" Nighthawk asked. "I would make some woman a widow and cause grief to many. And anger toward me as well. I'd be setting myself up for trouble with nothing to gain from it."

"It would show that your medicine is the strongest. That's what it would show."

"Then many more of the people would be angry with me. I don't want that."

"No one would blame you if the warrior challenged you," Gall insisted. "You would only be answering that challenge. If you didn't answer, you would be called a coward."

"Why are you asking me this? Do you know someone who wants to challenge me? Maybe you?"

"I don't want to kill you," Gall said. "If it was me that wanted to challenge you, I would not ride back and forth in front of you. I would come straight at you, and you would miss me, then die by my hand."

Nighthawk stared into Gall's hard eyes. "I'm not going to challenge anybody to a test like that," he said. "If someone challenges me, I will have to consider then what I should do. But I'll never dare anybody. That's not how I care to use my abilities. My medicine is for defense, not offense."

Gall smiled. "You *do* know what a warrior is all about. Most of the Bluecoats believe that a true warrior is always challenging someone. How is it that you know what's real?"

"I ask for guidance, the same as you," Nighthawk said. "I don't know enough about life to go without praying."

"You can fight beside me in battle any time you want," Gall said. "Come on. It's time for the third round."

It was late evening when Nighthawk left Sitting Bull. The sweat had been over for some time and he had just finished eating with Sitting Bull and the other warriors.

The Unkpapa wives and daughters of the warriors had fed them. Normally, the meal would have been in the village, but Sitting Bull had decided, even after the sweat, to keep Nighthawk's white blood away from his medicine.

Nighthawk hadn't been offended. Instead, he had thanked Sitting Bull for having invited him to the sweat and for having allowed him to eat with them. It had been an honor and he was grateful.

The last two rounds had been extremely hot and his arms were now covered with long red welts where the steam had scalded his skin. He had been asked to pray during the last round and had asked for blessings for his family and for the families of all those in the sweat with him. His father had come to mind and the emotional pain that had been with him from childhood had risen in him. He realized that he could do nothing about his father's life and asked the Creator for the strength to accept that fact.

Riding back through the village, Nighthawk noticed that the air was filled with joy and laughter. With all the people coming together, there were many relatives who had not seen one another for years. It took something like the coming of the Bluecoats to bring everyone together.

When Nighthawk arrived at his lodge, he found Ghostwind waiting expectantly. Talking Grass was playing with her dolls, but Young Horse was still out with Tall Deer and hadn't returned.

Also there, seated around a fire outside the lodge, were Ghostwind's adopted mother and father, Mountain Water and Five Bulls, and Day Lily and her husband, Red Bear.

Nighthawk took a seat next to Ghostwind, who was anxious to hear what had transpired.

"Did Sitting Bull tell you anything that can help us?" she asked.

"I don't think anyone can help us," Nighthawk said. "Sitting Bull was gracious, but he said that he couldn't see what was going on with either you or me. He said it was up to us to learn for ourselves."

Ghostwind frowned. "Did you ask for the presents back?"

"I just thanked him for the time," Nighthawk replied. "I believe the sweat helped me a lot."

Red Bear spoke up. "So, when are you going to share your medicine, so *I* can gain honors like you?"

Red Bear's personality had changed since the Rosebud fight. He was becoming increasingly hard to live with. Although less than a week had passed, Red Bear had already decided that he would never be the same man again. His injuries seemed to be getting worse instead of better. As a result of tearing up his knee, he couldn't walk very well, and his upper lip, sheared partly away by a bullet, was still so swollen that even drinking broth was painful.

Nighthawk had saved Red Bear from death, pulling him up onto the back of his pony. On the battlefield, Red Bear had thanked Nighthawk. But since then he had decided that he should have stayed and fought until he had been killed. "There would have been much more honor in that than in living the way I am now," Red Bear had repeated many times. "Next time I don't want anyone to save me."

Red Bear's bitterness reminded Ghostwind of her late husband, Kicks-the-Fox, when he had been injured. Nothing could make him happy; nothing could settle his angry feelings. When a warrior is hurt and cannot fight, it's worse than death.

"Nighthawk, do you hear me?" Red Bear continued. He was frowning deeply, making the open sore on his upper lip that much more hideous. "You're sweating with the big chief of all the bands in the village. You must have great medicine. So why don't you teach me some of your medicine?"

Day Lily spoke up. "Red Bear, what's the matter with you?"

"I'll never get to have those honors," Red Bear said. "He's white and I'm Indian, but I'll never sweat with Sitting Bull."

"Why don't you go with me next time?" Nighthawk asked.

"Next time!" Red Bear was pounding the ground. "See, there's already a next time. I can't go over there. I can't shoot a gun like you. I'll never gain honors now. I won't. Never. I can't even ride a horse, so how can I gain honors?"

"Your knee will heal and you'll ride again," Day Lily said. "Everything will be back to normal."

"No," he said, "nothing will ever be normal again." His eyes were glassy. "I'll have to gain honors on the Other Side. Yes. That's where." He stared into the fire.

Day Lily was weeping quietly. Five Bulls cleared his throat and said to Nighthawk, "I see that the sweat has made you nearly as red as us."

Everyone laughed but Red Bear. He continued to stare into the fire. "I'm going to show you all what honor really is," he said. "There are some young men in camp who are talking about having a Dying Dance one of these nights. I think I'll join them. That will bring honor to me. Nothing else can."

"What?" Day Lily said. "You aren't serious." Tears streamed down her face.

"Yes, I am serious," Red Bear said. "They say there may be some in the Sioux camps who want to join in. That would be good for me."

Five Bulls spoke up. "You already have honors, Red Bear. There's no need to become a Suicide Boy. You don't have to. You can gain more honors later, when you heal."

"But I don't want to wait. The biggest battle is soon to come, the battle that Sitting Bull saw in his vision. I want to be in that battle. I can't do it now."

"You can wait," Five Bulls insisted. "There will be other big battles. There always are."

"I would feel foolish if I stayed out of this battle," Red Bear said. "Besides, how do I know if I'll ever be able to fight from a pony again? Right now I can't even go for wood and water with the women."

"We'll have Horned Bull do a ceremony for you," Day Lily suggested. "His medicine is strong. He can make you well."

"I have nothing of worth to give him," Red Bear said. "I don't have many horses. I don't have anything, and I can't fight. I'm not worth anything to anyone."

Red Bear grabbed a crutch he had fashioned for himself. He struggled to his feet and limped away, Day Lily following after, weeping freely.

"I don't like to see him that way," Ghostwind said. "Day Lily has done what she can to help him."

"I remember when I first lived among the Cheyenne, after the battle on Powder River," Nighthawk said. "He really disliked me and didn't hide it at all. Then we grew to be friends. Now he's back to disliking me again, maybe even more than before."

"He's so upset that he doesn't know what he's saying," Five Bulls said. "He'll come around."

"I don't know," Nighthawk said. "He's angrier now."

"That was very hard on Day Lily," Ghostwind added. "She thought our friendship would end because Red Bear wanted nothing to do with you. Your name was Angry Heart then. Do you remember? Then you went up to the Yellowstone and stole horses from the Crows and the Bluecoats in the middle of the night, and got your new name."

"Maybe if Red Bear had gone along that time he would feel he had some honor now," Nighthawk said. "I don't know why he thinks he has to fight right away."

Mountain Water and Five Bulls had been listening intently. Mountain Water looked at Five Bulls and said, "Does this remind you of something? Do you remember the time I talked you out of becoming a Suicide Boy?"

"That was a long time ago. I wish I'd never wanted to do that."

"Think back on how you were feeling about things then," Mountain Water said. "You'd been injured in battle against the Pawnee and you didn't think you'd ever heal properly. I think it was your leg, too. Do you remember that?"

"Yes, it was my leg. I was hurt bad. An arrow had gone clear through and it burned like fire for a long time."

"Your leg healed and you went on more raids," Mountain Water said. "Red Bear could heal, too."

"That's what I was trying to tell him," Five Bulls said. "He'll heal in good time. He just wants to be part of the big battle Sitting Bull has foreseen. He doesn't have to do that."

"Maybe you should have told him that while he was here," Nighthawk said. "You should have told him that you had once wanted to die, like he does now. When he comes back you can tell him that, and then tell him how you changed your mind and how it was better for you in the end."

"*She* changed my mind." Five Bulls nudged Mountain Water with his elbow. "She talked me out of it. In fact, she did more than that."

Five Bulls went on to tell how Mountain Water had gotten him to go out in the hills with her, where they had spent the night together in a buffalo robe. While they had been gone, there had been a Suicide Dance in the camp. The next morning the Pawnee had attacked. The Suicide Boys had charged into the middle of the Pawnee and had all died fighting, enabling the rest of the Sioux warriors to surround the Pawnee and finish them off, to the last man.

"Had I been in the camp that night," Five Bulls said, "I would have danced and the next day I would have charged the Pawnee and died. I would have been thought of with honor, but I wouldn't have lived a full life."

"All those who danced charged and were killed?" Ghostwind asked. "Every one?"

"It's a pledge you make," Five Bulls explained. "You give yourself for the protection of the village. You know it will be a big fight, where the enemy wants to kill everyone. You give yourself in the battle so that the women and children may live and the people continue on.''

"I remember that day well,'' Mountain Water said. "When we got back to the village, the battle had just ended. The Pawnee were just leaving, what was left of them, riding over the hills as fast as they could. Dust was everywhere. Women were crying over their fallen, cutting up the dead Pawnee warriors. Many Lakota warriors died that day, but there would have been many more if it were not for the Suicide Boys.''

"It's good that you talked Five Bulls into going out into the hills with you,'' Ghostwind said. "Otherwise, I wouldn't have such a wonderful father today.''

"That's right,'' Mountain Water said. "I knew I couldn't find anyone so easy to boss around as him, so I didn't want him in the Suicide Dance.''

"She kept telling me that she knew how to take my mind off my sore leg,'' Five Bulls said with a smile. "I agreed that she could try and do that. It worked.''

"'It will be harder for Day Lily to keep Red Bear from the dance,'' Mountain Water said. "She can't get him out into the hills, no matter what she says. He couldn't go even if he wanted to. He can hardly make it around camp.''

"He can't dance if he can't stand up by himself,'' Nighthawk said. "Maybe we don't have to worry.''

"We have to worry, all right,'' Five Bulls said. "Red Bear is determined. If he has to, he'll just stand in place at the dance. That's a pledge, just the same as if he were dancing with the others. If he wants to bad enough, he'll be there, and he'll have his glory with the Suicide Boys. There's nothing we can do.''

SEVENTEEN

The eastern horizon was awash with crimson light. A gusty wind whipped from the west, drying the dew from the grass.

Red Moon awakened Garrett, smiling broadly. "I have a present. For you."

Garrett sat up in his bedroll and rubbed his eyes. He took the present from Red Moon's outstretched hand. A pocket watch. It read 5:00 A.M.

"Thank you, Red Moon. But why?"

"You will soon be my brother." He made sign as he spoke. "When the battle with the Sioux is finished. Then we'll have the ceremony." Garrett was amazed at Red Moon's vastly improved English.

Little Crane was kneeling beside Red Moon. The two had been up for well over an hour, preparing the horses for the day.

Little Crane said, "He's giving you a present now, just because he wants to. He's been practicing his English for a while now. You can probably tell. That's why he wasn't talking to you. He wanted to surprise you."

"Well, he sure did that," Garrett said. He examined the watch, gold-plated, with scrimshaw engraving on the back. He admired its gleam in the early sunlight.

"Where did you get it?" he asked Red Moon.

Red Moon pointed over into another camp, making sign about a game. "Don't know the white man words," he said.

Little Crane explained to Garrett. "He won it from another Ree scout in a hand game last night. You know, where you guess which hand the marked stick is in."

Garrett knew the game. He had watched it often in camp. Opponents took turns hiding two small sticks, one in each hand, one painted or notched. The object was to guess which hand held the marked stick.

"You should play it some day," Little Crane suggested. "You have medicine. You could win often." He laughed. "Do it before the Sioux take your fingers."

Garrett groaned, slipping from his bedroll. "Don't start with that again, Little Crane. It's much too early in the day."

The camp was already alive with activity. The soldiers were nearly ready for the day's march. The horses were being saddled, and the mules had already been packed.

"It will be a long day," Little Crane predicted. "The Crow scouts have gone already. They go far out ahead, to bring news of the Sioux and Cheyenne village."

"Are we that close already?" Garrett asked.

"No, we are far yet," Little Crane replied. "But there's much sign to be found, much to be learned about how the enemy is traveling and if they're preparing for battle."

"Do the Sioux and Cheyenne already know we're coming?"

"They have to believe Bluecoats are coming. That is sure. But maybe they don't know from what direction."

While the soldiers ate bacon and hardtack and swallowed coffee, Garrett's breakfast was gooseberries and fresh venison from a kill that Red Moon had made the night before. Red Moon had just finished cooking it. He handed it to Garrett on a stick.

"This ground gets harder every night," Garrett complained, accepting the meat. He sat with his back to the wind, trying to keep dust off his food.

Little Crane laughed. "Maybe you aren't tough like the other man-who-makes-the-paper-talk. See how hard he tries to get ready?"

Little Crane pointed over to where Mark Kellogg fumbled with his saddlebag, working to get his notes packed. He dropped a handful of paper and the wind scattered it everywhere.

"Oh, that's too bad," Garrett said. "His masterpiece on the General is headed into the four directions."

Little Crane smiled. "Why don't you help him? You could become his friend."

"No, I'm too savage for him."

"Maybe he should learn to be savage," Little Crane suggested. "Maybe he should ride a wild mule."

"Not that mule," Garrett said. "You couldn't get that old jenny to trot if you burned her butt with a torch. She's liable to die any minute."

"No," Little Crane said. "Not if you put this under the saddle."

Little Crane held up a burr that he had found along the river. It was the size of Garrett's thumbnail and very prickly.

"I suppose you had thought about putting that under *my* saddle," Garrett said.

"Oh, no." Little Crane shook his head vigorously, but he was grinning. "You're a good friend. And Red Moon would break my arm."

Garrett ran the burr between his fingers. "I suppose I should go help poor Kellogg round up his notes. I owe him that much. And I'll make sure his old mule doesn't go to sleep."

"Wake up mule," Red Moon said. "It's like a bee sting."

Garrett went over and began picking up Kellogg's loose papers, stuffing them into a saddlebag on the mule's back. Kellogg looked puzzled.

"Have you changed to a kinder fellow?" Kellogg asked, tightening his saddlebags. "Or do you just appreciate good literature and not want it lost?"

"It would be a shame to lose that valuable chronicle," Garrett said. "What would the world do?"

"You are a strange one, aren't you, Mr. Garrett," Kellogg said, preparing to mount. "I would rather think that you'd laugh at me, seeing me frantically chasing my work before it was scattered forever. But perhaps you've thought to become more civilized. I would hope so."

Garrett stepped back, and Kellogg climbed into the saddle. Kellogg had just raised his hand to salute in farewell when the mule flattened her ears and snorted. She lurched forward, taking Kellogg by surprise. Kellogg leaned backward, nearly falling off, putting even more pressure on the burr under the back of the saddle.

The mule snorted louder and lurched into a series of crow-hops that jostled Kellogg's hat loose. He bounced heavily in the saddle.

"Whoa!" he yelled, reaching up to hold his glasses in place. "Whoa! Please, whoa!"

The mule jumped sideways, flipping Kellogg to the ground. He landed on his hind end with a thump like a sack of wet flour, then rolled completely over in a backward somersault, his legs flailing, his coattails flying wildly.

The camp was roaring. Little Crane was rolling on the ground, laughing like a child. Red Moon was doubled over, laughing and crying at the same time.

Garrett caught Kellogg's mule and pulled the burr free. He dodged a quick kick from the mule's hind leg and led her over to Kellogg. At seeing Kellogg, the mule flattened her ears again and tried to pull away from Garrett. He settled her down, rubbing her neck gently.

Kellogg was on his feet, dusting himself off, his face a deep red.

"See what you've done," he told Garrett. He adjusted his crooked spectacles. "She won't even be civil now."

"Feed her a handful of oats," Garrett said, trying to stop laughing. "She'll forget all about it."

"I think you should ride her," Kellogg said. "That's what I think."

"Let's see how she is," Garrett said, climbing into the saddle. The mule flattened her ears again and started to buck, but Garrett held her head up and she settled down.

Garrett dismounted. "Sweet as honey, Mr. Kellogg."

Kellogg approached. "I believe the General will hear of this."

"Please don't tell on me," Garrett said. "I won't do it again. I promise. Can we be friends?"

Kellogg grabbed the reins. "I don't find you amusing, Mr. Garrett. You keep your distance. Do you understand?" The mule sidestepped away from Kellogg.

"You want me to help you up?" Garrett offered.

"You're really something, aren't you, Mr. Garrett?" Kellogg said. He began rubbing the mule's shoulder and neck, cooing, "Good girl. That man did it. I won't hurt you. That's it. That's a good girl." He struggled into the saddle and stayed on. In a moment Kellogg was gone, joining the troops falling in line for the day's march.

Red Moon brought Garrett's pony to him. Little Crane was already mounted.

"Are you ready for what is to come, Six Fingers?"

Garrett climbed on his pony. "I don't have a choice."

"You have a choice. We can turn around and ride away right now. No one would stop us."

"Are you asking me to give up now?" Garrett asked.

"I'm asking you to decide one way or the other," Little Crane said. "Your face is tight. Fear is eating at you. You wouldn't be a coward if you decided not to go any farther."

Garrett looked back down the Rosebud, along the twisting flow of water where a herd of deer was crossing, bounding into the timber that covered the red hills above the valley. To go back was so inviting. Going ahead seemed the most foolish choice he could ever make.

"Many of the scouts wonder if Custer and his Bluecoats are marked for death," Little Crane added. "The ghosts of those whose graves were destroyed are with us, dancing to war songs while we sleep."

Garrett watched lines of soldiers disappear around the bend of the stream. "There's no turning back now," he said, making sign. "I came to follow Long Hair and learn of his weaknesses. If I'm weaker than Long Hair, I have no right to make the paper talk about him. I must go on. Whatever comes, I must go on."

Evening, 23 June 1876
Rosebud Creek

Passed three deserted campsites today. Little Crane says that the camps show four hundred lodges, but that more will surely join Sitting Bull farther up the Rosebud.

Heard some of the men talking during supper about a cake packed on one of the mules. It seems that Lt. James Calhoun, Custer's brother-in-law, had one brought up on the steamboat for consumption after the battle with the Sioux. His preparations for celebration belie the test that awaits him.

Continual infighting among commanders. A lot of complaining about Tom Custer. Men are saying that he's very abusive and gets away with it because his brother's in command.

Custer sent Benteen on duty to help with the pack mules, which have been straggling behind. Benteen has just arrived in camp and is fit to be tied.

Custer becoming very moody. It seems that his personality changes with the wind. There has been talk among the soldiers about his short hair, that on every campaign before, he wore it long. When I asked him about it, he told me that he had it cut for Libbie before leaving. He said that she had had a dream in which a warrior was standing over him, holding up a scalp of long blonde hair. "I did it for her, so that she could rest easy," he told me. He seemed quiet and withdrawn.

I then asked him about facing so many warriors and he immediately turned gruff. He told me that he was tired of hearing that from everyone. He wanted the subject dropped. I suggested he consider talking with the Indians, demanding that they return to their reservations peacefully.

Custer told me that he didn't want to give them the opportunity to gather their things and run. He told me that if I wanted to write something about what was going to happen, I should be ready to fight. He said he had told me that in the beginning and nothing had changed. He gave me an unsettling, glassy stare, like one in a trance. He has his mind made up, there is no doubt. Maybe Little Crane is right in saying that Custer will ride to his death no matter what.

Want to write Ann in the worst way, but don't know what I'd say. I'm in a spot. She must be worried now, not having heard from me for so long. Yet I can't tell her that I have a feeling of impending doom. And I can't tell her that everything is going well. She knows me too well, and I'm afraid she could see it in my writing. Can't put anything over on her.

Is late but I will see if I can't find Major Reno before retiring. If I can substantiate Benteen's claim that Custer refused additional men for the campaign, it will be well worth noting to the Grants. Talking to Major Reno should be interesting to say the least.

At Reno's tent, Garrett found Reno's adjutant, Second Lieutenant Benjamin Hodgson, writing a letter. Hodgson rose and greeted Garrett.

"I'm looking for Major Reno," Garrett said. "I'd like to interview him tonight, if I could."

Hodgson, whom everyone called Bennie, was fun loving and well liked by all. His hair was dark and he wore a sweeping moustache.

"You're the writer with the Sioux scalp, aren't you?" Hodgson asked, smiling.

"Yes, I am."

"What business have you with the Major?"

"I'd like his thoughts on the campaign. I want to be thorough, you know."

"I thought you were the General's personal scribe."

"Personal scribe?"

Hodgson laughed. "I take it you don't confine yourself to the General solely."

"I'm trying to be more broad," Garrett said.

"You must be," Hodgson remarked. "You've already started killing Indians."

"It was him or me, Lieutenant."

"Very good," Hodgson said. "You'll soon have the chance to add to your collection. How does that sound to you?"

"It sounds like we'll have all the Indians we can handle, and possibly more," Garrett replied.

"You'll have your pick from over a thousand," Hodgson said. "If you've got a fast horse, you can catch them. In fact I'll challenge you: First one to shoot and scalp one of them collects five dollars from the other. How does that sound?"

"Why don't we make it ten?" Garrett said.

Hodgson laughed and clapped Garrett on the back. "It's your money. I'll be happy to take whatever you can afford."

"I've been interviewing the officers," Garrett said, "and I was wondering if the Major might be interested in talking to me."

"He told me if you showed up to send you to him." Hodgson pointed to the edge of camp. "You'll find him out with his horse."

Garrett thanked Hodgson and made his way to where the horses were on picket, grazing what scant grass they could find. Campfires burned here and there where troops on watch had gathered to talk. Soldiers were feeding their horses, and a number of the mule packers were preparing for the next day's work.

Garrett found Major Reno in the shadows, talking to a large chestnut gelding, holding a flask in his right hand. His voice was low and the tone rose and fell, as if he were airing his troubles. The horse lazily munched oats.

As Garrett approached, Reno turned, startled, hiding the flask behind him.

"Who goes there?" he demanded.

"Adam Garrett, the journalist. I understand you will grant me an interview."

Reno's boyish face was taut. He was of medium height and well built, with a dark moustache and streaks of gray in his dark hair. His eyes were pale blue, almost expressionless. He wore no hat and no uniform jacket.

"Mr. Garrett, is it necessary to do this now?" His words were slurred.

"No, sir, not if it's inconvenient for you. But I was hoping that I could talk to you before we meet the hostiles. I think that could be any day now. Perhaps tomorrow."

Reno turned to his horse and began rubbing its neck. "Tomorrow? Are you a scout, Mr. Garrett? I know that you dress like one, and I hear that you even fight Indians, but have you learned their tracking talents this quickly?"

"I just meant that the time was growing short, Major."

Reno took a drink and offered the flask to Garrett, who politely declined.

"I take it you're not a drinking man," Reno said.

"I tend to get moody if I drink while under pressure," Garrett said. "I partake during more festive times."

"I see." Reno laughed. "You don't consider this a festive time?"

"Not really, sir."

"Mr. Garrett, there is no more festive time than the present. You can look forward to riding into history with the Seventh. In but a few days this country will finally be rid of savages and safe for our fair citizens to travel through. It angers me deeply, though, that I won't be getting my fair share of the glory."

"I don't understand, Major."

Reno stepped over to a nearby cache of packs and supplies. He located a small wooden keg and refilled his flask. There were a number of such kegs arranged in a row on the ground. Garrett had seen them packed on the mules, but he hadn't known who had access to them.

Reno rustled in his saddlebags. He found a curry comb and returned to his horse. He held the flask out to Garrett.

"You sure you don't want a nip?"

"No thank you, Major."

Reno took a long drink. His voice was low and strained. "I, Mr. Garrett, am the only commander who knows what he's doing out here. But what is my reward? I've been exiled from my command."

"I don't understand."

"As a result of my terrible disobedience in gaining valuable reconnaisance information, I've been relieved of my command. You didn't know?"

"No, sir. I'm not very well informed, I'm sorry to say."

Reno began to comb his horse. "Well, you're not as sorry as I am. I should have gone after the Indians on my own, when I had the chance. They were just a way up Rosebud Creek, well within my grasp. I thought very seriously about going after them, don't you know?

"However, my scouts convinced me that the hostile force was much too formidable. Had I the decision to make over again, I would disregard their advice. As we now know, the Indian ranks have swelled considerably, with agency bands coming out all the time. I knew that to be true when I was leading my men on reconnaisance. I could have gotten it done myself. I wish now I had that day back again."

"But why would they relieve you of command?"

"It was Custer's doing, don't you see? He's afraid that someone else might take the honors in subduing the hostiles. He can't have that, you know."

"It doesn't sound like the General has been all that fair."

"Mr. Garrett, nobody ever accused that man of being fair. He doesn't know the meaning of the word. He might be an able commander, to a point, but he's no humanitarian." Reno pressed his fingers between the chestnut's ribs and shook his head. "He's losing weight. All the horses are going downhill. I sure hope we find some grass soon. The oats alone won't keep them going."

"Let me get to the reason I came to see you," Garrett said. "I need to substantiate a statement made to me by Captain Benteen last night."

"A statement about me?" Reno asked. "Benteen would say anything about me. Don't you believe a word of it."

"No, Major, it concerns the officers meeting called by General Custer the night before last. Captain Benteen told me of General Custer's reluctance to accept the services of the Sixth Cavalry. I need to know if, indeed, General Custer turned down additional soldiers for this march.''

Reno pulled hair from the curry comb, teetering slightly. ''Of course I know that he did. However, I heard it secondhand, as did Captain Benteen. No one else was present when Custer and Brisbin talked. So you can't make a case out of that, I'm afraid.''

''All I need to do is show that a number of officers know that the General turned down additional men. This constitutes very poor judgment on the General's part, wouldn't you agree?''

''Mr. Garrett, there has never been a time in George Armstrong Custer's bastardly life when he didn't exercise inexcusably poor judgment. Time after time he has caused undue hardship on others, yet we both see where he is today, don't we? We both see that *he's* the commanding officer, making all the decisions and setting himself up for the presidency.''

Garrett said, ''If you don't think he belongs in Washington, then you can help me.''

Reno turned. ''I won't have you quoting me, Mr. Garrett. I have a career to consider, you know. But you'd better get more than Benteen to testify for you. He's damned unreliable.'' Reno began combing tangles from his horse's mane. ''However, if you can get a number of officers and men here to sign something, I might reconsider. But you've got to have something very solid, and Custer's turning down Brisbin and his men won't do it.''

''You said yourself that Custer used poor judgment, that the extra men would have been of great benefit.''

''There's more to it than that, Mr. Garrett. Major Brisbin is sorely lacking in combat experience, and he also suffers terribly from rheumatism. When the weather was rainy, he spent much of the time during his march with Gibbon in an ambulance. You can't expect Custer to wait for an ambulance on this campaign, now can you?''

''Captain Benteen didn't mention that.''

''Captain Benteen hates Custer to the point where he will ignore a lot of facts completely. I wouldn't put it past him to strip down and paint himself up when the battle begins, and join with the hostiles.''

"But what about the additional men?"

"I don't know if Brisbin just offered his men and said he wouldn't go, or not. But I would imagine he would want to lead his own command, wouldn't you say? It doesn't matter now. We're without them. That's not an issue. The Seventh can do it alone, anyway." Reno went to combing knots from his horse's tail.

"I need facts to print about Custer," Garrett said. "I can't do it alone."

Reno took a drink and smacked his lips. "Mr. Garrett, far better men than you have tried relentlessly to knock Custer down, but to no avail. They have looked high and low for ways to undo him. Still, he manages to snake his way out of things." Reno was combing his horse with great energy. "However, this time you may have something on him."

"What would that be?" Garrett asked.

"Custer has taken civilians along on this campaign, in direct violation of a general order issued from department headquarters a year ago."

"You're talking about his younger brother, Boston, and his nephew, Autie Reed?" Garrett asked.

"Yes, of course," Reno replied. "Boston is listed on the quartermaster's rolls as 'forage master' and Autie is a 'quartermaster's employee.' Ridiculous! Insubordination is what it is."

Garrett was writing. "Why did General Terry allow it?"

"You're asking me?" Reno said. "You should have asked him back on the Yellowstone."

"I wish I'd been aware of it then," Garrett said. "I haven't had much to use, and I can't get anyone to vouch for anything."

Reno took another drink. "I don't know why we're bothering with this. It's too late now for anything, you see. The campaign is too far along. Custer foolishly believes he already has his glory. He's headed downhill, don't you know, and he won't be stopped, he thinks."

"I don't think it's too late," Garrett said. "If we handle it right, it's not too late."

Reno turned, leaning on his horse. He raised the flask toward Garrett's face. "I suggest to you, Mr. Reporter Man, that no matter the facts you obtain and substantiate, George Armstrong Custer is going to come out smelling like a rose. He always has. He always will. And you'd better be sure that he doesn't know what you're up to here. I've seen what he can do to a man who gets out of line."

"But I'm not on the army rolls. General Terry made that very clear."

"Is that so, Mr. Garrett?" Reno said. His voice was hard. "In case you've not been apprised, General Terry is not here. Custer is in command. *Everyone* here is under his control. He thinks he owns the birds in the sky. Surely he must have made that clear to you already."

"Yes, as a matter of fact he did."

Reno's face changed, his lips forming an odd smile. "I'll let you in on a little secret, Mr. Garrett. What the good General believes will happen and what will actually happen are two different things."

"What do you mean, Major?"

Reno's smile faded. "The battle is not going to be his, as he believes so strongly. No, not on your life. There are those who will see to that. I can promise you, Mr. Garrett."

"Could you explain that to me, Major?" Garrett asked.

Reno's eerie smile returned. "I would suggest, Mr. Garrett, that you take your pencil and paper and, when the time is right, find yourself a hill. From there, watch the battle and record whose command it is that wins the day. Be detailed, Mr. Garrett, so that the people reading your account will know who the real hero is. I can guarantee you that, one way or another, it won't be Custer. Not this time. It won't be Custer."

EIGHTEEN

The flames were whirling streaks of crimson rising into the night sky. It was hard to breathe. Garrett stood with the wall of fire in front of him, his feet rooted to the ground. The sea of red approached like a rolling tide. Garrett screamed.

Suddenly the fire broke before him and a huge black circle appeared. The fire rolled around the perimeter of the black circle, forming a huge ring of flame. The wall of red, with the black hole in the middle, continued to close in on Garrett, encircling him.

Garrett stared into the black hole. It was the only way out. But he couldn't make his feet move.

Don't be a coward! Come through the circle!

The words boomed like thunder in Garrett's head. Standing in the circle was the buffalo, shining white, staring at him.

What are you waiting for?

". . . I don't understand," Garrett managed.

Why must you understand? I'm telling you to come through the hole, to save yourself. That's all you need to know.

The circle began to draw shut, the flames spiraling inward. The perimeter of fire around Garrett drew ever closer.

Hurry! You haven't much time!

The hole grew smaller and smaller. The buffalo, shining white, stepped back.

"Wait!" Garrett yelled. "Wait for me!"

* * *

Garrett awakened with a yell and sat up in his bedroll. There was a hand on his shoulder.

"Can you hear me?" It was Red Moon. "Have you come back?"

Garrett was covered with sweat. He couldn't control his shaking, so he held his arms together across his chest.

"What happened?"

"The spirits are talking to you," Red Moon said. His face was stoic. "They come to help you."

The camp was in darkness, with only a faint light showing in the east. Little Crane kneeled close by, adding wood to a fire.

"It's cold," Red Moon said. "Stay covered."

Garrett lay back down. The air felt heavy on him. He reached out, expecting the ground to be hot from the fire. Instead, he felt grass cold with dew.

Little Crane spoke from the fire, filling a bowl with broth from a kettle. "The days are hot, the nights cold in this country. When we reach the divide, we will see fog in the morning."

Red Moon took the bowl from Little Crane. He returned to Garrett's side.

"Sit up."

Garrett sat up and took the bowl. "Thank you. I can feed myself."

He drank from the bowl, a hot broth made from roots and antelope meat. "Sorry, Red Moon," he said. "I didn't mean to snap at you."

Red Moon had no English for what he wanted to say. He made sign. Little Crane filled in what Garrett couldn't understand.

"He's telling you," Little Crane said, "that dreams and visions can make a person angry. Visions are hard on your mind. They sometimes cannot be understood, and you just have to live with them, wondering what you're seeing." He handed Red Moon a bowl of broth.

"I thought you said you'd find someone who could help me," Garrett told Little Crane. "What happened to that?"

Little Crane filled a bowl for himself and sat cross-legged in front of the fire. "It can't be just anyone. It has to be someone with a certain kind of medicine. I haven't found anyone yet."

"Why can't you help me?"

Little Crane looked into the fire. "I can't see what you see. I can only see my own visions. Maybe they're not the same, maybe they are. I cannot tell you what's inside of you. That's for you to learn. And it will come."

Garrett threw the bowl down, splashing the rest of his broth into the grass. He put on his buckskin shirt and pulled on his boots. Little Crane and Red Moon stared into the fire.

"I don't think either of you care at all," Garrett said. "Do you?"

Red Moon turned. His eyes were tender and slightly misty. "You're my brother. I *do* care."

Garrett walked away, past the horses, to the edge of the stream. The light in the east had turned to pink, laced with crimson. He sat just back from the water, in front of rose bushes filled with delicate blossoms.

The water rushed past, pushing through the valley toward the Yellowstone. Garrett took a deep breath, trying to release his anger and frustration. What were all these dreams about? Was he really about to die?

It wasn't fair not to know one way or the other. Sitting in the middle with no knowledge of the future was maddening. And seeing the fire and the white buffalo only complicated things.

"You can't run from it, or wish it to go away." Little Crane knelt beside him. "Let the spirits help you."

"Did you stop to think that maybe I wanted to be alone?" Garrett asked.

Little Crane stood up. "I came only to invite you to our sunrise prayers." He turned to leave.

"Wait," Garrett said. "I'm sorry. I'd like to go with you."

Garrett followed Little Crane and Red Moon to a hill at the edge of camp, along a trail that passed through juniper and yellow pines cooled from the night breezes.

The red rock buttes above the valley shone brilliant in the new light.

At the top of the hill, Garrett stood facing east with Little Crane and Red Moon. From a skin bag, Little Crane took a small pipe made of wood and red stone, with a red, black, and white design painted on the stem.

Little Crane filled the pipe with tobacco and lit it. Smoke curled from his mouth and nose, rising into the morning sky. He spoke softly in Arikara, lifting the pipe to the sky, then lowering it toward the ground, then turning to the four directions.

"Do as I have done," Little Crane instructed Garrett. "Say a prayer of your choosing, either aloud or to yourself."

Garrett repeated Little Crane's movements with the pipe, feeling awkward yet uplifted. "If I'm to die," he said, "please forgive me for my offenses against others. And help Ann survive my passing. If I'm to live, I promise to be faithful to you." Garrett thought a moment. Hadn't he been being faithful? What had made him say that? Fear. He was reaching a level of fear that he had never known before.

With nothing else to say, Garrett handed the pipe to Red Moon, who took it and began his own prayers. He felt foolish. Little Crane and Red Moon were so relaxed in their manner. They knew how to pray, Garrett concluded. They did so day in and day out, whether their fortunes were good or bad. Why hadn't he learned to pray when times were good?

When Red Moon had finished, Little Crane took the pipe and cleaned it. He placed it into the skin bag and, with Red Moon, sat down in the grass, cross-legged, instructing Garrett to do the same.

"See, the sun is rising," Little Crane told Garrett. "It's time to give thanks for life and to ask for protection during the day."

Little Crane and Red Moon began an Arikara sunrise song. Garrett listened, watching the sun's rim top the horizon, sending a burst of golden light across the hills. In the distance, a lone buffalo bull climbed a hill and began rubbing against a pine. Garrett leaned forward, thinking the bull was white. It was only the morning sunshine, he concluded.

When the song was finished, the three rose and started back for camp. Everyone was awake, preparing for another day.

At the creek's edge, Garrett looked into the sky. A half dozen crows were gliding down from the timber, cawing as they prepared to land in a dead cottonwood.

"Those birds really bother me," Garrett told Little Crane. "I see them everywhere."

"No need to dislike them," Little Crane said, walking toward the horses. "They don't make the laws, they just bring the news."

"The news?"

"They cross back and forth from this world into the Spirit World. For those in this world who listen and can understand them, they bring the news. They know what's coming."

Garrett tightened the cinch on his saddle and unhobbled his pony. "I've only seen them where there's death. On the battlefields."

"They've been to many battles, that's true," Little Crane said. "But they're always around, whether or not there's death."

Red Moon climbed on his pony and added, "Crows always around. Maybe you see them, maybe not. Always around."

"They're messengers," Little Crane said. "They have business in different places."

"Do you think they're here now because of death?" Garrett asked.

Little Crane mounted his pony. "Why don't you ask them? They'll tell you. They're loud and they talk roughly, but they never lie. Listen to them and wait for another dream."

"I don't want any more dreams." Garrett climbed into the saddle. "I've had enough of them."

"Oh, but they know that you're a dreamer," Little Crane said. He laughed. "Use your medicine fingers and write what your dreams say to you. You can never tell. Maybe you'll soon be talking in bird language.''

The morning was open; the sky a deeper blue than any Ann could ever remember seeing. But she was restless, anxious to renew her search for Adam, and time was of the essence.

They had been forced to remain in camp for the past two days; Lareaux had taken a high fever. He had gone in and out of delirium. Lareaux wanted to go on, but Tyrone and Water had both agreed that he could die if he didn't wait until the fever broke.

The fever had broken the previous evening, at the same time Water had returned from a scouting mission, announcing that a large soldier camp lay just downriver. Ann had been ecstatic and had seriously considered going ahead herself, but darkness had fallen and the men persuaded her that there could be danger in approaching the soldier camp by night.

Tyrone was hoping that Lareaux wouldn't have to lose his leg. Cauterizing the wound thoroughly had stopped infection and sealed off the blood vessels. There had been a lot of swelling, but no excess drainage from the slit Tyrone had left open. All three men had seen a number of knife wounds, and Lareaux's, for all its severity, seemed to be healing.

Lareaux was not anxious to surrender himself to army surgeons. ''They'll take my leg for something to do,'' he had told Tyrone. ''You can all go in. I'll wait out along the river.''

''We've given you some roots, but we don't have the medicines they do,'' Tyrone had argued. ''You can't keep up with us until your leg is healing well.''

''It'll heal well while I ride,'' Lareaux had said. ''*Oui!* It will heal well while I ride.''

Tyrone and Lareaux had argued back and forth the entire evening. Water had spent his time outside of camp, watching the horses and listening in the darkness. Ann, of course, was thinking of Adam, while Tyrone and Lareaux's voices droned beside her.

This delay frazzled her nerves even more, and learning that Adam might be just ahead, and her not traveling toward him, had made her crazy. Tyrone had seen it.

"We'll find him, Miss Ann," he said. "I know we will. You've just got to hold onto your faith."

"I know," Ann told him. "Thank you for your consideration, Tyrone. We'll find him tomorrow. He won't have left by then."

Ann hadn't slept the entire night, tossing and turning, often getting up to pace. Now, with the sun climbing, she was more than eager to get going.

"It's time we get you upriver," Lareaux told her as he waited for Tyrone to bring him his horse. "I've cost you enough time already."

"Nonsense. You shouldn't worry about it," Ann said. "Everything's fine."

"Had I been watching, it wouldn't have happened. She wouldn't have cut me. *Non,* she wouldn't have *touched* me. We'd have reached the soldiers by now and, *oui,* you would be with your man."

"Soon enough," Ann said.

Tyrone arrived with the horses. Water was sitting his pony on a nearby hill, watching in all directions, waiting. The Sioux scalps hung from his knife belt.

"I hope he don't spot no more of them Sioux," Lareaux said. "At least not until we get close to the soldiers."

Tyrone had fashioned a cane for Lareaux from an ash branch. Lareaux frowned.

"What's that?"

"Take it," Tyrone said. "You'll get around better."

"Is that why you were measuring me last night?"

"Yes," Tyrone said. "Here. Take it."

Lareaux took the cane and tested it. "I'd just as soon not have it," Lareaux said.

"You'll heal faster if you don't put a lot of pressure on your leg," Tyrone said. "The surgeons may want to keep you down, but if you have a cane they might not worry so much."

"What makes you think they would worry anyway?"
Lareaux asked.

"It's their job," Tyrone said.

"Maybe," Lareaux said. "Let's get upriver."

Tyrone moved to help Lareaux onto his horse.

"Back away from me, Tyrone," Lareaux bellowed.
"I'm no child. *Non*, no child."

Tyrone said, "If you fall off, it won't be me that picks
you up."

"I like it that way," Lareaux said. "*Oui!* Very
much!" He struggled into the saddle, groaning. "If I
don't stay on, just leave me for the wolves."

Tyrone helped Ann onto her horse. "Lareaux," he
said, "there's not a wolf on these plains that would touch
you. You'd just have to lie there and wonder."

Water rode down from the hill and joined them. They
rode slowly, so that Lareaux would not aggravate his
wound any more than necessary. It was nearly noon when
they reached the mouth of Tongue River, where infantry
soldiers guarded a large cache of military supplies.

"I don't like this," Lareaux said. "I say we turn and
ride away."

"Be patient," Tyrone said. "You need medical attention. And, more important, would you deprive Miss Ann
of her chance to find Adam?"

"He's not here! *Non*, not here!" Lareaux said with
disgust. "Are you blind, Tyrone? They're foot soldiers,
not cavalry. Surely you can see that for yourself."

Five soldiers mounted on mules rode out to meet them.
They spread themselves into a line and reined their
mules, their hands on their pistols.

The leader wore a sergeant's stripes. He addressed Tyrone. "Please state your business here, sir." The other
four soldiers stared at Ann.

"We've come out from Fort Lincoln," Tyrone said.

"Fort Lincoln?" the sergeant said. "That's a long way
from here."

"Yes," Tyrone said. "If you'd let me explain."

"Why wouldn't a lady travel by steamboat?" one of

the soldiers asked. "That's more suited, I would say."

"It was my choice to ride," Ann said. "I thought it would be much faster. And it's proven to be the case."

The sergeant tipped his hat. "Yes, ma'am. I'm Sergeant Arthur Sinclair, at your service, ma'am."

Sinclair was young and brimming with arrogance. His hair and complexion were light; the sun had brought out heavy freckles on his face and neck.

"I'm in search of my fiancé, Sergeant Sinclair," Ann continued. "He's a journalist named Adam Garrett, attached to General George Custer's unit. Does he happen to be in camp?"

"I don't remember a Mr. Garrett, ma'am," Sinclair replied. "But General Custer left this supply depot a good time back. He and General Terry moved upriver and had plans to go south. They're likely fighting Indians by now. Maybe they've even whipped them already."

"I see," Ann said. "Is there any way you might direct me toward the route they took?"

"You sure your fiancé was with them?"

"Yes. I'd like to find him as soon as possible."

Two of the soldiers snickered. Sinclair turned and glared at them. He turned back to Ann. "It might be advisable to wait for his return."

Lareaux leaned over toward Tyrone. "I told you this was a bad idea," he said.

"Relax," Tyrone said. "Everything's fine."

"It's not fine," Water said. "Lareaux was right. We should have gone around them."

Tyrone glared at them. "Enough!" he said in a harsh whisper. The soldiers, unable to hear what had been said, began to eye Lareaux and Water.

"I should think," Sinclair was saying, "that Generals Terry and Custer should be returning very soon. And certainly with a victory. I can assure you every hospitality until their arrival."

"I'd rather not wait, Sergeant," Ann said. "If it's all the same to you."

"I'm not authorized to allow you to go on," Sinclair said.

"You're not authorized to stop us in the first place," Ann said.

"*Oui!* That is right!" Lareaux said. "You have no business telling us what to do. You don't own this land!"

Sinclair and the other soldiers stiffened.

"Please!" Tyrone said, glaring at Lareaux. He turned back to Sinclair. "Please pardon him."

"Don't pardon me!" Lareaux said.

"He's in pain and he's speaking out of his head," Tyrone said. "Could we have a surgeon look at his leg? He recently sustained a rather nasty knife wound."

"One thing at a time," Sinclair said. "Addressing the matter at hand once again, I cannot allow you to pass on, not without a proper escort. And I don't know if we can spare the men at this time."

"This is free land!" Lareaux yelled. "None of you has any say over us. What makes you think that you do?"

Sinclair pulled his pistol and cocked it. "You, sir, will listen while I ask the questions." The other soldiers drew their weapons as well. Sinclair smiled at Tyrone. "You have a troublemaker with you, it would seem."

"Sergeant, none of this is necessary," Ann said. "We don't need any misunderstandings."

"Ma'am, I must insist that you submit to my authority," Sinclair said. "I can't let you roam free in this area, not with hostile Indians around."

"You're not responsible for me," Ann said. "You don't have to provide an escort for us. We didn't have one when we left Fort Lincoln."

"This is far more dangerous country, ma'am."

Ann continued to argue. "We chose to come out here. We can choose to go on in the same manner."

"I must disagree," Sinclair said. "It's my duty to protect this country's citizens. It doesn't seem to me that a lady of your obvious standing should be traveling with the likes of these three. Not of her own volition, anyway. Had you not spoken up earlier, I might have thought you a prisoner."

"That's nonsense, Sergeant," Ann said. "I told you before, I chose them to guide me out here."

"Whatever the case, ma'am," Sinclair said. "I'm going to have to take you and these men into custody until we have the entire matter straightened out."

Water suddenly kicked his pony into a dead run. Riding low over its back, Water turned it sharply, in zigzag patterns, heading over a hill.

One of the soldiers asked permission to give chase.

"Denied!" Sinclair barked. "We'll pursue him later. Fall into position. We'll escort the lady and the other two in."

Tryone had ridden close to Lareaux and was holding his hand so that he wouldn't pull his pistol.

"Don't be a fool!" Tyrone said. "They'll kill us all. That wouldn't be fair to Miss Ann."

"He's right," Ann said. "We'll find a way out of this. Just be patient."

"Sergeant Sinclair," Tyrone said, "I'm going to insist that we speak with your commanding officer."

"You'll have your chance to speak when the time is right, sir," Sinclair said. "For now, I would suggest that you do as you're ordered. If you will all follow me, please."

Sinclair led out and the other four soldiers fell into place at the sides and rear. Tyrone released his grip on Lareaux's hand. Ann rode forward and Lareaux took a deep breath.

"By the blood of Christ," he said, "we've been made prisoners."

NINETEEN

The column was a long line of blue twisting its way up the Rosebud. Custer rode in the lead, his two sergeants close behind, bearing the flags. Mitch Boyer and two of the Crows, Curley and Half-Yellow-Face followed. The other four had left camp early to scout ahead. Custer's staghounds remained on leash with John Burkman, Custer's orderly, who had cared for them ever since Bloody Knife's outburst two nights ago. It was apparent that Custer had taken Bloody Knife seriously and worried about the hostiles learning of the march, giving them the opportunity to strike their lodges and scatter.

Mitch Boyer, the son of a French trader and a Sioux mother, was known among the Crows as Two Bodies, because of his two heritages. He had married a Crow woman named Magpie Outside and was subsequently adopted by the Crow people. He was related by clan affiliation to Curley, whom he called Little Brother, and Curley's older brother, White Swan.

Among the Rees, he was called Man-With-the-Calfskin-Vest. Because of past differences with the Sioux, the Rees weren't particularly fond of him. They respected him, but felt no need to adore him, in the manner of the Crow scouts. Bloody Knife, who was favored by Custer, often felt the need to tell Boyer that his position was higher.

Boyer cared little about his popularity, good or bad. Instead, he had been concentrating on the campaign and was growing ever more uneasy. He had consented to scout in the belief that his advice would be taken by Long Hair Custer, who wanted to destroy the Sioux and Chey-

enne even more than he did. But Custer hadn't listened
to any of his advice, even from the beginning. It seemed
to Boyer that Custer had made his mind up about attacking the village even before starting up the Rosebud.

As they rode, Boyer recalled earlier times when he had
been in this country hunting or scouting for campsites.
Those days had been good. The coming days were going
to be the worst of his life.

He had felt this ever since turning up the Rosebud. His
medicine was leaving him. He wondered how he might
get it back. Curley, whose medicine was strong, had told
him to turn back, to let the six Crows do the work for
Long Hair. But Boyer had given his promise to see the
campaign through. He would stay and fight.

What bothered Boyer the most was the fact that the
Sioux and Cheyenne could be beaten, if all the Bluecoats
worked together as they were supposed to. Not once during the march had Boyer felt that Custer cared at all about
the other commands. In fact, Custer had totally ignored
them, despite orders to stay in contact with them, especially General Terry.

Now they were drawing ever nearer the hostiles. Boyer
wanted to see if he couldn't once again persuade Custer
to think about bringing all the Bluecoats together to fight
the Sioux and Cheyenne, so the odds might be more
even.

"I've talked a long time with my brothers, the Crow
scouts," he told Custer as they rode. "They've been out
and they've seen where the camps have been. You know
this. They've talked with you about it. When are you
going to send the courier to General Terry, so he will
know what's ahead of him?"

"Mitch, you worry about the scouting, I'll give the
commands," Custer said. "It sounds to me like you're
afraid to fight."

"That's not true!" Boyer snapped. "But I don't believe in a foolish fight."

"The Seventh has never fought a foolish fight," Custer
said. "The Seventh has never been beaten. That's the
way it's been and that's the way it will always be. I have

some good boys fighting for me, Mitch. I wish that you were one of them.''

''There are good times to fight,'' Boyer said, ''and there are times that aren't good, when the medicine says to go and leave things as they are. I've tried to talk to you before about that. Do you remember?''

''Mitch, my medicine is always good. I never have to worry about that.''

''But it's foolish to take a chance when you don't have to,'' Boyer persisted. ''I've heard Six Fingers Garrett say to you that the Sioux and Cheyenne might give themselves up to you, if you went to talk with them. Maybe he has a good idea. He has taken a scalp, so he can fight. But maybe his idea of talking is good.''

''I have no time for talk, Mitch,'' Custer said. ''My boys are chomping at the bit for battle. So am I. Besides, the Sioux don't want to talk. They'll stall while some of them come out, and the others will sneak around and snipe at us from all angles. I'm not going to let that happen. I'm ready to give it to them.''

''How do you know that the Sioux don't want to talk?'' Boyer asked.

''There's no sense in discussing it any longer,'' Custer said. ''Turn around and go home, Mitch, if you can't fight like a man.''

Boyer took a deep breath. ''Maybe you'll learn something up ahead,'' he said. ''You remember the scalps that my brothers brought to you last night? Don't forget them, because you'll see more. Very soon.''

Custer laughed. ''I'm not afraid of scalps, Mitch. There'll never be an Indian that will take mine.''

''Never is a hard word to live with,'' Boyer said. ''My brothers told you of a Sun Dance camp up ahead. When we get there, we'll see if the Sioux and Cheyenne think the same as you.''

''What do you mean by that?''

''You think they'll run. That's all you know, that they'll run. My brothers have told me the sign they've read, and it doesn't have to do with running.''

Boyer left Custer. He joined Curley and Half-Yellow-

Face. They were riding up a hill, looking across the country.

"Once again you're angry," Half-Yellow-Face said. "You've been talking to Long Hair. You shouldn't do that. It always turns out the same."

"You're right," Boyer said. "I wish I'd never consented to scout this time. I wanted a victory, but there can't be one if Long Hair thinks with a crazy mind." He looked at Curley. "What do you think, Little Brother?"

"I stay away from Long Hair if I can," Curley said. "When I first heard him speak about chasing the Sioux, even if he had to eat mule, I liked him. I thought he was a great leader for saying that. But I know now that he says things to make everyone follow him and do what he wants. He doesn't mean a lot of it. I think he really dislikes Indian people down underneath."

"He needs us to show him where the village is," Half-Yellow-Face said. "If he knew this country as well as we do, he wouldn't bother with us."

"He won't bother with us when the fight is over," Curley said. "I wish that wasn't so, but it is."

"We told Long Hair that we'd scout for him," Boyer said. "So we will. I just hope when this big fight is over we can all go home and tell the stories to everyone. Then, when the Sioux and Cheyenne are out of our country, life will be good again. That would be nice, to have life good again."

The morning grew warm, promising intense heat later in the day. The men were tired and there was little talking in the ranks. Custer remained in the lead, waiting for the return of the four Crows he had sent out. Curley and Half-Yellow-Face remained near the front and Mitch Boyer rode off by himself.

The only other change was that Lieutenant Varnum had selected some of the Ree scouts and was a short distance ahead, searching for the Sun Dance camp. The rest of the Rees kept to the flanks, as they had from the beginning.

Garrett rode with Little Crane and Red Moon along

the hills west of the column. Little Crane had wanted to be up from the valley floor, in case a large war party was lying in wait somewhere along the way.

"You're more nervous than I am," Garrett commented. "With all you've said to me, you ought to take your own advice."

"I'm no good at that," Little Crane said. "I want this to be over, and it's just beginning."

Varnum's scouts appeared, racing their ponies excitedly, pointing ahead. Watching them from the hills, Little Crane commented, "We've reached the Sun Dance village."

Over a ridge was a large flat that ran from the Rosebud up toward the hills. The Sioux and Cheyenne had camped all along the flat, but the village was deserted now.

At the near end of the flat Custer called a halt and began examining the area with his scouts. They counted lodge circles and searched the ground carefully for clues to the strength of the village.

Garrett remained with Little Crane and Red Moon, who took him to where the Sun Dance had been held. Garrett studied the lodge, a giant circle of planted poles over ten feet high, hewn from ash trees stripped of their branches, with shallow forks at the top. The circle was over a hundred and fifty feet across, large enough to accommodate over a hundred dancers. Garrett sat his horse, listening to Little Crane explain the meaning of what he was seeing.

"The Sun Dance is very sacred. Some call it the Medicine Lodge ceremony. All the Plains Indian tribes worship in a similar way. The dances may be a little different, but it's always to honor all life, to thank the Creator for giving us the sun every day, and with the sun, the water and the food that keep us alive. It is a renewal of another season where the grass greens once again, feeding the buffalo. The Earth Mother is cherished for her goodness and Father Sky is looked upon with wonder, for that's where the Great Mystery lives."

In the center was a large cottonwood, nearly forty feet high, also stripped of its branches, with two forks left about two-thirds of the way up the tree, complete with leaves and branches.

"That's the tree of life, where good things come," Little Crane explained. "A tree is very sacred. It reaches far down into the earth and also touches the sky. A tree unites everything together. That's why a cottonwood is used for the center pole.

"They are gone now, but two flags were tied to that cottonwood, one blue and one white. These are the two sides of everything: dark and light. It is up to the sponsor of the dance to order how the dance will begin and end. It is according to his vision."

He pointed to the ash trees. "During the dance there were long poles in the forks that were tied to the center pole. These are also gone now. After the ceremony is finished, the center pole is often chopped down, when a certain number of days have passed. Sometimes it stays up. Sometimes all the poles around the outside are removed. Sometimes they stay. It's up to the sponsor of the dance, according to what he's seen in his vision."

Garrett noticed a passageway constructed of ash poles leading from the west end of the main lodge to four small, dome-shaped lodges made of willows. Little Crane explained that they had been covered with buffalo robes, now taken off, revealing the ribs of the lodges.

"Those are sweat lodges," Little Crane said. "Sweat baths are taken every morning and every evening for purification. The dancers usually spend four nights in the lodge. Sometimes only three, depending on the sponsor. They dance to drums and sacred songs, and blow on eagle bone whistles, calling for their prayers to be carried into the sky on wings, to reach the Creator. The dancers go without food or water. Sometimes the sponsor will allow a swallow of tea after the morning sweat bath, or at some other time, depending on his vision."

"No food or water?"

"The body must be open, empty, so that a vision can come. When the time is right, the piercing takes place." He pointed to numerous scars on both sides of his chest, just above the breast, and also to scars on his back.

Garrett had thought they were battle scars. He studied Little Crane's scars, smooth circles of flesh the size of thumbnails, where the pierced skin had healed.

"During the ceremony," Little Crane explained, "the dancers are cut and skewers are placed under the skin and muscles. The dancers are then tied to the center pole by two long rawhide ropes, one attached to each skewer. They must dance and pull the skewers through their skin. Some are drawn up on the pole by having skewers put in their chest and back at the same time. These warriors have to shake themselves free."

Garrett stared at Little Crane. "What would you do that for? I can see the fasting, but why torture yourselves?"

"A man has only his body to offer to the Creator," Little Crane said. "Going through pain is a way of telling the Creator that we are giving ourselves to Him, that we have faith in Him and are not afraid to surrender our bodies. We offer the pain to Him to say that we are sorry for our bad deeds and that we are praying for good to come."

"That takes a lot of faith," Garrett said.

"And there are rewards for that faith," Little Crane said. "Many dancers are run over by the buffalo and receive visions that help them in their lives and help their people."

"What do you mean 'run over by the buffalo'?" Garrett asked, thinking again of his dream. "Is this part of the vision?"

"It's the beginning of the vision," Little Crane replied. "The buffalo comes from the spirit world to the dancer. When the dancer keeps dancing, the buffalo charges, and the dancer goes down, falling into a vision. They see something like what you saw in your dream. It's a very special thing. Every dancer wants that."

"It seems like a hard religion to me," Garrett commented.

"Isn't it the same as the white man's religion?" Little Crane asked. "The Black Robes say that a man came from the Creator as His son in a faraway land and suffered for the people, so that they might have good things come to them. The Christ, he is called?''

"Yes," Garrett replied. "Jesus Christ is the man you speak of.''

"I hear the Bluecoats saying the name," Little Crane said. "Sometimes out loud, when yelling at the mules or horses. The whispers come from Bluecoats who sit or kneel and have a necklace with a cross that has the Christ on it, hanging in death. They finger this necklace while they pray.''

"It's called a rosary," Garrett said. "There are a lot of Catholic soldiers. A rosary is a common method of praying among Catholics.''

"Yes, I saw the rosaries often as a child," Little Crane said. "The Black Robes had them, big ones tied around their waists. But I didn't stay at the Black Robe lodges, where they wanted to teach our children. My parents wouldn't allow it.''

Garrett knew that all missionaries, not just the Catholics, were trying to get the Indians to give up their own religion and adopt Christianity. The thought came to him that the white mans' civilization couldn't tolerate a religion it couldn't understand, especially one that included a ceremony like the Sun Dance.

Garrett wondered how Little Crane could compare the Sun Dance to Christianity.

"I don't know how you see Christ as a Sun Dancer," he said to Little Crane.

"Didn't Jesus Christ teach that the earth was sacred and that all life was part of the Creator?''

"Yes, he did teach that.''

"And didn't he teach that all men should love one another as brothers?''

"Yes.''

"That's what a Sun Dancer believes.''

"Yes, but Sun Dancers live through the ceremony," Garrett argued. "Christ died on a cross. He was tortured to death.''

"After that his spirit traveled all over, is that not right?''

"What do you mean?"

"Some of the people who followed him, the Chosen Twelve, they saw him after death. Isn't that right?"

"Yes."

"Well, that's just a white man's tale," Little Crane said. "Many more than the Chosen Twelve saw him. The old people among all the Indian tribes, from far in the north to far to the south, have told stories for many, many generations. They say that a man came from across the Great Waters, a prophet, and told of changes that would happen. This man didn't look like an Indian, but had long wavy hair that came down around his shoulders, and hair that grew on his face. At first the Indian peoples were all afraid of him. But he proved to them that he had come in peace, to help all people."

"I've never heard of that," Garrett said.

"White people never listen to Indian legends," Little Crane said. "Nothing that an Indian says could ever be true. Only the whites know truth."

"That's not fair."

"Sure it is. You know that's how it is."

"People who live in different cultures don't always understand one another," Garrett said. "Sometimes there's fear, and that can destroy anything good."

"It wasn't the Indian people with the fear," Little Crane said. "It was the whites. And they have more fear now than ever before."

"Why are we arguing this way?" Garrett asked.

"Because I want you to learn something about truth," Little Crane said. "You've been taught a lot of things. Not much of it is truth."

"You both should worry about that later," Red Moon said. He was pointing to the four Crow scouts who had left earlier. They had just ridden in and were dismounting in Custer's camp.

"They must have found fresh sign," Little Crane said. "We're getting closer."

Garrett rode with Little Crane and Red Moon to where Custer had called his officers together.

Custer was saying, "My Crows have told me about

fresh sign ahead on Lame Deer Creek. We will split into three divisions, taking three separate trails through the valley, traveling slowly, so that the dust we raise is minimal. I will lead off with two companies. The rest of you will march a half mile to the rear. I want no unnecessary noise of any kind. No talking or laughing. We're catching them, and we cannot let them discover us and run.''

The sergeant holding Custer's guidon had planted it in the ground while he listened. A sudden gust of wind blew it over. Custer turned.

''Pick that up, Sergeant. Secure it better, please.''

The sergeant planted the guidon. Once again, a gust of wind blew it to the ground. The sergeant picked it up and held it.

The wind seemed to scream, whipping through the village. Four large dust devils suddenly appeared, twisting their way past the Sun Dance lodge, filling the air with dust.

The men stirred, restless. Garrett held his hat. Little Crane and Red Moon turned away, covering their faces with their hands.

''Do you understand?'' Custer continued. ''I want it perfectly understood. We cannot let them get away.''

''We must leave this place now,'' Little Crane said. ''Death has come through here. I don't want to be marked.''

''Marked?'' Garrett said.

''There's no time to talk about it now,'' Little Crane said.

''We'll tell you later,'' Red Moon added. His face was twisted with fear. ''We've got to leave here now, before it's too late.''

TWENTY

Afternoon, Saturday, 24 June 1876
On Rosebud, near East Muddy Creek

Custer has called a halt. The Crow scouts have returned and he wants to learn from them what lies ahead. We've been stopped for three hours already and the men are restless. They believe the hostiles to be nearby and a battle is imminent.

Can't say my nerves are any better than anyone else's. The tension is thicker than pudding. But neither Little Crane nor Red Moon have sung any war songs, or begun painting themselves, so I'll try to relax.

But maybe *relax* is a word not suitable for the situation. Have just finished speaking with Little Crane and Red Moon about the Sun Dance camp. They told me about a drawing on sandstone that showed a battle being fought and won, something about a large buffalo and a small buffalo, the smaller being killed. I'm glad I didn't see the drawing as the buffalo dream will surely come again, anyway, and I don't need any added fear on top of what I have now.

The entire experience in the Sun Dance camp has left me with mixed emotions. Am grateful to Little Crane for his explanation of the ceremony and its meaning. I believe the ceremony to have good points, but it bothers me to know that they can reach God in their own way and have Him listen. I always thought my way of praying was the correct way. Little Crane is right: I have a great deal to learn about truth.

There are other matters of concern. Some of the scouts found white scalps, they say, in or near the Sun Dance lodge. Herendeen, one of the white scouts, said they came from soldiers on the Yellowstone with Gibbon who were killed in early June, before the Terry-Custer forces arrived.

There's talk that the scalps mean something in connection with the Sun Dance. I didn't see any scalps while there with Little Crane and Red Moon, and neither one of them mentioned seeing any. They just told me again that they would have seen them if they were present. Little Crane says the scalps were not connected with the ceremony.

Little Crane and Red Moon showed me a strange item. The skin from a buffalo calf was left tied by cloth to four poles. Little Crane believed it to be a sacred fixture. He thought it meant the buffalo spirit was going to be reborn. Perhaps someone had had a vision. Why else might it be there?

Also, three red-painted stones were found in one of the sweat lodges. Some believe that to be a sign of victory. But Little Crane isn't certain. He says it could be just the medicine color of the water pourer.

Little Crane explained to me that the Sioux have believed for as long as they can remember, based on the major colors that they use in ceremonies—red, black, white, and yellow, which represent the four races of mankind—that these four races will some day be combined into one. The four races of man coming together? That's interesting.

Of all the things I saw today, a sandstone carving that Little Crane and Red Moon showed me is the most bothersome. It showed Bluecoats riding horses with shod hooves falling headfirst from their saddles toward Indian figures on unshod ponies. Little Crane said over and over, looking into the distance, that someone in the Sun Dance ceremony had had a vi-

sion of a battle to come, where many Bluecoats
would be killed.

I have reason to believe the Rees and Crows more
than Custer and the soldiers. Maybe if the soldiers
laid off the whiskey for a little while, they'd see the
truth and mutiny. But Custer has them believing that
the Indians will run and that they'll simply be hard-
pressed to catch them and scalp as many as they
can. It's madness. Utter madness!

All this has given me cause to reflect on my buffalo dream, uncomfortable as that may be. Maybe
the hole in the flames symbolizes a journey to death,
to the Other Side. But why would the buffalo, the
symbol of strength and security, try to entice me into
death? It doesn't make sense, unless the black hole
really symbolizes a leap of faith into the unknown.

That would make perfect sense. The buffalo has
told me to run through the hole, to save myself and
not ask questions. Faith means trusting in the Hand
of God, as the minister used to say. I remember that
from childhood. Faith is wondering what's coming,
but releasing to that unknown condition, believing
that what's to come might be frightening, but that
it's growth toward God and has to be better than the
present. Hard to see that out here on these open
plains, with thousands of Sioux and Cheyenne
nearby.

I believe that I will take Little Crane's advice and
find Stabbed, who is supposed to have strong medicine and might answer some of my questions. I
guess I can't ask anyone else, as Little Crane has
said that Stabbed is the only one among the Rees
who could discuss it with me. The younger scouts
don't yet have the right to discuss spiritual matters.

I hope to have success with him, but will talk to
Mitch Boyer as well. I don't know what he can tell
me, but maybe he can direct me to one of the Crows.

Boyer seems to have a good head on his shoulders, but is like the others—loyal to Custer to a
fault. I guess I shouldn't criticize; they gave their

word and their honor is worth dying for. A com-
mendable if not a terrifying thought. Perhaps there
should be more of that kind of loyalty everywhere.
Then fighting would be limited to only just causes.
Unlike this one.

Garrett stuffed his diary into his saddlebag and lay
down to rest. He had suddenly become very tired. He
wanted to be somewhere else, anywhere else.

Little Crane, who had been combing his pony's coat,
mounted.

Garrett sat up. "Where are you going?"

"I'm taking my pony out to find grass. If you're smart,
you'll follow. Red Moon is already out there."

Garrett was tired, but he climbed into the saddle and
followed Little Crane through the surrounding hills until
they came to a spring. Red Moon was there, looking into
the distance. Garrett and Little Crane watered their ponies
and hobbled them to graze.

"Are we supposed to be this far out?" Garrett asked.

"I don't care," Little Crane said. "There's no grass
near the camp. If our ponies don't eat, they'll lose all
their strength. What's the difference if we die now or
later?"

During the ride, Little Crane had said nothing. Garrett
had thought that he seemed withdrawn and angry. Now
there was no doubt.

"You know something?" Little Crane suddenly said.
"I believe this: I believe that if all the Indian people
would put the past behind them and join together, we
could push the white man out of our lands. Forever. We
could rule our lands as we know how to rule them. But
that will never happen. There are too many problems between the tribes."

Little Crane was as serious as Garrett had ever seen
him. His eyes were narrow, his jaw muscles tight.

"What brought this on?" Garrett asked.

"It seems foolish that Indians are killing other Indians
when the white man doesn't like Indians, whoever they
are."

"You don't care for the white man?" Garrett said. "Then why fight with him?"

"I've already told you," Little Crane said, "if the Sioux and Cheyenne win, my people will be in trouble. The Sioux will kill us. If the white man wins, we'll still be in trouble, but maybe not so many of us will die. Either way, it's not good."

Garrett looked at Red Moon, who was staring into the distance.

Garrett turned to Little Crane. "I thought we were friends. I thought you told me that Red Moon wanted to be my brother."

"You and I are friends," Little Crane said. "And Red Moon already considers you his brother."

"I don't understand. You just said that all the Indians wished the white man gone, and that if all the Indians were to fight together, the white man wouldn't stand a chance."

"I said that the Indians should have a choice about their lands. The Indians should be able to accept the whites or tell them to leave. As it is, the whites want to take it all and we have to accept all of them, no matter what. There are good Indians and bad Indians, good whites and bad whites. The whites think they're all better than the Indians. If the Indians wanted to join together, they could make their choices about who came into their lands to live. But no one knows how an Indian believes. There's no way to make the whites understand us."

"Why can't you make the whites understand you?" Garrett asked.

Little Crane stepped toward Garrett. "Hold out your hand, palm upward."

Garrett frowned. "What? Why?"

"Give me your hand. I'm your friend."

Garrett hesitated, then held out his hand. Little Crane made no move to touch him. Garrett stood rigid, confused.

"Aren't you going to do anything?" Garrett asked. He drew his hand back. "What did you want my hand for, to just look at?"

"Did you think that I wanted your hand so that I could hurt you? That's the way you acted."

"I don't know."

"I think you do know. Has there ever been a time when you thought that I wanted to hurt you?"

"No, there hasn't. What does that have to do with anything?"

"Can't you see?" Little Crane replied. "I'm trying to show you how it is. It's hard for a white man to trust. I've never hurt you at all. Even so, when I ask for your hand, you're worried about it. Is that the way it is between us? Can't you trust me?"

Garrett thought about it. He had been afraid to extend his hand, perhaps in fear of physical pain; he didn't know for certain. Even though he knew Little Crane would do nothing to harm him, his instinct had been to be wary. Now he was embarrassed.

"I believe you have a good heart," Little Crane said, "but you don't let your heart make any decisions for you. Just your head. That's the way it is with the white man. Sometimes maybe your head is wrong. Think about that."

Little Crane mounted his pony and started back for camp. Red Moon followed. Garrett watched them leave and rode back alone. When he got to camp, he lay down on his bedroll, thinking he would rest.

Instead, his mind raced with what Little Crane had said about Indians fighting Indians. He recalled what Little Crane had said earlier when they had ridden through another deserted village a day beyond the Sun Dance camp.

"I told you what we would find," Garrett could remember Little Crane saying. "Even a blind man can see that this camp has been used by many Sioux and Cheyenne. The ground on the trails coming here has been chewed up by the many travois poles. There must have been nearly twice as many lodges here as there were down below, or even at the Sun Dance village. Sitting Bull's village is too large to fight. The enemy is more than the grass on the hills, except there is no grass left on the hills."

Besides the evidence of numerous lodges and campfire pits, horse droppings had littered the ground heavily, both within and outside the camp area, and the grass had been cropped to ground level for over a mile in every direction.

"There have been more ponies in this place than at any other time, ever," Little Crane had added. "Many warriors. A great many. This many Bluecoats cannot fight them alone. Long Hair had better take warning."

"Maybe Terry and Gibbon will show up in time," Garrett had suggested, voicing his constant hope once again.

"Long Hair is marching too fast for that," Little Crane had said. "Way too fast. He wants us to get there ahead of everyone else. And we will. We will take Long Hair to fight our enemies, though they shouldn't be our enemies. Long Hair is white, and we are all Indians. We should all be fighting Long Hair."

Garrett, his eyes closed, tried once again to get some rest. He could hear soldiers nearby, eating and discussing the Sun Dance village and the Indian trail along the Rosebud between Lame Deer Creek and East Muddy Creek.

Among the men was a scout named Charley Reynolds. Most knew him as Lonesome Charley, for his quiet ways and his preference to remain far from everyone. The Rees called him Lucky Man, for his hunting abilities. They maintained that Reynolds never went in search of meat without finding it.

Today Reynolds seemed to be in need of company. Garrett overheard him telling some soldiers, "I've had a good life out here in this country, damned better than most. I can't kick. If this is the end, I'll smile when it's over."

"If I'd have known what we were in for, I'd have found my way out back downriver," one of the soldiers said. "As it stands here, the Sioux will likely find those strung out on their own. And I don't intend to be found by no Sioux. I know what they can do to a man."

"Best to die quick," another soldier said. "Get it over

with. What happens after your last breath don't matter that much, I'd say.''

Garrett could stand no more. He jumped up and began to pace. He thought again about his buffalo dream, needing to know the answer to it. Now.

He would go to the Ree camp and find Stabbed. He searched through his belongings, finding four things to give Stabbed in exchange for his help analyzing the dream. Little Crane had always said that anyone who sought healing from a medicine man needed to present him four things in return for his help, one of the four items always being tobacco in some form—cigarettes, loose, or in a twist-tie. Tobacco was most important.

Garrett had little to offer Stabbed. He gathered together a slab of venison from the meat Red Moon and Little Crane had brought in, a small leather pouch of rifle bullets, a fifty-cent piece, and a plug of tobacco that he had bought from a soldier. It would have to do.

Garrett had spread his own bedroll, together with Little Crane and Red Moon, at the edge of the Ree camp, so he didn't have far to go.

As he walked, Garrett thought about the next few days. He had seen numerous large battles during the Rebellion, but he had never seen Indian warriors fight, riding with wild abandon, screaming war cries at the top of their lungs. He knew this would be happening very soon.

It would certainly be nothing like the battles of the Rebellion, he thought. The soldiers would fight as they had been trained, in skirmish lines, well defined and well ordered. But certainly not the hostiles. To think that Little Crane and Red Moon would confine themselves to a prescribed order was ridiculous.

Believing that the warriors would run seemed foolish to Garrett. Little Crane had said from the beginning that there would be a big fight, as had Mitch Boyer. Everyone knew this, but there were still those who refused to believe that the Seventh Cavalry could ever lose.

Garrett could only hope that he was well equipped when the time came. Certainly he knew how to use his firearms, and Little Crane and Red Moon had seen to it that he knew what an Indian pony was like and how to ride one. Staying alive among a horde of fighting Sioux and Cheyenne would take good weapons and a man who could use them, and a very good pony with a man who could stay on.

In the Ree camp, Garrett saw Stabbed, the older Ree scout, leading his pony to water. He also saw Little Crane and Red Moon, eating with friends.

"Can I talk to you?" Garrett asked Little Crane.

Little Crane got up. "What is it?"

"Are you still angry with me, or will you take me to see Stabbed?"

"I wasn't angry," Little Crane said. "Just hurt. I think you'd like to trust me, but you don't know how."

"I'll learn," Garrett promised. "Now, you told me that Stabbed could help me with my dream. I'd like you to introduce me to him."

Little Crane noted the gifts under Garrett's arm. "I told you that Stabbed *might* be able to help you. Follow me."

As they approached the river, Garrett's stomach tightened. What if Stabbed told him that the dream meant death? There was no stopping now; he had to know.

Stabbed had finished watering his pony and was now pulling burrs from its tail with a porcupine quill brush.

"Stabbed," Little Crane said in Ree, "Six Fingers has come to talk with you. I told you about him and you said to bring him sometime. Is this a good time?"

"Yes, this is a good time," Stabbed said. He shook Garrett's hand.

Stabbed and Little Crane were silent. Garrett shuffled his feet, trying to think of how to begin. Finally, Stabbed spoke and Little Crane translated.

"Little Crane tells me that you have strong medicine, that you've already killed a Sioux hand to hand and took his scalp. I've seen the scalp on your rifle, and I can tell you that you will always have followers if you want to lead Ree warriors into battle."

"I came to ask about a dream," Garrett said through Little Crane. "It's been bothering me."

Stabbed smiled, combing his pony. "A warrior with

your medicine should be having good dreams. Is it a good dream?''

"I don't know. I keep seeing a buffalo."

"Then it's a good dream. A powerful dream. Little Crane was right: You have strong medicine."

"But there's fire around the buffalo," Garrett said. "There's a huge wall of fire that surrounds me, and the buffalo turns white and runs through a circle in the fire. He wants me to follow him."

"Why don't you do it?"

"I don't know." Garrett shuffled his feet again. "I guess I'm afraid."

Stabbed nodded. "That's good. A buffalo comes to you and you're afraid. The next time, why don't you follow him through the fire and see what happens? I'd like to know."

Garrett was puzzled. Wasn't Stabbed supposed to know what was on the other side? He asked Little Crane.

Little Crane laughed. "It's your dream, Six Fingers. Stabbed can't see it the way you do. Maybe he can tell you whether you should be worried."

"Listen, I'm already worried," Garrett said. "I want to know what's going to happen as a result of my dream."

Little Crane asked Stabbed if he knew anything about Garrett's future.

"You're going with us into battle," Stabbed said. "And the buffalo will be with you."

"Can you tell me what's on the other side of the black hole?"

Stabbed listened to Little Crane's translation and shrugged. "How would I know? I can't see into it any better than you."

"You mean that you don't have any idea what the buffalo wants to lead me to?"

"No, I don't have any idea."

"Then why did Little Crane say you could help me?"

"I don't know. You'll have to ask him."

Garrett turned to Little Crane. "We're going in circles here."

"Life is filled with circles," Little Crane said.

"You know what I mean," Garrett said. "This isn't helping me at all."

"I never promised you that it would."

Garrett handed the gifts to Little Crane. "Would you thank Stabbed for having taken the time to talk to me? And tell him that I'm sorry I bothered him."

"Give him the presents yourself," Little Crane said. "He's helping you, not me."

"Sure," Garrett said. He handed the presents to Stabbed, who voiced his approval and shook Garrett's hand again.

Garrett turned to leave. Stabbed was saying something to Little Crane.

"Six Fingers," Little Crane called out. When Garrett turned, he said, "Stabbed says that the next time you have the dream, you'd better go through the fire with the buffalo. There may not be another chance and you don't want to let the fire catch you."

"Tell him that I'm worried there's something worse on the other side."

"Stabbed says," Little Crane told Garrett, "that there's nothing worse than the fire. He knows that for certain. What's waiting for you in the black hole, he can't say. But you'd better go there, Stabbed says. The buffalo won't wait for you forever."

TWENTY-ONE

Curley stood near a large sandstone rock, his face to the afternoon sky. He raised a burning cigarette above him, whispering a prayer, watching the smoke drift toward filmy, scattered clouds. In the distance, the air shimmered with heat, the hills beyond blurred. Scouting under these conditions was worse than darkness.

With Curley was his brother, White Swan, and also White-Man-Runs-Him, Goes Ahead, and Hairy Moccasin. The only Crow scout not to come was Half-Yellow-Face, who had stayed back with the soldiers, ordered to remain with Two Bodies Boyer and Long Hair Custer.

Continuing his prayer, Curley took a long drag on the cigarette and let the smoke balloon from his mouth. All of them had cigarettes and were praying, asking *Acaba-datdea,* the First maker, the Creator, for protection. Long Hair had sent them out again to search for new trails and find the Big Village. They had gotten precious little sleep since leaving Elk River, the Yellowstone, and were all very tired. They could not afford to make any mistakes, for Sioux or Cheyenne scouts must not see them.

Long Hair had told them many times to be very careful not to be seen. His face had been clouded with worry when he had talked, worry about losing his chance to attack the Big Village. If the enemy got away, he had told the scouts often, then they would be shamed in the eyes of their families and the Crow people. He would see to it.

Curley and the others had often wondered how Long Hair could be so certain of what was ahead. He seemed sure that victory was his without question, if no one else ruined it for him.

White Swan had never paid much attention to Custer and had told the others, "No one among our people thinks that much of Long Hair. He can say what he wants, but no one will listen."

White-Man-Runs-Him, prone to excitability, always voiced his anger at the threats. "That crazy yellow eyes had better give us our due and stop trying to scare us," he said. "We're doing a good job for him and still he isn't satisfied. What more does he want?"

Goes Ahead suggested, "Maybe we should all wear fancy buckskin suits all the time and lead the Bluecoats ourselves. We can send him out in front and see how well he does. He'd be lost in half a day and we'd find him curled up somewhere, sucking his thumb."

Hairy Moccasin felt he had been given an opportunity to gain honors for himself and his family. He had tried to get the others to stop talking about the bad things and just go ahead with the scouting. "We can all become famous among our people if we do this right," he would remind them. "Being angry at Long Hair isn't going to make anything happen. Forget about him and let's just find our enemies."

Curley laid his cigarette on the sandstone rock, to let it burn out and carry his prayers upward. He touched the small medicine bundle around his neck. His medicine helper was close, and Curley felt good that the medicine was protecting him. He worried, though, about White Swan, who had lost his medicine bundle twice, but had been lucky enough to find it both times in his bedroll.

Because of that, Curley wanted his older brother to be extra careful. It was ironic, for when the scouts had first volunteered, White Swan hadn't been interested. But when Curley had said he would go, White Swan had said, "He shouldn't go and do this without me along." He had pointed toward the east. "I will go with him."

To Curley and the others, it was important to pray and to stay in contact with the medicine. Earlier in the spring, before leaving on their journey, clan uncles in the village had held medicine bundle ceremonies for each of them, asking for guidance and protection, and for a special medicine to go with each of them as a protector. The closer they came to the Big Village, the more each of them realized that their medicine would have to be strong.

Curley jumped on his pony. They had come upon sign of a recent camp, perhaps only a few days old. The camp was one of many that they had found, moving toward the main village somewhere ahead. There were so many trails coming and going that it was very hard to tell which ones were the freshest. There was no doubt, though, that it meant a great many Sioux and Cheyenne were coming together.

"I don't know why Long Hair hasn't sent a courier to the Big Chief and One-Who-Limps, coming down the Big Horn," White-Man-Runs-Him said. "They should know what's ahead for them. And Long Hair should be telling them to hurry up, so they can help us fight."

"It's true," Goes Ahead agreed. "We'll need all the fighters possible. Never has such a big fight come to pass."

"We knew when we went with Long Hair that things would be hard to understand," White Swan said. "He told us that he would follow the Sioux as long as it took to find them, even if the food was gone and we had to eat the mules. We all thought that was an honorable thing to say, and maybe it was. But there's no sense in eating mules when you don't have to, just so you can say you did it."

White Swan's wisdom had never been questioned. It was true: Once they told Two Bodies Boyer that they would join the Bluecoats and scout for their enemy, they knew things would be very different from the way they were on their own war parties.

"You know that these Bluecoats fight differently," Two Bodies had said. "They won't decide whether or not it's a good day to die. They've come to fight the Sioux, no matter what."

Curley felt better that he was with White Swan and

the other three. As the youngest, he felt isolated without the others.

For part of the afternoon, the five had been split into smaller groups, studying the area. It was time now to decide what they would tell Long Hair when they returned. They had not discovered where the trail led, as Long Hair wished, but they had learned that a lot of fresh trails had joined with the main one along the Rosebud.

"It's important that someone tell Long Hair about all the new trails right away," Hairy Moccasin said. "This means many more enemy warriors to fight. One of us should go back, I think."

"I don't want to miss out on being the first to see the Big Village," White-Man-Runs-Him said. "I want to go ahead to the divide."

White Swan spoke up. "I think all of you want to see which way the trail goes after the divide. We've ridden hard already, and it's a hot day. I'll go back and report what we've found to Long Hair. Just use good judgment when you go ahead. Don't go too far."

"Don't worry, Big Brother," Curley said. "We don't intend to get so close to the village that they see us. All we'll do is find it if we can. And it may be too late in the day to see the village from the divide, but we can tell which way they went when they crossed the top."

"That will be good, Little Brother," White Swan said. "Then hurry back. I'll be worried about you all."

Garrett was napping when Little Crane shook him awake.

"One of the Crows has returned. They found fresh tracks not far from here. Long Hair and the Bluecoat chiefs are gathering. Let's go listen."

Garrett rubbed his eyes and stretched. He checked his watch. It was just after 4:00 P.M.

He walked with Little Crane and Red Moon to where the Ree scouts were sitting and eating. Stabbed was among them, his face stoic as he talked with another scout. Custer and his officers had already arrived. Custer had dropped to one knee and was speaking to Gerard.

"Ask them what they think about the large camps

ahead. Ask them what they think the outcome will be.''

Gerard spoke to the Rees. Stabbed came to his feet and began dodging about, simulating the way he would fight during an attack, speaking in Ree to Gerard.

Gerard told Custer, ''Stabbed says that the Rees move quickly so that they cannot easily be hit, while the Bluecoats stand in lines and wait for bullets and arrows to come. When the fighting starts, he wants to be with his own people, not the Bluecoat soldiers.''

''Tell him,'' Custer said to Gerard, ''that the Rees are good fighters and can do well in battle. My only intention in bringing them is to have them go into battle and take many horses from the Sioux.'' He extended his arms in a welcoming fashion. ''Some of you I see here have been with me on other expeditions, and to see you again makes my heart glad.''

The Rees listened further as Custer named many of them and said that they were brave young men and that if they were victorious, the Ree scouts could all be proud of themselves and could march with honor in a parade.

Garrett listened, jotting notes. Custer was a diplomat, there was no arguing that.

At the end of his speech, Custer turned to Gerard and said, ''I want you to tell these young men, these boys, that if we are successful, when we return, my brother, Bloody Knife, and I will represent you in Washington and perhaps we will take you in person to Washington.''

Garrett turned to Little Crane. ''Did you hear what I heard?''

Little Crane smiled. ''I think Long Hair wants to be the Great Father in Washington.''

''It sounds to me like he already *believes* that he's there,'' Garrett said. ''He's already won it all—the battle, the nomination, the election, everything! Incredible!''

Little Crane was impassive. ''Not everything a man desires comes to pass.''

''He speaks the truth,'' Red Moon said, reaching to cover his heart with his hand. ''I lost my family and I want them back. That cannot happen.''

The Rees were staring at Custer. Bloody Knife was nodding, smiling from ear to ear.

"What else is happening here?" Garrett asked Little Crane. "Nobody seems to like the idea of Bloody Knife representing them in Washington."

"It's a silly idea," Little Crane said. "Long Hair is insulting everyone. Bloody Knife has never represented the Arikara people before, in any way. He's a good scout, but he's never been a big chief or even the leader of a band. Why should he go to Washington?"

Garrett asked Little Crane, "Do your people believe Long Hair will actually take them all to Washington if he wins the battle?"

"It doesn't matter if he takes them or not," Little Crane said. "Long Hair might know Indian customs but he doesn't know Indian honor. They've already told him that they will follow him, so they will, no matter what. He doesn't have to make false promises now that he sees danger. We've already seen the danger. Way back."

Custer left the Ree scouts, waving to them. He gave the order to move out and the camp scrambled into motion. Garrett saddled his pony and tied his saddlebags in place.

"I wonder about the organization of this battle," he told Little Crane. "I'd bet that some of the officers would just as soon paint up and fight against Custer with the Sioux."

Little Crane laughed. "How do you feel?"

"A little that way, I'll have to admit."

Red Moon was already mounted. "Custer's a bastard," he said.

"You're learning a lot of English, Red Moon," Garrett said.

"I've always known those kinds of words," Red Moon said. "They were the first ones I learned. I haven't spoken much English since my wife and children died. Now I'll speak more. And I'll fight with Long Hair, even though he's really a bastard."

Garrett was adjusting himself in the saddle. There was

no way that he could sit that wasn't irritating a sore spot.

"I guess the Bluecoat chiefs will have to decide whether or not to paint up pretty soon," he said. "It won't be long now, it sounds like."

Little Crane jumped onto his pony. "Well, Six Fingers, you'd better decide now who you want to fight with. If you stay with Long Hair, he won't care about you in the end anyway. He won't want to see you again. If you go with the Sioux, they won't like you either. You're white and they haven't had good times with whites. So you'd better stay with Long Hair." He pointed to Garrett's hands. "At least you might save your fingers."

"That's not funny any more," Garrett said. "Not a bit funny."

"I didn't say it was funny," Little Crane said. "I just said it was a choice for you. But maybe you don't have a choice any more. Maybe none of us do."

Ann sat in a tent, staring at the canvas doorflap, wondering how to get out of her miserable situation. She had been placed there "for her own protection and good" and had been there ever since Sergeant Sinclair had brought them all in.

Tyrone had explained to her that they were in an army supply depot, likely in support of the Seventh Cavalry's efforts against the Sioux and Cheyenne. Many of its large number of bored soldiers were older, toward the end of their enlistment; the younger ones were incapacitated in some way.

Ann had told Sinclair numerous times that she wished to speak to someone in authority. Sinclair had told her that his immediate superior was out on a hunting trip and should be back soon. Someone else had told her that the commanding officer, Major Orlando Moore, had gone downriver on the steamboat and wasn't expected back until the next morning.

"We can't wait that long, Sergeant!" Ann had said to Sinclair.

"I'm sorry, but I've got to do what I think is right.

And that's keep you safe until I can consult with Major Moore.''

Again, Ann told Sinclair that he wasn't liable for her safety.

''Oh, yes, but I am,'' Sinclair had said. ''The U.S. Army is out here to see to it that our citizens pass through in safety. I must certainly follow through on that responsibility with you, ma'am, for you're the most admirable-looking citizen I ever laid eyes on.''

''I beg your pardon, Sergeant,'' Ann had said.

Through his ever present sarcastic grin, Sinclair had said quickly, ''With all due respect, ma'am. With all due respect, of course.''

''Sergeant, I find you rude and impudent to the utmost degree. Why don't you enroll yourself in a manners course, sir, and let others go on about their business?''

Sinclair had left the tent and Ann hadn't seen him since. She judged it to be well into the afternoon now, and besides her worry about Adam, her concern for Tyrone and Lareaux was increasing. They were in another tent, also being held ''for their own good.''

''It would be unfortunate if they tried something rash before Major Moore returned,'' Sinclair had said.

As Water had always been so aloof, she guessed that he had likely turned back for Fort Buford. It would have been so much easier had they listened to Lareaux in the first place. But their concern for his knife wound had outweighed caution. She didn't know if he'd been treated or not.

''An army thinks it owns everything,'' Lareaux had said when they were being taken in. ''You get involved with government things and you suffer. *Oui*, you suffer greatly! Look at us!''

Tyrone had tried to settle him down, but Lareaux hadn't let up until Sinclair had threatened him with leg irons.

''I don't care about your wound,'' Sinclair had said. ''Hold your tongue or else.''

Ann spent her time wondering what was going to happen when Major Moore showed up. If he was anything like Sinclair, he surely wouldn't allow her to go on after Adam. More likely, he would detain her further or force her onto the steamboat and make her remain aboard to take passage back to Fort Lincoln at some future time.

No matter what, she'd find a way to get away from this place. And she could start, she realized, by being civil to Sergeant Sinclair. In fact, she would be more than civil, just enough to make him feel he was getting somewhere with her. He might provide her with enough information and latitude to give her a chance to escape.

As Ann expected, Sinclair came back. She could hear him talking to the guard outside the tent.

"Allow me to apologize for my rudeness earlier," he said, entering without asking permission. He did remove his hat, but his smirk was plastered from ear to ear.

Ann batted her eyes. "Maybe I was a bit short with you," she said. "After all, you're very nice looking yourself."

Sinclair blushed. Ann realized she had come on a bit too strong and that he couldn't handle it. She turned sideways and peered through the open doorflap.

"It appears to be getting well into the day," she said. "I'll bet the evenings out here are beautiful."

Sinclair still hadn't adjusted to Ann's sudden change toward him. But he didn't appear suspicious.

"I came to invite you to dinner along the river," he said. "It won't be much—grouse and native vegetables—but it beats the regular fare of hardtack and bacon."

Ann thought a moment. "I don't know, Sergeant. It is a lovely offer, but . . ."

"I wish you would, ma'am. It's not right that you're cooped up in this tent."

Ann wanted to tell him that the simplest way to settle that would be to back off and let her go. But she maintained her poise.

"I suppose you're right," she said. "It might be good to get out for a little while."

"Of course it would," Sinclair said. "It would be simpler if you'd tell me your name. Ma'am doesn't fit a pretty woman like you.''

"My name is Sarah Parker. I'm from Minneapolis." She started out of the tent.

"How very nice," Sinclair said, following her closely. "You've come a very long way. I still can't imagine . . . You're looking for your fiancé, you say?"

Ann took a look around camp. Soldiers in all directions were staring at her.

"Yes. I know he's out here somewhere," she said. "I suspect far from here."

Sinclair offered his arm and Ann took it. They began walking.

"What would prompt you to come all the way out here after him?" he asked.

"Love, Sergeant. Isn't that what makes the world go round?"

"Are you sure he's worth the risk you're taking?"

Ann held herself. She had to be careful. If she wanted him to play into her plan, she had to do it right.

"We've known one another a long time, Sergeant Sinclair," she replied. "I always felt that I knew him quite well. But since he came out here entirely against my wishes, well, I don't know now."

"I can certainly understand, Sarah. May I call you Sarah?"

"Yes, that would be fine, Sergeant."

"Well, Sarah, it seems that his consideration for you is sorely lacking. Maybe he doesn't think as much of you as you'd like."

"I'm having to face that fact, Sergeant," Ann said, "however painful that is."

"I hope a good dinner will help you with your trail," Sinclair said. "The cook will be at his best, I can assure you, and we'll be by ourselves, along the beautiful river."

"That sounds simply wonderful, Sergeant." She looked over to where three soldiers were guarding a tent at the edge of camp. "Is that where Mr. Lareaux and Mr. Banks are staying?"

"That's where they're 'staying,' " Sinclair said with a chuckle. "I'm sure they'd prefer other quarters."

"I'd like to see them if I may."

"They're being well cared for."

"Oh, I'm certain that they are. But, please, Sergeant, if you would kindly humor me. They'll be glad to learn that I'm content. Perhaps the Frenchman will settle down then."

"That's sound reasoning and I can see no problem," Sinclair said. He escorted her to the tent and ordered the flap opened.

"I'll meet you in a few minutes, by the river, for a wonderful dinner," Ann said.

Sinclair looked to the three soldiers on guard. "Don't give her any trouble." He tipped his hat to Ann and left.

Inside, Ann met Tyrone and Lareaux, bound hand and foot. Lareaux was groaning from the pain in his leg.

"What's all this?" Ann asked. She began untying them.

"You'll get yourself in trouble, Miss Ann," Tyrone said.

"Nonsense! The Sergeant told the guards not to bother me." She struggled with the ropes. "This is ridiculous! How are we going to get out of here?"

"We've got to wait for Water, Miss Ann," Tyrone said. He worked his way from the bonds and rubbed his wrists. "Lareaux says he'll come."

Lareaux was breathing easier, rubbing his leg. "Water will free us soon. You wait, very soon."

"I thought maybe he'd left," Ann said.

"*Non*, not him," Lareaux said. "He and I, we practice the ways of escaping enemies. We've done this before. Don't worry, he hasn't left us. *Non*. You'll see. He'll be here."

"How did you get out of your tent, Miss Ann?" Tyrone asked.

"I'm charming the Sergeant," Ann said. "We're having dinner together. I was trying to decide how we could escape."

"Don't worry," Lareaux repeated. "Water will come. Soon. Shortly after dark."

"How will he get us out?" Ann asked.

"When you hear the sound of an owl, repeated four times," Lareaux said, "be ready to run south, along the Powder River. Stay to the east bank. We'll find you. Water will no doubt have the horses."

"Yes, just run south along the river," Tyrone said. "We heard the soldiers talking about Custer. He went up to the Rosebud and turned south. We can take a shortcut along the Powder and turn west. We'll catch them."

Lareaux was on his feet, testing his leg. "Remember to listen for the owl. Don't run before that."

"But what if I hear a real owl?" Ann asked.

"You won't hear a real owl four times," Lareaux said. "They don't count like that."

"He's right, Miss Ann," Tyrone said. "Owls can count, but not all the way to four."

"I'll be listening," Ann said. "I know I can keep Sinclair out there that long. I just hope I can keep him at bay."

"You go and have a fine dinner, Miss Ann," Tyrone said. "And you listen for the owl. When you hear it, you start running, and don't you stop for anything. You hear, Miss Ann? Not for anything."

TWENTY-TWO

With the sun nearing the western horizon, Ghostwind made her way toward the river, water skins in hand. The camp had moved downriver a way, taking up the entire morning and most of the afternoon. Now everyone was settling in, a major task for a village of more than five thousand people.

Ghostwind was amazed at the number of people who had joined the Big Village, many within the past few days. Some were Cheyenne, but the majority were Lakota Sioux who had come out from the agencies to hunt for food. Rations, they had said, were scarce and of poor quality.

They had brought news of marching Bluecoats, though no one knew exactly from which direction they were coming. Many believed the newcomers were talking about Three Stars Crook, who had taken a whipping on the Rosebud seven days ago and was still nursing his wounds in camp far to the south. Those who had fought told war stories of that day, and of the many honors gained in battle.

While many basked in glory, others argued that many more Bluecoats were coming out from the forts and everyone should look out for them, though no one really believed there would be enough of them to attack such a massive village, the largest anyone could remember, ever.

Everyone was in a festive mood. There was food enough for all and plenty of hides for making lodges and clothes. There had been many buffalo killed at the last camp, and in a few days hunters would go after antelope, which scouts had reported in large herds to the north and west. But during the next day, the horses would be allowed to graze and fatten up on the grass west of the village.

To celebrate the good fortune of the buffalo hunt, and of the victory over Three Star's Bluecoats, the camps were sponsoring dances of various kinds. Ghostwind had heard Young Horse talking to Nighthawk about a dance for young people in one of the Lakota camps. "There are a lot of new girls around," he had said. "Everyone is anxious to meet them."

Ghostwind found it difficult to get caught up in the revelry. Her visions had grown stronger since the newcomers' arrival. As more people arrived, the fire burned hotter in the skies of her dreams.

In addition, Nighthawk was increasingly restive. The majority of the Cheyenne people resented his presence, especially in light of the newcomers' stories of agency mistreatment. Even Eagle Wing, his war brother and best friend, couldn't make the council stop talking about sending him away.

While the villagers prepared for the evening's festivities, Ghostwind walked alone. At the edge of the village, she stopped at Day Lily's lodge to see if she wanted to go along. But Day Lily and Red Bear were fighting, their voices carrying outside. It would be better, Ghostwind decided, to leave them alone.

Ghostwind neared the river, swinging her water skins, trying to decide what she should do. If she took her children and went somewhere else with Nighthawk, they might run into Bluecoats. That would not be a risk worth taking.

At the river was a woman named Little Foot. Ghostwind hardly knew her, for she was a Southern Cheyenne and hadn't come north more than a few times in her entire life. She was married to a Southern Cheyenne warrior named High Cloud, who was well respected but not yet a leader.

Little Foot was the daughter of a prominent warrior under Black Kettle, who had camped for the last time along the Washita River in November of 1868. Every time Ghostwind heard mention of Washita, it brought back her childhood and the vision of the battle she'd had upon first coming to Old Bear's village. Though she had kept the band from harm that time, it now seemed that disaster would be coming soon.

Little Foot and High Cloud were part of a band led by the Southern Cheyenne warrior Lame-White-Man. They had come north to visit relatives, and like the other Sioux and Cheyenne bands had joined the Big Village for protection against the Bluecoats. Everyone knew that the Bluecoats were coming to kill all the Indian people immediately, or drive them back onto reservations, where they would linger in a slow death.

Little Foot was nearly ten winters older than Ghostwind and had already seen a very hard life. She had lost both her father and mother, as well as her husband and two brothers, when Long Hair's soldiers charged the village that cold November dawn.

After the Washita, she and a number of other Cheyenne women had been taken by the Bluecoats to be used by them. Among these women had been Little Foot's cousin, a woman named Monahsetah, Young-Grass-That-Shoots-Up-in-the-Spring.

For nearly a year Young Grass had belonged to Long Hair Custer, the famed Bluecoat leader. In the Indian way, she had become his wife. Some of her friends envied her, thinking that Long Hair was a handsome and courageous leader. Others thought that ridiculous.

She had been with child when Long Hair had taken her, but she had conceived again shortly after giving birth. When Long Hair's white wife had come out onto the plains to be with him, Long Hair had sent Young Grass back to her people, where she had birthed her second child, a son with light-streaked hair, whom she named Yellow Bird.

Little Foot had been among the Bluecoats herself most of that time. She had not been given to a particular Bluecoat chief, though, but had been used by all of them. She had conceived a daughter, Autumn Grass, born with light hair also.

Before she knew she was with child, Little Foot had managed to escape and find her way back to her people, many of whom did not welcome her. When she had given birth, there were those who wanted the child killed. "Get rid of it!" some shouted. "We don't want Bluecoat seed among our people."

Little Foot withstood the onslaughts and accepted High Cloud's proposal of marriage. High Cloud had lost some friends because of it, but the two were happy together.

Like Ghostwind, Little Foot had few friends among her own people. Ghostwind had heard the stories of both Little Foot and Young Grass, but had never approached Little Foot in friendship. Today, she felt the need to talk.

Little Foot was kneeling beside the river, filling her water bags, when Ghostwind knelt beside her.

"The river is clearing up," Ghostwind said. "The water isn't as muddy as before."

"The rains have stopped," Little Foot said. "It will be hot for the rest of the warm moons, I believe."

"I'm Ghostwind. I know that you are Little Foot, and I've wanted to meet you."

Little Foot smiled. "Yes, you're the prophet, the Owl Woman who saved Old Bear's band from what happened to us. I'm glad to know you."

"It seems there are a lot of people who wish I wasn't in this village," Ghostwind said. "I'm having a hard time with that."

"Ah, yes!" Little Foot said. "I know the feeling exactly. Things have happened to me that aren't my fault, yet I'm blamed. I don't believe that's fair."

"I understand," Ghostwind said. "Those people should walk our path. Then they would know better than to blame us."

"That's right," Little Foot said. "They yell, 'Kill your daughter! Kill your daughter!' But who among them would want to kill their own child just because her father was white? I don't know of many who would; and if they did, their hearts would be on the ground for the rest of their lives.''

"Children are often blamed, also, for things that they can't control," Ghostwind said. "It would be nice if we could all get along and quit the infighting. It's bad enough that the Bluecoats are coming. We shouldn't have to bicker among ourselves.''

"I've heard that you're married to a Bluecoat."

"He was never a true Bluecoat," Ghostwind said. "He was forced to join them, but then he saved my life on Powder River during the cold moons, when the Bluecoats attacked our village.''

"I heard he has special medicine with the rifle, that he can shoot a long way and hit anything he wishes.''

"He learned it as a child," Ghostwind explained. "He had to feed himself when he was young and learned to trick shoot so that people would pay to watch him. Like Young Horse can do anything on a pony, Nighthawk can do anything with a gun.''

"Is it true that you see more Bluecoats coming in your dreams?" Little Foot asked. "They say that you can see a battle in the sky.''

"Yes, and I can't get rid of those visions. Sometimes they come as dreams at night, and sometimes during the day when I'm just sitting somewhere. I see it coming all the time now. I don't like it.''

"Ah, the spirits are really talking to you, aren't they?''

"I wish they'd be quiet for a while," Ghostwind said. "It's beginning to make me crazy.''

"They say that you're like Sitting Bull, that you've seen dead Bluecoats. Do you know when this will happen?''

"No, and that's what troubles me. I can see it plainly, but I don't know when it's coming.''

"You shouldn't worry," Little Foot said. "Sitting Bull's vision said the Indian people would be victorious.''

"Maybe so," Ghostwind said, "but still a lot of Indian people will die. That will make a lot of us sad.''

"I just heard you say 'us.' Does that mean you believe

your husband will be killed? Can you *see* who will cross over?''

"I can't see that. I only know that it will be a very bad day. Very bad. Even if the Indian people achieve victory, the day will be bad.''

Ghostwind and Little Foot started back toward their lodges, but part way, they sat down to watch the sunset. From behind them, in the village, came the barking of dogs and the laughter of children.

"If only it could always be this way," Ghostwind said, "I would never complain about anything again.''

"Ah, I hear that!'' Little Foot agreed. "We take so much for granted. When it's all gone, then we'll wish we hadn't been demanding more all the time.''

The sky was lit with scarlet. A long bank of clouds, their bellies aflame, rested along the horizon. Overhead, nighthawks swooped and dived, twisting and turning in circling patterns through the darkening sky.

"Look at those birds," Ghostwind said. "They do that every night, no matter what has happened. As the warm moons come and go, there have been floods along the bottoms, fires in the mountains and grasslands, and sometimes even the ground shakes. Still, those birds ride the wind, sailing in front of clouds.''

"Yes, they're everywhere," Little Foot said. "I used to watch them every night when I was among the Bluecoats. They would remind me that some day I would return to my people.''

"It must have been hard living with them," Ghostwind said.

"I had a hard time, but Young Grass didn't have it so bad, living with Long Hair. At least that's what she told me. She's living on the southern plains now. Sometimes I miss her and want to go and see her.''

"Did she like Long Hair?" Ghostwind asked. "He must not have treated her badly.''

"Long Hair was a very unusual man," Little Foot said. "He had learned to sign well and could make Indians understand him. At times he talked as though he knew the Indian people and why they wish to remain free, and at other times he would degrade us. As a Bluecoat chief, he thought the same way as most white men. They want to own this land and will do anything to have it.''

"I sometimes think about that,'' Ghostwind said, "and I wonder. Nighthawk's stories told me of battles fought in times past, far to the east, by Bluecoats against Redcoats. Nighthawk said that the Redcoats wanted to control what the Bluecoats did. The Bluecoats won and pushed the Redcoats out. They left in boats, across the Big Waters, and went back to their homeland. Now the Bluecoats are doing to us the same thing that the Redcoats did to them. And Long Hair Custer is leading them.''

"What I knew of Long Hair was troubling,'' Little Foot said. "He was a confused man. He had different people all in one body. He would laugh, then suddenly turn sad. He would be quiet, looking across the land, then suddenly turn angry and violent. Some days he would stay the same the entire day, whether it was gentle or mean. Other days he would change often. You never knew.''

"How did he act when Young Grass conceived his child?''

"Many believe that Young Grass's light-haired son is his,'' Little Foot replied. "But Young Grass told me that it isn't so.''

"Long Hair didn't father Yellow Bird?''

Little Foot shook her head. "It was his brother who fathered her son, the one called Tom Custer. Long Hair didn't seem to mind if his brother lay with her. That's what she told me. I don't know how many know this, but a lot of people want to think Yellow Bird is Long Hair's son. He's not.''

"I don't understand,'' Ghostwind said.

"Young Grass told me that Long Hair lay with her, but he almost never took her as a man does a woman. Sometimes he did, but not often. That was part of his confusion. Young Grass said that he kept her to make the others believe that he wanted women, when he was actually confused about what he wanted.''

"Are you saying that he was a man-woman?"

"Not as we know a man-woman, no. Young Grass told me that Long Hair was never open about his feelings and always kept them locked away. He only showed what he wanted people to see. In the white culture, a man-woman is scorned, and he was a Bluecoat chief. He fought it all the time. Inside, he was a sad man. Young Grass told me this. And I knew it from being around him."

"If he was so sad, how could he lead men?" Ghostwind asked.

"He turned his sadness into anger," Little Foot replied. "He always drove hard for what he wanted, and always tried to outsmart everyone, even the Bluecoat chiefs above him. And he did outsmart a lot of them. But not my people."

"How did he try to outsmart your people?" Ghostwind asked.

"When Long Hair took us women, the other Bluecoat chiefs wanted us for their pleasure and thought of nothing else. But Long Hair knew that he could go into Cheyenne villages in peace and talk if he had Cheyenne women with him. He thought that he could go to the camps and have them believe that he cared about the Cheyenne people. But that didn't work; they all knew about the Washita. They didn't trust him."

"It's odd that the Cheyenne didn't kill him down there," Ghostwind said.

"Since Spring Grass was with him always, they never tried to kill him," Little Foot said. She looked into the darkening sky. "Maybe there was a time when Long Hair wanted peace with the Indian people. But there was too much bitterness, and the Cheyenne and Sioux warriors began killing whites, to avenge the deaths of their relatives. Then Long Hair was told to fight, and he decided that we weren't good enough and that he would win all the battles with us, no matter what. But he can't win. He's already dead."

Ghostwind's eyebrows raised.

"You know the story, don't you?" Little Foot made a sign with her fingers. "About the time Long Hair lied to Medicine Arrow and his council and the pipe ashes burned his boots?''

"Yes, I heard about that," Ghostwind said. "You were there?''

"I wasn't in the council, but I heard what happened from the wife of an elder who had been in the lodge,'' Little Foot replied. "Long Hair was sitting to the right of a prominent man, Medicine Arrow. They were having a pipe ceremony and Long Hair lied about wanting the Cheyenne people to live in peace. Long Hair was sitting under the Sacred Arrow bundle when he said this, and everyone knew it was a lie. The pipe did not burn after that, and Medicine Arrow knocked the ashes out on Long Hair's boots. A strange smoke rose and filled the lodge. The medicine was angry.''

"How did Long Hair feel about this?'' Ghostwind asked.

"He was too strong willed to know what he'd done,'' Little Foot replied. "When the ceremony began, he thought that he was being honored. But his words betrayed him. I believe he knew that the spirits were angry with him. Yet he was a man who didn't believe that he could lose. He'd always won in battle and believed that would never change.''

"Do you think that Long Hair and his Bluecoats are after us now?''

"There are scouts saying that they have seen Bluecoats up on Elk River, and some coming this way along the Rosebud. They know it isn't Three Stars, for he's still to the south, at the foot of the White Rain Mountains. But no one knows for sure who leads these Bluecoats, for their chiefs aren't familiar to anyone up here.''

"They should know not to attack us,'' Ghostwind said.

"Yes, they should know that,'' Little Foot agreed. "I've heard that there are Crow and Arikara scouts with them. They hate us, but they will know not to attack such a big village. They know that to do so would bring a lot of blood and death to them. Their families would have to mourn them, for they wouldn't survive such a battle.''

Ghostwind was listening, staring across to the horizon.

Suddenly the sky grew wild with fire and her vision returned, everything a boiling red, with both Bluecoats and Indian warriors churning and twisting, tumbling into a deep, dark hole, screaming as they fell.

"What's the matter?" Little Foot asked. "Are you seeing ghosts?"

Ghostwind closed her eyes. She bent forward and covered her head with her hands, rocking back and forth, tears streaming from her eyes.

"How can I help you?" Little Foot asked.

"It will go away," Ghostwind said. "I just have to wait for the vision to leave."

"You're seeing a battle?"

"Yes. When you talked about death, the vision returned."

"I'm sorry. I didn't mean to cause you trouble," Little Foot said.

Ghostwind took a deep breath and wiped tears from her eyes. "You aren't to blame for what's coming. And you don't have to feel bad about my visions. You didn't bring them, either. What's coming has been set to happen for a long time, and there's nothing anyone can do about it."

"This makes me afraid," Little Foot said. "Everyone knows that Sitting Bull has seen a battle, and people are beginning to talk about you now as well. And I've also learned that a Cheyenne man named Box Elder has been having visions. There are probably more. It must be going to happen."

"I'd better get this water back to my lodge," Ghostwind said, rising to her feet. "All I can tell you is that you should keep your children near. No matter how much we all want to believe that the Bluecoats won't attack us, they will. And when they come, it will be a surprise."

Young Horse sat his pony, watching Tall Deer as he stood grooming a fine pinto mare. Tall Deer had been training the pony for a warrior friend of Crazy Horse, teaching it to stop and start with knee and hand commands.

"I worry about my mother a lot," Young Horse was telling Tall Deer. "She feels bad all the time now."

"I'll bet it's because she believes Nighthawk will be forced to leave," Tall Deer said. "The warriors talk about it all the time."

"I worry about it, too," Young Horse said. "He's been good to me. And he's always making my sister laugh. Talking Grass thinks he's a better father than our real one was."

"It will be hard if he has to go," Tall Deer said. He gave the pony a handful of grass and ran his hands up and down its forelegs, working to gain the pony's trust. "Maybe you should do something to make your mother proud of you, so that she won't be so unhappy."

"What could I do?" Young Horse asked. "You train ponies for the warriors. They all respect you. I can't do that."

"Why not?"

"Because I don't know how."

"I'll show you how," Tall Deer said. "When we're finished, you will have Crazy Horse calling you brave."

Young Horse was intrigued with the idea. "It would have to be a very brave deed to impress a man like him."

"You know that young black stallion that Crazy Horse left up in the Wolf Mountains?" Tall Deer said. "If you could find that pony and tame him, Crazy Horse would think you a warrior already. Your mother would take her mind off her visions and take you around the village to show you off."

"That pony is pretty wild," Young Horse said. "Catching him would be a brave feat in itself."

"That's right!" Tall Deer said. "So if we caught him and you broke him to ride, all before Crazy Horse knew about it, you'd get plenty of glory. What do you say?"

Young Horse thought carefully. "How are we going to catch him?"

"I'll ride up next to him, on my pony, hiding on the opposite side of him, and then I'll lasso him. I'll tie him up and let him jump around until he's tired. Then we'll take him down to the river and tie him up. We'll keep him tied and you can get on him in the water. That should break him after a while."

"He's a wild one," Young Horse said. "Maybe we should take turns getting on him. You ride him for a while, then I'll take over."

"We can do it that way, if you wish," Tall Deer said. "When he's broke well enough, you can ride the pony to Crazy Horse's lodge and see him smile."

"That would make my mother very proud," Young Horse said. "But I've been thinking, how are we going to go clear to the Wolf Mountains? It was real trouble before when we went just a short distance outside of camp."

"We'll go first thing in the morning," Tall Deer replied. "Everyone will be in bed, still tired from tonight's dancing. No one will miss us."

"Are you sure?"

"Very sure. We'll catch that stallion and be back before anyone knows we're gone. You see, most everyone will be thinking about the Suicide Boys from your camp. They're having a dance tonight, for when the Bluecoats come again."

Young Horse knew about the Cheyenne boys and their dance, the Dying Dance, as it was called. There was already wailing in the camp because of the pledges some of the young men had given. They would fight until they died in the next battle with the enemy. Most of them were Tall Deer's age, or a little older.

"I'll make sure that Crazy Horse hasn't gone and gotten that stallion," Tall Deer said. "I can find that out and then meet you tonight at the Dying Dance. We'll talk about where to meet tomorrow morning to go after the pony."

"Do you think that my pleasing Crazy Horse will help my mother stop worrying about her visions?"

"Of course it will," Tall Deer said. "I told you before, she will show you off. She'll be laughing, not crying."

"Good," Young Horse said. "That's what I want."

"Don't forget, tonight at the Dying Dance," Tall Deer said. "Get ready for tomorrow, when you'll be brave!"

TWENTY-THREE

8:00 P.M. Saturday, 24 June 1876
On Rosebud, near Davis Creek

In camp for the night. Resumed march at 5:00 P.M. and just halted. Everyone very tired and irritable. Little Crane with the Rees again, learning what the Crow scouts have found up ahead. There's news that they've returned and were in a hurry to see Custer.

Am very concerned about getting my letters out to the Grants. Custer is not allowing couriers to go back with mail, not until after the battle. Have a great deal of information that I'd like sent before the battle, so that it might appear in print ahead of Custer's glorious muse, Mr. Kellogg.

Despite my dislike for the man, I've decided to lay off him. Red Moon discovered that Kellogg had recently lost his wife and had left two daughters in the care of relatives. Red Moon can sympathize with losing family, and asked me to go easy on Kellogg from now on.

I tried to apologize during the march late this afternoon, but Kellogg would have none of it. Instead, he told me that he had a surprise to spring when the time was right. I asked him what that might be, and he refused comment.

Lieutenant Charles DeRudio approached me earlier and asked to be interviewed. He stated that he was certainly not part of Custer's "royal family" and had some information that would be of interest to me. I didn't have time to ask him how long he's known Custer or what has provoked him, but I would suppose it has to do with the "royal family" and the fact that many of them are now in commands within the regiment, displacing many of the senior officers.

Soldiers do what they're trained to do, and do what they're told to do. Otherwise, I doubt if many outside the "royal family" care a plugged nickel about the upcoming fight.

Garrett laid his diary down and sipped coffee. While he had been writing, Red Moon had traded some soldiers a bag of pemmican for a pack of bacon and hardtack.

Smiling, he sat down next to Garrett. He skewered the bacon with a small stick and held it over the fire to cook.

"We'll share," he said to Garrett, making sign that they would eat together.

"Thank you, Red Moon," Garrett said. "Bacon will taste good. I'm not sure about the hardtack."

Red Moon turned the bacon in circles. Drippings popped in the fire.

"The big fight will come very soon now," he told Garrett. "Many will cross over to be with the Grandfathers."

"You and Little Crane talk about death all the time," Garrett said. "It would seem that you want to die."

"The Creator makes the choice," Red Moon said. "It's not up to us. We must be ready to go and die with honor."

"How could there be any honor in this? It seems to me that the Sioux and Cheyenne are fighting for survival, the Crow and the Ree are fighting to keep the Sioux and Cheyenne from surviving, and the soldiers just have a job to do."

"Long Hair believes there's glory," Red Moon said. "Doesn't he?"

"Long Hair cares about his own glory," Garrett said. "And it doesn't seem anybody can stop him."

Red Moon stripped a piece of bacon from the skewer

and handed it to Garrett, who accepted it gingerly and quickly dropped it onto a tin plate.

"I don't know how you and Little Crane can handle hot food the way you do," he said, whistling and shaking his fingers. "It's amazing."

Red Moon smiled, handing Garrett a piece of hardtack. "We have medicine fingers, too, but not such strong medicine as yours."

"Pretty strong medicine, though," Garrett said. "To be able to stand heat like that takes something I haven't got." He chewed the bacon and the hardtack together. The taste was pleasurable, a good change from the wild meat and berries.

Red Moon chewed and pointed to Garrett's diary. "What will you do with the talking paper?"

"I will send words that will go on big sheets called newspaper." He made sign. "Many people in the east will know what is happening out here. Many people will learn how Long Hair is leading his Bluecoats, so that they will not want him leading them."

"You've been making the paper talk against Long Hair, so that he doesn't become the Great Father in Washington?"

"That's what I hope to do. I want to talk to more soldiers and get as much as I can. I have an appointment with Lieutenant DeRudio tonight."

"I don't know who he is, but I thought you had stopped that."

"What?"

"Talking to people who don't like Long Hair."

"No," Garrett said. "I'm working for some men in the east. They hired me, like I hired you and Little Crane. You've known that from the beginning. I can't stop now. I have a job to do."

"How many of the Bluecoats here know what you're doing?"

"Not many. Just the officers who hate Long Hair and wish me well."

"What if one of them tells Long Hair?"

"They wouldn't do that. They don't want him to succeed."

"Maybe not," Red Moon said, "but if they hate him bad enough, they'll tell him so they can make him angry."

"I don't think they'll do that," Garrett said. He chewed his food hard. "They'd better not."

"You're doing a dangerous thing," Red Moon cautioned. "Long Hair is not one to make bad talk about and have everyone know. He might do something bad to you. Maybe he'd even shoot you."

"He wouldn't do that in front of everybody. And not now, so close to the Big Village."

"What if he told everybody that you were a spy?" Red Moon was staring hard at Garrett. "What if he said that the Sioux and Cheyenne sent you here?"

"Spying would be impossible to do, wouldn't you say?"

"You couldn't do that and be able to march with the Bluecoats every day. But you know Long Hair: If he thinks something, it doesn't matter if it's possible or not. He's made up his mind and you can't change it."

"He already knows that I'm working for a paper in St. Louis."

Red Moon shrugged. "I just want you to be careful. I wouldn't want to lose you as a brother so soon. I've lost many already."

"I'm going to be very careful from now on," Garrett promised. "Very careful indeed. I've discovered that the Bluecoat commanders under Long Hair are as crazy as he is. Maybe crazier."

"Very crazy," Red Moon agreed. "That's what I'm saying. They might do something foolish." He pointed to the diary again. "Will you make the paper talk about you and me, as brothers, when the battle is finished and the ceremony is done?"

"I will do that, yes."

Red Moon smiled, offering more bacon and hardtack to Garrett. "I will take you as my brother to our people.

If you wish, you can stay with me and find a wife among my people.''

Garrett thought about his answer. He didn't want to offend Red Moon, or hurt his feelings. ''We will talk again about that when the big fight is finished,'' he finally said. ''I told you, I will have to travel back to where I came from and make the big papers talk about what I've seen out here. But I do want to come back and see you, and maybe live with you for a while.''

Red Moon looked into the fire. ''It would have been good if my wife and children had met you. They would have liked you very much. My wife would have been proud to know you as my brother.''

''I wish I could have met them.''

''The children laughed a lot. They were so little. The sickness finished them quickly. My wife lasted for many days. She suffered greatly. I don't worry, though. They're on the Other Side and I know they're living well. But I wish they could have been with me longer in this world.''

Garrett ate in silence.

''My son was little; but even so small, he talked of becoming a warrior. He loved to ride horses. I would put him on and lead the horse around. He would hold on to the mane with one hand and swing his other arm and yell. He always yelled loudest when I stopped the horse. He never wanted to get off. He would have been a fine rider.

''And the girl. She would have become well known with her beading. She would sit and help her mother. She wanted her mother to bead all the time. Her mother would tell her to find a blue bead and she would pick one and hold it up. Then she would find a red one, or a yellow one. Her hands were so tiny, so soft and tiny.''

''I'm sorry, Red Moon,'' Garrett said. ''It wasn't fair that you had to lose them.''

''There is always loss,'' Red Moon said. ''It's a part of life. It's hard, but we have no choice.''

Little Crane returned from the Ree camp. His face was somber.

''The Crow scouts are still meeting with Long Hair. I

don't know if they've brought news about the Big Village or not. I'll bet they have, though, and I'll bet the Big Village isn't far away.''

Little Crane accepted some bacon from Red Moon. "It will make you feel better," Red Moon said.

"It will make me feel less hungry," Little Crane said, "but it won't make me feel better."

Everyone looked up as a man strode deliberately to Garrett and stood over him. Mark Kellogg told Garrett to get to his feet, his lips parted in a smirk.

"I'm comfortable the way I am, Mr. Kellogg," Garrett said. "If you'd care to have a seat, though, that would be fine."

"I'm afraid not, Mr. Garrett. I have news for you. The General will see you right away, and I don't mean after you finish your meal."

"The General wants to see me?" Garrett said.

"Right away," Kellogg said. "Right *now*, Mr. Garrett."

Garrett took another bite of bacon. "Why did he send you, Kellogg? Why not one of his orderlies?"

"You're the one to be answering the questions, Mr. Garrett. And the General is waiting."

"What's this about?"

"Your friend in conspiracy, Major Reno, has given you away. While in a drunken rage this evening, he threatened Lieutenant Cooke with physical harm and added a remark that will prove most embarrassing to you, I'm afraid."

"What kind of remark?" Garrett asked.

Kellogg was grinning broadly now. "Reno told Lieutenant Cooke that when you were finished with the General in the press, the General would wish that the Indians had gotten him instead."

Garrett tried to hide his shock. "I don't know why Reno would say a thing like that," he finally said.

"Don't be coy with me, Mr. Garrett. What I've said all along is precisely the case: You intend to gather slanderous information on the General. Then you intend to have it published far and wide."

"Mr. Kellogg—" Garrett broke in.

"Who hired you, anyway?" Kellogg was shouting now. "Surely not a paper. It had to be somebody with political aspirations. Whoever it was, they've made a mistake. And so, Mr. Garrett, have you. The General wishes to see your notes, your diary, everything. Don't forget to have them with you."

Kellogg stomped away. Garrett set his bowl down. Little Crane and Red Moon sat in silence.

"I didn't think Reno was that stupid," Garrett said. "I should have known better. I can't show Custer my diary and my notes. Who knows what he'd do to me."

Little Crane laughed. "Don't worry. Go and see Long Hair, but without the talking paper. Tell him the talking paper is lost." He stood up and picked up Garrett's saddle. "This is how it happened. I took your pony out to graze, and I forgot to unsaddle him. The cinch was loose and when I took the pony across the creek, the saddle turned. The talking paper was in your saddlebags and fell out. Now it's all lost."

Garrett laughed. "Oh, that's brilliant. I don't know if he'll believe that, though."

"Make him listen. Tell Long Hair that you intend to whip me. Tell him how angry you are about it."

"I can't go that far, Little Crane."

"You must. That's the only way he'll believe you."

"But what if he makes me do it? What if he comes over here and insists on watching?"

"That is not how Long Hair behaves. He will likely tell you to make me stand on a barrel for a long time, with one leg up. When Bloody Knife got drunk, he didn't do anything."

Red Moon had been listening intently. He said, "If Long Hair comes, I will say that I'm to blame also. I went out with Little Crane to graze the ponies."

"I appreciate your support, Red Moon," Garrett said. "Let's hope Long Hair isn't interested in coming over here to check." He turned to Little Crane. "Where are you going to hide my papers?"

"Hide them? No, I will drop them in the water for

real. That's the only way you can come out in this. If Long Hair learns you still have the talking papers, something bad will happen."

"There's got to be another way," Garrett said. "I don't want to lose all that work."

"You have no choice," Little Crane said. "It's either that or risk what Long Hair will do."

"I can't lose my work. It will take too long to reconstruct it, and I'll surely forget things."

"Do you want Long Hair to know what the talking paper says?" Red Moon asked.

"Of course not!"

"Red Moon is right," Little Crane said. "Don't be foolish. Let me drop your saddle and many of your things into the water. The talking paper must be lost. Now, you'd better go to meet with Long Hair. Hurry."

Garrett approached Custer's tent, trying to envision the conversation. It would be foolish to deny that he had ever talked to Reno; Kellogg wasn't capable of fabricating such a pernicious story. But what else had Reno told Lieutenant Cooke? How far had Reno gone in his drunken anger?

At the tent, Garrett stopped and composed himself. The time had come to face up to Custer, and there was no way out of it.

There was conversation inside the tent. Custer was giving commands to someone. Near the doorflap his two staghounds lay chewing on deer bones. Garrett tried to listen, but could only hear something about attacking the village as soon as it was located.

Two officers left the tent, followed by Lieutenant Cooke, who frowned deeply upon seeing Garrett.

"Good evening, Lieutenant," Garrett said, as cheerfully as possible. "I've just learned that the General wishes to see me."

"You've got a lot of nerve," Cooke said. "I, for one, am in favor of sending you off, hostiles or not."

"That would be a bad idea, Lieutenant, and you know it," Garrett said. "What if Sioux scouts discovered me wandering around out here? They'd surely know there was a force of Bluecoats somewhere near. Don't you think?"

"Then how does a firing squad sound?"

"Gunshots make a lot of noise."

"Not if the muzzle of the gun is up against your head." Cooke turned and leaned into Custer's tent, announcing Garrett's arrival. "If it were up to me," he said, "you wouldn't live another minute." He held the flap open for Garrett.

Inside, Custer was sitting cross-legged on the ground, a map spread out before him. Bloody Knife was on his right, Mitch Boyer on his left. Curley and Goes Ahead sat across from them.

They were all watching the map, which had been drawn from descriptions of the area by Mitch Boyer and the Crow scouts. Custer traced a line up over the Rosebud–Little Bighorn divide. Custer had traced the column's route up the Rosebud and had penciled in X's along the Little Bighorn River.

Custer looked up. "So, Mr. Garrett, where do you think the village is?"

Garrett shifted from foot to foot. "I don't know the country, General. I couldn't even begin to guess."

"Well, then, take a look." Custer motioned Garrett to come over and sit down with them.

Garrett took a seat between Boyer and Curley. He rubbed his hands together, and Curley said something in Crow that made Mitch Boyer and Goes Ahead laugh out loud.

Mitch Boyer told Garrett, "He says that you rub your hands together to make the medicine come into your fingers, but that you'd better keep your fingers close to you and away from Son-of-the-Morning-Star. He can use a knife."

Garrett laughed nervously. Custer was frowning, studying the map, as if he hadn't heard the conversation.

"If you were in command of the Indian village, Mr. Garrett," Custer said, "where would you locate your camp?"

Custer waited for his answer, while the scouts looked on stoically.

"They would need plenty of grass and water," Garrett said. "And—"

"No, Mr. Garrett," Custer broke in. "Not '*They* would need plenty of grass and water.' You're supposed to say '*We* would need plenty of grass and water.' You're playing the part of the enemy here. Remember? You seem to have earned that position. At least that's what I've been led to believe."

"I understand, General." Garrett realized this was no time to appear weak or demoralized. Instead, he would take the offensive. He allowed his voice to become firm, almost demanding. "We will need to camp where there's plenty of grass and water," he said. "And also wood. Lots of wood." He turned to Curley. "Where's a camping place that has all of that?"

Boyer interpreted for Curley, who then put his finger on the map and traced the Little Bighorn from its mouth at the Big Horn River to the upper Little Bighorn, the Greasy Grass. He made circles in various places, including the foot of the Big Horn Mountains, in what the Crow called the Valley of the Chiefs.

"He says that the entire Little Horn—we call the Little Bighorn the Little Horn—has good wood and water," Boyer told Garrett. "There is usually plenty of game. But such a big village would have to send hunters out often for enough meat to feed everyone."

"I would have to think of another, very important condition for my camp," Garrett added. "I don't want to camp in a narrow valley. I want to be where there is plenty of space to flee, so that the women and children aren't trapped if we're attacked."

Custer's eyebrows raised. "That's very astute, Mr. Garrett. Have you studied military science somewhere?"

"I learned some things from covering the Rebellion, General," Garrett said. "I would suppose some of the same strategies would apply here."

"But you don't know quite enough, Mr. Garrett," Custer said. "You'll soon see why I was chosen to command this regiment." To Bloody Knife and the two Crows he said, "You are all dismissed for now. You may return to your camps. I'll send for you when I need you again." When the scouts were gone, Custer turned to Garrett. "Now, my good man, make yourself comfortable, for you're going to be here a while."

TWENTY-FOUR

A lone in the tent with Custer, Garrett felt as though he were in a courtroom, on trial by a one-man jury. Custer had turned his attention to the maps. Garrett felt the sweat rolling off him. He took a handkerchief from his pocket and wiped his face and neck.

Custer noticed Garrett wiping his brow and smiled.

"A gentleman scout. How quaint."

"It's a warm evening, General," Garrett said.

"That it is," Custer agreed. He took a red cloth from a large bag near him. Something was wrapped in the cloth, something that gave off a disagreeable odor.

Custer unwrapped the cloth, exposing a half dozen scalps, taken from men with short, light-colored hair.

"What do you think about this, Mr. Garrett? Curley and Goes Ahead brought them in."

Garrett noted that the scalps were not entirely dry, which meant they weren't a week old. He knew how long it had taken the scalp on his rifle to dry. This meant these scalps hadn't come from the Sun Dance village, where other scalps had been found earlier. They had to have been brought from somewhere up ahead.

"From white men, certainly," Garrett said. He was studying them. "Those two look odd to me."

"Those were taken from a man's face," Custer explained. "They were long sideburns, like Lieutenant Cooke's."

"Yes, I can see now," Garrett said. He was envisioning Cooke with his face bloody and raw, his sideburns gone. "Who would these men have been?"

"Would you venture to guess, Mr. Garrett?"

"Where did the scouts find the scalps?"

"Just ahead, in an abandoned village at the foot of the divide."

"Do you suppose they were couriers, General?"

"Possibly," Custer replied. "But not likely. These came from soldiers, Mr. Garrett."

Garrett immediately thought of Terry and Gibbon's commands coming up the Big Horn River.

"General Terry's men, you think?"

"I doubt it," Custer said. "My scouts would have seen or heard a battle like that. I believe this must have happened before we started up the Rosebud."

"You don't mean Crook's forces?"

"I do mean Crook's forces. There are no others out here that I'm aware of. And I would be aware of them were they here."

"Certainly, General," Garrett said. "But I still think that maybe they were couriers."

"Couriers don't travel in large groups, Mr. Garrett. If you want couriers to get through, you send them out separately, one at a time—two, three, or maybe even four men, spread way apart, if the news is that important. That way one of them is bound to get through."

"Yes, I can understand," Garrett said. "So you believe these were soldiers with Crook's regiment?" He thought about Ann's cousin, Mason Hall, wondering if he was still alive.

"I can see no other explanation."

"Then does that change your plans?"

"Only from the standpoint that the hostiles have another direction to turn and run. South. If they've met Crook and have taken scalps and are still traveling, that means that they won the battle and Crook is either wiped out or on the run. In any event it's certain he was whipped." Custer stared hard at Garrett. "And that means we must march as fast as possible. I cannot give the hostiles time to discover us, go into council, and run from me."

"Why would they run from you, General, if they

didn't run from Crook? Wouldn't a victory like that give them an added boost of courage?''

"You don't understand, Mr. Garrett." Custer's face was red. "I know how to fight Indians. These other commanders do not. If you strike a village the right way, you're going to rout them. I don't care what the numbers are, one soldier under me can take care of ten hostiles. Remember that, Mr. Garrett. *Ten* hostiles. When you think of it that way, there aren't that many of them up ahead. Do you understand?''

"I hear you, General."

"I'm disappointed in you, Mr. Garrett." Custer was leaning over the map, his eyes narrowed. "I've been hearing some annoying things about your discussions with Major Reno. It appears that you really don't know me all that well. I thought you told me early on that you knew what kind of commander I was. Didn't you?''

Garrett struggled to keep his poise. "Of course you're a good commander. There's never been any doubt about that.''

"Then why have you decided to side with Mr. Reno and Mr. Benteen? Or were you siding with them all along?''

"To get a full view of the campaign, I must talk to everyone, General. Any good reporter would do that.''

"Mr. Kellogg, in my estimation, is a good reporter," Custer said. "He finds no need to listen to drivel from jealous and insubordinate underlings.''

"Yes, Reno and Benteen would fit that description.''

Custer took a deep breath. "You see, Mr. Garrett, the time of our battle with the hostile Sioux and Cheyenne is very near. It is then that you'll become convinced of my abilities as an army commander and leader of men. I say again, Mr. Garrett, that it deeply disappoints me that you don't already see that in me.''

"Maybe I haven't been around you enough," Garrett said. "After all, Mr. Kellogg hasn't exactly welcomed me, and you seem to have taken his side.''

"Is that any reason to turn against me?''

"I would like to spend more time riding with you and learning how you command," Garrett said quickly. "If that's possible at this point."

Custer wasn't listening. He was circling an area along the Little Bighorn River, just below the divide.

"It would seem they would have to be somewhere in this vicinity," he said. He looked up at Garrett. "I remember you asking me to talk to those people, to try and reason with them. That's impossible, Mr. Garrett. You see, I know their ways. I know what they're thinking. Again, you don't know me, who I am, otherwise you wouldn't doubt my decisions."

"I believe you're right, General. I need to get to know you better."

Custer frowned. "Can you remember all this, Mr. Garrett? I don't see you taking notes. I don't even see any pencil and paper. Didn't Mr. Kellogg make it clear to you that I wanted to see your notes?"

"He did tell me that, General," Garrett replied. "But one of my scouts was careless and lost them in the creek." Thinking of Little Crane dumping all his work actually made Garrett angry and depressed, which Custer could plainly see.

"How did that happen?" Custer asked.

"Little Crane was out grazing my pony and foolishly left the saddle on. I had loosened the cinch and the saddle slid sideways, dumping my work. I've decided that I'm going to whip him for it."

Custer studied Garrett. "Perhaps you should reconsider. Whipping your scout will only cause him to hate you. Maybe you should take a look at yourself instead. You should have been more cautious with your work. You shouldn't have left your saddlebags on your horse."

"You're right, General," Garrett said. "But I was so tired from marching that I dismounted, dropped down, and fell asleep. He took my horse out before I'd awakened."

Custer grunted. "Do you have more paper?"

Garrett thought carefully. "I'm afraid I've lost it all, General."

"Perhaps you can borrow some from Mr. Kellogg."

"I don't believe he'd share. Especially not with me."

"I believe I can persuade him to give up some paper, and maybe a pencil or two," Custer said. "Then you can give Mr. Kellogg your work each day as you finish it and he will keep it for you."

"Give my work to Mr. Kellogg?"

"Yes. I believe that would be the best thing you could do. Mr. Kellogg watches over his work like an old hen. I'm sure he'd keep yours as well. Especially if I recommend it to him."

Garrett couldn't find any words.

"I'll have him bring you some paper and a pencil or two," Custer added. "Then, each evening shortly after the meal, you will bring your work to him. When Mr. Kellogg is ready to send his work off, he can send yours as well. There'll be plenty of news for everyone."

Garrett stood up. "Well, I'll look forward to seeing Mr. Kellogg before long, then."

Custer shouted for Lieutenant Cooke, who opened the tent flap. "Have a good evening, Mr. Garrett."

Garrett stepped out of the tent and strode toward his camp. First, he had allowed Little Crane to dump his work, then he had consented to work with Kellogg. He felt like the drunken soldier Custer had trapped in the wooden barrel.

When he met Little Crane and Red Moon, his frustration had grown.

"What did Long Hair say to you?" Little Crane asked. "Did he tell you to leave?"

"No," Garrett replied. "Worse. He wants me to write about him the same way Kellogg does. I don't know whether or not he believed the story about you having lost my work in the creek, but he's insisting that I accept paper from Kellogg and, after I've finished, give my notes back to him so that he can take it to Long Hair."

"So you won't be able to make the paper talk the way you want to?" Red Moon asked.

"I'll have a hard time," Garrett said. "They'll be

counting the sheets of paper, expecting the same number back that they gave me.''

Garrett noticed his saddle, resting nearby, damp from having been dunked in the creek. Beside the saddle were various personal items—clothes, and an extra pair of boots—also wet.

"I knew that you were going to get rid of my talking paper," Garrett said, "but did you have to ruin *everything?*"

"We expected Long Hair to come back and watch you whip me," Little Crane said. "Or watch me stand on a keg. He would be looking for your things, and your saddle would have to be wet if it fell into the water. And also your clothes."

"Yes, I suppose," Garrett said. He slumped to the ground. "All that work gone and nothing to do but wait until this campaign is over to redo it."

Red Moon could contain himself no longer. He rolled over and began laughing, as he had the day Mark Kellogg had been bucked off the mule.

"What's so funny?" Garrett asked.

Little Crane was smiling. "Red Moon has your talking paper tied into a blanket. He will keep it on the back of his pony."

"You mean you didn't toss my paper into the water?"

"That would have been a waste," Little Crane said. "But we thought it would be funny to tell you that we did. And we were right. It's funny."

Garrett was both angry and filled with elation. "Where is my work, did you say?"

"You can't go to it now," Little Crane warned. "That would be stupid."

"You're right," Garrett agreed. He walked over to Red Moon, who was still doubled over on the ground. "Can you keep my notes and diary safe? Are you listening, or are you just going to roll around laughing?"

Red Moon sat up. He had become suddenly serious. "I will guard the talking paper with my life."

"There will be times when I'll want you to bring me my diary. Can you do that without being noticed?"

"I can bring you whatever you want and no one will know," Red Moon promised. "I'm good at sneaking."

Garrett sat down and loosed a deep sigh of relief. His work was intact after all. He laid back to rest and fell asleep. It seemed he had just closed his eyes when Little Crane shook him awake.

"The Sioux and Cheyenne are not far, maybe just over the divide on the Little Bighorn. Long Hair says we will march tonight."

"Tonight?" Garrett said. "But the men and horses are so tired. How can anyone fight when they're exhausted?"

"Long Hair is as fresh as if he had slept a week," Little Crane said. "They say that he needs little rest and can march forever. He wants to reach the divide and stay in hiding during the day tomorrow. He wants to attack in two sunrises."

That would be the morning of the 26th, Garrett thought to himself. Maybe he's decided to wait for Terry and Gibbon after all.

"Are you ready to ride?" Little Crane asked Garrett. "I'll get your pony."

The camp was in motion, men grumbling and complaining, stumbling in the darkness. Garrett felt a surge of relief. Custer might have finally come to his senses, realizing that the scouts were right. Attacking without Terry and Gibbon's support was too big a risk.

Little Crane brought his pony and Garrett saddled up with new energy. For the first time in many days, he began to think that maybe he wouldn't die after all.

TWENTY-FIVE

Water sat in the shadows, watching as the fires in the Bluecoat supply camp died down one by one. His pony, picketed along the river, grazed on fresh grass, adding strength to legs that must soon run very fast.

He had watched the camp throughout the day and well into the evening. No Bluecoats had come after him, and at present he didn't expect that any would.

In a way, he wished some had ventured out. It would have been fun to lead them a good distance away and then kill them one by one.

Water realized that killing Bluecoats would have put Lareaux and Tyrone's life in danger. Not the woman's, though. The Bluecoats would never hurt the woman. Bluecoats never hurt women, unless they were too old to use for pleasure.

As a child Water had seen his mother raped by Bluecoats who were meant to be protecting his people from the Sioux. Fort Berthold was supposed to have been a place of refuge. Instead, for him, it had been a place of pain.

His mother had never recovered from the rape. She couldn't understand how the Bluecoats had professed to be protectors and then forced themselves on her. She could expect as much from an enemy, but not from a friend.

Water's older brother, Little Crane, had been hunting with their father and an uncle at the time. He was lucky. Watching was something Water would never get over.

Water had been slow to learn English. The elders, even those who had fought the first whites, the Long Knives who had come up the river for furs, had said often that the Arikara people must learn to live in two worlds. For Water, learning to live in the white world had been very difficult.

Not so for Little Crane. English had come easy to him; he had followed the White Man's Road with ease. Water had watched him learn the traits of the conquerors, yet retain his own identity and keep to the spiritual teachings that had been passed down among the Arikara people for as long as they could remember.

Little Crane, to his credit, had not swallowed the teachings of the Black Robes, who wanted the Arikara to stop their old ways and turn themselves into different beings. Little Crane had argued that not all of the Black Robe people were mean. They were like all people: some very good, some very bad, and very many in the middle.

Water, though larger in stature, had always felt inferior to Little Crane, to whom everything seemed to come easy. But Little Crane had left with his friend, Red Moon, to guide a man-who-makes-the-paper-talk to find Long Hair Custer. No matter how easily things had come before, Water knew that this journey would be very hard for his brother.

Water had been wondering how Little Crane was doing. Had they found Long Hair, and had they gone into battle against the Sioux and Cheyenne? As much as he worried about his brother, Water hadn't found a reason to go out by himself and find out.

If Lareaux, his close friend, hadn't agreed to come on this journey with the woman and her people, Water would never have left his home. He had always known there would be a long, hard war between the Bluecoats and the Sioux nation. It had been building for a number of years.

He had been hoping in his heart that Little Crane would never catch up with Long Hair and would avoid the fighting. Even though the Sioux were old enemies, Water had hoped for their success. To him there was no enemy like a Bluecoat.

As he studied the camp from the shadows, Water decided that it was time for his plan. More and more fires had gone out. Only a few remained in the camp.

First, he would steal the horses and hide them nearby, where they could be easily caught and ridden for escape. This would not be difficult, for the horses were picketed at the edge of camp with only one guard. Then he would signal Tyrone and Lareaux to be ready, using the soft call of a ground owl.

Water and Lareaux had practiced this many times back at Fort Burthold, for use in cases such as this. Tonight there would be no difficulty giving the signal. The Bluecoats were holding Tyrone and Lareaux in a tent at the edge of camp, close to the river. Smart soldiers would have kept their prisoners nearer the center. Escape would then have been almost impossible.

Also, the horses, even more important than enemy captives, should never be kept where they could easily be stolen. The Bluecoats knew little about keeping horses or prisoners for very long.

As for the woman, she was sitting near the river with the lesser Bluecoat chief who had taken them in. They had been there a long time—walking, talking, eating, more walking and talking. As the darkness settled, the lesser chief was getting closer to her and she kept moving around, putting her hands up to ward him off.

Water wondered why she hadn't gone back to her tent long ago. He had watched her go into Tyrone and Lareaux's tent a while back. Perhaps Lareaux had told her about the escape plan, that after four calls from an owl, she should be ready to run.

No matter how bad the Bluecoats were at defending their camp, it wouldn't be easy to get everyone away safely. Water wished Lareaux's leg hadn't been so bad; he would have come back at the Bluecoats, firing arrows into one or two of them, scattering the rest, and Lareaux could have ridden away with Tyrone and the woman. Then they would now be drawing closer to Long Hair Custer's Bluecoats.

Water drew down close to camp along the west end and signaled Lareaux, the four owl calls echoing over the slumbering camp. Had he heard? Water knew that his friend would be listening; Lareaux never rested in the hands of an enemy.

Water smiled, his face to the gentle west breeze. Perfect. The grass was dry and brittle. He pulled a match from a cloth bag. Now was the time.

By the river, Ann noticed the smoke drifting in, growing ever heavier. Sinclair, who had been holding her arm, trying to get her to kiss him, released her and ran back into camp, yelling into the tents.

"Fire! Fire! Get up and fight it! Get up, all of you!"

Not far away, a soldier was screaming. Gunshots sounded, followed by yells and curses. Ann heard hooves rushing past her and saw the shadowed form of an Indian with a bow in his hand, riding low over the back of a pony. Lareaux was right behind him on another horse. A third horse followed, riderless.

Lareaux had been right. Water had come to set them free. But where was Tyrone?

Ann knew she couldn't leave him. She ran toward the tent where Lareaux and Tyrone had been held. Suddenly, a form ran straight toward her from the darkness.

"Miss Ann?" Tyrone said, gasping for breath. "Why aren't you running in the other direction?"

"I came to find you," Ann said. "The others rode away without you and I thought something had happened."

"No, Miss Ann, I just fell off the horse."

Ann touched his arm. "Tyrone, you're bleeding!"

"It's a scratch. Nothing more. Now, let's git from here!"

The air was thick with smoke. Soldiers ran through the shadows, fighting fire with shovels and saddle blankets while others formed a bucket brigade from the river. Shouts came from every direction.

Ann and Tyrone ran through the brush along the river. She heard Sinclair's voice calling for her.

"Don't stop, Miss Ann. Don't stop for nothing!"

Tyrone tripped in the brush, slamming his wounded

arm into a tree. He yelled and fell to his knees. Ann turned to help him.

"Miss Ann," Tyrone said, clambering to his feet, "I told you to get along. Go! I'll catch up."

A figure suddenly appeared from the smoky shadows. "Halt, or I'll shoot!"

It was Sergeant Sinclair, panting heavily, his pistol drawn. Other soldiers could be heard not far behind.

"You will both come back with me," Sinclair said, "and I'll have no backtalk from either one of you."

A shot rang out from behind Ann. Sinclair dropped his pistol and staggered backward against a tree. Another shot bounced him off the tree and he fell heavily to the ground.

"By the Good Lord! You two having a picnic?" Lareaux asked, holding a smoking pistol. "A lovely picnic?"

Water was with him, holding the horses.

"We need to hurry," Lareaux said. "*Oui*, quickly!"

They mounted and kicked their ponies into a run. Behind them, shots rang out from the shadows, buzzing past like angry bees. Soon they were deep in the darkness, the shouting and shooting behind them, riding south toward the Little Bighorn.

Darkness had long since fallen. The Dying Dance continued, the drums growing stronger. Each dancer was dressed and painted like a warrior who had gone on many war parties. They had been painted by family members or medicine men hired to give them the best possible journey to the Other Side.

Mothers, fathers, and other relatives stood in a circle around the dancers, singing praise songs. More young men joined the circle all the time, as if the dance itself were drawing them in. Parents stood back, allowing each son to make his own choice, filling some with pride and others with deep sorrow.

Among them, Red Bear stood in place, moving his feet up and down with the drums. His face showed pain. Day Lily was nowhere to be seen.

Nighthawk watched with Ghostwind and Young Horse. Ghostwind had talked a long time with Day Lily about Red Bear. There was nothing anyone could do; Red Bear had made his choice. But Day Lily had said that she didn't have to watch it.

Ghostwind had left Talking Grass in the lodge with Mountain Water, going to the dance only because she didn't want Tall Deer talking Young Horse into something he couldn't get out of. She didn't think that Tall Deer would want to become a Suicide Boy, but he would do just about anything for honor.

Among the dancers and around the lodges knee-high shadows appeared, darting here and there, some gathering together. Ghostwind had noticed them since sundown. The Little People. They hadn't taken full form yet, but sometime in the night they would.

Some of the Little People would come to the dancers later in dreams, and perhaps to others in the village as well. The Little People were special, Ghostwind knew, for they were healers. But they often foretold death.

Ghostwind hadn't seen the Little People since the night she had prayed in the hills, when Nighthawk had come to find her. They would stay in the village until the battle, she thought, waiting for the time when they would be needed to help spirits of the dead cross over. Their presence frightened her deeply, for it meant that the battle couldn't be far off.

Nighthawk saw the look on her face. He noticed her eyes following something low to the ground.

"What are you seeing?" he asked.

"I don't want to talk about it," she said. She grabbed Young Horse and held him close to her, embarrassing him.

"Why are you worried about me?" he asked her. "I'm not old enough to be accepted for the dance."

"Are you sure of that?" she asked, fighting fear and sorrow.

Young Horse pointed to the dancers. "Do you see anyone my age in there?"

"I see some very young men, almost boys," Ghostwind said. "It's such a terrible thing. Why should they want to die so young?"

Nighthawk asked Young Horse, "Would you ever want to do this dance?"

"I don't think I ever would," Young Horse said. "I feel bad for them, especially Red Bear, but I feel that I'll live until I'm an old man. I don't know if that's good, but that's what I feel." He felt his teeth. "I just hope I can still eat then."

A group of Oglala warriors joined the onlookers. Among them was Crazy Horse, who stood nearby with his arms crossed, watching the dancing.

Young Horse pulled away from his mother. "I don't want Crazy Horse to think that you're nursing me," he said. "He gave me a pony for my very own. If he saw you holding me like a toddler, he might take it away."

"No one would mistake you for a toddler," Nighthawk said. "I think you're growing up pretty fast these days, with the help of Tall Deer. You're mother's right: You shouldn't do everything he suggests."

Young Horse wasn't listening. He was watching Crazy Horse.

"What do you suppose he's thinking?" Young Horse asked.

"Why don't you ask him?" Ghostwind suggested.

Young Horse didn't hesitate. He darted over to stand beside Crazy Horse.

"I'm making sure that the pony you gave me stays fat," he told Crazy Horse. "Every day I take him to fresh grass."

"I know that," Crazy Horse said. "It's good. It means you'll have pride in your ponies when you grow to be a warrior."

Young Horse thought about Tall Deer's plan to catch the black stallion in the morning. He held his hand over his mouth, so that he didn't say anything to Crazy Horse about it and spoil the surprise.

"Where's your friend Tall Deer tonight?" Crazy Horse asked.

"I don't know," Young Horse replied. "He said he

was coming, but I haven't seen him yet.'' Surely Crazy Horse liked Tall Deer better than him, because Tall Deer was an excellent rider. Why else would Crazy Horse ask about Tall Deer if he didn't wish to see him?

"Are you going to give Tall Deer a pony, too?" Young Horse asked.

Crazy Horse laughed. "Tall Deer will have plenty of ponies, I'm sure. He won't need to have anyone give him one. He'll catch all the wild ones for himself. That's an honorable thing.''

Young Horse smiled. "Did you say catching wild horses was honorable?"

"Sure it is. I wish I could have done that as a young man. I saw horses in dreams, but I had trouble catching them.'' He laughed. "I couldn't even dream them to me.''

"Do you have any wild horses that you wish were tamed?" Young Horse asked.

"Not anymore," Crazy Horse replied. "I had a few that I really liked once, but they're in the hills now. They got away when we moved camp here. There was a two-year-old black stallion among them, a very good-looking pony. But he's no good to me if he runs away all the time. And I can't keep going after him when there could be danger near the village.''

"Yes," Young Horse agreed. "It's much better if you can catch the ponies and not have to chase around after them. That's a lot better.''

"Are you going to be a wild horse breaker and trick rider like Tall Deer?" Crazy Horse asked.

"Maybe. Do you think I'd be a good one?"

"You would be pretty good at just about anything you'd want to do," Crazy Horse said.

Young Horse stuck his chest out. "Really? Do you mean that?''

"Of course I mean that. But you shouldn't choose breaking horses just because Tall Deer's good at it. Maybe there's something else that you can do that would bring just as much honor. Look into your heart and ask. You'll get an answer.''

Young Horse pointed to the dancers. "Why do you

think they decided to become Suicide Boys?"

"They believe that it's a sure way of dying an honorable death," Crazy Horse replied. "But you can see that some of them shouldn't be there." He pointed to various dancers. "You see the fear in their eyes? They should have made their peace with death by now if they're going to fight to die. They shouldn't be afraid. It will be hard for them to cross over."

Young Horse stared at the dancers. Crazy Horse was such a powerful man, yet so kind and filled with wisdom. He would never tell someone not to do something, but he would certainly ask them if they were ready. It's not so easy to be ready to die.

Young Horse was proud that Crazy Horse talked to him as if he were a man, a grown warrior. With Crazy Horse, there was no such thing as "You're not old enough for that yet," or "You're not old enough to hear that." If someone was old enough to ask, he or she was old enough to get the answer.

"You take good care of yourself," Crazy Horse said to Young Horse. "I'm going to a ceremony. Maybe I'll see you tomorrow."

"I'll see you tomorrow for sure," Young Horse blurted, and immediately worried that Crazy Horse would wonder how he could be so certain.

"Good," Crazy Horse said, smiling. "Until tomorrow, then."

When Crazy Horse had left, Young Horse returned to Ghostwind and Nighthawk.

"Did you see me talking to him?" Young Horse asked. "Did you?"

"You talked to him for quite a while," Ghostwind said. "What did he say?"

"He made me think about the Dying Dance," Young Horse replied. "I know for sure that I won't ever be joining them. I won't be ready for death until I'm very old."

Ghostwind was smiling. "That's good to hear. Are you ready to go back to the lodge with us?"

"I'll stay for a little longer," Young Horse said.

"Don't be too late," Ghostwind said. She was watching the shadows again. More and more Little People were coming all the time.

"Are you sure you don't want to come with us?" Nighthawk said. "I'm going hunting tomorrow. You can come along and see how I shoot the rifle. But we'll be leaving early."

Young Horse was sorely tempted to go back with them. But he had promised Tall Deer he'd meet him at the dance.

"I'll be along soon," Young Horse said. "I'll get up and go hunting with you tomorrow. I'll be there."

Young Horse watched Nighthawk and his mother disappear into the shadows. Tall Deer suddenly appeared at his side.

"I was watching you talking to Crazy Horse," he said. "What did he tell you?"

"We talked about the Dying Dance," Young Horse replied. "He said that anyone who does it should have already made peace with death."

"I don't think I'd care to die yet," Tall Deer said. "Are you ready to go after Crazy Horse's stallion?"

"Not yet," Young Horse said.

"It will be light before long," Tall Deer said. "A lot of warriors are going out beyond the boundaries. We can cross the river with them."

"Why are they going out there?"

Tall Deer said, "Scouts say that a large number of Bluecoats are somewhere on the Rosebud. They want to go out and fight them. A warrior named Wolf Tooth is taking them."

"I thought we were going to catch Crazy Horse's pony and break him."

"Maybe we will," Tall Deer said. "But if there's a fight, it's more important to be there. Just think, if you stole a Bluecoat horse or counted coup on a Bluecoat that had fallen, you would be a warrior already! Crazy Horse would think much more of that than breaking a pony to ride."

"I'd rather go after the pony," Young Horse said. "I'm not old enough to fight Bluecoats. You aren't either."

"We can go after the pony, then," Tall Deer agreed. "But we still have to leave now if we're going to find the horse and catch him and break him all in one day."

Young Horse thought a moment. Maybe it would be a good idea to catch the stallion early and bring him back right away. Then he could go hunting with Nighthawk, like he'd promised.

"Let's go," Young Horse said. "I'll have to catch my pony."

Tall Deer smiled. "I've already caught him for you. Both our ponies are waiting just outside the village. Already Wolf Tooth and his warriors are across the river. They're going to stay in the trees and brush until dawn, then go toward the Rosebud."

Young Horse followed Tall Deer through the shadows to where the ponies were tied.

"Are you sure this is a good idea?" Young Horse asked.

"This is your time to be brave," Tall Deer said. "The police are all watching for Wolf Tooth's warriors. They won't see us, because we'll be very careful." He jumped on his pony. "Are you ready?"

Young Horse mounted. "I don't know."

Tall Deer had already eased his pony into the water and was riding low over its back. "Come on!" he hissed. "Don't go back on me now."

Young Horse lowered himself over his pony and followed, splashing through the current. The water was high and cold, surging up over his thighs, taking his breath away.

On the opposite shore, he turned for one last look at the village. The drums were loud in his ears, almost as loud as his heart. The singing carried out through the deep shadows, into the hills.

"Young Horse! Come on!"

Tall Deer was partway up a hill, waving frantically, hissing loudly. Young Horse nudged his pony with his heels. There was no turning back now. The time to be brave had come.

TWENTY-SIX

G arrett rode with Little Crane and Red Moon through the darkness. They stayed below the ridges, to one side of the command.

The march had begun shortly after midnight. Though Custer had emphasized the need for quiet, there was more noise than at any time during the campaign. In addition to the usual sounds of marching—the creaking of saddle leather and the banging of pots and pans—the irate soldiers cursed and whipped their tired horses. The horses snorted and puffed up the trail, a difficult one to follow even in the daylight. The mules brayed constantly, their packers yelling oaths that could be heard up and down the line.

In the middle of the column, someone was singing "Annie Laurie," while another soldier farther back sang "The Goodbye at the Door."

"If there are Sioux scouts out tonight," Little Crane said, "they will surely hear us."

Garrett felt as if the hills might explode with warriors at any time. Little Crane explained that Indians normally fought in the early morning hours. Many times horses were stolen under cover of darkness, but death was not good in the night.

Garrett glared through the dark at Custer, wondering how he could think the Seventh Cavalry would win another victory, no matter the odds, just because that's the way he wanted it. Watching him today, he'd known that Custer was paying little attention to what was happening around him. Reaching the Big Village held his mind like a vise.

Curley and the other Crow scouts had returned earlier to report that the trail had crossed the divide and had entered the Little Bighorn valley. Custer had immediately sent a large detachment of scouts ahead to a high ridge above the divide, called the Crow's Nest, where they would wait for daylight, then look down upon the Little Bighorn valley and search for the hostile village.

"Long Hair told Peaked Face Varnum to go and take some others with him," Little Crane told Garrett. "Five of the Crows went, along with six of the Ree scouts, Boyer, and Lucky Man Reynolds. They will find the village and tell Long Hair how many lodges there are."

Little Crane then announced that he would ride ahead and talk with Bloody Knife and some of the Ree scouts. Garrett rode silently with Red Moon, too tired to care.

Mark Kellogg approached and pulled his mule alongside Garrett's pony.

"Good evening, Mr. Kellogg," Garrett said. "Are you enjoying the march?"

Kellogg ignored the question. "Mr. Garrett, you haven't come to me for paper and pencil, as the General ordered. The General is wondering if you've given up your journals."

Garrett was careful how he answered. If he said he had given up his writings about the campaign, Custer might dismiss him. Prudence was the answer here.

Garrett said, "I miss keeping track of things."

"Well, I've brought you something to write on." Kellogg pulled a wrapped bundle of paper from his saddlebag and handed it to Garrett. "I'll expect you to have something for me by noon today."

"Noon today? If we ever stop, I intend to sleep until noon."

"You'd better take some time to write," Kellogg said. "The General is eager to read your thoughts about the campaign."

"Are you sure the General is as eager as you?" Garrett asked.

Kellogg chuckled. "It doesn't really matter, now does it, Mr. Garrett? The General is in charge and it was he who sent me. I trust that you won't disappoint him.''

Kellogg started to turn his mule. Garrett stopped him.

''Where do you plan to be during the fight?'' Garrett asked.

''With the General, of course. If you're wondering about yourself, you'll be with another commander. I don't believe the choice of which commander has been made yet, but you'll be informed when the time is right.''

''Did the General tell you that himself, or did you just make it up?''

''I have every reason to believe you won't be with the General,'' Kellogg said. ''Why should he need you when he has me?''

''That should be obvious.'' Garrett knew he shouldn't have said it. Again, he had shown lack of control. Somehow, Kellogg got deeper under his skin than anyone he had ever known.

''I'm sorry, Mr. Garrett. What did you mean by that?''

''Forget it,'' Garrett said. ''I'm too tired for this conversation. Thank you for the paper.''

''When can I expect your notes?''

''When I get them to you.''

''Very well,'' Kellogg said. ''I'll report that to the General.''

When Kellogg was gone, Red Moon said, ''You would do better to take your notes to Long Hair personally. Don't give them to that man.''

''I don't intend to give them to Long Hair, either,'' Garrett said. ''My diary will be written on *my* paper, kept by you until I need it back. The paper Mr. Kellogg gave me will remain blank.''

''But Long Hair expects you to make the paper talk about him.''

''If he lets me go with him into battle, then I'll write something and give it to him,'' Garrett replied. ''Otherwise, he can whistle Dixie, which is something he would never do.''

'' 'Whistle Dixie'?'' Red Moon said.

''The Greycoats who fought the Bluecoats in the war to the east were from Dixie,'' Garrett explained. ''You already know what Long Hair thinks of Greycoats."

"Ah, yes, I do understand," Red Moon said with a laugh. "I'll give you five ponies to whistle Dixie for Long Hair."

"I don't know the song."

"Oh, that's interesting. You must have forgotten it just now."

"I'll teach it to you, Red Moon," Garrett said. "Then you can whistle it for him."

"How many ponies do you have?"

"Maybe I'll steal some from the Sioux," Garrett said. "Wouldn't that surprise you?"

"No, nothing you might do would surprise me," Red Moon said. "Not even whistling Dixie."

Little Crane returned, filled with rumors about Long Hair's plans for the upcoming battle. They were all speculative, for no one had heard Long Hair say what he was going to do.

"The scouts tell me that no one knows what's in Long Hair's mind, not even his lesser chiefs," Little Crane said. "Everyone is guessing that, with so many in the village, he will attack in full force, straight on. Others say that he's so worried about the Sioux running away that he will split the force and try to come at them from different directions."

"A head-on, frontal assault would show power," Garrett said. "That would put the women and children at risk. Wouldn't they likely surrender then?"

"They would surely surrender if the women and children faced danger," Little Crane said. "Either that, or fight to the death. They have nothing to lose. Going back to the agencies is a slow way to die, without honor. Death in battle is the greatest honor. If I were a leader among the Sioux, that's what I would want."

Garrett listened to Little Crane and Red Moon discuss the battle further. He offered little to the conversation, other than his thought that Custer would be wise to ask the hostiles to surrender before attacking, possibly saving many lives on both sides. But he had already talked to

Custer about that and had learned that Custer wanted to fight, not talk.

Around 2:00 A.M. a halt was called. Garrett slid from the saddle and pulled the bit from his pony's mouth, as did Little Crane and Red Moon. Garrett tied the reins to his wrist and lay flat in the grass, his hat askew on his head. He was asleep immediately.

"I'll take the ponies to graze," Little Crane told Red Moon.

"I'll join you soon," Red Moon said, starting a small fire.

As Little Crane untied Garrett's pony and led the ponies away, Red Moon blew on the kindling and watched tiny flames burst upward. He scooted over and removed Garrett's hat from under his head and placed it neatly to one side, then straightened Garrett's hair across his forehead.

"Sleep well, my brother," Red Moon said. "We have a hard road ahead of us."

Mitch Boyer awakened in the dawn light. Curley was shaking him, his breath condensing as he spoke.

"Hairy Moccasin and White-Man-Runs-Him have seen the Big Village. Let's go up and look."

Boyer sat up. His blanket was covered with heavy dew. "How big is it?"

"Not enough light yet to see well," Curley said. "But they said that the Little Horn was filled with smoke."

Boyer looked back toward where they had come. The draws were still in deep shadow, the tops of the ridges bathed in a reddish glow. After Custer's orders, they had ridden for nearly five hours through the darkness before making their way up a timbered draw to the base of the ridge. There they had settled in to sleep until daylight.

Restless, Hairy Moccasin had awakened before dawn. White-Man-Runs-Him had accompanied him to the Crow's Nest, where they had waited for enough light to see into the Little Bighorn valley. What they had found had startled them.

The Crow's Nest was a short climb away. Everyone was in a hurry to get there and see.

"It's a big village," Hairy Moccasin was telling Curley and Boyer as they climbed. "Bigger than any village ever. Smoke rolls from their lodges like clouds on a winter day."

Boyer followed Curley up the last stretch of slope to a notch in the divide, a saddlelike depression that resembled a huge nest. From there it was easy to see out and not be detected by anyone looking into the hills from below.

The Big Village lay nestled in the valley bottom, some fourteen miles distant.

Varnum, the commander, had come up behind and settled in next to Hairy Moccasin and White-Man-Runs-Him.

"I don't see anything," Varnum said. He rubbed his tired eyes, swollen from dust and lack of sleep.

The air was cool and slightly damp, trapping the smoke in the valley below. Boyer and the other scouts were used to such conditions, their eyes trained to pick out detail no matter the light conditions.

"Are you sure there's a village down there?" Varnum asked. "We can't be wrong, you know."

White-Man-Runs-Him offered his spyglass. Boyer interpreted.

"White-Man-Runs-Him wants you to look through this. Then you'll see that what we've been telling you is true. The enemy is great in number."

Charley Reynolds, who had a set of field glasses, looked long and hard. He took the field glasses away from his eye, his face twisted with worry. He said nothing, but sat back and stared into the valley.

"I still can't see anything," Varnum said.

White-Man-Runs-Him was losing his patience. Boyer told Varnum, "He's asking you to look hard. You won't see many lodges, because they're hidden by the bluff along the river. But you'll see the smoke. You can't miss that. And look into the hills across the river. That's the main thing. There are many horses. See them? They look like maggots crawling on a fresh buffalo hide, they are so many.''

Varnum shook his head. ''I can't see anything. Are you sure?''

Boyer noted deep lines of anger in White-Man-Runs-Him's face. Goes Ahead and Hairy Moccasin were asking Boyer if Varnum had gone blind. Curley and White Swan continued to look down into the valley, discussing the amount of horses.

''Maybe with more light we can see better,'' White Swan told Boyer. ''When the sun rises fully, then Peaked Face can see what we see.''

Varnum continued looking, trying to see what was being pointed out to him. White-Man-Runs-Him turned around and spoke angrily, pointing back to the east.

''Surely you can see that, Peaked Face,'' Boyer said.

The sky to the east was filled with light, showing plainly where Custer had called a halt. Breakfast fires were sending plumes of smoke skyward.

''Why doesn't Long Hair just ask us to go down into the Big Village and announce that we're here?'' Goes Ahead told Boyer. ''He makes all kinds of noise marching and he burns fires at dawn, so that the enemy will see and hear us plainly. Is this what he calls surprise?''

The other Crow began to add their own comments. Boyer was glad that Varnum couldn't speak Crow. Red Star, one of the Rees, made sign to Varnum that Long Hair should be told what they had found.

''What do you think, Boyer?'' Varnum asked. ''Is the village that big?''

Boyer was tired of repeating himself. He told Varnum, ''If Long Hair orders an attack without waiting for Terry and Gibbon, we'll be run over by the Sioux and Cheyenne like a herd of buffalo crushes the grass beneath their hooves.''

''Well, my job is to report that we've found them,'' Varnum said. ''Maybe you boys are making too big a thing of all this.''

Boyer got up and walked away. He stood for a time, looking out across the Little Bighorn valley. The sun had passed the horizon and there were signs of activity in the village—milling horses with the tiny figures of men among them, and the movement of women and children along the river.

Though he was seeing only the upper end, Boyer realized that a village that size had to have scouts. If they didn't know that Bluecoats were very near by now, they soon would.

Red Star and Bull, another Ree scout, had saddled their ponies and were mounting. Red Star held a note from Varnum.

Boyer watched them ride away. Long Hair would soon be in a hurry to see the village. Maybe, once he did, he would shake off his strange idea of gaining glory and wait for more soldiers. Maybe, Boyer hoped, but not likely.

Garrett awoke to the smell of bacon. The sun was well into the sky and the camp was alive with activity. Little Crane was checking his gear. He turned to Garrett.

"You've finally awakened. We've already said our morning prayers and eaten. It's almost time to march."

Garrett looked at his watch. It was after 8:00 A.M.

"Where are we?" he asked.

Little Crane said, "Not far from the divide. But we're trapped. The Sioux are all around us, brother. Your snoring awakened them in their lodges."

Red Moon laughed. "Hide your fingers. They're looking for you."

"Now you're starting with the fingers thing?" Garrett asked Red Moon, packing up his bedroll. He reached over and took a strip of cold bacon from a bowl.

"Red Moon is right," Little Crane said. He had turned serious. "I hope you're ready for a fight today. Word has come back from the Crow's Nest that the Big Village is just ahead. Long Hair is going around telling everyone to get ready."

"Are they close enough to attack?" Garrett asked. "I thought we had a way to go yet. I thought he was going to wait for Terry and Gibbon."

"The Sioux and Cheyenne are camped on the bottom, up and down for a long way," Little Crane said. "There was much smoke, and the ponies were so many that when you saw them through a spyglass, they looked like piles of maggots."

"And Custer wants to attack without reinforcements?"

"Yes. Bloody Knife told him that there were enough Sioux and Cheyenne to fight for two or three days. Long Hair laughed and said that we could get through them in less than a day." Little Crane loaded bullets into his gun and filled a leather pouch at his side. "Long Hair has left to ride to the Crow's Nest with more scouts to look for himself. If it's true that the village is close, then they will have seen our campfire smoke. They will either be leaving or getting ready for battle."

Garrett forgot about eating. He checked his rifle and his pistol. "Do you think they'll come out and attack us?"

Little Crane mounted. "No one can say. But we must be ready."

Garrett's watch showed 8:45 A.M. They would certainly reach the Little Bighorn by late morning or early afternoon.

Well, perhaps Custer was thinking of taking position and awaiting nightfall, preparing for a dawn attack. All his successes had come just at daybreak.

But the scouts believed there was no way to surround a village that size without being seen. Three separate forces from three directions would be the only way to trap the Big Village.

Garrett realized that Custer might in fact have no choice but to attack as soon as possible. If the hostiles fled upstream toward the Yellowstone, they would run into Terry's smaller force and no doubt annihilate the entire command.

So it seemed that Little Crane and Red Moon had been right all along: The soldiers had desecrated Indian graves along the Yellowstone, and someone in the Sioux and Cheyenne camp had foreseen an upcoming victory over the Bluecoats for their people. The spirits now hated the

Bluecoats. There was no getting away from it.

Garrett climbed on his pony and looked around him, uneasy. He thought about the whirlwinds in the Sun Dance village, and what Little Crane had said about the spirits of the dead following them. He was sure they were behind him now, and he could hear them. They were laughing.

TWENTY-SEVEN

Young Horse sat his tired pony, watching Tall Deer approach the black stallion. Tall Deer rode on one side of his pony, holding a coil of rope in his hand.

The young pony's sides heaved with exhaustion. Young Horse and Tall Deer had taken turns running him in circles, switching off so that their mounts didn't become too tired. The stallion had lasted a long time before they had finally worn him down.

Young Horse was deeply worried. They were a very long way from the village. Shortly after crossing the river, they had evaded the police and headed into the hills at the edge of the Wolf Mountains. They had planned to rest there until daylight, but had suddenly come upon the stallion drinking at a stream.

At first they hadn't recognized the horse. He had been drinking with five other horses, all gone wild. Then Tall Deer had gotten a good look at him in the moonlight. His extra-long tail swept nearly to the ground.

"It's him!" he had whispered. "It's Crazy Horse's black stallion."

The chase had begun, and throughout the night they had tried to catch the stallion. The black horse, a deep shadow in the darkness, had taken them farther and farther from the village. Finally, at first light, Tall Deer had the idea to run him in circles until he was winded.

It had been hard on both their ponies, but now they would have the stallion. Still, Young Horse was very worried, knowing that he was in serious trouble. He couldn't possibly get back to camp in time to go hunting with Nighthawk, and he wouldn't be able to lie about where he'd been. No amount of glory in catching the stallion was going to appease his mother's anger, especially now that she feared her vision was about to come true.

Tall Deer slipped the noose over the black stallion's neck. The stallion didn't fight, but led perfectly. Now all they had to do was get him back to the village and saddled for Crazy Horse.

"We shouldn't have to ride him that much," Tall Deer said. "He's already pretty tame. Crazy Horse must have worked with him some."

Tall Deer petted the stallion, watching his reaction. His ears went back and he struck at Tall Deer with a foreleg. But the attempt was feeble.

"Let's keep him moving," Tall Deer said, jumping on his pony. "That way he won't get his strength back on us. We don't want to chase him any more."

"We're lucky it's not any later than it is," Young Horse said. "Maybe we can slip past the police lines, but I'm afraid my mother will be grinding rocks with her teeth when I get back."

"Don't worry," Tall Deer said. "She'll be so proud of you she won't have time to be angry."

"You don't know my mother," Young Horse said. "She'll have plenty of time to be angry."

Tall Deer rode in front, leading the stallion. Young Horse, right behind, began to look over the country. The sun had risen fully and the air was still, promising another hot day.

They climbed a long ridge and stopped near a large lone pine. Tall Deer tightened the knot at the stallion's neck, placing a stick in the knot so it wouldn't pull too taut.

"I don't want him choking," Tall Deer said. "I just want him to keep from breaking away. This will hold him."

Young Horse pointed toward a parallel ridge to the north, to a place known as the Crow's Nest.

"Someone's up there," Young Horse said. "Who are they?"

Startled, Tall Deer turned. "What? At the Crow's Nest?" He looked closely. The small figures of men moved in and out of sight. "Maybe it's Wolf Tooth and his warriors."

"Maybe," Young Horse said. He felt the bottom of his stomach contracting. "But I don't think so. Why would they go up there and show themselves? Does that make any sense?"

"You're right," Tall Deer said. "Wolf Tooth and his warriors wouldn't do that."

Young Horse suddenly pointed. "Look! One of them is wearing blue, I think."

"You're right," Tall Deer said. "One of them *is* a Bluecoat. They have to be enemies. Can you see that? A Bluecoat?"

"They're watching us," Young Horse said. "See them pointing? Do you think there are a lot of them?"

Tall Deer continued to look. "All the rest are Indians, probably scouts. I can't tell if there are any more Bluecoats, but I'd bet there are."

"You don't want to go fight them, I hope," Young Horse said. His stomach was knotting ever tighter.

"No. Let's get down off the ridge and hurry back," Tall Deer said. "We can't fight them alone. We'll warn the village."

Young Horse was eager to leave. "What about the stallion?" he asked. "Should we let him go?"

"We'll just hurry and go," Tall Deer said. "If we can tell about the Bluecoats and bring the stallion both, we'll be honored by everyone." He was yelling. "Let's go! The Bluecoats are here! The Bluecoats are here!"

Boyer crouched in the Crow's Nest, watching two riders in the distance. One of them led a pony and the other rode behind. The scouts referred to them as Sioux, making sign that they should go and kill them.

"They'll warn the village," White Swan said. "We should go and run them down."

"One of them is just a boy," Boyer said.

"He can tell the village just as easily as a man," Goes

Ahead pointed out. "And maybe they'll catch Bull and Red Star. We don't want them stopping the message to Long Hair. And we don't want them seeing the smoke from the breakfast fires. I believe as White Swan does. We should go after them."

Varnum ordered it done. Boyer mounted his pony. Lucky Man Reynolds, Varnum, and the Crow scouts all rode quickly toward a small divide in the ridge, straight north, hoping to intersect the two riders.

Near the divide, everyone dismounted and spread out, easing up the slope toward the top, their rifles ready. Varnum stayed close to Boyer, while the others took positions all along the ridge.

Boyer peeked over the top, his rifle ready. The hills were empty, and as quiet as a falling leaf.

"What do you see?" Varnum asked.

"Nothing," Boyer replied. "They're gone. But I don't know where. They can't have vanished."

Varnum squinted into the distance. "How could you see anything out there? It's so vast."

Boyer continued to search, his eyes scanning the bottom and the ridges carefully. No one could ride the area without crossing a hill or a ridge somewhere. But there was no one to be seen.

"Maybe they slipped around us," Varnum suggested. "Along the bottom."

"No, they couldn't do that," Boyer insisted. "We would have seen them. They must be hiding in a ravine somewhere."

"Then we'll go after them," Varnum said.

"I think that would be foolish," Boyer said. "The farther we go, the closer we'll be to the village. Maybe they're leading us into a trap."

From above, along the ridge, came a loud caw. Answering calls came from below.

"Birds?" Varnum asked.

"The Crow scouts are signaling one another," Boyer explained. "Look over there. A number of Sioux riders."

Varnum could see them, riding in single file along a ridge nearly two miles distant.

"I count seven," he said.

"There may be more," Boyer said. "There are a lot of places to hide in this country."

"Maybe you're right," Varnum said. "We might have ridden right into a trap."

More calls came from the Crow scouts, longer and louder.

"Do they see more Sioux somewhere?" Varnum asked.

"I don't know what the matter is," Boyer replied. "But we should get back to the Crow's Nest." He was pointing behind them. "There's dust coming from the trail below. Maybe Custer's on his way up here."

"Yes, you're right," Varnum agreed. "Signal your boys to come together and we'll go up there. I don't want to be gone when the General arrives. That would be trouble, serious trouble. We've enough of that as it is."

Nighthawk rode with Eagle Wing and three other village police from the Cheyenne camp. They had left well before dawn, searching for Young Horse and Tall Deer.

Nighthawk had been sure that Young Horse wouldn't go out this far from camp, certainly not after what had happened last time. He had to believe something had happened to them.

But in all the searching, no one had seen either one of the boys, and there was a lot of resentment because of it.

The police had gathered to discuss where the boys might be. A warrior named Calls-at-Night suggested that the boys might never come back to camp.

"Maybe they both know the whipping they're going to get when we find them," he said. "Maybe they don't want to face that."

Nighthawk had remained silent throughout the search. Playing the horseback coup game with Tall Deer, out from the village, had seemed innocent enough at the time, but had turned out to be a very serious problem, the most serious he had encountered since coming to the Cheyenne and marrying Ghostwind.

Nighthawk knew he couldn't afford another problem like that. Now Tall Deer and Young Horse were again past the boundaries, and this time much farther out.

No one could understand why the boys would go so far. Surely they wouldn't have initiated the journey on their own. In fact, Calls-at-Night had suggested that Nighthawk had led the boys out and had somehow managed to get back to camp without being discovered. If this could be proved, Nighthawk would surely be sent away or killed.

Nighthawk did not understand why Calls-at-Night had turned against him. He had never met the warrior before.

Out from the village, they split into two groups to cover more ground. Nighthawk had gone with Eagle Wing, who explained the situation to him.

"Calls-at-Night lost his only brother at the Rosebud fight," he told Nighthawk. "He has always hated Blue-coats. Now it's worse. He sees you as a Bluecoat, and he always will. He has many relatives who feel the same way. They're a powerful family."

"Can't you tell them any different?" Nighthawk asked.

Eagle Wing said with a sigh, "I can't change their minds. I can't change anybody's mind. I've tried. Every-one is angry because the Bluecoats are trying to kill us all. Anyone who's even partly white is now called an enemy."

"That isn't fair," Nighthawk said.

"Nothing about any of this is fair," Eagle Wing said. "None of it."

Nighthawk thought about the conversation with Eagle Wing and tried to remain calm. Had Calls-at-Night directed his anger solely at him, Nighthawk wouldn't have been so upset. But Calls-at-Night was going to try and get to him through the boys.

"Those two boys are going to be very sorry," Calls-at-Night said. "I think we'll have to whip them a long time to make them understand." He was staring hard at Nighthawk. "I'll be the first, and they'll remember never to break the rules again."

"Maybe there's more to it than their desire to break the rules," Nighthawk suggested. "Neither one of them would go this far without a very good reason. And whipping an eight-year-old boy severely isn't going to teach him any lessons. Making him stay inside the lodge during the day, and carry water and wood with the women for a very long time, will do much more toward teaching him to follow the rules."

"Why do you think you know so much?" Calls-at-Night asked Nighthawk. "You're not Cheyenne. You might speak our language, but you're not one of us. The Cheyenne hate you."

Nighthawk looked at the faces of the other three police. Eagle Wing appeared saddened. The other two remained impassive.

"Some of the Cheyenne hate me," Nighthawk told Calls-at-Night. "Not all."

Calls-at-Night was smart enough not to involve Eagle Wing. So he said, "There are far more who want you gone than want you to remain."

"You aren't strong enough to run me off," Nighthawk said.

Calls-at-Night's face clouded with anger.

Eagle Wing spoke up quickly. "Let's not argue. Let's find the boys and take them back to the village. That's what's important."

Calls-at-Night glared at Nighthawk.

Eagle Wing told Calls-at-Night, "Forget your anger."

"No, I want to talk to him." He rode next to Nighthawk. "There's no reason the boys should be this far from the village unless you told them to go. Maybe you sent them here."

"No, I wouldn't do that," Nighthawk said.

"You did it before."

"I wasn't with them this time."

"Maybe it's you who should receive the whipping." Calls-at-Night raised his quirt and began striking Nighthawk.

"Calls-at-Night! What are you doing?" Eagle Wing asked.

The warrior paid no attention. Nighthawk snatched the quirt away. Small streaks of blood lined his face and neck.

"You had no reason to do that," Nighthawk said.

Calls-at-Night demanded the quirt back.

"You'll get it back down below," Nighthawk said. "Not until then."

Calls-at-Night pulled his knife. "I said I want my quirt back."

"Stop!" Eagle Wing said. "Calls-at-Night! Put the knife away!"

Calls-at-Night slashed at Nighthawk. The blade nicked his arm.

Nighthawk's eyes hardened. "You've gone too far."

Calls-at-Night lurched from his pony toward Nighthawk. After blocking the knife thrust, Nighthawk slammed the butt end of the quirt into Calls-at-Night's face, knocking him sideways to the ground. He landed with a heavy thud.

Nighthawk jumped to the ground. "You just won't listen to reason, will you?"

Eagle Wing reached to grab Nighthawk. "Stop! Don't do it!"

Nighthawk had already lifted Calls-at-Night by the hair. He slammed a fist into Calls-at-Night's jaw and had pulled back to hit him again when he was overwhelmed by the police.

"Nighthawk, I told you not to fight!" Eagle Wing said.

Nighthawk jerked free. "Did you expect I'd let him kill me?"

Calls-at-Night had come to one knee. He shook his head and spat out a tooth.

"The blow to his face with the quirt was enough," Eagle Wing said. "If you'd hurt him so that he couldn't ride, you'd be in real trouble."

Nighthawk looked at the faces, each one staring hard at him. He asked Eagle Wing, "If Calls-at-Night had killed me, then what?"

"He would have paid," one of the police said quickly.

"Certainly," Nighthawk said, "but not so much that he couldn't ride back to the village. Isn't that right?"

Eagle Wing remained silent.

"Isn't that right, Eagle Wing?" Nighthawk demanded.

"We don't have time to argue," Eagle Wing said. "We need to mount and find the boys."

Nighthawk jumped on his pony. Eagle Wing wouldn't look at him. The other two police helped Calls-at-Night into the saddle and turned back with him toward the village.

"You're leaving us?" Eagle Wing asked. "We haven't found the boys."

One of them turned in the saddle. "We're taking Calls-at-Night back. You can stay with the *Wiheo* if you choose. All white men are *Wiheo*."

When they were gone, Nighthawk apologized for having lost his temper.

"He could never have overpowered me," Nighthawk said. "I should have just struck him and left it at that, like you said."

"It's easy to look back," Eagle Wing said. "Now you've made things that much harder for yourself. I said that Calls-at-Night had a very influential family. He'll do all he can to get you sent away. I'm sorry to say it, but he'll probably succeed."

"No amount of hunting or fighting will help me?"

"I can't say," Eagle Wing replied. "We'll just have to wait and see. Right now we've got to find those boys."

They rode on, looking carefully in all directions. The sun had topped the horizon, filling the land with gold. Only the deep ravines were still in shadow.

When Nighthawk left the village, Ghostwind was up in the hills, seeking an answer to her visions, so Nighthawk had left word with Mountain Water and Five Bulls that he was going out with Eagle Wing to find the boys.

Five Bulls had seemed to know what they.were up to. "They want glory," he had told Nighthawk. "They want to become warriors all too soon."

Nighthawk had asked Five Bulls, "Do you think they joined Wolf Tooth's warriors going toward the Rose-bud?"

"No, and Wolf Tooth won't go far, either," Five Bulls had said. "I can remember trying to get past police lines to count coup on an enemy. There's great honor in that. But we never went very far in the darkness. I believe that the boys are looking for some way to gain honors, but not by fighting. They both know they're too young." He corrected himself. "Young Horse knows the limits of his age."

"If they're not out to join Wolf Tooth's warriors," Nighthawk had asked, "then what are they doing?"

Five Bulls had taken a deep breath, saying, "I don't know. Find them if you can. Just try hard and find them."

Now, Eagle Wing pointed toward a high, twin-peaked ridge called the Crow's Nest.

"Look! Someone's up there watching us."

Nighthawk, his eyesight less keen, tried to see into the distance.

"A Bluecoat!" Eagle Wing said. "I see one, but surely there are more."

Nighthawk's mind raced. It could be Gibbon from the west, or Terry from the east. Both commands could be in the area. "What if they've got Tall Deer and Young Horse?" he asked.

"We'll go forward carefully," Eagle Wing said. "We don't want to jump into a trap."

They rode along a ridge, taking their time, looking in all directions. A series of birdcalls sounded—cawing, like crows. The lone Bluecoat and the scout left the ridge.

"Indian scouts are signaling," Eagle Wing said. "Our old enemies, the Crow. They've surely brought a great many Bluecoats to fight us."

Nighthawk pointed to another ridge, lower and closer than the Crow's Nest. There, seven warriors rode north.

"That must be the Oglalas who left camp this morn-ing, on their way back to the agency," Eagle Wing said.

Nighthawk had met them the night before, at the Dying

Dance. A warrior named Black Bear and six others had come clear out from the agency looking for stolen horses. Not finding them, they had decided to go back.

"I don't know what to do about the boys," Eagle Wing said. "We should find them, yet we should go back and warn the village about the Bluecoats."

"We *have* to find the boys," Nighthawk said. "I can't leave here without them."

"And it's equally as important to warn the village about Bluecoats nearby," Eagle Wing said.

"Maybe we could ride a way further and see if there are more Bluecoats," Nighthawk suggested.

"That's too dangerous," Eagle Wing said. "We could be easily trapped if there are very many."

"Bluecoats don't fight like that," Nighthawk said.

"Scouts do," Eagle Wing said. "They could be Crow or Pawnee or Arikara, if they come from the north or east. Any of those people would gladly kill us."

Suddenly, Nighthawk spotted Young Horse and Tall Deer, riding down a ravine toward Ash Creek. Tall Deer led a black pony behind him.

Eagle Wing yapped like a coyote and the two boys stopped to look back. Nighthawk and Eagle Wing joined them.

"I don't have to tell you the trouble you two are in," Eagle Wing said.

Tall Deer pointed to the pony, which was dancing impatiently. "Look, we've captured Crazy Horse's young stallion. Won't he be happy with us?"

"A horse, no matter whose, isn't important right now," Eagle Wing said. "Did you know there are Bluecoats up on the Crow's Nest?"

"We saw them," Tall Deer said. "That's why we went down here to the bottom. They can't catch us."

"What about their scouts?" Nighthawk asked.

Young Horse bowed his head. "I knew this would happen," he said. "I'm sorry."

"What will you tell your mother?" Nighthawk asked him.

"She'll be proud of him," Tall Deer said. "It's not every day that a woman's young son captures and tames a pony for Crazy Horse."

"And it's not every day that the Bluecoats come to kill us," Eagle Wing pointed out. "We're all in grave danger here. Let the pony go, and we'll hurry back."

Tall Deer frowned. "Let the pony go?"

"You heard me, Tall Deer. We have to hurry back. We can't be slowed by a half-broken pony."

"Let me show you how slow he is," Tall Deer said. He kicked his pony into a run, leading the stallion behind.

Nighthawk got ready to give chase.

"No, let him go," Eagle Wing said. "I'm afraid he'd come back out here to catch that horse. Let him take the stallion to Crazy Horse."

Young Horse continued to sit his pony, his head bowed. "I knew better, but I thought it a brave thing to do. I was wrong."

"Your mother is worried enough about everything else," Nighthawk said. "If something were to happen to you, she would have a very hard time. She loves you very much."

"I know," Young Horse said. "I told her last night that I would never want to become a Suicide Boy. Now I'm out here acting like I want to die. I can't grow old this way, I guess."

Eagle Wing smiled. "You're already growing wise. Have you learned anything?"

"Yes," Young Horse said. "If you follow Tall Deer out of the village in the middle of the night, you're bound to get into trouble."

"Don't blame Tall Deer," Nighthawk said. "You made your own choice to follow him."

"Okay," Young Horse said. "What I meant to say is that I won't take chances like this again, day or night."

"That's better," Eagle Wing said. "Now, if *any* of us want to grow old, we need to get back to the village. And fast!"

TWENTY-EIGHT

B oyer stood in the Crow's Nest, watching Custer's approach along the bottom.

Custer was raising enough dust to be seen for several miles. He rode to the base of the slope below the Crow's Nest and stared up. With him were Fred Gerard, Bloody Knife, and three Ree scouts from the camp.

Varnum started down the hill immediately, followed by the Ree scouts who had come to the Crow's Nest the night before.

Lucky Man Reynolds, who had been watching Custer's arrival, walked over to Boyer. "This is plumb crazy," he said. "Do you think I can get Custer to hold the troops at the divide and have him send couriers to Terry and Gibbon?"

"No," Boyer said. "I don't think Long Hair will listen to you. He hasn't listened to anyone else."

Custer dismounted and yelled up the hill to Varnum.

"Why doesn't he come up here?" Reynolds asked.

"He already believes in his victory," Boyer said. "He's put that into his mind. He doesn't need to come up here and see anything else."

"Well, I'm going down and tell him what we've found," Reynolds said. "Varnum can't tell him; he can't see that far. Custer had better take a close look down through them hills. If he's human, he'll shit when he sees that village."

When Reynolds was gone, White-Man-Runs-Him and Hairy Moccasin joined Boyer.

"I hope Lucky Man asks Long Hair why he allowed breakfast fires so close," White-Man-Runs-Him said.

"All the Sioux know we're here and are waiting for us."

"Don't be so sure," Hairy Moccasin said. "The village is so big that news in one camp takes a long time to reach another. Maybe it will never reach all the camps."

"The news of Bluecoats reaches all camps in a hurry," White-Man-Runs-Him argued. He turned to Boyer. "What do you say, Two Bodies?"

"I don't think it matters," Boyer replied. "If we attack a village that size, we'll be met by so many warriors we won't know what to do. That's for certain, and it won't take long to happen."

Custer started up the slope with Varnum and the scouts. Reynolds met him partway up and pointed toward the village. Custer looked across, shaking his head. Reynolds handed Custer his field glasses. Custer looked for a time, shaking his head again.

"Is Long Hair blind?" White-Man-Runs-Him asked.

"Only to what he doesn't wish to see," Boyer said.

Boyer descended the hill, with White-Man-Runs-Him and Hairy Moccasin right behind. Custer greeted them and they all sat on the ground in a circle.

Custer had removed his buckskin jacket and rolled up his sleeves. His two Bulldog pistols jutted from the holsters at his sides. He tilted back his broad hat and stared at Boyer.

"Mitch, they tell me there's a large village down there. Did you see it?"

"Yes, there's a very big village down there," Boyer replied. "Too big to attack by ourselves. We should wait for the rest of the soldiers."

Custer frowned. "Do you suppose your boys are making too big a thing of this?"

"No, General," Boyer said. "We've all seen what's down there."

Custer pointed to Varnum. "The Lieutenant here concurs with my belief that there aren't as many of them as you think, that maybe you're too excited."

"Either you believe me or you don't, General," Boyer said. "Why didn't you bring Six Fingers, the man-who-makes-the-paper-talk? Let him look and see what he tells you. Hasn't he been wanting to learn about fighting Indians?''

Custer disregarded the question. He said something to Bloody Knife, congratulating him and his fellow Rees for finding the village.

"*We* saw the village first!" White-Man-Runs-Him yelled. He rose to his feet. "It was Hairy Moccasin and I who saw it first. And why do you let cook fires burn and tell the Sioux we're here?"

"What's he saying?" Custer asked Boyer.

"He said that he and Hairy Moccasin found the village, that the Rees were asleep. He also wants to know why you allowed cook fires. There are enemy scouts out here everywhere."

"If there really is a camp out there, they haven't seen our army," Custer said. "None of their scouts have seen us."

Boyer by now had decided he would pull no punches with Custer. This was an important decision, whether to attack the village or wait. He told the two Crows what Custer had said, provoking another outburst from White-Man-Runs-Him.

"He says that you should know," Boyer told Custer, "that we saw two young boys going fast toward their camp. And there were other groups of riders out here. They were all close enough to see the smoke from your fires."

Custer leaned forward and pointed a finger at White-Man-Runs-Him. "I say again, we've not been seen! That camp has not sighted us!" He sat back, suddenly calm and detached. He turned to Boyer. "Tell your two boys what I said. Make them understand."

Boyer said nothing. The two Crows were staring at Custer. White-Man-Runs-Him sat down. Varnum, Reynolds, and Bloody Knife all remained silent, as did the Ree scouts.

Custer addressed Boyer and Gerard. "Both of you, tell your boys what I'm going to do, so they'll be ready to scout for me. We'll march when darkness falls and surround the village. Then we will attack at dawn.''

Gerard interpreted for the Rees. They nodded in agreement. Boyer told the two Crows. Hairy Moccasin was silent. White-Man-Runs-Him spoke angrily again.

''He says the plan is no good,'' Boyer told Custer. ''We've already been seen. If you're going to attack, do it right now, he says, and capture their horses so they will be slowed down at least.''

Custer restated his plan. Boyer interrupted him.

''Why aren't you listening? The village is too large to attack the way you want to. If you don't find more Indians down there than you've ever seen before, you can hang me!''

''Oh, come now!'' Custer said. ''It would do a damn lot of good to hang you, now wouldn't it?''

Varnum's eyebrows raised. Everyone stared at Custer.

''Wait for more Bluecoats,'' Boyer said.

Custer was livid. ''I shall attack them! If you're afraid, then . . .''

Boyer shouted, ''I can go anywhere you can go!'' He calmed himself. ''But if we go in there, we won't come out alive.''

Custer stared at White-Man-Runs-Him. Finally, he said to Boyer, ''Tell your boys that it shall be as they wish. We'll go down there right now and keep them from getting away. You decide if you want to fight with me or not.'' He rose to his feet. ''I'm going back down and give the order to march. If you're ready to fight when I get here with the boys, you'll be part of all this. Otherwise, no one will ever know who you were. Ever.''

The Big Village slept soundly, even as the sun rose higher in the morning sky. The dancing had carried on late into the night, and afterward a large number of warriors had gathered to eat and tell battle stories until dawn.

At first light, the Suicide Boys had paraded through the Cheyenne and Oglala villages to the singing of ancient war songs by their brothers and uncles. Some rode fine war ponies while others marched. All were painted and dressed for battle, and given presents by those who looked on.

Nighthawk watched Crazy Horse groom the young stallion, pulling a porcupine brush through its sleek black coat. The pony had calmed down considerably since Tall Horse had brought it to the village, but it had been hobbled tightly to prevent flying hooves.

"That was quite something, those two boys catching this pony," Crazy Horse said. "If it wasn't so dangerous outside the village right now, they would have gotten honors, not a scolding."

"What do you think of Bluecoats so close?" Nighthawk asked. "No one believes me. They think Eagle Wing and I are making it all up, so the boys won't be punished."

"I heard about your trouble with Calls-at-Night," Crazy Horse said. "He's powerful among the Cheyenne and also has family among the Oglala. I can speak for you if I choose to do so, but a great many will disagree, I believe."

"It appears that I'll be leaving before long," Nighthawk said. "Ghostwind will have to decide whether or not to come with me."

"It will be very hard for her, no matter which way she decides," Crazy Horse said. "Where will you go?"

"I have no idea," Nighthawk said. "I guess I'll find a circus somewhere and go back to trick shooting."

"If the Bluecoats are near, as you say, we can use your shooting to keep them out of the village," Crazy Horse said. "Or maybe you've decided now that you want to fight with them again."

"You know that I never did fight with them."

"You wore their colors."

Nighthawk knew he couldn't convince Crazy Horse otherwise. He hadn't been able to convince anyone else; and after his trouble with Calls-at-Night, many would be certain he was a Bluecoat.

"There are some in the village who think you're helping the Bluecoats, that you rode out to tell them where we're camped," Crazy Horse said. "They believe you came to the village for that purpose."

"Don't you think that's rather silly?" Nighthawk asked.

"When people are worried for their very lives, their minds work in unusual ways."

"They can ask Eagle Wing," Nighthawk said. "He knows me. He's been with me enough to know that I couldn't have sneaked away to tell the Bluecoats anything."

"Eagle Wing is but one voice," Crazy Horse said. "And I'm Oglala. When the Big Village breaks up, I will take my people one way and Two Moon and the other Cheyenne leaders will take their people another. Do you see the problem?"

"I can see that my choice has already been made," Nighthawk said. "I might as well leave now, before someone decides to kill me."

"You can't leave now, not if what you say is true," Crazy Horse told him. "The Bluecoats will have scouts out, and they'll kill you faster than the Cheyenne will. There's nowhere to run."

"Who said I was running?"

"Sometimes you have to face the worst things in life wherever you are," Crazy Horse said. "I've had my share of problems. And here comes someone else who's going to have a hard time of it when he grows older."

Crazy Horse motioned toward Tall Deer, who had taken a seat a distance away along the river.

"He's supposed to be in his mother's lodge," Nighthawk said. "He wasn't supposed to go anywhere until he was told he could. I'll send him back."

"Don't bother him," Crazy Horse said. "He's hurting inside. You know that as well as I do. I think the only reason he took the chance of capturing this pony is because his father left and he wishes I would become his father now."

"I look over at him and I see myself," Nighthawk said. "I went through the same thing. It's very strange. And we both have the same father."

"Maybe when the Bluecoat fight is over, I'll give this stallion to him," Crazy Horse said. "Then both he and Young Horse will have a pony from me."

"You're a generous man, Crazy Horse," Nighthawk said.

"And a tired one," Crazy Horse said. "I'll be back later and take this horse out to graze. Maybe I can get Tall Deer to go to his lodge and rest. Bluecoats like to attack at dawn. We'll get rested up, then maybe go out in the morning and wait for them."

Crazy Horse walked over to Tall Deer. The two began talking and soon headed into the village together, Tall Deer walking proudly.

Though tired, Nighthawk was too troubled to sleep. He wanted to talk to Ghostwind, but couldn't bring himself to do it.

If Terry or Gibbon, or both together, charged the village in the morning, he would once again prove his worth to the Cheyenne people. He would gain more honors than anyone else, he vowed. He would drive the Bluecoats away by himself. He had to. That would be the only way they would let him stay.

The sun climbed ever higher, yet the village slumbered. A few had awakened and had gone to swim or lounge under the trees along the river, but many would stay in their lodges, even upon awakening, until after the heat of the day had passed.

Young Horse stood at the river's edge, content to be carrying water skins for his mother. He would be doing a lot of things with and for his mother, including carrying wood and water from now through all the cold moons, until the first thunderstorm the following spring.

It seemed a long time to be doing women's work, but Young Horse was pleased that the punishment hadn't been far worse. When he had arrived back in the village with Nighthawk, his mother had been waiting in the lodge. She had met him with sobs, clutching him tightly until he couldn't breathe.

At first he had thought that he would suffer inside the

lodge forever. Five Bulls had fashioned a seat of rocks and sharp sticks at the rear of the lodge and had told him to sit there and not to move until he was released. If he so much as slid one small rock out of place, he was told, he would face something worse.

Outside, they had discussed his punishment. He had overheard them, first Five Bulls and then his grandmother and then his mother, all discussing what should happen. They had talked a lot about keeping him off his pony for a long time, perhaps throughout the rest of the warm moons. That had caused him tears he was glad no one had seen him shed. All were in favor of that, until Night-hawk had spoken.

"Don't take his pony away so long. Let him instead learn how hard it is to stay in camp and work with the women. Maybe he should learn that following the rules and riding is better than disobeying and not riding for seven days and helping his mother for seven months."

All had agreed that Young Horse should continue to improve his horsemanship; that was very important. So working with his mother, with the menial daily tasks, would help him appreciate his station in life and give him ample time to think about the importance of following the rules.

Young Horse had smiled inwardly. Helping with the chores would get him laughed at by the other boys, yet they wouldn't laugh very hard, and certainly not in front of him. If they did, he would remind them that he had sneaked past the village police in the night and had helped capture a wild stallion belonging to Crazy Horse himself. How many of them could boast of that?

If the truth were known, most of the boys Young Horse's age would likely do chores for a full year if they could boast of the same honor.

Young Horse didn't feel that everything would go smoothly, though. The hardest part of the chores was going to be the washing, especially Talking Grass's dresses. Since the coming of various Cheyenne bands from the agencies, the availability of trade cloth in the village had increased greatly. Reds and yellows and blues were popular, sewn into small dresses for the girls.

As Young Horse stood beside the river, water skins in hand, he watched as his mother showed him the finer points of scrubbing fabric to clean it.

"Put those skins down," she said, "and do this with me. That's the way you learn."

Young Horse wanted to groan, but knew he didn't dare. Talking Grass sat beside her mother splashing her feet in the water. As Young Horse sat down, she doused him.

"Hey!" he said.

She splashed him again.

"Mother, make her stop that."

"Is she hurting you?" Ghostwind asked him. "Don't you like water?"

"Ah! How am I supposed to work when she's doing that?"

"Ignore her and she'll quit."

"Yeah, when she drowns me, maybe you'll care then."

Talking Grass laughed. "Ha, ha, you have to wash my clothes. Make sure they're clean."

Young Horse was tempted to rub his sister's face with a wet dress. His mother told him to move over to the other side of her, away from Talking Grass. When Talking Grass got up to join him, Ghostwind asked her to go look for some more clothes to wash. Talking Grass hurried away, eager to find more work for her brother.

Young Horse took a small dress from his mother and rubbed the material together to clean it, as he was directed. He looked out into the open beyond the village, where boys of all ages were gathered near the horse herd. They were playing with hoops and tossing balls around. He should be out there, boasting. This was no fun.

Besides, the warm weather was making him drowsy. He hadn't slept at all since the day before.

Ghostwind noticed his eyelids falling.

"How would you feel if your eyes closed and never opened again?" she asked him.

Young Horse looked up. "What?"

"And how do you think your sister would have taken it if she had never been able to see you again? 'Mother, where is Young Horse?' 'Lost. We can't find him.' 'Lost? No, Mother. He can't be.' 'I'm sorry, Talking Grass, but he is. He left with Tall Deer. He'll never return and we'll never know where he died.' "

Young Horse fought back tears. He hadn't realized how his foolishness had affected his family. He thought of how he would feel if Talking Grass were lost somewhere, never to be found.

"I won't do it again, Mother," he promised.

"I know you won't," Ghostwind said. "I'm proud that you're such a brave young man, but save the bravery for times when you really need it. Catching a stallion way out from the village is a waste, even if the pony does belong to Crazy Horse. Think how he would have felt if someone had told him that you and Tall Deer had been killed trying to please him. No pony, no matter how wonderful, is worth your life."

"I understand," Young Horse said. "I guess it's easy to believe that you'll never die, especially at my age."

"And you promised me that you would become an old man," Ghostwind said. "You're not working very hard at it. In fact, you're working hard *against* it."

"I'll grow old, like I said I would," Young Horse said. "I'll work harder at it than I ever have before. It's important to me."

Ghostwind smiled. "Now, go back to the lodge and get some sleep. I'll finish the washing. This evening, you can come out and help me again."

Ghostwind hugged Young Horse and watched him walk back to their lodge. Tears rolled down her cheeks; she wasn't yet certain that Young Horse would be alive much longer.

The night before, after the Dying Dance, she had gone into the hills to pray. Seeing the Little People had frightened her. She had felt it was time for some answers to come.

While in the hills praying, Ghostwind had seen the sky change before her eyes. Red owls had appeared, flying low over the village. She had then watched the sky catch fire—the darkness blow up into flaming red. Men began falling, turning over and over; women and children screamed and cried. She had not been able to see them clearly; they had just been ghostly figures, all tumbling down into a steaming crimson river.

She had rolled over and over on the ground, yelling. Even when she had closed her eyes, she had seen the vision.

When the vision passed, she had run back to the village, tripping and falling often. There, in the lodge, she had learned from Mountain Water that Young Horse and Tall Deer were gone, and that Nighthawk had gone with Eagle Wing to look for them. She had believed then that she would never see Young Horse again.

When Nighthawk had brought him back to her, she hadn't wanted to let him go. Just now, as he had headed into the village, she had wanted to call him back, for her fear was rising again.

Ghostwind thanked the Creator for bringing him back to her, asking Him to allow her son to grow old. But everything belonged to the Creator, every man, woman, and child. When she had stood in front of the lodge, looking into the night sky, she had realized there was nothing she could do about what was soon to come.

Ghostwind once again looked into the sky. Though only midmorning, it was changing, as it had the night before. Fear gripped her tightly. Owls appeared from no-where, silent red shadows sailing over the village, bring-ing the message of death.

Turning her head, Ghostwind ran toward the village. She stopped Talking Grass, who was returning with more laundry. She would go into her lodge and spend what time she could with her children and with her husband. She could do no more than that, hoping and praying that the owls would leave and the sky would close again. But she knew better. Soon the sky would fall completely.

TWENTY-NINE

11:00 A.M. Sunday, 25 June 1876
Divide between Rosebud and Little Bighorn

Day turning very hot. Column has been halted. Custer back from Crow's Nest, and Little Crane has gone to Ree camp to learn what new orders will come.

News of hostiles following us. It seems that a Capt. George Yates sent a Sgt. Curtis back to find a pack of food supplies lost from a mule during the night. Sgt. Curtis discovered Indians eating the food supplies and fired on them. Curtis and his party returned, reporting that the hostiles scattered. It's feared they will warn the village.

Tom Custer and Lt. Calhoun rode toward Crow's Nest to find Custer. He was already on his way back. Little doubt in my mind now that he will order an immediate attack.

Now is the time to persuade Custer to let me accompany him. Have no idea how to approach him yet, but I must. To hell with Mark Kellogg. My career hangs in the balance.

Garrett closed his diary and stuffed it into Red Moon's blanket.

"Are you finished making the paper talk?" Red Moon asked.

"Yes, I've some business to attend to."

Red Moon studied him. "Will you seek out Long Hair and ask to go with him?"

"That's why I came in the first place," Garrett replied. "It would be crazy not to try."

Garrett started toward the Ree camp. Red Moon fell in behind.

"You won't try to stop me, will you?" Garrett asked.

"No," Red Moon said. "You're right. You came all the way out here for this. No one should tell you not to go with Long Hair if you can. But if Long Hair gets angry, I'll be there to stop him from harming you."

Garrett and Red Moon entered the Ree camp. Little Crane had been talking with some of the scouts. He came over to Garrett.

"There's going to be a fight soon. You'd better not stay here. Long Hair is coming to talk to the scouts, and he'll ask you about your talking paper."

"I came to see Long Hair," Garrett said. "I've decided to ask him if I can go with him during the fight."

Little Crane smiled. "You have a strong heart. Long Hair might do anything to you."

"No, he won't," Red Moon said.

Little Crane pointed to Red Moon. "He will die for you. He is right to feel this way. And I feel the same. If Long Hair tries to harm you, I'll fight, too. We'll both fight."

"I appreciate both of you," Garrett said, "but I don't think there'll be any trouble. That wouldn't be a good idea just before a battle. Even Custer wouldn't do that."

"Maybe you're right," Little Crane said, "but I wouldn't gamble on it." He pointed. "Long Hair's coming to talk to the scouts. He has Gerard with him."

Custer entered the Ree camp and was met with solemn faces. He told Gerard to say that the battle would be fought very soon. Through Gerard he added, "Boys, I want you to take the horses away from the Sioux camp." He waited while Stabbed told the scouts to obey, to be brave, and to take as many horses as possible.

"Make up your minds to go straight to their camp and capture their horses," Custer continued. "You're going to have a hard day; you must keep up your courage. You will get experience today."

The scouts talked among themselves. Arguments broke out here and there. Some of the scouts thought it crazy to attack so large a village. Others said that they had to uphold Arikara honor and go into battle, no matter the odds.

Custer listened. He had started to tell Gerard what to say to the quarreling Rees when Boyer stepped next to him.

"General," Boyer said, "I've been with these Indians for over thirty years, and this is the largest village I've ever heard of."

"Don't you believe in me, Mitch?"

"You are a good chief, Son-of-the-Morning-Star, but I've told you many times before that there are far too many of the enemy for us. We should wait for the other Bluecoat commands, Terry and Gibbon, and Three Stars Crook."

"You know as well as I do that Crook's forces already engaged the hostiles," Custer said. "Those scalps that Curley and Goes Ahead brought in the other night were from that command. I have no doubt of that. You told me yourself that you believed that."

"Maybe that's true," Boyer said. "We talked about that. But why don't you send couriers to Terry and Gibbon, and to find Three Stars Crook? Wait for help, so we can attack from all sides."

"Even if I sent someone, there's no time," Custer said. "We must march right away, or they'll strike their lodges and be gone. Are you going to scout for me now, or are you going to quit?"

"I'll do as you say." Boyer turned and left for the horse herd.

Custer noticed Garrett and Little Crane standing nearby. He turned to Lieutenant Cooke. "See to it that my things are in order for the remainder of the march. And have the officers in charge of the mule train await my instructions. Thank you."

Cooke saluted, glared at Garrett, and was gone. Custer walked over and stood before Garrett, his hands behind his back.

"I've been expecting you, Mr. Garrett. Do you have some journal entries you wish to give me?"

"Actually, I came to ask permission to accompany you into battle."

"And why should I grant that wish, Mr. Garrett?"

"The more journalists with you during the fight, the better coverage."

Custer smiled and began to pace. "Actually, Mr. Garrett, I don't believe you've been too good at your 'coverage,' as you put it, thus far. Do you?"

"I've tried to do as much as possible."

"Mr. Garrett, who do you think you're fooling?"

"Perhaps we had a misunderstanding."

"I don't believe so, Mr. Garrett. I can rely on Mr. Kellogg. Sorry to say it's not the same with you."

"General, maybe Mr. Kellogg has been talking a bit too much, and maybe he doesn't know every side of the issue. You know Mr. Kellogg dislikes me intensely."

"Hate is a better word, Mr. Garrett."

"Exactly my point, General. How could you expect him to do anything other than try to turn you against me?"

"You've done a more than adequate job of that on your own, Mr. Garrett." Custer's eyes narrowed under his hat. "You consort with Mr. Reno and Mr. Benteen. And I've heard that of late, Mr. DeRudio has offered you his nasty tales. But my question to you, Mr. Garrett, is why haven't you spoken to my brother Tom? How about Boston, or Autie Reed? You haven't spoken with Lieutenant Calhoun or Captain Keogh. No, you've interviewed malcontents. What does that say, Mr. Garrett?"

"I interviewed those gentlemen," Garrett said. "Boston, Reed, and your brother. Calhoun and Keogh. Each of them just once. That was enough, General. I can learn nothing from them about the complexities of this campaign."

" 'Complexities,' Mr. Garrett? What do you mean?"

"I mean that there are problems among the officers here, sir. You can't deny that. This is not a cohesive force. I need to know the odds you face both from the hostile Indian forces and the dissenters within your own command.''

''I've been told, and would have to concur, that you head the list of 'dissenters,' Mr. Garrett.''

''I'll be honest with you, General: There's nothing negative I could say to anyone about your abilities as a commander. I might not agree with you on a number of things, but I'm sure you're a fit leader. You know your tactics in the field.''

''I trust you've already put that in writing.''

''I wrote it on the paper provided to me by Mr. Kellogg during the night march.''

''You wrote it this morning?''

''If you have the time, General, you can see for yourself.'' Garrett held his breath.

''So, you have nothing to hide from me?''

''Not a thing, General.''

Garrett could feel his brow warming, the sweat forming. Had it not been a hot day, he would have given himself away.

''It appears that you've left your notes back at your camp,'' Custer said. ''I told Mr. Kellogg explictly to have you bring me them by noon.''

''I was in such a hurry to get over here and talk to you. Well, General, it's not far. We could go over there.''

Custer looked at Little Crane and Red Moon, whose faces were chiseled in stone.

''Or I could hurry and get my work for you,'' Garrett suggested. ''I'd love to have your comments.''

Custer frowned. ''Well, I suppose there's no time for that now. Perhaps later, after the fight.''

''Does that mean that I can accompany you?''

''I'll give it some consideration, Mr. Garrett. Meanwhile, prepare yourself to ride hard. Stay with your scouts. I'll let you know my decision when the time comes.''

''Maybe if I could start out with you now . . .''

''That's all, Mr. Garrett.'' Custer turned and left.

When Custer was gone, Little Crane broke a smile.

"What if he had waited to see your talking papers?"

"I didn't really believe he'd wait. He wants to march; and more important, he doesn't believe he has anything to fear from me. No matter what I say, if the battle is won, he'll be the Great Father, like he told the scouts."

"None of that matters now," Little Crane said. "The battle is near. We must call on our medicine helpers."

The Ree scouts were already preparing for battle. Stabbed had mounted his pony and was riding around the camp, shouting words of encouragement.

"You men, keep up your courage," Stabbed said. "Don't feel that you are children; today will be a hard battle. We have been told that there is a big Sioux camp ahead. We attack a buffalo bull and wound him. When he is this way we are afraid of him, though he has no bullets to harm us with."

"You need to get ready for the fight," Little Crane said. "Take off your shirt and Stabbed will rub you with medicine."

Stabbed had finished his speech and was dismounting. He took a bag of white clay from his saddle and lifted his eyes to the sky, saying a prayer for help and guidance. He then went to the first scout, took a handful of clay from the bag, spat into it, and rubbed it onto the scout's chest. He went on to the next.

Garrett stood in line and watched Stabbed paint Little Crane and Red Moon. When he had finished with Garrett, Stabbed said to him, "You'll have a hard time of it. No one will get out of this day without having hard time of it. Live or die, it will be terrible. Harder than you can know. Harder than your dream has told you."

Trembling, Garrett put his shirt back on. Stabbed was daubing more of the scouts with clay, praying that the Creator might protect them. Little Crane led Garrett's pony over and handed him the reins.

"Are you ready for this?"

"No," Garrett said. "I'm scared to death. I'm about to throw up."

"You are the same as all of us," Little Crane said. He

pointed over to Red Moon, who was preparing his pony for war. "He is praying harder for you than he is for himself. He's afraid for you."

Garrett felt sweat beading on his forehead. "I'm glad that he's praying for me. I don't know if it will do any good."

"Let him prepare your pony for battle," Little Crane said. "He wants to."

Little Crane started getting his pony ready for the fight, tying up its tail and singing horse medicine songs. Red Moon walked over and Garrett handed him the reins to his horse.

"Will you get my pony ready?"

Red Moon smiled. "Yes. It would do my heart good."

"While you're doing that, I'll take my talking papers back from your pony and tie them on mine," Garrett said.

Red Moon frowned. "I can keep them."

"You've done a very good job," Garrett said. "It's time that I take them back now."

"Are you sure?"

"Very sure. Thank you, Red Moon."

Garrett took his notes from a buckskin pouch tied on Red Moon's pony and transferred them into his saddlebags.

Red Moon began preparing Garrett's pony for the battle. "I hope it's good that you did that," he told Garrett.

"It's good that I did," Garrett said. "I need the talking paper with me now."

"As you say." Red Moon steadied Garrett's pony and placed his hand in front of its nose. He said a prayer and blew herb dust into the pony's nostrils. "That will give your pony strength," he told Garrett.

Garrett climbed into the saddle, his heart beating wildly. They hadn't even begun fighting, and yet his nerves were shattered.

Red Moon repeated the prayer and dusting of his own pony and mounted. "We are ready for war," he told Garrett. "You and I will fight bravely. Very bravely. Brother!"

*   *   *

Ann tried to sleep, but the day was too hot and the flies and mosquitoes too thick. She had tried covering her face and hands with bear grease, as Tyrone and Lareaux had, but the smell had been too strong and she had washed it off, using an entire bar of soap in the process. Only a single bar was left for the duration of her journey.

Now she covered her head with a blanket and tried to rest. Even in the shade, it felt like an oven.

Tyrone and Lareaux slept nearby, seemingly unfazed by the insects and heat. Ann feared that their snoring might attract Indians from miles in all directions. Water, who seemed to need no sleep, was scouting the area ahead.

It had been much harder to adjust to the conditions than she had ever imagined. She had believed that her love for Adam and her intense desire to find him would give her strength. Instead, the journey had sapped her energy, forcing her to think more about herself than Adam.

This land was a continuous trial. She was careful of the water she drank, for Tyrone had warned her more than once about alkali and a condition referred to as the Dakota Quick Step.

In addition, she hadn't eaten since her dinner with Sinclair. There had been no time to pick berries, and there would be no fires from now on, so she would have to be content with pemmican.

Sleep had proven nearly impossible. Since escaping the soldiers, they had traveled only at night, finding areas in deep cover to rest during the daylight hours. Indians traveling with families remained in their lodges at night; and as for finding another soldier encampment, they would take no more chances with "friendly" army personnel.

They rode over old tracks that Lareaux and Water said had been made by soldiers following an Indian trail. The country was open and rolling, filled with the smell of sage. The clay soil lay heavy and dense; the bottoms were thick with greasewood, the slope rising to scattered cliffs, and pockets of pine and juniper.

Water believed that the column they now followed wasn't as large as the Custer force, but reported that there had been scouts who had ridden out ahead to look for Sioux camps. The trail had left the Powder River, following the Mizpah River, where they were now camped until nightfall.

"We're sure they were cavalry, Miss Ann," Tyrone had said. "Water says the trail is old, but that it likely leads the direction we want to go."

The trail had taken them through an old Sioux camp and Ann had found a pair of small dolls carved from cedar, complete with hair. One doll was male and the other female.

"Love dolls," Water had told her. "Someone made medicine for a young man to win the love of a young woman. Maybe it worked, maybe it didn't."

Ann had kept the dolls and told herself that if she could hold the dolls close, praying that she and Adam might come together soon, then her dream of finding him before disaster struck would come true.

She had tied them together and now kept them on a rawhide string around her neck. She didn't care what anyone thought. They had all stared, but no one had asked. Tyrone had already begun to question her sanity.

"If you're not feeling good, we'll turn back," Tyrone had said just before stopping for the day. "You look a little peaked."

"I'm tired and I'm starving," she had told him. "And, sure, I'm worried sick about Adam. Otherwise, everything's going well, thank you."

There were times when they all questioned their sanity, traveling in a small number like they were, through open country with the constant threat of hostile Indians. But Water scouted continuously and assured them the main body of Sioux and Cheyenne lay at least two days ahead.

As she lay in discomfort, Ann thought about Adam and what she would say to him when she found him. "I'm so glad to see you" didn't seem strong enough.

"Are you glad you came out here and made me search for you?" would sound silly in front of a lot of staring men. Maybe she would just take him aside and say, "Damn you, Adam Garrett! I've been so worried about you. Promise me you'll never do this again."

Ann held the two dolls and studied them. The figures had been carved with great skill, the arms and legs life-like, the faces bearing smiles of contentment. The eyes had been fitted with tiny black seeds. They were shiny, like happy eyes. And both dolls were completely naked, as happy lovers should be.

"Oh, Adam, why can't you be here with me now?" Ann said to herself. "We could be as happy as these two dolls. I would see to it."

She thought of Adam's strong frame, the muscles of his chest and arms, his flat stomach, and the firm feel of his tight buttocks. She saw herself running her hands down the small of his back, trailing her fingers around his slim waist.

He would take his time, nuzzling her neck and ears, moving his lips across her shoulders and over her breasts, stopping for just the right amount of time at just the right places. If only he were here to do it now. If only they could be together, alone somewhere, with nothing but a soft night breeze surrounding them.

Ann closed her eyes. Suddenly the ground came alive with the drumming of horses' hooves. She sat up quickly. Water had returned, riding hard into camp.

"Sioux!" he yelled, pointing. "Sioux, right behind me!"

Tyrone jumped from his bedroll and grabbed his rifle. Lareaux came to his feet, holding his leg, cursing loudly. Water had tied his pony to a tree and was taking position, his rifle ready.

"Miss Ann!" Tyrone yelled. "You keep your head down. You hear?"

Ann checked her pistol. "I'm not going to sleep through this, Tyrone. Don't worry about me."

Tyrone hurried over anyway. "This could be bad, Miss Ann. We'll just have to wait and see."

Five Sioux warriors came into sight, reining their ponies just under the brow of a hill. They talked among themselves, pointing.

"They're out of range," Lareaux said. "Or I'd give them what for. *Oui,* I'd give them what for. Where did you run across them?"

"A small village, moving east, maybe back to the agency," Water said. "They'll come, just to see what we're made of."

The warriors remained on the hill for a short time, talking. Then they began riding at a gallop, back and forth across a flat in front of the trees.

"They'll come closer and closer," Water said. "They're testing us."

"We'll hold our fire until they're nearly on us," Tyrone said. "Make every shot count."

Ann trembled. She watched the warriors ride ever closer. They were on the far sides of their ponies, yelling war songs. Lareaux could hold himself no longer and fired a long shot at the lead warrior.

The bullet struck the warrior's pony in the foreleg. It tumbled head over heels, squealing, rolling over on the warrior's leg.

"Lareaux!" Tyrone yelled. "Why'd you do that?"

The other four Sioux retreated a short distance. The fallen warrior came to his hands and knees, shook his head, and pushed himself up. He began hopping toward the other four warriors.

"Oh, no you don't!" Lareaux yelled. "*Non,* you won't get away from me!"

Lareaux lurched to his feet and ran, limping, toward the hobbling warrior. Two of the warriors charged him on their ponies. The other two raced their ponies forward and dismounted, taking position with their rifles, firing heavily into the camp.

"Lareaux! Come back!" Tyrone started out, but Water tackled him.

"You'll die, too," he said. "Leave it. Lareaux is crazy."

The two warriors providing cover fired wildly. Bullets

zipped into the trees overhead and a rain of leaf and branch clippings poured down.

Ann's stomach churned as the two charging warriors closed in on Lareaux. Both fired their rifles from the sides of their ponies while Lareaux struggled to take aim. Lareaux doubled over as a bullet struck him in the stomach.

"I've got to do something!" Tyrone yelled.

He started out, but Water tackled him again. Bullets ripped the dirt near them. Water hauled Tyrone, screaming and crying, back into cover.

The injured warrior hobbled over to the two firing into the trees. He climbed onto a pony and tied himself on, then lay across its back, breathing heavily.

Lareaux struggled to his feet, clutching his stomach, then fell to his knees. A Sioux warrior dismounted beside him, his knife gleaming in the sunlight. He threw Lareaux's hat to one side and grabbed his hair.

Ann turned away as the warrior cut into Lareaux's head and tore the scalp free. Lareaux screamed and fell forward. The other warrior jumped from his pony and counted coup, then the two of them tied a rope to Lareaux's feet. They both mounted, one taking the rope binding Lareaux's feet. They joined the remaining warriors and all rode away, yelling in triumph, dragging Lareaux behind.

Tyrone pounded the ground. "We shouldn't have let them take him! We shouldn't have!"

"Did you want us all to die?" Water asked. "Did you want them to get to the woman? What then?"

Ann looked into the distance. The warriors were out of sight and everything was calm again, as if nothing had happened. The only evidence was the leaves and bark that covered the ground under the trees, and the wounded horse, lying on its side, screaming.

Water took his rifle and walked to the horse. He placed the muzzle behind its ear and fired. The horse jerked spasmodically, stiffened, then lay still, a deep snort escaping its lungs. When Water returned there were tears in his eyes.

"We'll go now," he said. "We can't stay here in this place of death."

They packed and mounted. Tyrone took one last look to the east before following behind Water. Ann fell in, thinking, "Damn you, Adam Garrett! Damn you, anyway!"

THIRTY

Garrett rode with Little Crane and Red Moon, looking over the vast sea of hills and ravines ahead. Below, at the end of Ash Creek, lay the Little Bighorn and a valley filled with Sioux and Cheyenne.

Garrett wondered if he wasn't entering the last few hours of his life. He had been composing a letter to Ann, working it through his head, searching for just the right words. But who would carry it for him?

Little Crane and Red Moon had been singing death songs since the march had begun, touching their weapons and paint often while they sang. Which of those two would he give the letter to? Should he write two copies? His mind raced as he tried to decide.

Upon realizing fully that the odds of death were great, Garrett had felt drained and saddened. His life had hardly begun and he would soon end it of his own volition. Then euphoria had engulfed him; it hardly seemed so bad to die after all.

The entire command had felt the emptiness of impending death. Though the scouts had been open about predicting their own deaths, voicing their fears and sorrows to Custer and others, many of the soldiers had been equally as candid.

A private named Thompson had had a chilling dream during the first halt. He had talked of seeing a warrior coming at him with an upraised ax. Thompson had lurched awake, terrified. Completely exhausted, he had fallen back asleep, only to have the same dream resume, with the same warrior coming at him. He had remained awake, fearing that sleep meant the same as death.

Charley Reynolds had come back from the Crow's Nest with a blank stare in his eyes. He had given away all his possessions, even his rations of food.

Garrett had felt fortunate in not having the buffalo dream. But now its absence made him wonder if it was too late for him to follow the white bull through the ring of fire.

Just over the divide, Custer called a halt. The commanders waited. Custer had not yet divided the twelve companies or assigned battalion commanders.

Garrett took paper and pencil from his saddlebag and started his letter to Ann.

An orderly rode up and addressed him. "The General requests your presence, sir. Right away, sir."

Garrett turned to Little Crane and Red Moon.

"Here is your chance," Little Crane said. "You can make the paper talk now, like you wanted."

Garrett followed the orderly to where Custer sat his horse. Four battalions were forming, consisting of three companies each, their commanders shouting orders.

Mark Kellogg was writing furiously. He ignored Garrett. Mitch Boyer rode up to Custer, pleading with him to wait.

"I don't want to hear this any more, Mitch," Custer said. "If you say another word, I'll have you leave the command."

Boyer didn't want the disgrace of dismissal. He nodded.

"You and I are going home by a strange trail," he told Custer. "I hope you've made the paper talk to your wife and said goodbye to everyone."

Boyer turned his horse and rode out from the column, awaiting orders to march.

Bloody Knife, who had been nearby listening, looked into the sun. "I shall not see you go down behind the mountains tonight," he said.

Custer turned to Garrett and raised his finger.

"Mr. Garrett, if you would come here." When Garrett had arrived, he said, "I'm still concerned by your lack of faith in me, Mr. Garrett. So I'm going to allow you to hear my plans. Are you ready?''

"I'm ready, General," Garrett said.

"As you're familiar with military order, I won't bore you with the details, but please note that I have a plan of attack formulated.'' Custer leaned toward Garrett, smiling. ''An attack that will rout them early on.''

"I hope so, General," Garrett said.

Custer frowned. He began writing in the air with his index finger. ''My intention is to separate my men and trap the hostiles between forces. I'll send Major Reno with three of the left-wing companies to attack their flank, at the south end of the village. Captain Benteen shall command the remaining three left-wing companies and scout the hills to the west, looking down into the valley for hostiles camped farther up the Little Bighorn. If he finds nothing, he will report to me and rejoin us, either in support of me or Major Reno's forces.

"I will have Captain McDougall hold back with one right-wing company, to watch the pack train traveling behind. Then I will take the five remaining right-wing companies and turn north, striking the village at the top, pushing straight through toward Major Reno.''

"Do you know where the strongest part of the village lies?" Garrett asked, furiously taking notes. "Won't that make a difference how you divide your men?''

"Mr. Garrett," Custer said, obviously irritated, "this movement I've outlined for you is guaranteed to work, no matter what part of the village supports their strongest force. You see, Mr. Reno will engage them at their flank, drawing the warriors to him. If Mr. Benteen sees that Mr. Reno needs help, then he will enter at his discretion. Meanwhile, I will lead my forces to the top of the village and sweep through, engaging the warriors fighting Mr. Reno from their rear. They will be trapped and forced to surrender, or die. They'll make that choice. It's an infallible plan, Mr. Garrett. Are you learning something?''

Garrett knew it would be useless to argue. Custer had already made up his mind. "I'm learning, General," Garrett said. "The strategy appears sound, if the warriors behave as you suppose they will."

Garrett wondered why the General couldn't see the obvious holes in his plan. If what Custer had said about his experience fighting Indians was true, the women and children wouldn't remain in the lodges, but would seek safety away from the fighting. So, what if a number of warriors stayed back to protect the fleeing women and children? Or, with a great number of warriors, why wouldn't some of them think of trying to outflank Reno's men? What if these warriors crossed the river and rode right into Custer's forces before he reached the village?

Even if Custer met no warriors on the way to the north end of the village, any warriors defending the women and children would engage him, and they would be fighting to save their families. It would not be a running fight, and this would surely delay Custer's movement through the village to assist Reno.

Garrett straightened himself in the saddle. Risking Custer's anger again, he asked, "General, if there are anywhere near as many warriors as the scouts say, can you really expect Reno to engage them for very long? I mean, what if he's driven back?"

"I just told you," Custer said, "Mr. Benteen's job is to provide support! If there are no enemy camps upriver, and he should be able to see them clearly, then he will be free to help. I don't anticipate that need before I make my strike, though. Mr. Reno will have a number of sharp-shooters with him, using their Springfield rifles, keeping the enemy at bay. You do understand that warriors will not ride headlong into that kind of fire, don't you?"

"Likely they won't, General," Garrett agreed. "Providing Reno's ammunition holds out."

"They'll be running from him before he's used half of his cartridges," Custer assured Garrett. "Maybe you'd like to be there to see it, with Major Reno?"

"I'd prefer to ride with you, General," Garrett said. "That's the reason I came out here."

"Mr. Kellogg will be with me," Custer said. He studied Garrett, smiling. "I'm certain there will be enough news for all. It wouldn't hurt if you were along as well, I suppose."

"Thank you, General," Garrett said.

Custer's smile widened. "On the other hand, someone able needs to accompany Major Reno to keep an account of his activities. It wouldn't be fair to slight that end of the battle, now would it?"

Garrett didn't speak.

"Mr. Garrett, don't you think Major Reno's part in this should be documented?"

"I suppose so, General," Garrett said.

"I'll tell you what," Custer said. "Mr. Kellogg has just borrowed a pair of spurs from Mr. Gerard, in order to keep his mule up with the horses. He wants to be at the front, you know. He intends to go forward with the scouts. You ride out with them as well, and I'll have my decision for you when we get down to the village."

"Fair enough, General," Garrett said.

Garrett rejoined Little Crane and Red Moon. Curley and White-Man-Runs-Him rode their ponies over.

"I told Bloody Knife that today we die," White-Man-Runs-Him said to Garrett. "I go as a Crow. You will go as one of your people. We will be together and it will be the end."

Curley asked Garrett in sign, "Could you make the paper talk about me and tell it to my family?"

"What do you want me to say?" Garrett asked. His hands shook as he held his pencil.

Curley took his time, so Garrett would understand everything. "Tell my loved ones and all my people that my brother, White Swan, and I are going to the Other Side with good hearts. Our homes have been good and we will miss being there. We died a good death. They can all be proud. We will be with the Grandfathers and wait for them to join us."

Garrett finished recording Curley's words. Mitch Boyer had ridden back. He told Garrett, "Don't do this foolish thing. Turn back now. It's a bad day for all of us."

"I don't intend to leave," Garrett said. "Besides, I

told you before, where's there to go? We're so close to the village, there'll be Sioux and Cheyenne all around us.''

"Not if you wait for the battle to start, then go back up the trail," Boyer said. "Go and then come back when the battle is finished. Make the paper talk about what you find. Make everyone know what craziness this is and what a bad day it was. If you stay, you will die and no one will know.''

"Do you really think *everyone* will die?" Garrett asked.

"If anyone lives, it's only because the Creator wills it," Boyer replied. "There are enough Sioux and Cheyenne to cover us over like a blanket on so many ants.''

A trumpet sounded for the march to resume. Boyer and the other scouts took their positions. Garrett sat with Little Crane and Red Moon, waiting for the column to move.

"Are you going with Long Hair?" Little Crane asked.

"He hasn't decided if he wants me yet," Garrett replied. "He's taking Kellogg, of course; but for the time being, he's content to toy with me. He says he'll tell me farther down, near the village.''

"A lot can happen between here and there," Little Crane said. "You heard what everyone has said. How is he planning to fight so many?''

"He has a battle plan," Garrett said. "He's certain it will work.''

Red Moon was turned toward the sun, praying. He had lit a cigarette and raised it to the sky.

"Long Hair still believes the enemy will run," Little Crane said. "No one can tell him different. If they were going to run, they would have gone by now. They will stand and fight. Just hope the medicine Stabbed gave you is good this day.''

Ash Creek flowed through a narrow bottom with steep, grassy slopes on either side. Ponderosa pine and juniper grew in isolated colonies, mixed with sage and scattered stands of skunkbush.

Though the hills were open, the creek bottom was choked with dense stands of ash trees and berry bushes, enough to hide a great many hostiles.

Garrett rode with Little Crane and Red Moon, crossing from one side to the other, keeping their eyes open for signs of movement. They had joined the Ree and Crow scouts, under the leadership of Lieutenants Varnum and Hare, riding ahead of the column, looking for higher hills from which they could look down into the valley. Mitch Boyer and George Herendeen were also along, interpreting back and forth for the Crow and Ree scouts.

The heat was intense; and everyone stopped often to water their tired ponies. Little Crane, who had been closely observing the soldiers' horses throughout the march, remarked to Garrett, "You'd better keep your pony happy with water today. Don't be like Long Hair and his Bluecoats. You can't give them water just once and believe that they'll run well."

"They have too many to water very often," Garrett said in Custer's defense. "There's not enough room to get them in. It would take a long time."

"Time is what bothers Long Hair the most," Little Crane said. "He feels there's not enough time, that the enemy will flee. He wants to shoot them all. It's a silly way to fight a battle. Ponies are more important than rifles."

The day grew ever hotter. Varnum, Boyer, and Herendeen had moved ahead with the Crow and were scouting from the hills above the valley bottom. Many of the Ree, whose ponies were tiring, had fallen back. Gerard had gone back to get them and they all were hurrying forward again, shouting that Long Hair was catching up.

"Long Hair is pushing the horses way too hard." Little Crane got down from his pony and rubbed its neck as it drank. "When the horses are tired, it's not good."

A short way further some of the scouts began waving and pointing. Garrett rode forward with Little Crane and Red Moon. Just across the creek, under a high bluff of white clay, stood a single lodge. The doorflap had been sewn shut.

"A death lodge," Little Crane said. "There's a dead Sioux inside."

Garrett stared. Some of the Ree scouts were gathering around the lodge, singing war songs. The Crow, with Boyer and Herendeen, watched from a nearby hill. Varnum and his orderly, a private named Elijah Strode, had broken ahead of the others and were a good distance downstream.

The Ree attacked the lodge, whipping it with their quirts, yelling oaths to the Sioux. One scout slit the lodge open with a knife. A dead warrior lay on a wooden scaffold, dressed in his finest clothes, painted, and wrapped in a buffalo robe.

"We shouldn't stay," Little Crane said. "It's a death lodge."

"Varnum's gone," Garrett said. "So who's in charge?"

Little Crane pointed. "That man. You said his name was Hare. No one's listening to him."

Some of the Ree were robbing the lodge, taking food that had been left for the dead warrior. Gerard, who had been hurrying up the stragglers, rode up, yelling, "What are you all doing? You were supposed to go right on into the Sioux village." The Rees stopped their war songs.

"See," Gerard said, "Long Hair is here, and he's angry."

Custer rode in at a gallop. He reined his horse, his face red. "I told you to dash on and stop for nothing," he yelled. "You have disobeyed me! Move to one side and let the soldiers pass you in the charge."

The Rees stared at Custer. Little Crane leaned close to Garrett and said, "They shouldn't have torn the lodge open, but Long Hair should understand that they would stop and count coup. It would make them bolder for the battle. Long Hair's not thinking very well today."

Custer continued to yell at the Rees. "If any man of you is not brave, I will take away his weapons and make a woman of him."

One of the scouts said something and all the Rees laughed.

"He said," Little Crane told Garrett, "that if Long Hair does the same to all his Bluecoats, who are not as brave as the Rees, it will take a very long time, indeed."

Gerard was signaling to Custer that the Rees were now eager for battle.

"Send them on, then," Custer said. "Tell them to get the Sioux horses. I want the Sioux horses!"

By now some of the soldiers had dismounted and were examining the lodge and its contents. One of them tossed a match onto the scaffold, igniting the buffalo robe. Shortly, the entire lodge was in flames.

"That's crazy," Little Crane remarked. "Now we have one more ghost to follow us and give us bad luck."

Many of the Rees were shouting at the soldiers, "Bad luck! Bad luck!" There was an argument between those who had set the lodge ablaze and a few others. A sergeant had to restore order.

At the same time, Lieutenant Hare rode up to Custer and pointed toward the valley. Stabbed had joined Little Crane and Red Moon, and was talking in Ree, also pointing toward the valley.

Little Crane told Garrett, "Stabbed says that there are Sioux just ahead, riding down into the valley, kicking up dust. He says the Sioux are already moving horses, which means they must know we're coming. We'll have to hurry to reach them."

"Are you saying they're running away?" Garrett asked. "Was Long Hair right?"

"I just said *some* Sioux just ahead were running away," Little Crane explained. "I don't know about the Big Village. I don't think any of the scouts can see the Big Village yet. We're still too far away."

Garrett turned from his discussion with Little Crane to see Reno moving out at a fast trot with his troops. Lieutenant Cooke, who had been speaking with Reno, rode clear and let the column pass.

"Ah!" Little Crane said. "Long Hair is angry and is sending his Bluecoats ahead of the scouts. It would be better if the scouts went first and stole the horses.''

"It doesn't look like the scouts want to go," Garrett said. "Maybe there are more horses than they know what to do with.''

"More horses than *anyone* knows what to do with," Little Crane agreed. He laughed. "Long Hair should try stealing them himself. Maybe if he saw how many there are, he wouldn't be so anxious to ride down there.''

"I'm going over to Long Hair and join him," Garrett said. "Are you ready?''

"You lead the way," Little Crane said.

"Red Moon?" Garrett asked. "Are you ready?''

Red Moon raised his rifle in the air and yelled. "We'll kill our enemies today. It will be a big fight. However it ends, I'm ready to go down there.''

Garrett rode up to where Custer and his orderlies sat mounted, watching Reno's men advancing down the creek. Little Crane and Red Moon remained a distance back.

Garrett waited for Lieutenant Cooke to notice him. Ignoring Garrett, Cooke turned his horse and rode on the other side of Custer.

Holding his pony steady, Garrett took position beside the sergeant carrying Custer's guidon. He would simply act as if he were going with Custer and not even ask permission.

Custer noticed him and yelled, "Mr. Garrett, you're losing them." He pointed toward Reno's troops.

"I beg your pardon, General?''

"Get with it, man!" Custer was up in his stirrups, his hat off waving Garrett forward. "Go on with Major Reno and fill a ream of notes. I'll want a full report.'' Custer waved his hat again. "Go on! Be quick about it!''

Garrett rode forward, declining to argue. He could catch up with the General on the bottom, after the battle.

But he wasn't comfortable with Reno, who had already betrayed him to Lieutenant Cooke. Had that not happened, perhaps he would be with Custer now, taking notes on the beginning of the biggest battle of the entire Sioux campaign. Perhaps the biggest Indian battle ever.

THIRTY-ONE

Garrett rode with Little Crane and Red Moon, flanking Reno's column on the east side of the creek. Custer led his column right behind, staying to the west bank.

Reno led with a flurry, his white straw hat plainly visible. The Crow rode out in front, racing their ponies over the hills toward the village.

In the lead with Reno was Bloody Knife, who would be helping steal Sioux and Cheyenne horses. "Bloody Knife is along to give them courage," Little Crane had told Garrett. "Like you, Bloody Knife wanted to go with Long Hair, but Long Hair said he wanted someone strong with the young warriors."

The two columns rode from the narrow bottom out onto a flat. Garrett's pony wheezed for air. Though it was moving only at a trot, the heat and the long marches had taken their toll. Garrett wished that he had taken his pony out with Little Crane and Red Moon to graze more often.

Little Crane rode back and forth among the Rees, learning what was ahead, while Red Moon stayed right beside Garrett. Having promised to fight with Garrett as a brother, Red Moon would stay beside him throughout the battle.

The Crow scouts broke into yells. Red Moon pointed to where two riders were racing their horses up out of the bottom.

"Sioux!" Red Moon said. "They must stop them before they get back to the village."

Garrett watched as the Crow and Ree scouts ran one of them down, shooting him and then finishing him with repeated blows from their rifles. Another group of warriors appeared from the hills to the east, stopped for a short look at the oncoming soldiers, and broke for the village.

Gerard, who had been riding with the Rees just ahead of Custer's column, waved his hat and yelled down to Custer, "Here are your Indians, running like devils!"

Custer sent Lieutenant Cooke and Captain Keogh ahead with orders for Reno to charge the village. Garrett watched them pass in a cloud of dust.

"Brave up, my brother," Red Moon told Garrett. "We are almost to battle."

Just ahead, Ash Creek met the Little Bighorn River, and just beyond, along the broad valley bottom, lay the massive Sioux and Cheyenne encampment.

The village was tremendous. It began a few miles north of the mouth of Ash Creek and ran for over three miles along the bottom. Just the upper end itself, where the Unkpapa camp circles were located, appeared massive.

Bloody Knife rode next to Reno, screaming war cries, anxious to meet his old enemy, Gall. Reno led his troops to the river, where they watered their horses. Cooke and Keogh rode back toward Custer, their horses at a full gallop.

At the stop, Garrett was approached by Reno's adjutant, Second Lieutenant Benjamin Hodgson. Garrett knew why he had come.

"Mr. Garrett, sir," Hodgson said, his eyes wide with anticipation. "Do you recall our wager the other night?"

"Yes," Garrett said, remembering the night he had met Hodgson, just prior to his talk with Reno. "Are you still up for that wager?"

"Indeed I am, sir," Hodgson said. "Would you care to up the ante?"

"As I said before, Lieutenant," Garrett replied, "whatever your pocketbook can tolerate."

"Very well!" Hodgson was laughing. "Ten full Yankee dollars. How does that sound?"

"Fair enough," Garrett said. "Have your money ready within the hour."

The command dismounted to tighten the cinches on their saddles. Garrett felt a sudden high, an excitement that overwhelmed him and doused his fear of death. He checked his rifle and pistol, and made certain his ammunition pack was tightly closed. He thought about his letter to Ann, but his notepaper was sealed in his saddlebags. It would have to wait.

Little Crane and Red Moon made their last preparations for battle, singing battle songs and checking their rifles. They made certain the ropes that held them on their ponies were secure. Little Crane helped Garrett tighten the ropes around his legs and under his pony's belly.

"Whatever you do, stay on your pony," Little Crane advised. "If you fall off and your pony runs away, you're a dead man."

Garrett nodded and readied himself for the charge. Sweat poured from his brow and soaked his back, running in a thin line from the back of his neck to his tailbone.

Bloody Knife broke ahead toward the horse herd with the Ree scouts and two of the Crow, Half-Yellow-Face and White Swan. The soldiers cheered them on.

Garrett wondered how the two Crow had ended up with Reno's command.

"It's a mistake," Little Crane said. "They went ahead without watching where Long Hair went. Now they're with us."

Or was it a mistake? Garrett wondered. Perhaps the two scouts hadn't felt comfortable with Custer. But why would White Swan leave his younger brother, Curley?

Things were happening fast, and a lot of mixups could occur in the confusion.

Garrett secured himself in the saddle and checked his rifle again. His mind was spinning, his heart thumping in his chest. At the order, "Left front into line!" the troops took position for the charge toward the village.

Someone yelled that Custer's men had reached the bluffs and were cheering them on. Yells and waves rose from the ranks.

In the distance, Garrett could see mounted warriors

riding in circles, yelling war cries and blowing eagle bone whistles, sending clouds of dust into the hot sky. His stomach squeezed into a knot.

"Look!" Little Crane said. "They aren't running away. They're getting ready to come at us." He stared at Garrett and Red Moon, his eyes wide. "Fight hard! Fight hard and die proud!"

The formation galloped forward, dodging brush growing along the bottom. After nearly two miles, they reached a prairie dog town. There was no brush here, the ground open and level.

At the edge of the village, painted warriors gathered by the hundreds, their rifles raised. Beyond them, the Ree scouts had charged into the pony herd, causing the horses to bolt and run en masse. Huge clouds of dust rose skyward like brown fog.

Reno raised his hand in the halt command. Officers screamed orders. Troopers jumped from their horses, every fourth man holding the reins of four horses, while the other three took position. Two young soldiers screamed, struggling to stay in the saddle. Out of control, their horses ran headlong into the village, where they were engulfed by screaming warriors.

Ignoring the two casualties, Reno gave orders for battle. Garrett worked to control his pony as the soldiers formed a skirmish line that reached from a heavy stand of timber near the river clear across the bottom. Some knelt on one knee while others lay flat on their stomachs, using the prairie dog mounds for breastworks.

"Why didn't we finish the charge?" Garrett asked Red Moon. "At least we might stand a chance of chasing them out. We're trapped if we stay here."

"There're too many to charge," Red Moon said. "Long Hair shouldn't have sent us down here. There's nothing right about any of this."

Little Crane, who had returned with Sioux horses, rode up beside Garrett and Red Moon. "Stay on your ponies," he said. "Don't get off, even if you're hit."

Garrett heard the order, "Fire!" The troops loosed a

volley of bullets directly into the village. From the distance came the screams of women and children.

"Hold the lines, boys!" Hodgson yelled. "Here they come!"

From the village rode a horde of screaming warriors, their yells and the shrill tones of their eagle bone whistles filling the air. They rode directly toward the skirmish lines, their horses pounding forward at a dead run.

From both sides rifles cracked, spitting flame. Bullets and arrows whizzed into the skirmish lines. A sea of dust rose, obscuring nearly everything.

Garrett's pony, crazed with fear, tried to bolt, Garrett held the reins tightly in one hand, his rifle in the other. Unable to see anything clearly, he held his fire.

The dust dispersed momentarily. The warriors had turned back and were regrouping. Here and there a warrior lay still. The wounded tried to rise, only to be shot by a sharpshooter from the skirmish lines.

Dead horses lay everywhere. Wounded horses were screaming and flailing on the ground, or limping in circles, their reins hanging free.

Near Garrett a wounded soldier lay on his back, his eyes blinking, his face blank. A feathered shaft had run itself cleanly through his neck.

Bloody Knife returned with stolen ponies, ordering some younger Rees to take them behind the battle lines. "This is what Long Hair told us to do," he said. "We want him to know that we're doing it."

Bloody Knife had intended to go after more horses, but saw that the Sioux were chasing the scouts back from the herd. Some were caught and killed.

In front, even more warriors had come to the aid of the hundreds already there.

"Fire!" Another volley sounded.

The troopers holding the horses struggled to keep the reins. Garrett's nostrils filled with the pungent odor of mortal fear. The horses exuded it strongly, their eyes rolling, waiting for the warriors' coming charge.

Hodgson walked up and down the lines. "Keep cool,

boys. We've got them. Remember to fire low. I say, fire low."

Reno was near Bloody Knife, pacing, his white straw hat covered with dust. Someone near him yelled, "Where's Custer? Where the hell is he?"

Another soldier said, "He sat up there and watched us charge. Now he's gone, damn him! He's left us all here to die!"

Boyer rode with Custer, his pony making a turn around a bend deep in Cedar Coulee. Just ahead, Medicine Tail Coulee, filled with travois marks and pony trails, would lead directly into the village.

They had halted earlier atop a high ridge to survey Reno's progress below. Seeing that Reno had formed his soldiers into skirmish lines, Custer believed he had time enough to reach the upper end of the village and capture every man, woman, and child.

"It's the job I came here to do," he had told Boyer after starting the march again. "I told you before, I'll get it done, or die trying."

After separating from Reno's command, Custer had called a halt to water the horses hurriedly on the North Fork of Ash Creek. "Hold them back, boys!" he had yelled. "Don't let them fill up. We can't be slowed down."

Then Long Hair had asked Boyer to take the Crow scouts to a hill overlooking the valley and learn what they could about the village.

Boyer had called the Crows together and they had watched Long Hair Custer bend to one knee and pray.

When he had finished, he shook hands with each of them. Through Boyer he said, "If we win this battle, you will be the noted men of the Crow nation. If I die today, you'll get this land back from the Sioux and stay on it, happy and contented.

"I'm a great chief, but I don't know if I'll pass through this battle or not. If I live, I'll recommend you boys, and you'll be the leaders of the Crow. There's nothing good can come of this for the Sioux. If they kill me, they will suffer. Even if they do not kill me, they will suffer, for they have disobeyed the orders of the Great Father in Washington.'' He pointed into the hills. ''Now go on up there and look at the village. Come back to me with what you find and we'll charge ahead.''

Partway up, Half-Yellow-Face and White Swan became separated. After Reno ordered the charge, sounded by the bugler, Half-Yellow-Face and White Swan had ridden down to join the Rees. Boyer and the other four scouts had ridden the rest of the way up to look at the village.

Boyer saw that the upper end of the village, where Reno was headed, appeared inactive. He couldn't see farther downriver because bluffs stood in the way.

While on the hill, Boyer and the Crows watched couriers going from Reno to Custer.

''The Sioux aren't running away,'' Boyer said to the others. ''It will be a big fight, as I have said.''

Boyer and the Crows rejoined Custer, who had been anxious about Benteen's return. Not wishing to wait, Custer ordered the march up into the hills above the valley floor.

Toward the top, the soldiers began cheering, waving at Reno's troops charging through the valley. Some of the horses bolted out of formation, prompting Custer to say, ''Hold your horses in, boys. There's plenty of them down there for all of us.''

Custer waved his hat at Reno and his troops on the bottom, yelling, ''Get in there! Go after them!''

Boyer pointed north, toward the end of the village obscured by bluffs.

''If we can see that many lodges already,'' he told Custer, ''how many more must there be?''

Custer sent back a courier to speed up Benteen, and to tell McDougall, who commanded the pack train, to hurry as fast as he could.

Boyer wondered at another remark Custer made. While peering through binoculars he said, ''Look, boys! We've caught them napping! We'll finish them and return to our station.''

Boyer was surprised to see little movement in that portion of the village now visible to them. Children and dogs roamed about, along with a few women, but few warriors could be seen.

But Boyer knew full well that most of the village was still concealed by bluffs. And soon couriers from the upper end of the village would warn those in the hidden camps.

Before resuming the march, Custer ordered the men to load their carbines and prepare to dismount if ordered, because a small contingent of hostiles had been seen flanking them. The column formed into fours and the march resumed.

Finding the north end of the village and crossing the river to attack had been foremost on Custer's mind since leaving Reno. Boyer decided he needed to make Custer understand that he should waste no more time with halts, but move as quickly as possible without wearing out the horses.

Now Boyer looked to a high peak just to the west, where White-Man-Runs-Him waved down to him.

"They've seen something," Boyer told Custer.

Hairy Moccasin and Goes Ahead were pointing into the valley, making sign for heavy battle.

Curley, who rode beside Boyer, remarked, "Dark Face is getting killed."

Boyer signaled for the scouts to come down. When they reached the command, Custer asked, "How goes it?"

Hairy Moccasin replied, "Dark Face is fighting hard. There are too many Sioux for him to win."

"Are they all killed?" Boyer asked.

"Not yet," Hairy Moccasin said. "But if we don't fight soon, they will be. You can go look."

Boyer started up the hill. Curley rode behind, singing a death song under his breath. Custer called two officers to him, and they followed.

Boyer and Curley reached the top of the peak, with Custer and his officers right behind. They sat their horses, peering into the valley.

"I see a lot of dust," Custer said.

Boyer pointed. "There are soldiers in a line, shooting at the Sioux, coming at them on ponies. Do you see them?"

"If you say so," Custer said. "Where is Benteen, anyway?" He turned his horse and descended the hill, his two officers behind.

White-Man-Runs-Him and Hairy Moccasin came to the top, followed by Goes Ahead. They all dismounted and crouched down to study the village.

"Long Hair is sending another messenger to find the pack train," Hairy Moccasin said. "He's going to have one of his Bluecoats make the paper talk this time, so they'll understand."

"Who's going?" White-Man-Runs-Him asked.

"A trumpeter," Hairy Moccasin replied. "Long Hair thinks his horse is fresh. He's telling him to ride hard."

"It's too late," Goes Ahead said. "There are too many. It's all lost already."

Hairy Moccasin pointed toward the west side of the village. "If the Rees keep stealing their ponies, maybe it will be easier for us."

Goes Ahead was shaking his head. "No. There are too many. Way too many."

"Maybe Long Hair shouldn't have come this way," White-Man-Runs-Him commented. "Maybe he should have gone in behind Dark Face. They should have all charged at once. Then the Sioux would have run away."

Boyer climbed on his pony. "I'm going back down and see what's going to happen."

Hairy Moccasin turned to look behind him. He pointed over to an eastern ridge.

"There's that little bunch of Cheyenne we saw earlier, sneaking up from the back. They didn't return to the village. Long Hair had better send some Bluecoats after them or they'll cause trouble."

"Look!" Goes Ahead pointed downriver. "The camps are coming alive. Criers are running everywhere. Long Hair had better get down there before the warriors make their medicine."

Boyer returned and dismounted.

"Long Hair says we're all to leave him now and go back toward the pack train. We're released. I'm not going, but all of you can, if you wish."

"Why?" Goes Ahead asked.

"Long Hair says he brought us to find the village," Boyer said. "We've done that, and he wants no more from us."

Hairy Moccasin looked down into the village. "The Rees are stealing ponies. I want some of them. Maybe I'll do that."

"Yes, if you want," Boyer said. "Maybe it would be easier if you weren't with Long Hair. You know how he fights."

"So why are you staying?" White-Man-Runs-Him asked.

"He told me before that I was afraid," Boyer replied. "I don't like him to think that. I'm braver than he is."

"If he called you afraid, then you should stay," Goes Ahead agreed. "I'll see you again, sometime in another land."

Boyer bid them all good luck going back to the Crow village. They said no goodbyes, for there is no such word in the Crow language. "Until we meet again" is used, for everyone meets again sometime, someplace.

Boyer mounted and turned to leave. Curley jumped on his pony and sat. The other three rode a short distance away, then stopped and jumped from their ponies. They sat down with their rifles and began shooting down into the village.

"Hah!" Boyer yelled. "Drive them all out!" He turned to Curley. "Why aren't you with them?"

"I changed my mind. I'm staying with you."

"Go with them, Little Brother," Boyer said. "Save yourself."

"No, I'm staying with you," Curley insisted.

"You can if you want," Boyer said. "But it's going to be bad. You know that."

"Yes, I know that," Curley said. "But wherever you can go, I can go."

THIRTY-TWO

Garrett joined Little Crane and Red Moon, riding in circles behind the skirmish line. From the village came a barrage of yells. The warriors charged again, this time riding in formation, firing from under their horses' bellies or necks, hundreds of them coming, still coming, with no end to them.

Soldiers' screams pierced the dust-clouded air as the warriors flanked the left wing of the skirmish line, their bullets ripping through men, their arrows slicing into arms and chests and backs.

A bugle sounded retreat. The surviving soldiers scrambled into their saddles, panicked at the thought of being completely surrounded. Reno led the way to the timber along the river.

Garrett kicked his pony into a dead run. Little Crane and Red Moon rode alongside. All three shot back into the oncoming sea of Sioux and Cheyenne.

Warriors poured through the dust, screaming as they rode, knocking soldiers from their horses with war clubs and rifle butts. A warrior in front of Garrett raced alongside a terrified private and buried his knife in the trooper's backbone.

Garrett, his pony running at full speed, fired forward, knocking the warrior from his pony. He fired again into a painted chest coming alongside. Two warriors rode up, one on either side, and Garrett shot at the closest one, on the left. The hammer clicked on an empty chamber.

The warrior to Garrett's right was arming his bow. Garrett brought his rifle back and slammed the barrel into the warrior's face, knocking him to the ground. The second warrior had his war club raised when Red Moon placed the barrel of his pistol against the warrior's ribs and fired.

They reached the timber together. Red Moon reloaded his pistol while Garrett checked his rifle.

"Where's Little Crane?" Garrett asked.

Red Moon peered through the dust and smoke. "I can't see anything. I can't hear anything. It's all too much."

Garrett rode forward. A bullet snapped a tree branch in front of his face, driving splinters into his cheek, just missing his left eye. He barely felt it.

"Where's Little Crane?" he yelled again.

"There!" Red Moon was pointing to their right.

Little Crane on his pony emerged from the fog of dust. He gripped the reins tightly.

Garrett had dismounted and stood behind a tree, shooting his rifle into the circling warriors.

"Why are you on the ground?" Little Crane asked. "You'll be killed."

"I can't shoot from my horse," Garrett said. "I can't hit anything."

"Get back on your pony and don't worry about killing Sioux," Little Crane said. "There are too many to matter. We can't stay here. Long Hair's not coming to help."

"We're killed if we don't leave," Red Moon added.

Garrett mounted. "Where's Benteen? He was supposed to come up from our rear."

"It's only us," Red Moon said. "And we're not enough."

The Sioux continued to circle the trees, loosing arrows and rifle fire in a continuous hail. The Sioux were like ghosts, emerging from the thick clouds of dust, then disappearing only to return.

Garrett smelled smoke. Little Crane pointed to the edge of the trees. "The Sioux have set us on fire! Now we have to leave, or it's too late."

Though some of the bottom was too wet to burn, among the timber lay dead cottonwoods, which the Sioux had lit with flaming dried grass. Garrett could see warriors coming through the smoke, shooting bullets and arrows into the soldiers.

A short way away, Reno worked to remove a spent shell jammed in his Springfield rifle. He broke his knife point and threw the rifle to the ground.

Bloody Knife, fighting beside him, pointed to where more warriors poured from the village. Reno shouted commands and a bugler blew retreat.

"We'll have to fight our way through them," Little Crane said. "Brave up!"

A bugle sounded again. Reno started to mount his horse. Bloody Knife, holding his own pony just a few feet away, turned to speak to him. A bullet slammed into his head, blowing blood and brains into Reno's face, covering his straw hat with crimson.

Bloody Knife slumped like a sack to the ground, his pony running away. Reno tore off his hat and wiped his face, his eyes wide and rolling. The hat fell to the ground. He reached into his pocket and pulled out a small flask, but dropped it from his trembling fingers.

Reno shouted for the men to mount, then to dismount, then to mount, staring down at Bloody Knife's convulsing body.

"Dark Face was crazy before," Little Crane said. "Now he's worse. He can't lead anybody now. We'll all have to run for it, or we'll be dead. All of us."

Boyer rode down off the high point with Curley, joking about the other scouts shooting into the village.

"Maybe they'll get Sitting Bull and it will all be over," Boyer said.

"Or even Crazy Horse," Curley said. "He'd better not show himself to them."

To the south, the trumpeter rode as fast as he could up the hill, carrying the message toward Benteen. The small group of warriors on the distant hill to the east began firing at him.

Boyer pointed toward them. "Goes Ahead said they would cause trouble. Long Hair should have sent some Bluecoats to run them off."

At the column, Custer said to Boyer, "What are you two doing here? I dismissed you."

"I told you before," Boyer said, "I can go where you can go. I'm going to stay and fight it out."

Custer pointed to Curley. "What about him?"

"He's old enough to know what he wants to do," Boyer said. "I won't make him leave if he wants to stay with me."

Custer ordered his men ready to march. "What more did you see up on that hill?" he asked Boyer.

"It's bad," Boyer said. "We'd better hurry down there. The warriors who were sleeping are catching their ponies by now. And maybe there'll be others who'll come from the south, where they've been fighting Dark Face."

"Are you saying Mr. Reno is finished?"

"I don't know if he's finished, but he could be. It's very bad down there."

"Go back up on the hill and watch for me," Custer said. "We'll go on down. If Mr. Reno can hold on just a little longer, we'll go in at the Medicine Tail and support him."

"I think we should go farther on," Boyer said. "Warriors will come from behind us and trap us. We should go farther on, now, to the end of the village, and not waste more time."

Custer pointed up the hill. "Mitch, get up there and watch the camp for me. Signal what you see."

Tired of arguing, Boyer turned and rode back up, Curley right behind. They reached the crest and saw the other three Crow scouts riding hard toward the south, a number of Sioux warriors in pursuit.

"Ahh! The Sioux are already coming up here," Boyer said. "Those three had better ride hard. And we'd better tell Long Hair. I told him we should move fast."

"And look over there," Curley said. "Dark Face is getting killed."

In the distance, smoke curled up from the timber. More Sioux warriors poured from the village to surround Reno's men.

A bugle sounded and soldiers began to break from the timber, engaging the Sioux on horseback and hand to hand.

Boyer turned around and yelled down to Custer, who was too far away to hear, so Boyer made the sign to Custer that Reno was being killed. Custer and his brothers removed their hats and cheered.

"I don't think Long Hair read the sign right," Boyer said, confused. "We'd better catch him."

Before leaving, Curley stared into the bottom. The shooting and yelling were even louder.

"I wonder if Six Fingers will make it through all that," Curley said. "If he does, he'll have a lot of things to make the paper talk about."

Reno's retreat across the river to the bluffs had begun in earnest. Little Crane and Red Moon rode ahead of Garrett, stuck like glue to the sides of their ponies.

Garrett rode close behind. From every side came the screams of men and horses, echoing through the dust and smoke like the wails of the damned.

Just ahead, a wounded soldier rose to his knees, reaching out for help. Garrett reined his pony. He leaned over and lifted the wounded soldier up behind him.

Garrett turned for the river and met a mounted warrior coming straight at him. Feeling himself slipping, the wounded soldier clutched at anything he could, tearing Garrett's rifle from his hands.

"Don't let me fall!" the soldier screamed. "Please, don't let me fall." A passing warrior shot into his side and he slid off.

The warrior was drawing his bow when Garrett pulled his pistol and fired. The bullet clipped the warrior's fingers from his right hand, and the shattered arrow flew in pieces.

Screaming with pain and anger, the warrior pulled his knife with his left hand and turned his pony toward Garrett.

The wounded soldier had come to his knees, holding his side. The warrior tried to run him down on his way to Garrett, but the soldier grabbed his leg and held tightly.

The warrior began stabbing the soldier in the face and neck. As the soldier fell backward, Garrett rode up and fired into the warrior's head, then turned for the river.

In front of him, grass and dead cottonwoods formed a maze of fire. Suddenly, the buffalo dream exploded into his head. Flames rose all around him.

Garrett nearly fell from his horse. He turned his pony in a full circle, looking for an escape. The flames surrounded him, but for a small opening leading to the river.

In the small circle in the fire, a figure appeared.

"Six Fingers!" Red Moon yelled. "Come on! What are you waiting for?"

Garrett, frozen with fear, could only stare. Red Moon screamed at him again and was gone, leaving the ring of fire before him, a hole of darkness on the other side.

"No, no, this can't be," he said to himself, holding his pony back. "What's going on here?"

The hole began to disappear, the flames closing in, and Garrett knew his choice had come. His heart in his throat, he kicked his pony into a dead run for the burning trees.

Garrett, his eyes wide, found himself at the mouth of the black hole. An arrow zipped past his ear; a bullet whizzed just over his head. Then he burst through the smoke and flame.

Outside the flames was another world, violent beyond description. Spent powder, dust, and smoke covered the valley like a dank gray cloud. Garrett's ears rang with the screams of men and horses, the shrill notes of the eagle bone whistles, and the loud blasts of rifles and pistols going off everywhere around him.

His pony crashed over a warrior scalping a fallen soldier. He passed another soldier crawling on his hands and knees, an arrow through his ribs. To his right a warrior was riding down upon another soldier, raising a war club, then striking the soldier in the side of the head.

Pull your pistol! Garrett told himself. *You've got to pull your pistol!*

Just ahead was the river. If he could get across, the

chance of making it up onto the bluffs was good.

Between him and the water were two warriors who turned their ponies toward him and came straight on, racing one another to see which one could count first coup.

Garrett lowered himself over his pony's back and cocked his pistol. One of the warriors broke into the lead, brandishing a war lance. Garrett fired and the warrior dropped the lance and rode past, clutching his throat, falling sideways from his pony.

The second warrior pulled up, but Garrett had turned his pony straight at him. He galloped up and fired point blank into the warrior's chest. The bullet tore completely through and out the warrior's back, blowing blood and lung tissue in a cloud of pink mist.

Just ahead, Benjamin Hodgson's horse stumbled and fell forward. Hodgson rolled free and came to his hands and knees.

Garrett's pony balked at the river. The water was frothy with blood and mud, filled with screaming soldiers. The bank on each side was steep, and the soil had been plowed into a greasy slide.

Men and horses churned feverishly to climb the far bank to the grassy slope beyond, then scramble through a tight ravine and up to the top of a high hill for cover.

Sioux and Cheyenne marksmen had taken positions along the slopes above the river and were shooting down into the retreating soldiers. Garrett worked his pony along the steep bank, looking for a place to ford.

Little Crane appeared beside him, yelling, "Get your pony across! Go! Go!"

"Where's Red Moon?"

"I'm behind you!" Red Moon shouted.

"Go!" Little Crane yelled. "Don't wait! Go!"

Garrett kicked his pony hard, holding on tightly as it lurched down into the current. A short way away, Lieutenant Hodgson was being pulled across, struggling to hold onto a trooper's stirrup. Hodgson reached the other side, spitting water from his lungs, and began to limp up the hill. Partway up, he jerked with the impact of a bullet, fell, and slid to a stop near the river, where he lay still.

In the current, Garrett struggled to hold onto his pony. His pistol slipped from his grasp as he clutched handfuls of mane. A dead soldier washed into him, the head coming to rest on his arms, the mouth open in a pallid face, rolled-back eyes staring up at him.

The dead soldier rolled off and Garrett choked. A rifle bullet ripped the water just under his horse's neck. Another struck the pommel of his saddle.

Wheezing for air, Garrett's pony pulled itself from the current, only to slide back down, struggling again to climb the bank. Grunting with exertion, the pony gained firm ground and was rising when a bullet slammed into its left eye.

The pony reared, squealing, its eye and a chunk of skull missing. Garrett felt himself going over backward, falling under the kicking pony. Desperately he freed himself from the stirrups and came up to see his pony grow limp in the current and lodge against a snag on the opposite bank.

My pony! Garrett said to himself. *My notes! All my notes!*

Red Moon was beside him, reaching down, yelling for him to take hold.

Garrett clasped Red Moon's arm with both hands and Red Moon pulled him up behind, urging his pony out of the river. Garrett held on tightly, both arms around Red Moon's middle.

Red Moon's pony struggled up the hill. From a slope just behind them came the report of a rifle. Garrett felt a hot sting along his upper left arm. Red Moon gasped as the bullet tore through his ribs and into his left lung, coming out his chest at an angle. Blood streamed from the wound, coating Garrett's arm.

Red Moon slumped forward. Little Crane was beside them, taking the reins.

"Hold on!" he told Red Moon. "Don't get off until we reach the top."

With his left hand, Garrett clutched the pony's mane, holding Red Moon with his other arm. He could hear

Red Moon singing his death song, a high, wailing sound interrupted by gasps for air.

"Hold on," Garrett told him. "You're not going to die. You're *not*."

Little Crane led the pony to the top of the hill. Reno's troops were gathering, placing the wounded in the center of a hilltop. Others. were building breastworks of saddles and any loose gear they could find. Some were trying to dig trenches with pocketknives and gun butts.

Garrett, numbed with shock, eased Red Moon off his pony and laid him on his back. Red Moon's eyes looked unfocused.

"Ah, my brother," he said to Garrett, "there's a trail that I'm supposed to take . . ."

"Hold on," Garrett said, gently probing Red Moon's side and chest with his fingers. "We'll get you fixed up." He turned and yelled, "Where's a doctor? We need a doctor!"

The wounded wailed and moaned. Near Garrett, a terrified soldier cried, clutching his face with trembling hands. Garrett turned back to Red Moon.

"Hold on, brother," he said. "You'll make it."

Red Moon reached up and touched Garrett's face. "You made me laugh. . . . The hell flies." He coughed. "You should have seen my children."

"I wish I had," Garrett said.

"Some day," Red Moon said, "when we meet again."

Little Crane knelt down. "Can you hear me, Red Moon?"

Red Moon nodded. "I can . . ."

"The Sioux are leaving. They're going to fight Long Hair. He'll learn now what he brought us into."

Red Moon nodded. "They're killing Long Hair . . ."

"We can move you out of here and take you home," Little Crane continued. "Can you come?"

Red Moon smiled. "I'm going home. . . . I see my wife, my children. It's good. It's good."

"No, Red Moon," Garrett said. His eyes filled with tears.

"It's good," Red Moon said again. The air left his lungs and his eyes lost their sheen. His head tilted slightly to one side.

Little Crane stood up. He wept loudly, his hands over his face.

Garrett pulled Red Moon to his chest and rocked him. "Oh, I've lost you, my brother," he said. "Dear God, I've lost you."

Ann sat up in her bedroll, drenched with sweat. The dream had been terrifying.

She rose and awakened Water and Tyrone.

"What is it, Miss Ann?" Tyrone asked.

"We've got to go," Ann said. "Now!"

"Where do you want to go?"

Ann pointed, her eyes filled with tears. "We have to find Adam."

"I don't understand, Miss Ann. We're headed where he is."

"You don't understand, Tyrone. The buffalo died. I saw it fall."

"You dream, Miss Ann? You had another dream?"

"Yes," Ann said, tears running down her cheeks. "I don't have time to explain."

Water had risen to his feet. He unhobbled the horses.

Ann stared into the distance. She had seen the buffalo again. Adam had come through the flames and had jumped from its back, just as the buffalo had turned red. The buffalo had fallen and Adam was turning in circles. He couldn't stop himself, turning circle after circle.

"You'd better sit down, Miss Ann," Tyrone advised.

"I'll sit in the saddle," Ann said. "That's the only way I'm getting off my feet." She packed her bedroll hurriedly.

Water held the ponies. He pointed into the distance, where dust rose high into the air.

"Something's happening far down there," he said. "Something very big is happening."

"Can we get there now?" Ann asked.

Water frowned. "Now? It will take a full day of riding, through the night, to this time tomorrow."

"That's not soon enough," Ann said.

"Miss Ann, we don't have wings," Tyrone said. "We've got horses. That's all."

"Then let's get on them," Ann said. "And I'm not getting off mine until I find Adam."

THIRTY-THREE

Nighthawk awakened from a sound sleep.

Tall Deer crouched at the doorflap. He was yelling, "Bluecoats! Bluecoats have attacked the Unkpapas! And there are more coming along the bluffs!"

"Where's your mother?" Nighthawk asked.

"Headed into the hills with the others."

Ghostwind pulled Talking Grass close to her. Young Horse stared at Tall Deer.

"Are you coming with me?" Tall Deer asked him.

"He's staying with me," Ghostwind said. "If you're smart, you'll go find your mother and stay with her."

Tall Deer popped back out of the lodge. Nighthawk followed quickly, looking for him, but he was lost in the dust and confusion.

The village had erupted into a storm of screaming people. Women and children rushed everywhere. Mothers searched for young ones, tearing their hair. Toddlers not in their mothers' arms rolled under the stampede.

From the south came yells and rifle fire. The sky was filled with dust and smoke, rising up like a thunderstorm as the pony herd churned across the hills to the west. Across the river, a long line of blue weaved in and out of sight among the hills, flags flying at the head of the column.

Ghostwind emerged from the lodge, Talking Grass and Young Horse at her side. She wondered aloud about Day Lily and where she might be. It would be impossible to look for her now.

Nighthawk ducked back inside and returned with his Henry and the Springfield he had acquired the day of the buffalo hunt.

"You can't shoot them both," Ghostwind said.

Nighthawk handed her the Springfield and a pouch of bullets. "Use this if you have to."

Ghostwind's eyes filled with tears. "Now it's certain that you must leave, isn't it?"

They had talked a long time earlier in the day, when he had returned from his visit with Crazy Horse. Both Nighthawk and Ghostwind had realized that his trouble with Calls-at-Night, together with another battle that would cause more grief and suffering, would necessitate his leaving. No matter his skills with a rifle or his contribution against the Bluecoats, there would be many who would want to kill him.

"I'm afraid so," Nighthawk said. "After this, there'll be even more anger toward me. But I'll come back, when there's been peace for a while. I'll find you."

"The children and I are going with you."

"You can't. Someone will kill you. We talked about this. Stay with the safety of the village."

"No," Ghostwind sobbed. "I don't want you to go."

Nighthawk felt his heart tearing inside. He dropped his rifle and held her tightly. Young Horse and Talking Grass looked on, tears rolling down their cheeks.

Nighthawk held each of them in turn. "I'll be back to see you. I promise. Now, hurry to safety with your mother."

Ghostwind, sick with grief, gave Nighthawk a long kiss, and held him tightly once more. Then she picked up Talking Grass and clutched the Springfield with her free hand.

"Take care of yourself, my husband. Please."

"This is not goodbye," Nighthawk said. "I'll see you again. I promise."

Nighthawk watched Ghostwind disappear into the crowd. Young Horse turned back momentarily and waved.

After a deep breath, Nighthawk picked up his rifle. Eagle Wing ran up, holding two ponies.

"I've come from the Unkpapa village. The Bluecoats are running across the river. Many are killed."

"So there are a lot of warriors coming this way?"

"A great many," Eagle Wing said. "Gall lost his entire family to Bluecoat bullets. They shot them in their lodge. There are huge holes where the slugs tore through. Gall is coming with a big force to go up the Medicine Tail and fight the other group coming through the hills."

Nighthawk looked around the village, where older men were singing songs and helping prepare the younger warriors for battle.

"Everyone is getting ready to fight," Nighthawk said.

Eagle Wing said, "Sitting Bull is now in his lodge, making strong medicine. Everyone can feel it. Crazy Horse's black stallion, the one that Tall Deer and Young Horse brought down from the hills, is running wild up and down the camps. There are many who say the stallion has a rider on its back, but no one can see the rider."

"Where's Crazy Horse?" Nighthawk asked.

"The Oglalas are preparing to fight from the north end," Eagle Wing said. "They are all making medicine now. You and I should stop here for a short while and I'll help you with your medicine. Do you remember the songs?"

"Yes, you taught me well," Nighthawk said. "Who do we fight with?"

"Two Moon is gathering a lot of warriors," Eagle Wing replied. "Lame-White-Man came from a sweat and he's going to take a bunch straight up." He put a hand on Nighthawk's shoulder. "It won't matter who we fight with. Take your pony and get on, while we sing the songs. Then we'll go together. Brave up! It's a good day to die!"

Boyer and Curley rode hard down off the ridge. Custer had called a halt in the Medicine Tail. His younger brother, Boston, had just joined the column.

"Mitch, you know my brother Bos, don't you? He couldn't miss it."

"That's good," Boyer said. "Dark Face is running to the river. We'd better start fighting soon, or all the warriors will be charging us."

Custer frowned. "Are you sure?"

"I'm telling you that Dark Face and his men are running. They're being killed."

"Where's Benteen? Did you see him?"

"We didn't see him," Boyer said. "I don't know where he is."

"There's no reason he shouldn't be here by now," Custer said. "Absolutely no reason in the world."

Mark Kellogg, who had been taking notes, called Boyer to him.

"What did it look like?" he asked Boyer. "I mean, could you see the Sioux fighting the soldiers?"

Boyer tossed his head over the hill, toward the river. "Wait until we get over there. You'll know what it's like. You can make the paper talk as long as you can hold out."

Custer ordered a trooper to him and scribbled a note onto a piece of paper.

"Maybe General Terry and Mr. Gibbon are arriving up ahead. Let's hope so."

"Why didn't you send someone before?" Boyer asked. "You should have."

Custer ignored him and handed the note to the courier. "Ride hard, boy! Tell them we need help here, and quickly. Do you understand?"

The trooper saluted and assured Custer he would get through. He kicked his sorrel roan into a full run, north over the hills.

"We'd better go back and find Dark Face," Boyer suggested. "Maybe some of them are alive and maybe Benteen is there." He pointed through the coulee, into the village. "There are a lot of warriors with ponies now. They'll be here soon. That will make it a lot harder for us."

Custer pointed to a high ridge just ahead. "I want to have another look."

At the top of the ridge, Custer scoured the south hills with binoculars, fuming. He removed his hat and slapped it against his leg.

"I don't understand where Benteen is," he said.

He turned to look into the valley. The northern end of the village, and the country beyond, lay in plain view. The valley was filled with the screams of women and children running for safety.

"A-ha! Can you see that!" Custer yelled. "Mr. Reno must have pulled together for another attack, or maybe Mr. Benteen joined forces with him down below and they rallied! They're running away! They are, for a fact!" Custer yelled back to his command, "We've got them, boys!" but no one cheered.

"We're seeing the women and children, and the old people," Boyer explained. "There are some young warriors and horse tenders with them, but the fighting men aren't here yet. I'm telling you, they will be coming soon, and we'll be trapped."

"Mitch, I have no intention of running from them." He pointed into the village. "*They're* doing the running. Can't you see that?" He adjusted his red cravat and smoothed his buckskin pants.

"Then let's hurry up and fight!" Boyer said. "We've been here too long."

Custer called Captains Miles Keogh and George Yates to him. Both officers saluted.

Yates, four years younger than Custer, also wore buckskins. His blonde hair was cut short and neatly trimmed and his boots were polished like a bathroom mirror.

Keogh had already acquired battlefield honors. His service in the Papal Army had earned him Catholic medals, awarded by Pope Pius IX. He carried both medals, one a large cross, with him at all times.

Keogh had served in the Union Army against the Rebel forces. Among the enlisted men of the Seventh Cavalry, though, Keogh's reputation as a hard drinker and stern commander overshadowed any merit they might have seen in him.

Custer ordered Yates to bring his battalion to the left. Keogh frowned.

"Mr. Keogh, I'm going to give you the opportunity of a lifetime," Custer said. "I want you to remain at this position and hold it. I'm taking Mr. Yates and his boys with me. Brother Tom and brother Boston will go with me, also."

"Yes, sir, General." Keogh saluted. His expression was pained. There was no honor in any company other than the General's.

"Mr. Keogh, this is an important assignment. I hope you realize that."

"Yes, I do, General."

"Your performance here today could well gain you a number of honors. Do you understand?"

"Yes, General, I do."

"I want you to hold this position, for all you're worth." He pointed into the Medicine Tail. "If Mr. Benteen arrives, then you will assume command and go through that crossing into the village. I'll go north, to the front end, and hope to meet the column coming up the Big Horn. With or without them, I'll sweep down through the village to meet you. Is that understood?"

"We'll do our best, General."

"Miles, I want you to hold this position!" Custer said. "If I have to come back, I want a place to come to. Do you understand?"

"I understand, General. We'll hold the position."

"See that you do. You're a good man and a good fighter, Miles. I believe it with all my heart. Help me here. We've got a hard situation, but by the grace of God, we'll go back to our station as victors today. I can't do it without your help, Miles. Do you understand?"

Keogh blinked hard. He saluted again, shouting, "Go and fight them, General. We'll hold the position for you. I promise."

Ghostwind held Talking Grass tightly, keeping Young Horse close beside her at all times. The women and children had gathered north of the village. Mothers and grandmothers milled through the throngs of frightened villagers, looking for lost family members.

With Ghostwind was Day Lily, who stared across at a group of young men. Red Bear, painted for battle, had been tied to his pony. This would be the day he would cross over and join the Grandfathers with honor.

As one of the Suicide Boys, Red Bear had flanked the women and children north of the village and would fight to the death any Bluecoats who came near. If no Bluecoats came near the river, they would seek them out in the hills.

Mountain Water arrived and stood beside Ghostwind, worried about Five Bulls, who was still in the village, urging young warriors into battle.

"I hope he doesn't think he needs to fight," she said. "He's too old for that. I don't want to have to search for him among the dead."

Ghostwind pushed the thought from her mind. Enough friends and relatives would die before the afternoon had ended. She couldn't bear to think that Nighthawk would never come back to her.

Looking to the south, Ghostwind could see more dust clouds forming over the village. What did they mean? Perhaps the Bluecoats were attacking again.

Little Foot, the Southern Cheyenne woman, sat by herself on a knoll overlooking the river. She had gone to the upper ford, where the river went from a straight run into a series of small loops. Some of the women had taken their families across and into the trees and brush, thinking the cover safer than the open.

Ghostwind joined Little Foot, who smiled faintly in welcome.

"This is the day your vision foretold, isn't it?" Little Foot said. She pointed into the sky. "The sun shines through the smoke and dust like a ball of fire."

"Is your man fighting?" Ghostwind asked.

"He's with Lame-White-Man's warriors." She pointed toward the hills. "They're going to try to stop the Bluecoats from getting down to the river."

"I won't see Nighthawk again," Ghostwind said. "Not for a while. Maybe not ever again."

"Did you see his death?"

"No, but he can't stay in the village now. There are too many who want to kill him, even if the Bluecoats don't."

"It's a sad day for you, no matter what," Little Foot said.

To the south, warriors began moving up into the hills. The Suicide Boys sang a song together and started forward on their ponies.

After watching Red Bear ride away, Day Lily walked aimlessly up into the hills.

Ghostwind wanted to go after her, but noticed that Tall Deer had ridden out from the village and was dismounting near Young Horse.

Ghostwind listened from nearby as Tall Deer showed Young Horse a rifle he'd been given.

"Look what I've got!" Tall Deer told Young Horse. He held a single-shot Springfield. "One of the Cheyenne warriors who went down to fight the Bluecoats with the Unkpapas gave it to me. He just tossed it to me. I don't even know his name. He said that I could become a warrior today."

"You aren't going out to fight, are you?" Young Horse asked.

"I'm thinking about it," Tall Deer said. "The warrior told me to come up here and watch for Bluecoats, but I think the fighting is going to be up in the hills now."

Ghostwind approached. Tall Deer saw her and mounted his pony.

"Where are you going?" Ghostwind asked.

"I know that you don't like me any more," Tall Deer said. "I'm sorry I took Young Horse out from the village so far."

"Young Horse made his own decision to go with you," Ghostwind said. "You're right, you shouldn't have done it. But Young Horse is old enough to know better."

"Is Nighthawk going out to fight?" Tall Deer asked.

"Yes. He's going with Eagle Wing," Ghostwind said. "Nighthawk's not a Bluecoat, though many in the village think he is."

"I never thought he was," Tall Deer said. "He's a kind man, and he's said some good things to me. I only wish I could shoot as well as he can."

"Get down and stay with us," Ghostwind said. "I'm not angry with you."

"Good," Tall Deer said, jumping down. "Maybe I'll have to defend us all when the Bluecoats come."

"Let's hope the Bluecoats don't get this far," Ghostwind said. "Besides, you don't even know how to shoot that rifle."

"I'll bet I can shoot this one better than you can shoot that one," Tall Deer challenged.

"I won't argue that," Ghostwind said. "I'm not going to fire this unless I absolutely have to. Let's see if you know anything about that rifle you've got."

Tall Deer frowned. He took a bullet from a pack he wore on his belt and fumbled with the gun.

"Let me have it," Young Horse said.

Young Horse took the rifle and opened the breech. Taking the bullet, he carefully loaded it into the barrel and locked the breech in place.

"I won't pull back the hammer," Young Horse said. "You don't do that until you're going to shoot it."

"How did you learn that, Young Horse?" Ghostwind asked. "Did Nighthawk show you?"

"No. I asked him and he said that I was too young. But I watched how he did it anyway."

Tall Deer took the rifle back. "Is that all there is to it?"

"You have to know how to aim it," Young Horse said.

Tall Deer put the rifle to his shoulder and sighted.

"No," Tall Deer said. "Use your right eye. If you put the gun against your right shoulder, use your right eye."

"Actually," Tall Deer said, "the rifle feels better against my left shoulder."

"Then shoot that way," Young Horse said. "Use your left eye to sight."

"That feels good," Tall Deer said. "What should I shoot at?"

Young Horse pointed. "Look! Bluecoats, on the hill up there. Can you see them?"

"It looks like they're fighting our warriors," Ghostwind said.

"If they come down here, I'll shoot them," Tall Deer said.

"That's dangerous," Young Horse pointed out. "They'll shoot back."

"Young Horse is right," Ghostwind said. "You'd better come back up into the hills with us."

"I'll go down there, into the trees," Tall Deer said, pointing to the crossing. "If they come, I'll shoot at them."

"You're going to be killed," Young Horse warned.

"Don't worry about me," Tall Deer said. "Crazy Horse gave me his black stallion and then I watched him paint his pony for the fight." He pointed toward the village. "He's coming this way soon, with a bunch of warriors. They'll come by here and they'll keep me from being killed."

A group of horse tenders rode to the crossing, warning the women and children to stay back. Two of them, young Santee warriors, staked their ponies up along the slope and went down into the trees at the river crossing.

Tall Deer staked his pony with theirs and checked his rifle.

"I've got a feeling that the Bluecoats are coming down here," he said. "I'd better get into cover at the crossing and help the Santees."

"You'll be killed, Tall Deer," Ghostwind said. "Come with us."

"No, I'll live, and I'll gain honors," Tall Deer said. "Crazy Horse gave me some medicine."

Young Horse turned to go into the hills with Ghostwind. "I hope you're right, Tall Deer," he said. "I'll miss you if you're killed. I'll miss you a lot."

*   *   *

Boyer and Curley rode together, just behind Custer at the head of the column. They were descending a high hill toward a gentle slope that led to the river below.

Curley had been watching to the west, where a small group of warriors had gathered along the slopes, some mounted and some afoot. They didn't appear aggressive until the column turned toward the river. With loud cries, the warriors now rode and ran straight toward the troops, stopping to shoot into the lines.

Arrows and bullets raked the column. Curley heard an arrow zip past his face. His horse grunted as a bullet tore into its stomach.

Boyer grabbed his side, just above his belt.

"I'm shot, Little Brother."

Curley's horse was bucking. Curley jumped to the ground and the horse fell, squealing, a short distance away.

Boyer also dismounted, his horse limping badly. A bullet had torn open its right knee.

Many men and horses were wounded. Custer ordered a dismount and a skirmish line. At the order, the soldiers fired into the warriors, driving them back down over the hill.

Custer ordered the men to mount. Boyer, believing Custer had taken position permanently, called Curley to him.

Boyer held his side as he spoke. "Little Brother, quickly. Change your hair and braid it like a Sioux. You have to run from this place."

"I want to stay with you."

"Don't stay with me. You're young and don't know much about fighting." He pointed east. "Go that way and stay clear of the Sioux."

"Come with me, Big Brother," Curley begged.

"No, I'm shot and I'll fight it out. I'll get some of them before they finish me. Go tell the Bluecoats coming from the north that we are all killed." He pointed to Custer. "That man will stop at nothing. He's going to take us right into the village, where there are many more warriors. We have no chance at all. Now, go and tell what you saw.''

Boyer, grimacing with pain, hugged Curley. He found a loose horse and mounted, and watched as Curley disappeared down the slope and into a ravine to the east.

''Go, Little Brother!'' he yelled after him.

Custer, at the head of the column, ordered full speed down the slope toward the village. To the west, coming at a dead run through the village, rode a horde of warriors, yelling loudly. They were headed for the same crossing.

Boyer rode low over his pony, holding his side. The pain was like fire. It was all he could do to hang on. He slowed down and veered off, letting soldiers pass him. He watched the force close in on the crossing. Women and children were screaming on both sides of the river, running for their lives.

Boyer looked south. Lines of warriors rode up into the Medicine Tail, gathering around the hill where Long Hair had left the other group of Bluecoats. The air was filled with the sounds of battle.

Along the bottom, Custer neared the crossing. At the base of the hill, the river ran straight for a short section, then curved north into a series of twists and turns. The crossing lay between the first two curves.

To the west, the warrior horde from the village closed in. Custer might make the crossing; but soon after that, Boyer knew, the end would come.

THIRTY-FOUR

Garrett sat with Little Crane in the circle of survivors on a high hill, looking north. Intense firing had begun. Every man knew that Custer's men were under siege.

Benteen had arrived not long before. He stood conferring with officers, pacing back and forth. Reno had gone down to the bottom of the hill, near the river, to look for Lieutenant Hodgson.

Reno had watched Bloody Knife die in front of him and had learned of Hodgson's death from Garrett. One shock had been added upon another. Not a soldier thought he was fit to command.

The wounded were screaming, the one surviving doctor unable to help everyone at once. Men were digging graves for the dead, whispering under their breath about the possibility of the Sioux returning. If Terry and Gibbon didn't show up soon, they'd all be lost.

"There's no need to stay here," Little Crane told Garrett. "The Bluecoat leaders are afraid to charge. When the Sioux are finished over there, they'll be back. We don't want to be here."

Garrett stared at Red Moon's body. Little Crane had wrapped him in a blanket. Garrett reached into his pocket, pulling out a pencil—the only fragment left of his writing career.

"What are you waiting for?" Little Crane asked. "We should get ready to leave."

"Won't there be warriors out there?"

"All the warriors have gone to fight Long Hair," Little

Crane replied. "They'll start coming back soon, though, when they see that they can kill us all."

"I'm willing to go, then," Garrett said. "What about the other scouts?"

"They've already left, most of them, anyway. They've got Sioux ponies with them." He pointed to the south. "We'll take Red Moon and let him cross over in the hills out there. Nothing is good about this place. Nothing."

Garrett and Little Crane loaded Red Moon on the back of Little Crane's pony and tied him securely. The soldiers watched them without comment.

Garrett mounted, hoping one of the officers might try to stop them from leaving, but none did.

Little Crane took a ravine to the south that led back into Ash Creek. They climbed up for a distance, then turned south, up a small creek that wound back into the hills.

To the north, dust rose high into the air. Screams and shots could be heard plainly. Garrett didn't look back. He didn't want to think about Custer's fate.

Tall Deer rested his rifle over the branch of a box elder tree, sighting in on the oncoming Bluecoats. They rode at a gallop along the flat, parallel to the river, following the travois trail to the crossing.

The lead rider, in flashy dress, with buckskin pants, a bright red tie, and a broad white hat, was eager to reach the crossing. Tall Deer believed him to be a scout. He would be important to kill, for scouts were even more hated than the Bluecoat leaders.

Tall Deer decided he would shoot this one. Then he would take his scalp and be honored by all the people.

The two young Santee warriors armed their bows and waited. The other horse tenders crouched in the trees and brush, unarmed, there just to say they had come close to the fighting.

The Bluecoats rode closer. His hands trembling, Tall Deer clutched his rifle tightly. "Don't pull the hammer back until you're ready to shoot," Young Horse had instructed. "And wait until they're very close, or you'll miss."

Tall Deer forced himself not to pull the hammer back and fire. Within a few heartbeats, they would be at the crossing—and the scout would be his.

Then, just before reaching the crossing, the Bluecoats saw Crazy Horse and his oncoming warriors. The Bluecoats began to shout among themselves. Half of them stayed with the flashy scout, while the other half turned back, following a different leader dressed in buckskins.

Tall Deer took a deep breath as the remaining Bluecoats followed the scout into the crossing.

Tall Deer leveled his rifle. The flashy scout, a pistol in his hand, rode right toward him. He could see the scout's wide eyes, his mouth, open and yelling, the blonde hair soaked with sweat.

A thought flashed through Tall Deer's mind: A scout with light hair was unusual.

Tall Deer pulled the hammer back and aimed at the scout's middle. He was so close.

Gritting his teeth, Tall Deer touched off. Smoke and flame poured from the barrel. The butt slammed into Tall Deer's shoulder, knocking him off balance. He stared, watching the scout fall from his horse into the water.

Everyone in the brush cheered. The young Santees loosed their arrows at the other Bluecoats, who reined their horses at the crossing. One arrow flew high, but the second drove itself into one of the horses, who bucked off a Bluecoat into the water.

Another rider dressed in buckskins jumped from his horse and tried to lift the fallen scout, whose lower stomach was soaked with blood. He held the scout, crying, as the Santees loosed arrows at him, hitting him in the leg.

Most of the Bluecoats turned and scattered back up the hill. Two Bluecoats remained behind and began shooting into the brush at the young Santees. The Santees crouched low, one of them yelling that he had been hit.

Tall Deer opened the breech and tried to remove the spent cartridge, but it was stuck fast. Another Bluecoat had jumped from his horse and pulled the first Bluecoat away from the fallen scout. They both mounted and started back toward the hills, just as Crazy Horse and his warriors approached the crossing.

The flashy scout fell back in the water, losing his hat, and was swept a short way downstream before he caught hold of a tree root and held tightly.

Tall Deer ducked to one side as Crazy Horse and his warriors burst through the crossing, yelling and screaming, splashing water in all directions.

When they had passed, Tall Deer stood up, drenched, and watched Crazy Horse ride up toward the hill in pursuit of the retreating Bluecoats.

With the exception of a few stragglers, whose horses had given out, the Bluecoats all made it back to the hills. Some had gone the same way they had come, while others had ridden along the river, turning up a ravine that led to the top.

The Bluecoats would be able to run only a short way, Tall Deer knew, for many hundreds of warriors were already crossing the river in many places, riding toward the hills.

The stragglers who hadn't been caught by Crazy Horse's warriors were now fleeing into the brush along the river, pursued by young warriors, their knives out, who had rushed down from the hills to count coup.

One of the soldiers put his pistol to his own head and fired.

Among the Bluecoat horses that had fallen from exhaustion stood a lone mule, grazing lazily a short distance from the river. Its rider lay still in the grass, a young warrior standing over him, holding a scalp in the air. Another warrior held up an ear.

Tall Deer helped the wounded Santee out of the brush. Women poured down from the hills, including the young Santee's mother, who rushed to care for him.

Young Horse ran to meet Tall Deer. "I saw you shoot that scout!" he said, pointing downstream. "Is he dead?"

"Yes, I shot him," Tall Deer said. He continued to struggle with his rifle. The stuck shell wouldn't budge.

"But he's not dead yet. I think I broke this thing when I shot it."

Ghostwind hurried down the slope, holding Talking Grass. Mountain Water was close behind.

"Tall Deer shot that scout who led them," Young Horse said. "He'll get honors for that."

Ghostwind looked downstream to where the scout had pulled himself out onto the bank. She handed Talking Grass to Mountain Water and checked her rifle.

"I don't want him to live any longer," she said.

"It's only fair that I finish him," Tall Deer said.

"No, you should stay back," Ghostwind warned. "He might have a gun."

"He can shoot you just as well as me," Tall Deer argued.

"I'll shoot him again before I go up to him," Ghostwind said. "Maybe two or three times. I won't take any chances."

A group of warriors rode up, mixed Sioux and Cheyenne. They noticed the fallen Bluecoats across the river, and the young horse tenders who had come down from the hills and were now shooting arrows into one of them.

"Did they shoot those Bluecoats?" one of the warriors asked. "Or did Crazy Horse get them?"

Young Horse pointed to the scout on the bank. "Tall Deer got one of them himself. He shot that one. He was the leader."

The warriors voiced their approval. "Did you touch him with your rifle?" one of them asked Tall Deer. "Did you count your first coup?"

Tall Deer turned and ran toward the fallen scout. Young Horse hurried after him. Ghostwind caught him from behind.

"You stay back. I told you that you might get shot."

"He can't shoot me," Young Horse argued. "He can hardly move."

Ghostwind and Young Horse eased up behind Tall Deer, who stared down at the scout.

The scout looked up at them and groaned.

"He doesn't have enough hair to take," Tall Deer said.

The warriors rode up behind. One of them shouted, "Go ahead and touch him! Ahhh! Count your coup!"

Young Horse put the muzzle of his rifle against the scout's back. The warriors yelled war cries. One of them dismounted with a rope.

"We'll take him into the village," he said. "We won't finish him off right away. We'll leave him for anyone who wants him."

The other warriors had already crossed the river and were tying their ropes around fallen Bluecoats, dragging them behind their ponies back to the village.

Some of the warriors had stripped the uniforms from the Bluecoats and were wearing them. Tall Deer looked at the scout's clothes, but knew they wouldn't fit him.

"Go catch your pony," one of the warriors told Tall Deer, tying the rope around the scout's middle.

Tall Deer hurried up the slope and untied his pony from the stake. He rode back down and the warrior handed him the rope.

"Here, take this one back to the village yourself. Tell everyone you see that you got him. Tell everyone that today you're a warrior."

Boyer knelt in the skirmish line, firing at warriors who rode toward their position. His side had become numb, but he knew the bleeding hadn't stopped. Dizzy spells came and went.

Yates had led the first half of Custer's batallion back from the river, taking the highest ground possible for a stand. Boyer had joined them, knowing in his heart the end would come soon.

They had staked their horses, hoping to get a chance to mount and join Keogh's command to the east. But they were surrounded, and warriors with blankets had flapped them continuously, scaring the horses so badly they had pulled their pins or snapped the bridle reins.

Now there was yelling and screaming in all directions. Dust and smoke hovered over the field in a thick, dank cloud, mixed with the heat of the day and the smell of blood.

Horses and men lay all along the route near the top, having been shot by warriors positioned along the sides of the hills.

The firing suddenly eased and the dust and smoke lifted. Boyer felt hope. Perhaps Benteen had arrived and the enemy was leaving.

Then into their position rode a force of warriors painted white like ghosts. Boyer's stomach fell. No one could save them now. Suicide Boys had come to break up the skirmish line.

The hill exploded with gunfire. The soldiers killed or wounded many Suicide Boys, but others took their place and still others came behind them. The soldiers fired their rifles and threw them aside, bringing out their revolvers. There was no time to reload; when the revolvers were empty, the fighting turned hand to hand.

Boyer had been shot again, high in the left shoulder. He grabbed a pistol from a fallen soldier beside him and aimed at an older warrior riding straight at him.

He fired, hitting the horse in the chest. The horse staggered and fell, landing on the warrior's leg. The warrior, tied to the pony, cut himself loose and crawled toward Boyer on his stomach, his knife between his teeth.

Boyer aimed the pistol and pulled the trigger. It clicked on an empty chamber. The warrior, riding with the Suicide Boys, appeared grotesque, covered with paint, his eyes wide, his entire top lip missing.

Boyer tried to shoot again. Again a misfire. He threw the pistol aside and drew his knife as the warrior reached him, screaming, clutching at him.

Boyer stabbed the warrior, breaking the blade in his shoulder joint. The warrior screamed louder.

His left arm useless, Boyer tried to hold the warrior off with his right hand, but the warrior stabbed him repeatedly in the right arm and shoulder. After getting a foot under the warrior, Boyer kicked him away.

The warrior came at him again. Boyer found a rifle and used it as a club, slamming the butt into the warrior's face and head until he lay still.

Boyer caught his breath. The fighting had grown so

intense that a number of soldiers suddenly broke and ran downhill toward the river. Boyer saw them briefly. As they became lost in the dust, a warrior grabbed his hair and slammed a war club into the left side of his face.

Boyer slumped, and the world fell into darkness.

Nighthawk sat against the side of the hill, resting his rifle over his knees. Only sporadic fire sounded from the top. The dust had begun to settle, and the sun broke through.

Disheartened, Nighthawk had decided not to fight. What good would it do? He had to leave anyway. There had been no sense in risking his life.

At one time he had wanted to find Calls-at-Night and kill him. Who would know, with all the confusion, who had killed him? But with so many warriors fighting, finding him would have been impossible.

Nighthawk considered going down to where he had tied his pony. But he wanted to say a final goodbye to Eagle Wing, who had rushed over the hill with Lame-White-Man's warriors in a charge against the batallion that had retreated from the bottom.

Warriors began to filter off the hill, some talking among themselves while others helped the wounded.

Finally, Eagle Wing appeared, limping. As he drew closer, Nighthawk saw that his chest was covered with blood.

"Eagle Wing!" Nighthawk said. "I'll help you down to the village."

"No, I'm killed," he said, his eyes glassy. He held a scalp in his hand. He spit on it and tossed it aside. "I got this one, though, before he shot me."

Eagle Wing began his death song. He fell and Nighthawk caught him, laying him down gently.

"It's time for you to go," Eagle Wing said. "Remember me . . . will you?"

"I'll remember you," Nighthawk said. "Always."

Nighthawk knew he must leave as quickly as possible. His one real friend was gone; if Calls-at-Night had survived, he would already be looking for him.

The best direction for him was west. There were settlements along the upper Yellowstone, and over into the Madison and Gallatin. While with Crook's army, he had heard about the gold towns; numerous soldiers had talked about deserting.

All that seemed a hundred years ago, but somehow it also felt like yesterday.

Nighthawk hurried to his pony and mounted. The villagers were returning in almost as much confusion as they had left. He crossed the camps while women and children passed him, going toward the battlefield, searching for missing husbands and fathers. Already the wailing had begun.

From the upper end of the village came the screams of men being tortured. He saw fires burning and naked men staked to the ground, soldiers who had been captured alive.

His vision of warriors carrying heads returned to him. He rode quickly through the village.

From the hills, Nighthawk looked back to the battlefield. The slopes and ridges were littered with dead horses and men. The soldiers' bodies were being stripped, and women in mourning for fallen warriors worked their way along, hacking and pounding, chopping off fingers and arms, so the Bluecoats couldn't cross over as whole men.

Along the tops of the hills, warriors rode south in groups, yelling war cries, brandishing rifles they had taken from the fallen troopers. Nighthawk knew that the soldiers who had opened the battle at the upper end of the village now lay trapped in the hills. He could see them and the little puffs of smoke that rolled from their rifles.

Nighthawk wanted badly to turn around and find Ghostwind. But he realized that he couldn't do that and expect to stay alive. It was better to go now and come back another time. He had to believe she would be waiting for him. That's what he would live for.

Curley wrapped himself in a red blanket he had found on the hillside. Though the air burned, he felt cold inside.

He was sitting on a high hill east of the battle, watching as Long Hair's Bluecoats fell under the onslaught of Sioux and Cheyenne warriors.

Tears streamed down Curley's face. Mitch Boyer had been lost, and he was sure now that his brother, White Swan, must have been killed. All the scouts must be dead. There was no one left but him.

Soon the warriors would be combing the area, looking for stragglers and survivors. He didn't want to be there. He would find some high country, where he could see out, and watch until it was safe to travel. Then he would tell of the last minutes of Long Hair Custer, for it was something he would never be able to forget.

Ghostwind descended the hill back into the village. Tall Deer was still riding around, with Young Horse behind him, telling of his coup on the scout. Everyone cheered them. A warrior even promised to compose a war song in his honor.

The scout had been dragged into the village, along with several other Bluecoats. They had been stripped and burned to death. Three of them had been beheaded, and warriors had ridden from camp to camp, showing the heads around. Then the charred heads had been tied together with a wire and suspended from a pole.

Ghostwind wanted no more of this day, though the bad part was really just beginning. The keening and wailing had started already, as fallen warriors were discovered among the dead Bluecoats strewn upon the hills above the village.

Among the mourners was Little Foot, who sat in front of her lodge, gashing her arms and legs with a knife. Her husband lay beside her wrapped in a blanket. She had already cut her hair short.

Ghostwind approached her and voiced her sympathy.

"Have you heard if Nighthawk was killed?" Little Foot asked.

"No one has seen him since the fighting started," Ghostwind said. "And there's been no report of him on the battlefield. I believe he lived through it and he's left by now.''

"That's good for you, I guess," Little Foot said.

"Only if he comes back again some day," Ghostwind said. "Until that time, I'll feel as if he had died.''

A Northern Cheyenne woman rode down into the village and dismounted at Little Foot's lodge.

"You should come with me and look at one of the Bluecoats we found," she said. "Two women from your camp believe it's Long Hair Custer."

"It's been a long time since I've seen him," Little Foot said. "What does the man you found look like?''

"This man has light hair and wears buckskins. He died at the top of a hill. They say he was the leader. The two women from your camp say they think it's him, but they're not sure. They want you to look.''

"I don't want to look," Little Foot said. "I've seen enough death today. If they think it's him, then maybe it is.''

"They said he came into your village down south, winters past, and sat in council with some of the Southern Cheyenne leaders.''

"Yes, Long Hair Custer did that," Little Foot said.

"They said that after that day, he was marked for death.''

"Yes, that's true. Maybe it is him, but I don't want to go and look.''

The woman mounted her pony. "I'll go and tell them you think it's him.''

"Wait," Little Foot said. "Before you go, I have something for you." She entered her lodge and returned with a large bone awl. She handed the awl to the woman. "Have them punch holes through Long Hair's ears, into his head. Maybe he'll listen better in the next world.''

The woman rode away. Ghostwind left Little Foot and returned to her lodge. Mountain Water sat rocking Talking Grass, who slept in her arms.

"I've seen this day and I'm sad," Mountain Water said. "Not for me or you, but for the children. This will change their lives and make them suffer greatly.''

"Our world is different now," Ghostwind agreed. "And there's nowhere to go that we won't be found. The Bluecoats will come again and again, until they find us all."

"Are your terrible visions over now?" Mountain Water asked.

"I haven't had any visions since last night," Ghostwind said. "It's been fulfilled. I can only hope the visions never return. No matter what, I hope a day like this never happens again."

"What about Nighthawk?" Mountain Water asked. "Do you want to go and be with him?"

"I believe that he'll return to me, when it's safer," Ghostwind said. "If he comes back now, he would have to kill Calls-at-Night. And then he would have to kill others. It wouldn't be good."

"Yes. I believe, as you, that he'll be back," Mountain Water said. "Until that day, you can live safely within the village. But great changes are coming, and maybe you won't want to stay with the people always." She looked hard at Ghostwind. "I'm sure your visions will return when you need to learn something."

"Yes," Ghostwind said. "My visions will surely return. Of this I have no doubt. I just hope Nighthawk stays safe until he can return again. That's what I'll live for."

THIRTY-FIVE

Garrett studied the land from a wooded hillside. The sun had fallen and the horizon bled crimson.

Far to the south, rolling hills and gentle flats stretched from the Bighorn Mountains across to the level-topped Pryor Range, drenched in gentle shadow.

From over the mountains came dark thunderheads, spitting jagged light into the hills. Rain had not yet fallen, but it would come in the darkness, when the heat had drifted out.

So ironic, Garrett thought, that rain would come and wash the battlefield.

Nearby, Little Crane prepared Red Moon's body for burial. The smell of burning cedar filled the air.

Garrett stood quietly while Little Crane spoke softly in Arikara, lifting a pipe to the sky. Above, a golden eagle circled, descended in a slow circle, then soared into the flaring sunset.

Below, along the Little Bighorn, occasional gunfire sounded. Garrett tried to block it from his mind.

Little Crane handed the pipe to Garrett. He hadn't smoked or prayed since the sunrise ceremony far back up the Rosebud. Though he still remembered how to handle the pipe, he wished he had participated more.

"Say a prayer of your choosing," Little Crane said. "Either aloud or to yourself. It makes no difference."

Garrett raised the pipe, asking for blessings for Red Moon and for his safe journey to the Other Side. "You are the same God as mine," Garrett said. "Hear me praying to you in a humble way. Such a good man as this must have lived in your favor. Grant him the happiness he searched so hard for. Allow him the peace he so greatly deserves.''

Garrett's hands trembled. ''And thank you for granting continued life in this land to me and to my friend and brother, Little Crane. Help me to follow your path from this day forward. I will listen and I will learn. I promise.''

In finishing, Garrett asked that those who had died down below, and those who would soon die, might travel across in good favor.

He handed the pipe back to Little Crane, then knelt beside Red Moon. He removed the pencil from his pocket and placed it in Red Moon's hands.

''This isn't much of a gift, brother, but I know that you always wanted to learn how to use one. You would have been very good at it.''

Garrett and Little Crane then carried Red Moon up to a crevice in a nearby cliff. Gently, they laid him in and covered him with pine boughs and rocks, filling the opening completely.

''He will sleep well here,'' Little Crane said. ''Very well.''

The sky boomed over the valley and streaks of rain fell over the Little Bighorn.

''We'll travel now, under cover of darkness,'' Little Crane said. ''When we reach the Crow's Nest, we'll rest.''

Garrett wondered what he was going back to. How would Ann feel now that the Grants no longer needed him? If he wasn't given a position in Washington, would she still want to marry him?

He knew she would. Worrying about every little thing was a waste of time. The battle had taught him that anything might happen at any time. It's the journey that counts, not the end.

On his pony, Garrett followed Little Crane through the twilight, onto a trail that would take them back to the divide. Roiling clouds moved down from the mountains, bringing rain in a heavy torrent. It didn't last long.

Wolves appeared in small packs, headed for the battlefield, skimming the slopes like fleeting shadows. The smell of blood traveled far in an open land.

The night was a dense black when they reached the Crow's Nest. They camped at the base, along a timbered draw, picketing their ponies and sharing pemmican. No fires tonight, or for the next few nights at least.

Despite the lack of warmth, Garrett fell into sound sleep. For the first time since leaving St. Louis, he was headed away from the battle and not into it. His sleep might be filled with nightmares, but at least the scenes he would see had already happened and, God willing, he would never have to live them again.

Ann rode behind Water and Tyrone, barely able to stay in the saddle yet clutching the love dolls around her neck. The night had been long and hard, the ground slick from heavy thunderstorms, yet she had no desire to stop.

To the east, a line of gray light swelled on the horizon. Just ahead, through scattered reaches of timber, lay the Rosebud.

Tyrone turned back to her. "We'll find him today, Miss Ann. I promise."

"I know we will, Tyrone, thank you. We'll ride until we do."

We'll find him. We'll find him. Wherever he is, we'll find him. Ann had said it over and over to herself, so many times now that it echoed in her head.

Her thoughts had gone from euphoria to complete despair, back and forth endlessly. She had seen Adam, alive and well, running to greet her, ecstatic over his great success. She had also seen him drop beside the fallen buffalo, unable to return to his feet. Reality, she knew, lay somewhere in between.

At the timber, they stopped while Water surveyed the country. They had climbed steadily since leaving the Powder River and would soon reach a high divide.

The morning was cool, the grass wet with dew. Birds sang from the draws, their voices high and filled with glee.

No matter the trials, Ann took strength from the birds. They were always there, sending her a message of hope.

At the Rosebud, Water stopped to read sign. A great many Sioux and Cheyenne had passed this way, he said, followed closely by a large number of soldiers.

"A great battle was fought yesterday," he said. "The dust we saw was from that fight. Today the sky is clear from the storms. But the country may now have a lot of Sioux and Cheyenne."

"How will we know?" Tyrone asked.

"If the Bluecoats won the fight, there will be some who escaped, and they'll be angry," Water said. "We don't want to meet them. If the Sioux and Cheyenne were victorious, they won't split up for a while yet."

"If the Sioux and Cheyenne won," Ann said, "then that means things were hard for Adam. If the soldiers won, that will make it that much harder for us to find Adam."

"That's right," Water said. "It will be hard, no matter."

"Are you saying that we can't win either way?" Tyrone asked Water. "That doesn't seem right."

"It may not be right," Water said. "But that's the way it is."

The light in the east grew to a pink glow. Soon the sun would peep over the horizon.

Farther up the Rosebud, they stopped while Water again looked over the country. He sat his pony along a high ridge. When he waved down, Ann and Tyrone rode up to join him.

"What do you see?" Ann asked.

"Are there more Sioux to fight?" Tyrone asked.

"No, the country is empty," Water said. "But far out, you can see smoke rising from the valley."

"Is that where the battle was fought?" Ann asked.

"Yes," Water replied. "I'm sure of it."

Ann took a deep breath. "How soon can we get there?"

"A battle that size would leave many dead," Water said. "The field would be covered with blood. You don't want to see that."

"I'm asking you to take me to Adam," Ann said. "If

that's where he is, that's where I want to go.''

"Even if he's dead?''

"I want to find Adam, no matter what.''

Water smiled. He moved his eyes toward a high ridge with a saddle in the middle.

"Would Adam still be with my brother, Little Crane?''

"I would think so, yes. What's so funny?''

Water pointed. "There are two riders at the top of that high place with the saddle between the two peaks. Can you see them?''

Ann squinted. "Way, way, out there?''

Tyrone looked as well. "I see two riders, sitting their horses on a ridge. One is waving to us.''

"Yes,'' Water said. "That's Little Crane. He's seen us and he's making the sign that we do when we talk to each other from afar.''

"Are you sure?'' Tyrone asked. "You wouldn't be funning us, now, would you?''

Water laughed. "It's fun, but it's not the kind of fun that you mean. Yes, that's Little Crane. I know it is.''

"Are you really sure?'' Ann said. Her heart was pounding.

"I'm really sure,'' Water said. "See? They're riding down to meet us.''

"Oh, God in Heaven!'' Ann said. "What are we waiting here for? Let's go!''

Adam rode with Little Crane down off the Crow's Nest. At first light, Little Crane had awakened and climbed into the saddle to look for Sioux and Cheyenne. He had seen no enemies, for they were all still concentrated down in the valley, working to kill the rest of the soldiers.

He had been content that there were no enemies close enough to worry about. They could travel safely.

Then he had seen three riders coming up the Rosebud. After watching them for a time, he had gone back down and awakened Adam.

"There's a woman coming this way,'' he had said. "A white woman, with two men.''

Adam had jumped to his feet. In the Crow's Nest, he had looked hard through Little Crane's spyglass, but he hadn't been able to see anything in the dim light. Why would a white woman come into this country?

As the riders had drawn nearer, Little Crane had looked again. "The woman has red hair. It's long and flowing. Didn't you tell me that Ann looked like that?"

"Red hair? That woman is redheaded?"

"That's what I said. What does Ann look like otherwise?"

Adam described Ann's build, and the way she held herself on a horse.

Little Crane handed the spyglass to Adam. "I think you described this woman. Is she Ann?"

Adam didn't have to look long. "Yes, I would say that it is." He wanted to be sure. His heart beat wildly. "He looked again. "Yes, I'm certain. But what in God's name is she doing out here?"

Now, with the sun just topping the horizon, Adam mounted his pony and rode with Little Crane to a high ridge, so they were plainly visible.

"I've signaled down below," Little Crane said. "I received a signal back from the warrior. It's my brother, Water. So the white woman is no doubt Ann."

His whole being alive with anticipation, Adam hurried with Little Crane down the slope and toward the divide. The distance was but a few miles, but the time seemed to drag on endlessly.

Finally, they approached the three riders, and Adam shouted, "Ann! For God's sake, what are you doing out here?"

Ann's breath left her. "Adam! Oh, Adam, is that you?" She slid from her horse, running as soon as her feet touched the ground.

Adam, off his pony, rushed to greet her. The two met, holding each other tightly. Adam picked her up and twirled her around and around. Ann's face glistened with tears.

"What happened to you?" she asked, noticing the

blood and dirt on Adam's clothes. "Are you hurt?"

"The blood isn't mine, Ann. I'm fine. Why in the world are you here?"

"Because I wanted to find you, Adam Garrett! You were in danger, and I knew it. I don't ever want you to pull a stunt like this again. Do you hear me? Never again!"

"What are these?" Adam asked, touching the love dolls.

"I found them back in one of the deserted villages. They brought us together. I would have gone crazy without them. You can ask these two."

Adam greeted Tyrone, thanking him for his devotion. To Water, who had just finished hugging Little Crane, he said, "Your brother is the best friend I have now. I want you to know that."

Water looked to Little Crane. "We saw the dust yesterday. How bad was it?"

"The worst fight ever," Little Crane said. "Very bad for everyone, especially Long Hair and his soldiers. I think they're nearly all killed. I don't know, they're still fighting."

Water motioned to Garrett. "You brought him through it, and you brought yourself through. Red Moon isn't with you. Did he cross over?"

"Red Moon died honorably, and he crossed over well," Little Crane said. "He's with his wife and family now. He's happy."

Adam looked into the distance, blinking. "He wanted to adopt me as a brother. I'll always think of him that way, and wonder why he had to die."

"I'm sorry, Adam," Ann said. "You must have gotten very close to him."

"He and Little Crane were the only reason I survived," Adam said. "The only reason."

Ann studied Little Crane, who was peering into the distance. His clothes, like Adam's, were covered with dirt and blood. Both he and Adam, she realized, had been holding their friend Red Moon as he died.

Tyrone spoke up. "We lost one of ours as well. Little Crane, do you remember Lareaux?"

"Yes," Little Crane replied. "He's also gone?"

"He came out to help us," Tyrone said. "He was a good friend. The Sioux came and we fought them. They were too much. Lareaux didn't go well. I just hope he died soon after they dragged him away. You don't want to know the details."

"It's good that all of us are alive, here and now," Water said. "It wasn't that way down below, I'll bet."

"I'll tell you again, it was the worst I ever saw," Little Crane said.

"A lot of men died, on both sides," Garrett said. "Yesterday was a day I'll never forget. No one should ever have to go through that."

Little Crane pointed to Garrett. "Six Fingers fights as well as he makes the paper talk. But he lost it all in the river, when his pony was shot from under him."

"Adam?" Ann said. "You lost everything?"

"It's all gone," Garrett said.

"But what about your reports to the Grant administration?"

"Custer's dead. Or at least he's lost the battle. I think he'd rather die than face that. The Grants don't have to worry about him now."

"So all this was for nothing?" Ann asked. "You put me through hell for nothing?"

"How was I to know how it would end? Besides, maybe I can tell the story sometime. I don't know if I can start over, though. There was so much."

"Be glad that you still have your fingers to do it," Little Crane said.

"That's what's important." Ann had turned serious. "You can consider yourself very lucky, Adam Garrett. I don't ever want you to travel into anything like this ever again. Do you promise?"

"There couldn't ever be anything like this, ever," Garrett said. "You don't have to worry."

"Will you write about this for the *Democrat*?" Ann asked.

"I'll see what they say," Garrett replied. "It will be hard to compete with the stories that come from the soldiers, if any of them live."

"Yes, it will be hard for Six Fingers to tell the real story," Little Crane agreed. "The Bluecoats will want to have people think one way. Six Fingers will tell the truth, and no one will want to hear that."

"I don't care whether you tell the story or not," Ann said. "And I don't care where you work or how much they pay you. I've got you now, and I'm not letting you go. Now, we've got to get back and plan the wedding."

They rode to the river and watered the horses. The sun had risen, filling the land with gold. The Rosebud ran softly, and the trees and brush were filled with birdsong. Overhead, four crows flew into the pines, stared down at Garrett, cawed, then flapped away into the morning.

"That was interesting," Ann said. "Were those birds talking to you?"

"You don't know the half of it, Ann," he said. "Not even the half of it."

"Well, I'm glad we're together, finally," Ann said. "I never want to go through this again." She placed the male doll around Garrett's neck. "I had nightmares you wouldn't believe."

"We'll talk about our dreams, yours and mine," Garrett said. "Especially the good ones that are to come. Maybe this evening, when we're resting and the hills are cooling off."

As they left, Garrett thought of his buffalo dreams and the ring of fire he had ridden through during the retreat. He took a long look across the land. The sun spread light farther than the eye could see. A cloudless sky stretched a deep blue overhead, leading straight to heaven.

Soon, Garrett knew, fire would again mix with the gentle sky. Far down below, on the valley floor, hell had come for an afternoon, leaving the land in tears. So many had died and now so many wept. When the news reached the nation, shouts of anger would overpower the mourning, and then hell would return.

Perhaps things would change in time. Maybe the gentle

winds would heal the hearts and minds of those who had lost a father or a son, and the birds flying over would bring back the wings of joy.

But such a change would be a long time in coming, and the buffalo would have to rise again.

AFTERWORD

George Armstrong Custer's end at the Battle of the Little Bighorn has been retold many times over. Various military accounts have been used to suggest Custer's whereabouts at certain times during the fight; and, during the early stages, the documentation is likely accurate. However, the reality of Custer's last moments is in direct conflict with where he was supposedly found on the battlefield.

The truth is, Custer never led his men to Last Stand Hill. He didn't direct a monumental attempt to withstand the charging Sioux and Cheyenne hordes. Unlike the many portrayals of the gallant commander standing on the hill, shooting his pistols or waving a sword, gravely wounded, urging his troops against insurmountable odds, Custer was certainly not the last man killed, nor was he anywhere in the vicinity.

Indian oral history has always maintained that Custer fell at the river. Historians long believed that "the river" meant the Medicine Tail Ford. Soldiers in Reno's command and others with Terry and Gibbon, upon finding Custer's men, studied the mouth of Medicine Tail Coulee and found that few, if any, soldiers had crossed there. Recent archaeological findings concur: some skirmishing occurred, but no major confrontation took place there.

Custer fell not at Medicine Tail Ford, but above the Indian village, at a crossing just south of U.S. Highway 212's junction with Interstate 90.

Besides Indian oral history and recent archaeological evidence, a major consideration lies in the location of Mark Kellogg's body.

Despite a marker on the east side of Battle Ridge that bears his name, it is clearly documented that Kellogg's body was found down on the flat, "a stone's throw from the river." Colonel John Gibbon's account reads, in part: "We suddenly came upon a body lying in the grass. It was lying on its back and was in an advanced state of decomposition. It was not stripped, but had evidently been scalped and one ear cut off."

Gibbon stated that the clothing was not that of a soldier. He ordered that a boot be cut off and the stockings and drawers examined for a name. None could be found. However, Kellogg had reinforced the instep of his boot with a strip of leather, buckled along the side. "This led to the identification of the remains," Gibbon continues, "for on being carried to camp the boot was recognized as one belonging to Mr. Kellogg, a newspaper correspondent who accompanied General Custer's column."

As with every good journalist, Kellogg would have wished to remain close to the action, and certainly close to Custer. Upon being met overwhelmingly at the river by Two Moon and Crazy Horse's warriors, Custer's troops turned and fled back into the hills. Kellogg, riding the slow mule, couldn't catch up, and was overtaken. He was likely shot or knocked from the mule, in much the same fashion as many of the soldiers under Reno during their retreat at the south end of the village.

Custer's determination to—in his own mind—keep the villagers from escaping led him to divide his command at Medicine Tail Coulee, leaving the senior officer, Captain Miles Keogh, behind with three companies. Custer's intent was to hurry ahead and encircle the fleeing villagers. Should he succeed in capturing the women and children, he would have the warriors at his mercy.

Custer rode beyond the location of the present Visitors' Center and cemetery and onto the flat just past the north end of the village, where he approached a river crossing. There, a group of young men lay in ambush, protecting the women and children as best they could, hoping for Crazy Horse and Two Moon to arrive.

Custer was shot at this crossing, nearly at the same

time that Crazy Horse and Two Moon arrived. His command scattered back into the hills and regrouped in the vicinity of Last Stand Hill, possibly under the next senior officer, Captain George Yates, a strong leader with blonde hair who emulated Custer and was also dressed in buckskins that day. On Last Stand Hill and vicinity, the entire command was wiped out.

After the battle, could Yates possibly have been mistaken for Custer?

It was nearly three days before the aftermath was discovered by the Terry-Gibbon forces coming up the Big Horn River. The dead were unrecognizable. Grieving Indian women had dismembered, beheaded, and in some cases, disemboweled the fallen troops. In addition, a brief evening thunderstorm had soaked the remains, causing bloating and discoloration during the following period of intense heat.

The burial detail, also well documented, spent little time with the bodies, covering them as quickly as possible with thin layers of soil and pieces of grass and sage. Reno and his men, delirious from battle fatigue, wanted no more of the Sioux and Cheyenne. After seeing the field of battle, it is certain that the Terry-Gibbon forces had to be worried about another attack.

Custer's body may never have been found, at least not in a recognizable state. Many of the soldiers, including some of the officers, were never accounted for.

Custer's reasons—or perhaps lack of reasoning—for even initiating the attack have been the topic for continual discussion. Ample evidence exists that the Crow scouts warned him many times that the village held more warriors than they could handle, that if they attacked without the Terry-Gibbon forces, they would all die.

However, upon examining the events leading up to the Sioux campaign, it would seem obvious that Custer believed he had no choice but to win a victory for himself against the Sioux and Cheyenne.

Foremost, Custer's bitter feud with the Grant administration forced him into a power struggle, a struggle Custer felt he could win only by acquiring the Democratic nomination for President. To gain enough notoriety to be placed on the ballot, he had to perform some heroic feat—like defeating the Sioux and Cheyenne.

Also, much has been written, and much omitted, concerning Custer's personal life. It has been suggested that he was a latent homosexual. Therefore, his personal struggles within himself would have overshadowed even the intense political battles around him, prompting a ''do or die'' mentality, which unfortunately cost the lives of a great many men in his command.

Today, the majority of Custer historians no longer subscribe to the notion that Custer led his soldiers down Medicine Tail Coulee and then back to Last Stand Hill, where they gave it their best to the end. No, something else occurred. But there was no way the U.S. Army could release the truth, especially if they weren't certain of having found Custer's body.

Lieutenant James Bradley, who led a scouting detachment ahead of the Terry-Gibbon forces coming up the Big Horn River, initially discovered the remains of Custer's command. Upon entering the abandoned Indian village he noted in his diary that campfires were still smoking and that numerous items littered the ground, including food and cooking utensils, weapons, and clothing, suggesting a hurried departure.

Also in the village were abandoned lodges sewn shut—death lodges containing one or more slain warriors. Bradley noted seeing wounded horses hobbling around in a daze, clothing belonging to Seventh Cavalry soldiers, and three scorched heads wired to a pole. Could one of these heads have belonged to Custer?

Custer, dressed in buckskins and riding in front, may have been mistaken for a scout. The Sioux and Cheyenne were not fond of enemy scouts and treated their remains with added vehemence.

That afternoon, few if any of the Sioux and Cheyenne knew whom they were fighting. To them, the attackers were simply Bluecoats, enemy soldiers who had come to destroy them and drive them from their rightful homes.

Many warriors assumed that General George Crook

had returned with his forces to try and gain revenge for his defeat on the Rosebud eight days earlier.

Dr. Thomas Marquis interviewed a Northern Cheyenne warrior named Wooden Leg, who was eighteen at the time of the battle. Wooden Leg took part in all phases of the battle, including the fight against Reno's forces at the south end of the village.

While chasing Reno's men back across the river, Wooden Leg was quoted as saying, "Our war cries and war songs were mingled with many jeering calls, such as: 'You are only boys. You ought not to be fighting. We whipped you on the Rosebud. You should have brought more Crow and Shoshone with you to do your fighting.' "

After the battle, Wooden Leg was walking with friends among the dead when they discovered a fallen Arikara warrior, whom an older warrior referred to as a Corn Indian. Wooden Leg became confused.

"I examined again the one I had helped in beating to death," he told Marquis. "I learned he also was a Corn Indian. . . . Now there began to be talk that maybe these soldiers were not the same ones we had fought [on the Rosebud]. Or, perhaps they had added the Corn Indians to their forces since that time. There were different opinions on the matter."

A few days later, after the camp was moved, Wooden Leg was stationed as a wolf, or lookout. There, a young Santee Sioux warrior told him, "I think the big chief of the soldiers we killed was Long Hair. One of my people killed him. He has known Long Hair many years."

Wooden Leg remembered, "That was the first time I had ever heard of any such person as Long Hair. The news was interesting to me at first, but after I had thought a few moments about it the story seemed not very important. I recalled myself having seen at least three soldiers having long and light-colored hair."

That night a council was held. An Unkpapa war chief stated that he had killed Custer, for he couldn't mistake his long and wavy yellow hair.

Yes, there were soldiers with long wavy yellow hair

who died on the Little Bighorn. But none of them was Custer. Back at Fort Lincoln, he had cut his hair short to appease Libbie, who had had a dream of a warrior holding up a scalp with flowing golden locks.

Nevertheless, Libbie's vision came to pass. Perhaps it could have been avoided, perhaps not. There are those who say that the destiny of Custer and his men was marked from the time they left Fort Lincoln. Pretty Shield, a Crow woman married to the scout Goes Ahead, once said, "Son-of-the-Morning-Star was going to his death, and did not know it. He was like a feather blown by the wind, and *had* to go."

Today, the Battle of the Little Bighorn is as vivid within the American conscience as at any time in history. Custer Battlefield is now the Little Bighorn Battlefield, in memory of *all* the fallen. It serves as the West's major landmark to the horrors of interracial war. Men, women, and children died there. It is a sacred place. It will forever be a sacred place.

But perhaps, as with any sacrifice, it has become a starting point for the acceptance of all humanity as equals and one under the Creator.

In the tradition of the Sioux, there are four colors present during religious ceremonies—red, black, yellow, and white—the four races of mankind. "These colors were given to the people by the Creator, way back in time, well before Columbus or any of the explorers found the Americas," says Ben Cloud, a close personal friend of mixed Plains Indian heritage. "These colors came in visions, to be used in sacred ceremonies, for it was known that some day these four colors would merge, to form a unity of the human race."

Today, thousands of visitors come to the battlefield each year, representing the four races of mankind. They come to learn about the battle and about the lives of the soldiers and the Indians who were camped there. These visitors look across the open hills, feeling the memory of that day, still very much alive, still as horrible as when the actual fighting took place. And into their hearts and minds comes a message from the Creator: "Let no more events like this happen. Learn to respect one another and live in peace.''

—Earl Murray
Yellowstone River Valley
Laurel, Montana
January, 1995

SELECTED
BIBLIOGRAPHY

Barnard, Sandy. "Mark Kellogg's Role During the 1876 Campaign." *Proceedings. 1st Annual Symposium, Custer Battlefield Historical and Museum Association, Inc.* (1987), 1–10.

Bourke, John G. *On the Border With Crook.* New York: Scribner's, 1891. Reprint, Lincoln: University of Nebraska Press, 1971.

Brinninstool, E. A. *Troopers with Custer.* Harrisburg, Pa.: Stackpole Co., 1952.

Carroll, Matthew. "Diary on Gibbon's Expedition, 1876." *Montana Historical Society Contributions* 2 (1895), 229–40.

Chandler, Melbourne C. *Of Garryowen in Glory: The History of the 7th U.S. Cavalry.* Annandale, Va.: Turnpike Press, 1960.

Cleckley, Hervey, M.D. *The Mask of Sanity.* New York: New American Library, 1982.

Custer, Elizabeth B. *Boots and Saddles.* New York: Harper and Bros., 1885.

Doran, Bob. "Battalion Formation and the Custer Trail." *Proceedings. 3rd Annual Symposium, Custer Battlefield Historical and Museum Association, Inc.* (1989), 9–23.

Fox, Richard A. *Archaeology, History, and Custer's Last Battle: The Little Bighorn Reexamined.* Norman: University of Oklahoma Press, 1993.

Graham, W. A. *Abstract of the Official Record of Proceedings of the Reno Court of Inquiry, 1879.* Harrisburg, Pa.: Stackpole Co., 1954.

———. *The Custer Myth: A Source Book of Custeriana.*

Harrisburg, Pa.: Stackpole Co., 1953. Reprint, Lincoln: University of Nebraska Press, 1986.

———. *The Story of the Little Big Horn.* Harrisburg, Pa.: Stackpole Co., 1926.

Gray, John S. *Centennial Campaign: The Sioux War of 1876.* Fort Collins, Col.: Old Army Press, 1976. Reprint, Norman: University of Oklahoma Press, 1988.

———. *Custer's Last Campaign: Mitch Boyer and the Little Bighorn Reconstructed.* Lincoln: University of Nebraska Press, 1991.

Grinnell, George Bird. *The Fighting Cheyennes.* New York: Charles Scribner's Sons, 1915.

Hammer, Kenneth. *Men With Custer: Biographies of the 7th Cavalry, 25, June, 1876.* Fort Collins, Col.: Old Army Press, 1972.

Hanson, Joseph Mills. *Conquest of the Missouri: Being the Life and Exploits of Captain Grant Marsh.* New York: Murray Hill Books, 1946.

Harcey, Dennis W., Brian R. Croone, and Joseph Medicine Crow. *White Man Runs Him: Crow Scout with Custer.* Evanston, Ill.: Evanston Publishing Co., 1993.

Hardorff, Richard G. *Markers, Artifacts and Indian Testimony: Preliminary Findings on the Custer Battle.* Short Hills, N.J.: Don Horn Publications, 1985.

Hofling, Charles K. *Custer and the Little Big Horn: A Psychobiographical Inquiry.* Detroit, Mich.: Wayne State University Press, 1981.

Innis, Ben. *Bloody Knife!* Fort Collins, Col.: Old Army Press, 1973.

Kellogg, Mark H. "Notes on the Little Big Horn Expedition Under Custer, 1876." (May 17–June 19), *Montana Historical Society Contributions* 9 (1923), 213–25.

Kuhlman, Charles. *Legend into History.* Harrisburg, Pa.: Stackpole Co., 1951.

Lackie, Shirley A. *Elizabeth Bacon Custer and the Making of a Myth.* Norman: University of Oklahoma Press, 1993.

Libby, Orrin G. "The Arikara Narrative of the Campaign Against the Dakotas, 1876." *North Dakota Historical Society Collections* 6 (1920).

Mails, Thomas E. *The Mystic Warriors of the Plains.* New York: Doubleday and Co., 1972.

Marquis, Thomas B. *She Watched Custer's Last Battle.* Privately printed pamphlet, 1933.

————. *Wooden Leg: A Warrior Who Fought Custer.* Lincoln: University of Nebraska Press, 1931.

Merrington, Marguerite. *The Custer Story: Life and Letters of Gen. George A. Custer and Wife, Elizabeth.* New York: Devin-Adair Co., 1950.

Michno, Greg. *The Mystery of E Troop: Custer's Gray Horse Company at the Little Bighorn.* Missoula, Mont.: Mountain Press Publishing Co., 1994.

Powell, Peter J. *Sweet Medicine: The Continuing Role of the Sacred Arrows, the Sun Dance and the Buffalo Hat in Northern Cheyenne History.* Norman: University of Oklahoma Press, 1969.

Rickey, Don. *Forty Miles a Day on Beans and Hay.* Norman: University of Oklahoma Press, 1963.

Scott, Douglas D., Richard A. Fox, and Dick Harmon. *Archeological Insights into the Custer Battle: An Assessment of the 1984 Season.* Norman: University of Oklahoma Press, 1987.

Scott, Douglas D., Melissa Connor, and Clyde Snow. "Nameless Faces of Custer Battlefield." Custer Battlefield Historical and Museum Association's *Greasy Grass* 4 (1988), 2–4.

Sills, Joe, Jr. "Were There Two Last Stands?" *Proceedings. 2nd Annual Symposium, Custer Battlefield Historical and Museum Association, Inc.* (1988), 13–20.

Stands in Timber, John, and Margot Liberty. *Cheyenne Memories.* New Haven, Conn.: Yale University Press, 1967. Reprint, Lincoln: University of Nebraska Press, 1972.

Utley, Robert. *Cavalier in Buckskin: George Armstrong Custer and the Western Military Frontier.* Norman: University of Oklahoma Press, 1988.

————. *The Lance and the Shield: The Life and Times of Sitting Bull.* New York: Henry Holt and Co., 1993.

Weibert, Henry. *Sixty-Six Years in Custer's Shadow*. Billings, Mont.: Bannack Pub. Co., 1985.

Welch, James. *Killing Custer: The Battle of the Little Bighorn and the Fate of the Plains Indians*. New York: W.W. Norton, 1994.